THE H

It's not always beautiful...

Marco Morelli is pleased tha ... she is very much like her father. This time he's aiming for the jugular with his plans to bring his brother to his knees once and for all. Meanwhile, Erin still suspects things are far from how they should be. Unable to keep the promise for a fresh slate with the young girl who ties Zane to his past, she's ready for problems, but these could be closer to home than she bargained for.
And it isn't just Erin and Zane who are in the sights for the fallout. What will happen to Skye's boyfriend and the other people who have put their love and trust into her?

They say that the truth will set you free, but on many occasions it does the exact opposite...

What readers are saying about *The Hard Truth*:

- *"Brilliant. Absolutely brilliant!"*
- *"Probably my favourite in the series so far..."*
- *"A great read. Looking forward to number five!"*
- *"Let Edie take you into a world of gangland..."*
- *"Talk about hard hitting!"*

Also by Edie Baylis

Scarred Series

Mirrors Never Lie (Scarred #1)
The Price of Betrayal (Scarred #2)
Trusting Blood (Scarred #3)
The Hard Truth (Scarred #4)
The Last Promise (Scarred #5)

Allegiance Series

Takeover (Allegiance #1)
Fallout (Allegiance #2)
Vendetta (Allegiance #3)
Payback (Allegiance #4)
Judgement (Allegiance #5)
The Allegiance Series Box Set

Retribution Series

An Old Score (Retribution #1)
Finders Keepers (Retribution #2)
The Final Take (Retribution #3)
The Retribution Series Box Set

Hunted Series

The Status Debt (Hunted #1)
The Family Legacy (Hunted #2)
The Target of Lies (Hunted #3)
The Hunted Series Box Set

Downfall Series

Until the End of Time (Downfall #1)
Escaping the Past (Downfall #2)
Vengeful Payback (Downfall #3)
The Downfall Series Box Set

THE HARD TRUTH

SCARRED #4

EDIE BAYLIS

ATHAME press
- LONDON -

First published in Great Britain in 2024 by Athame Press.
This paperback edition published in 2024 by Athame Press.

Cover photography: Simbiothy/depositphotos; Maliy/depositphotos; Stetsik/depositphotos; aleksokur/depositphotos

Paperback ISBN 978-1-916977-04-4
e-ISBN 978-1-916977-03-7
Hardback 978-1-916977-06-8
Large Print 978-1-916977-07-5

Athame Press
Unit 13230 - PO Box 6945 – London – W1A 6US

PROLOGUE

May 1983

'I am ashamed that you would do such a thing!' I stare at my youngest son, knowing that the look in my eyes alone is enough to render him quaking in his boots. It's the same effect I have on anyone who disappoints me.

A lot of people disappoint me, but I never expected this kind of disappointment from my own blood, yet here it is.

I pull my ice blue eyes away from Marco. My glare has little effect when the recipient lacks the courage to look at me. Instead, I glance around my office. Furnished with carefully sourced antique pieces, all meticulously hand-picked to complement one another underlines the level I have achieved.

I run half of London - a far cry from the little boy accompanying his parents to England with the aim of expanding the family business.

The Morellis flourish in Sicily. There, we have control of everything. But my grandfather's family firm had to expand abroad to conquer pastures new and out of his seven sons, my father received that task.

At eight years old I only saw it as an adventure, but as I grew, taking my place in the firm my father worked hard to establish in foreign climes, I realised how hard it was to break into and keep a foothold on the English scene.

In Sicily, our family were renowned. In England, we were no one. My father and subsequently myself and my brothers worked extremely hard in this cutthroat industry to rise to the top. We took no prisoners and still don't.

But only after fifty years since first stepping on English soil as that eight-year-old, I can say that I've achieved what the family set out to do and that I intend to maintain and further grow the Morellis' standing and reputation in London.

But Marco has jeopardised that.

Now he thinks I'm not looking, I can feel him studying me. Whether my eyes are on him or not, I see all.

I also saw what he did last night.

It's an image that makes me want to rip Marco's head from his neck, the same way I would to anyone else I caught doing what he did.

My sudden cold, unwavering glare catches Marco unawares. His eyes are as blue and hard as mine, yet he has more to learn than I realised.

'Have I not brought you up better than this?' I growl, determined to get an explanation. 'You've let me down, Marco. Your actions will jeopardise the arrangement I've been working hard to broker with the Buscemis.'

Marco shuffles awkwardly in his handmade Italian brogues. Fourteen years old, he dresses like a man; looks like a man but acts like a child. My temper spikes. 'Nothing to say for yourself?'

I slap my hand on the leather inlay of my mahogany desk. I'd stab Marco through the heart for putting me in this position if he wasn't my son. 'Answer me, boy! That girl was your brother's guest!'

Whether I wish for Zane to have interest in an English girl or not is irrelevant. I'd planned to deal with that, but not this *way. If this got out...*

'But you don't want Zane to marry Shirley. You said...'

I stand up faster than Marco expects. The back of my hand connects with his cheek, causing a crack to echo around the wood panelled room. 'When did I say that? Eh? I do not and would not speak of such things to you!'

I cannot fathom where this boy of mine got his impudence from. Speaking to me like I am an equal? I am not his equal - I am his father.

'I-I overheard you talking to Salvatore last night. I... I heard you say you needed a way for Zane to lose interest in Shirley so he would marry Sofia. I'll *marry her if Zane won't!'*

'Over my dead body would I ever foist you *on anyone's daughter after what I saw yesterday!' I roar. 'Zane will marry Sofia regardless.' I snatch up the decanter, my fingers trembling with rage. 'Furthermore, what I discuss with my men is no concern of yours!'*

I pour a large measure of the finest Scotch and ignore the glossy film of tears forming in Marco's eyes. The stupid, stupid boy!

'I'm sorry, father,' Marco mumbles. 'I was trying to help... I want to learn how things run.'

I narrow my eyes at my youngest son. He speaks like he will one day have a say in how the Morelli firm operates, but he won't. The running of the empire I've nurtured and built from what my father before me started, will pass to Zane. As the eldest, Zane gets that honour as default. It's how our family works and Marco knows that.

Marco raises his chin defiantly. 'Zane won't want Shirley Wilson when he learns she is a slut.'

Enraged, I follow up from the first backhand Marco received with another. This time, I make sure it's a full upper cut to his jaw which lifts him off his feet to crash onto the rug in the centre of my office.

Storming from behind my desk, I drag him up by the neck, seeing the first hint of fear behind his eyes. 'Zane will not learn of this and neither will anyone else. I will sort it.'

And sort it I would. As much as I do not justify or agree with what Marco did last night or the reasonings behind it, he is my son and so therefore I will ensure his name and reputation, along with mine and our family is protected.

I throw Marco in the direction of my office door before I completely lose my temper. 'Never breathe a word about what you've done. Now get out of my sight!'

Sitting back down, I finish my whisky and ponder how to ensure no one else learns of this. Once that is decided, I'll arrange a meeting with the Buscemis and make the decision as to when Zane and Sofia should marry.

One

26th June 2001

MAKING SURE he wore his most flirtatious smile, Zane Morelli grinned at the nurse on the ward reception. Leaning on the counter, his leather jacket sleeves squeaking on the laminate, he was close enough to detect the beginning of a flush on her cheeks. He knew how to play the game when required.

He was getting good at being Damon Sandler's brother. Not that he had the first clue whether Damon had a brother, but Zane cared little.

For all intents and purposes, *he* was that brother. Phoning around hospitals pretending to be the concerned relative was the only reason he'd located this bastard in the first place. 'It doesn't surprise me that he's asked for no visitors. Knowing my brother, he's keeping it quiet from our old Ma that he's got himself into such a scrape, but I'll cheer him up.'

'Well, I don't know, Mr...'

'Sandler, Keith Sandler.' Zane finished the nurse's sentence and jerked his head in the direction he presumed the tosser was lying. 'You'd have thought being the oldest, Damon would have more sense! Do you know exactly how this happened?' Not that he knew what had befallen Sandler, short of that one of his best men had watched the prick being dragged from his fleapit of a flat into a waiting ambulance. But if, like they all suspected, Zane's *real* brother was behind why Sandler was lying in intensive care, he could hazard a guess.

The nurse played with a tendril of her hair and blushed once again at the handsome stranger. 'Your brother's memory about the incident is sketchy, so we're not sure exactly what happened.' Lowering her voice, she leant closer, covering Zane with her peppermint breath and a waft of floral perfume. 'If you ask me, with the damage to his knees, it looks like criminal retribution…' She raised her eyebrows. 'Is he involved in gang-type stuff, your brother?'

'Damon?' Zane laughed. 'You must be joking! The only thing he gets involved with is playing dominos at the Bridge and Anchor on Tuesday nights! Christ, no. It can't be anything like that! Unless it's a case of mistaken identity?'

Perhaps he should have picked acting as a career, Zane wondered. His lies almost convinced himself! As far as he knew, Sandler knew sod all about dominos. Saying that, having ended up in such a shit position, the man also knew less about how *this* life worked than he should.

Zane then frowned, feigning shock. 'This sounds more serious than I was led to believe. Are... are you saying he's been… kneecapped?'

The nurse smiled kindly. 'I shouldn't really speculate, Mr Sandler. I may be barking up the wrong tree, but your brother's injuries are certainly very serious. You're aware he's lost both legs?'

Zane sucked in his breath in mock horror. 'Jesus! I-I didn't realise. Oh my God! If this is a case of mistaken identity from a criminal gang, then surely the police are involved and...'

'The police have questioned your brother several times, but he can't or *won't* give them any information.'

'Are the police still here?' Zane refrained from peering around the nurse to see if he could spot anyone he didn't want recognising him but seeing her shake her head he relaxed.

'They've given up for the time being.' The nurse's eyes then brightened. 'But if you can get further information from Damon, then we'll pass it on to them. We all want to know who's responsible.'

'I'll try my best. And please call me Keith.' Zane smiled. He'd be getting information from Damon-fucking-Sandler, but not for the police's benefit. 'Can I see him now?'

'Yes, okay,' the nurse winked. 'I'll show you where he is, but don't blame me if he's angry I've let you in.'

The fixed smile dropped from Zane's face the moment the nurse walked ahead in the direction Sandler lay. Sandler definitely wouldn't want him there, but the fucker had no choice. Neither did he have a choice about telling him what he wanted to know. Once he had that, he'd kill the cunt.

Zane owed Sandler plenty - none more so than for trying to kill the woman he loved and most recently for murdering Hazel Grimes. Whether Hazel had or hadn't betrayed him, Sandler would still pay for it. And now, he thought with a cold smile as he approached a side room with 'Sandler' scrawled on the board clipped to the door, this wanker wasn't in a position to get away.

• • • •

DAMON SANDLER stared at the wall. A hospital issue clock with a yellow face and black plastic casing - the type that every single room, ward and corridor he'd spent time in, sported. It taunted him with its slowly moving hands, but the clock was the only thing breaking up the stark whiteness of the walls. It was like going snow-blind. Or worse.

But then, not much was worse than *this*...

Against his will, Damon's eyes moved down the bed to where his legs had once been.

Actually, he still had his legs. Part of them, anyway. But the bits required for walking and functioning like he'd done every other single day of his life were no longer there.

Clenching his jaw to prevent the sob escaping his mouth,

Damon blinked away the burn of tears and forced himself not to dwell on what had happened.

But how could he not?

How the fuck was he supposed to do anything now? The simple truth was that he couldn't. He'd be stuck like this - a fucking cripple, getting jammed in doorways with a wheelchair nowhere accommodated.

And he could still feel where his legs had once been. Surely the bloody doctors could have saved them if they'd wanted to?

Damon swallowed dryly, unable to remember the exact chain of events surrounding being rushed into hospital. Through the fog of excruciating pain, he had vague memories of hearing *'too badly damaged'*, *'nerve endings'* and *'high risk of gangrene'*.

Maybe they'd lopped his legs off to spite him?

He didn't know, but he *could* recall with startling clarity who had done this. The person took it upon themselves to blow both his kneecaps to smithereens was the same person who would, at some point, return to finish off the job.

Marco.

And after discharging the bullets from Damon's very own gun, Marco Morelli wouldn't forget his promise: *'Being crippled and living in fear as to exactly when I'll come to finish the job is a much more satisfying outcome'*, were his exact words.

And the psycho would leave it as long as possible before making good on that promise.

Struggling to push himself upright in the bed, Damon reached for his glass of water. That fat bitch of a cleaner had moved the fucking table and now he couldn't reach the damn thing. The water might be warm and taste like crap, but he was thirsty.

Stretching as far as possible, Damon's fingers fumbled along the rim of the glass. *If he could scoot it forward just a little bit, then he'd...*

He stared in horror as the glass fell from the table, taking the stale, tepid water with it.

Frustrated tears brimmed. He could do nothing properly. How would he cope?

Not that there was much point in trying. His block of flats had no lift and Marco was waiting to kill him. It was a royal fucking set up from all sides.

Why hadn't he just walked away when he had the chance instead of scheming and plotting to take Marco's empire?

He could have disappeared or even gone abroad.

But no...

Damon stared up at the ceiling, a snarling sound coming from the back of his throat. It had been a dead cert Marco would go to prison. The man had no defence and no way of getting one. Damon certainly had no intention of following orders of getting that bitch, Marco's wife, to sign the statement to get the charges dropped. With accusations of sex trafficking and murder hanging around Marco's neck, his fate was sealed.

Then it all went wrong…

Damon trembled with rage. He'd found Hazel Grimes dead. Thanks to Martin Bolt taking it upon himself to kill her and set him up, even if he'd wanted to force Hazel to sign that statement, he couldn't. Then the little twat running off with Zane's daughter was the icing on the bloody cake because now Zane Morelli was after him too.

It *had* to be Martin who'd killed Hazel. Who else could it be?

Damon choked back another sob, the throbbing pain in his smashed teeth closely matching the burning nerve pain where his legs abruptly ended.

He'd almost achieved the end result too. He'd escaped detection from Zane's retarded gorillas at the Starbright Centre; he'd avoided being fitted up and tortured for a murder he hadn't committed and he'd successfully returned to his flat.

Twenty-four hours was all he'd needed to get through before Marco got sent down for the foreseeable, so how the hell had the charges been dropped and the man released?

The minute Damon had woken to find Marco standing in his bedroom, he knew it was over.

Except it wasn't over.

This was *worse...*

He didn't even know who'd called the ambulance, but whoever had, Damon wished they hadn't. He'd rather get eaten by rats than this.

And no, he hadn't told the police anything. They could turn up as much as they liked, but he'd remain silent. He would say nothing. After all, it wasn't like they'd offer him protection, was it? Not without telling them everything, and that would only incriminate *him*.

But being in hospital didn't make him safe either. Marco was still out there somewhere, as was Zane. And that was why he'd made it clear to every single person working in this bloody place that he wanted no visitors.

Not *one*.

And that included the physiotherapist. Learning to live with no legs and how to move around was irrelevant when it was only a matter of time before he was brown bread. He also couldn't rule out that Marco wouldn't send someone here under the guise of being a physio when really they were tasked to finish him off in his hospital bed.

Marco wasn't winning *that* easily.

Hearing footsteps outside his room, Damon glanced up. *About fucking time.* The lunch orders should have been collected long before this. He'd be fucked if he was ending up with a shit leftover dinner no one else wanted again just because people couldn't be arsed.

That daft bint could fetch him another jug of water while she was at it too.

As the nurse entered, Damon wore his most ferocious scowl. It wouldn't hurt her to be reminded to do her bloody job. 'Ah! Finally!'

'Morning, Mr Sandler. I know what you said, but as you need cheering up, I'm overriding you. Look who's here to see you!' The nurse reached to pick the fallen glass from the floor, revealing Zane behind her.

'Oh mate, what have you done?' Zane strode into the room wearing a concerned smile.

Damon's tongue stuck to the roof of his mouth, a horrible ringing in his ears. 'Wha…?' His eyes darted to the nurse. 'No! You can't le…'

'I'll fetch some fresh water, Damon, while you chat to your brother.' Lightly placing her hand on Zane's shoulder, the nurse smiled. 'See if you can cheer this one up, Keith. I'll be back shortly.'

Keith? Zane Morelli was calling himself Keith? Pretending to be his goddamn brother? Damon hadn't even got a brother! Damon froze in fear, the words he longed to scream sticking somewhere between his stomach and his throat. He dug his elbows fruitlessly into the hard mattress to lever himself further up the bed away from the man who was about to steal Marco's pleasure.

No! He wouldn't die like this. Not here. Not now.

But then, what could he do? Fucking run away?

As the door closed behind the nurse, the smile slid from Zane's face. Moving quickly to the bed, he shoved his hand underneath the sheet and gripped one of Damon's stumps. Then he squeezed hard.

Really hard.

'AAAARGH!' Damon's scream was silenced by Zane's other hand clamping over his mouth. 'Shut the fuck up! We don't want to draw attention!'

The strong stitches securing the end of Damon's left stump buckled and broke under the onslaught of Zane's tightening grip. Vomit rushed into his mouth and blood seeped steadily through the thin sheet as Zane's thumb pushed into the raw flesh of his wound, the excruciating pain making lights flash behind his eyes.

'Who did this?' Zane hissed. 'Marco, I take it?' Seeing Damon's frantic nod, he twisted his thumb and pushed deeper into the ravaged flesh. 'Where is he? Tell me where my brother is, Sandler, or I'll kill you right here, right now.' His eyes narrowed into slits as he leant lower over Damon's sweating face. He removed his hand from over his mouth. 'Talk.'

'Marco shot me, then took the keys to the penthouse. He's gone there,' Damon gibbered, all instincts of giving up the fight diminishing. He wanted to live. He didn't want to die. He'd manage without legs. *Somehow*. 'Look! Please! He'll kill me! I'll do anything you want. I'll work for you. I'll...'

'Why would I want a cunt like *you*, working for *me*?' Zane moved his attention to Damon's other stump where he quickly performed the same manoeuvre. 'You tried to kill the woman I love.'

'I'm sorry, I'm sorry,' Damon gabbled, his brain swirling in light-headed agony. 'It was a mistake. I was confused. I...'

'And you killed Hazel!' Zane shoved his thumb deep into the space where Damon's right kneecap once lived.

'AAARGH! No! It wasn't me. It wasn't me!' Damon panted, his lungs heaving with unbearable pain. 'Martin Bolt did it. He's in on it with Marco! He's got your daughter too. Marco will take her, rape and kill her. They'll...'

'Stop lying or you'll wish it *was* Marco here rather than me! Did you forge Hazel's signature on that statement?'

'What? No!' Damon squawked. 'I don't know what her writing's like. She was dead when I got there and…'

'You're getting on my wick now,' Zane hissed. Pulling out his flick knife, he snapped it into position. 'Bleeding out is a shitty, slow way to go, Sandler…'

'Oh my God!' A nurse barged into the room, rushing straight over to slap the emergency buzzer.

Stepping back, Zane rapidly stowed his flick knife and reinstated his panicked expression. 'Damon went berserk! He tried to rip out his IV and pulled at his wounds,' he cried, his face a picture-perfect mode of distress. 'I couldn't stop him.'

'Step back please, sir,' the nurse cried, removing the blood-soaked sheets to reveal Damon's ghastly wounds as more nurses and doctors ran into the room. 'This one needs to go back to surgery and quickly!'

Retreating against the door, Zane kept his worried look in place. 'I'll leave you to it.'

Exiting the room, his crafted expression fell to be replaced by a thunderous one.

Bollocks! Damon Sandler had got away with that by the skin of his teeth and there was slim chance of a repeat opportunity.

He quickened his pace down the shiny corridor, the smell of antiseptic and bleach stinging his nostrils. He may not have finished Sandler, but now he knew for definite where Marco was this hadn't been a complete wasted journey.

Two

SITTING ON THE END of the bed Martin Bolt had recently begun sharing with Skye, he watched her apply her makeup.

How things had changed in a matter of days. This time last week after being run off the road; battered by Damon Sandler; been forced to risk his life by breaking into the place where his girlfriend worked to save her from the people he believed were holding her hostage and then taking refuge in a cupboard while Skye's father and his men combed the vicinity in order to kill him, his outlook had appeared bleak. But things had now changed and his life couldn't have transformed more dramatically.

He didn't think he'd ever been happier.

He watched Skye Wilson slick another coat of mascara onto her lashes. She didn't need makeup. She was so beautiful it was unnecessary, but Skye could do whatever she liked, providing she remained in his life.

The thought of not being with her filled Martin with off-the-scale angst. That angst was why he'd put himself in the position which most people would run a mile in the opposite direction from rather than risk in the first place. But he'd risked it. He'd risked everything for Skye and he'd do it all again if required, no questions asked.

'Are you trying to tell me something, Marty?' Skye eyed Martin in the reflection of her dressing table mirror. 'You're watching me so intently it's like you're after makeup tips!'

Skye's infectious, melodious laughter made Martin smile. In fact, *everything* about Skye made him smile. He glowed with happiness. 'I'm just thinking how gorgeous you are.'

Getting up, Skye moved to sit on Martin's lap. Wrapping her arms around his neck, she kissed him, knowing her plump lips always left him longing for more. 'I'm hoping today will be the day that we can start getting back to normal,' she said. 'I'll go out of my mind without something to do.'

Extracting herself from Martin before he got carried away, Skye returned to the mirror to inspect herself. Her jet-black hair shone with a blue sheen, just like that of her father's. She owed the same piercing blue eyes to him too. Luckily, all the Morellis shared the same physical traits otherwise it would be impossible to get away with what she'd successfully concealed.

And *that* couldn't be uncovered until the time was right.

For Skye, that time couldn't come soon enough because being nice to everyone was wearing thin.

'It's good of your Dad to let me stay here,' Martin said, his smile almost permanently engraved into his face. 'He didn't have to. With everything that happened, things could have turned out very differently.'

Skye's face fell. *Would Martin ever stop bleating about that?* Rather than revealing her irritation, she pulled on a hurt look. 'I don't know how many times I can apologise for what I did, Marty.'

'Hey!' Getting up, Martin pulled Skye into his arms. 'You explained your reasons and we've started again, have we not?' He kissed the top of her head. Skye *had* explained why she'd lied about his existence; why she'd made out he was stalking her and the other awful things she'd said. It had hurt - *really* hurt and he wasn't sure whether he completely understood why she'd done it, but they had agreed to start again - or rather, *he'd* begged for them to start again. They'd had such a good relationship before Skye became thrown off kilter with the stress of searching for her father and he didn't want to lose her. Plus, he loved her, so that was all there was to it.

But sometimes he couldn't help but wonder *why*...

Still, that was in the past. The future was what mattered. Despite residing in the house of an infamous and feared criminal gang leader, who up until a mere few days ago had wanted him dead, he was happier than ever. Life moved in mysterious ways and it was working out well.

However, there was one thing Martin really did need to do and that prospect of touching base with his parents hung over him like a dark cloud. But he wouldn't think about that just now.

Not while he was so happy.

• • • •

THERE WERE WORSE PLACES Leo Holland could be tasked to watch than a luxury apartment complex overlooking the Thames. But knowing *why* he was sitting outside watching it and exactly who was *inside* wasn't the best.

That Marco Morelli lounged around in the lap of luxury inside the penthouse Zane owned, but being unable to do anything about the insult was torturous. All Leo wanted to do was go in, gun the fucker down and be done with it.

After all, that's what would happen in the end and patience wasn't one of his strong points.

However, there was one upside of watching for signs of Marco leaving the building or for anyone entering that might signify them to be a new member stupid enough to do his dirty work. And that was catching up with his friend and colleague.

Handing Tiger Shoreham a cigarette, Leo chucked the packet on the dashboard. 'It's good to see you, mate,' he smiled, bringing his lighter to life. 'I know it hasn't been long, but hey - I guess I miss you!' He playfully punched Tiger's arm. 'I also wanted to personally say that it was good of you to check on Sandler before leaving town. Given the circumstances, no one expected you to do that, but if it wasn't for you, I'd have walked into an attempted murder scene and been the prime suspect.'

He glanced at his watch. 'Thanks to your eagle eye giving us the gen about what happened in order to track him down, anytime around now, Zane will have personally dispatched Mr Sandler from within his hospital bed.'

Tiger grinned. 'Glad to be of assistance! Besides, when your existence has revolved around a certain way of life since the off, it's impossible to just turn your back like *that.*' He clicked his fingers for emphasis. 'That's why I'm here now. When I got your text saying you'd been sent to watch the wanker in there, how could I resist?'

Leo had promised not to broach the subject burning the tip of his tongue. He'd told himself over and over that it wouldn't be discussed unless Tiger brought it up, but it was impossible. Sitting here like brother-in-arms only brought home with stark reality that he'd be on his own again the moment Tiger got out of the van.

The pleasure of Damon Sandler's expected demise evaporated.

Taking a long drag of his cigarette, Leo exhaled, the smoke pooling around the low ceiling of the van. 'Have you reached a decision about returning to the firm?'

Tiger's gaze remained fixed on the double doors of the apartment complex visible from where they'd parked just out of sight. 'I do nothing *but* think about that.' He sighed. 'It's only been a few days and I miss you all like crazy. You lot have been my life for so long it's unnatural not being part of it.'

Leo looked up hopefully. He'd do anything to have Tiger back in the fold and put right the disastrous reactions to the events which forced this man into taking time out in the first place. 'Does that mean you're...?'

'I'm not sure whether I'm coming back yet.' Tiger shrugged. 'I want to. Of *course* I do, but then I remember what Zane presumed and what you *all* gave credence to. It might not have been for long, but everyone still believed it feasible and that isn't something I find easy to ignore.'

Leo's huge shoulders sagged. 'I know, mate. It wasn't something any of us found easy to stomach, but...'

'But you all thought I *might* have done what that little bitch alleged,' Tiger hissed. 'And that grates like fuck!'

Leo nodded. He understood completely. He and Tiger were Zane's two most trusted right-hand-men and that Zane's daughter had successfully fabricated and manipulated things, accusing Tiger of assaulting her, alleging that rape was on the cards, was one thing in a long list the girl had done to cause grief. Tiger leaving being one of the most detrimental. That, and almost succeeding in convincing Zane that Erin – his fiancée, was mentally unstable.

Just because Skye had since admitted Tiger had done nothing and it was all part of her resentment over Zane's absence from her life, didn't change the accusation of something so heinous. Or for a moment in time, they'd all considered it plausible.

Okay, so everyone had struggled to believe that Tiger would even *think* of doing such a thing. It wasn't in his nature and he'd always been 100% trustworthy, but Skye had made it seem convincing. Masterminding it for Zane to walk in just after she'd ripped her own clothes off and thrown herself at Tiger was perfectly executed. That Tiger had been horrified and merely restraining her wasn't visible when Zane burst in, finding his daughter half naked with one of his most trusted men.

Skye had the opportunity to throw a cat amongst the pigeons and she'd chucked it with both hands. No excuses or apologies made that better.

'Does it make a difference by me telling you that the guards on duty that day were put right?' Leo pressed. 'Zane made Skye explain to them what she'd done. She didn't like doing that, believe me.'

'I bet,' Tiger muttered resentfully. 'But whatever she said to redress it, mud sticks.'

'Only if people talk and Zane's made sure none of those men will say a bean. Not if they want their job.'

Tiger flicked his cigarette end out of the van's window and thought for a moment. 'Skye's still at Zane's house and therefore will be around somewhere wherever I go. Aside from not being altogether confident I can look at her without ripping her fucking face off for what she's done, it would be awkward.'

'Only as much as you allow,' Leo shrugged. 'The girl's a bitch. Whatever she's saying and doing to "make it up to everyone" means jack shit to me. I don't like her and don't trust her, but as Zane's daughter we're stuck with her. With any luck, she'll fuck off back to her mother's soon and take that deluded boyfriend with her!'

For Martin Bolt to remain by Skye's side like an infatuated puppy after what she'd also said about him, made Leo want to sling the lad out of the window to put him out of his misery.

'Perhaps I'll shortly have that talk with Zane like I promised after all,' Tiger said, still staring intently at the penthouse complex entrance door. 'But back to this - there's sod all happening in there. Marco must be lying low.'

Leo grinned. While Marco remained holed up and Sandler hopefully by now on a one-way descent to hell, things were good. And until that changed, it was clear that no one needed to be kept under lock and key. Plus, from what had been said, there was a chance that Tiger would be back within the inner circle sooner rather than later, therefore today looked promising.

THREE

CUTTING A LINE of coke between the large breasts of the woman he'd booked to relieve his frustration, Marco snorted it then nipped the blonde's left nipple with his teeth.

Sneering at the muffled yelp from the spreadeagled figure on his bed, Marco listened to the voice coming from his mobile. There was no need to worry that this slag here would repeat anything. The amount of gear he'd plied her with, she wouldn't remember a fucking thing.

He didn't want conversation from this paid encounter - he just needed to lighten the load in his balls and give this tart a bit of a slap. It wasn't like he wanted to marry the bitch!

His lips curled into a sneer. He'd done marriage once and that wouldn't be happening again! All the years he'd hankered over Hazel Grimes, AKA Lisa Tequila - the golden star of the adult film industry, and the cow turned him over. She'd even gone as far as palling up with the other side, the devious slut.

Nope. Never again.

But now Hazel was dead, courtesy of his daughter, it showed it never paid to pull a fast one on Marco Morelli.

Because that's who he was - Marco Morelli - and he ruled this city.

Or he had...

Zane stealing his territories whilst he'd languished in a shitty Battersea police station cell was a low move, but his brother hadn't pulled *everything* off in the way he'd planned, had he? Plus, the stupid bastard hadn't possessed the nous to take back his own penthouse when he'd had the chance either.

No matter. *He* was out now and back to reclaim what had been his mere *weeks* ago.

'Yeah, I'm still listening,' Marco barked in the direction of the mobile balanced on the bedside table. He frowned at Skye's voice screeching through the speaker like a petulant child. 'What do you mean, you can't stand it anymore?' His eyes narrowed. 'You'll stand it as long as you have to in order to sort this.'

The last thing he wanted was hysterical demands just because of fluctuating hormone levels! Skye may be the daughter he wasn't aware he'd even got until recently, but he wasn't having histrionics. He'd have to put up with the way she did things to an extent because he needed her. Not only to sort this, but to get the ultimate revenge on his bastard brother by unveiling that the child he'd been led to believe was his, was in fact, not.

Skye had done bloody well so far. *Better* than well. But she was correct in saying that they had to move forward and take advantage whilst they could. However, Skye needed to have a word with herself about her expectations regarding living here. Marco didn't want her here. It would cramp his style.

And style he had bucket loads of...

He glanced in the floor to ceiling mirror covering an entire wall of the master bedroom and admired his well-built physique and rippling muscles. *Yep, still looking shit hot.*

Marco then checked the woman on his bed was still off with the fairies, then turned his attention back to his daughter on the other end of the line. 'Okay, this is how it's going to go. I'll send you names of men I want you to touch base with and where to find them. I want their allegiance and you're going to arrange that.'

He frowned. 'Yeah, some of them have worked for me in the past. They're decent enough and aren't connected to anyone else... Yeah, that's right. No, that bit is up to you to sort out. I'm entrusting you to broker this, Skye, so give them what they want in order to work for me.'

And that's what a sizeable chunk of his nest egg would go on. Unfortunate, not to mention galling, but necessary nonetheless.

'What? I don't know, but whatever happens, not here. I'll leave it up to you to find a suitable base where discussions and further instructions can be given… Yeah, a place to meet away from prying eyes and flapping fucking ears.'

Getting irritated by the questions, Marco knelt between the thighs of the barely conscious woman and spread out another thick line of cocaine on her supine body. 'Yeah, I'll text you shortly. Keep me posted.'

Leaning across, Marco ended the call. That was enough conversation. Skye could get on with the job. Even as a woman and a very young one at that, the girl was hard-headed enough to sort it. Now it was a question of whether his instincts were correct. This was his daughter's chance to show him what she was made of and he was pretty certain she would succeed.

With that set in the pipeline, he'd get on with achieving some much-needed release. He'd text Skye the relevant details later.

Pulling the unconscious woman's thighs wider, Marco lined up his engorged erection and slammed home.

• • • •

PULLING HIS YAMAHA FJ1200 up outside the rented home in Dalston, Zane rushed inside. Barrelling into the kitchen, he swooped Erin Langley off her feet and spun her around. 'I have news!'

Squealing in surprise as Zane pressed his mouth hungrily on hers, Erin heart surged with both excitement and anticipation. That her relationship with Zane was back on track was fantastic, but did his unexpected return to the house mean *good* news? And if so, then *how* good?

Erin didn't think anything could be better than hearing news that Zane's brother and Damon Sandler had both been swallowed by a freak sinkhole never to be seen again, but she doubted anyone could be that lucky.

Pulling his mouth from Erin's, Zane grinned, his piercing blue eyes twinkling and her heart jolted once again at the sheer masculinity the man held. He exuded raw power and the magnetic pull he held over her, even when driving her to distraction, hadn't waned regardless of the immense pressure lumped on them during their short, yet full on, unconventional relationship.

Always a ruggedly handsome man, when the lines of stress and fierceness usually present on his face were absent, his features transformed into what Erin believed to be the most gorgeous man in the world. One, whom whichever face he wore, had won her heart and soul all but from their very first meeting. Even the deep scar running below one eye down his right cheek, done via Marco's orders as an act of retribution, was a part of Zane that Erin wouldn't change.

'Are you going to tell me what the news is or shall I guess?' Erin asked breathlessly, hardly daring to hope something really good had happened.

'Well, it could be better, but it's not bad either.' Zane chucked his leather jacket over the back of a kitchen chair. After the ill-timing which put paid to his plan of permanently removing Sandler from this world, he'd managed to transform his initial rage. During the ride home, he'd floored his bike along every available stretch of road at full throttle so that the wind blasting over him at over 100 miles an hour would temporarily rid him of his resentment over the failed attempt and replace it with the positives.

He could revisit the screw-up with Sandler shortly, but for now, it was vital that he brought home good news. Sitting down, he pulled Erin astride him. 'Sandler won't be going anywhere for a very long time, if ever. And it's been confirmed that Marco is indeed inside the penthouse.'

Erin frowned. 'Okay, but didn't we kind of think that anyway?'

Zane smiled - a crooked smile using just one side of his mouth. 'Yes, we *thought* that to be the case, but you know presumption is dangerous. Now these presumptions are facts because after my interesting "visit" to see Sandler in intensive care, I sent Leo to watch the penthouse and he's confirmed everything.'

Erin's heart soared. 'So, does that mean...?'

'It means that you're not at risk from Sandler and neither is Skye. Marco's got no one so he'll be holed up for as long as it takes to find anyone stupid enough to work for him.' Zane's eyes sparkled. 'With no money, no contacts, no territories and no safe way of stepping foot outside his self-imposed prison, it means that not only is time on our side to ensure we're ready and waiting to cut him off any which way he moves, but we - or rather you and Skye specifically, are safe to get back on with life until the situation changes. And,' he added with a wink, 'there'll be someone continually watching the penthouse to see if a) Marco leaves and b), anyone goes in.'

Erin's breath caught in her throat. The avalanching relief wasn't down to the disintegration of the threat of Marco or Sandler which had been hanging over her like a miasma for so long, but because she could finally leave this house without an armed escort.

'What about when Sandler recovers?' Erin frowned. 'When he gets better, then he...'

'Sandler won't be getting better,' Zane said, his voice becoming cold. Sandler would *never* recover because he'd find a way to finish what he'd gone to do today. *That* time there would be no interruptions.

'Then this *is* good news!' Erin cupped Zane's face, her mouth searching for his.

'It's such good news that it would be rude not to celebrate...' Zane's hand reached down to unbutton Erin's jeans.

'Oh God, no!' Skye laughed as she entered the kitchen. 'I come in for a drink, only to find you two about to get down and dirty. Can't you guys get a room?'

Zane immediately withdrew his hand and Erin swallowed the urge to point out that this was *their* home, not Skye's and they could do what they liked. Enough time had been wasted in firefighting the shit between them that this girl had caused but voicing that wouldn't keep their unspoken truce going.

'Actually, I'm glad you're here,' Zane said, deflecting from the unusual red hue of his cheeks, relieved Skye hadn't walked in ten seconds later. 'I wanted to talk to both you and Erin about the Starbright.'

FOUR

PETER BOLT stared out of the large bay window onto his driveway, his face screwing up at the sight.

It wasn't like he hadn't seen it before - he'd stared at it at least a thousand times, but the fact remained the same: the police, no longer needing to keep hold of the car which had crashed, sparking panic that Martin who'd borrowed it had been inside, had dissipated once he'd got in contact, safe and well. Hence the car had been released back to the registered keeper.

Peter.

But he was not happy.

Peter's eyes drifted over the mangled metal of his beloved Range Rover, his blood pressure increasing.

Bloody ruined, it was. A complete write-off. That was the last time he'd *ever* lend a car to Martin, the stupid boy. To make matters worse, Fiona shrugged off the ruined motor, like it didn't matter.

Well, it *did* matter. It mattered a *lot.*

'Staring at it won't change anything, Peter.' Fiona eyed her husband. 'You should be glad that Martin is safe. A car isn't important in the grand scheme of things.'

Peter scowled. *Yes, it was.* He liked that bloody motor. Out of all his cars, that Range Rover was one of his favourites. It was useful for transporting his golf clubs. Not that he played very often but that wasn't the point. 'I'd like to know when that son of ours will bother showing his face,' he moaned. 'Phoning you to say he's all right after the worry he put us through is all very well, but to then remain somewhere in London with that... that *girl*, saying they'd be back "soon", isn't acceptable as far as I'm concerned.'

Fiona made a point of inspecting her manicured fingernails rather than revealing the worry coursing through her veins. It had been the same since Martin phoned. She did not buy her son's explanation as to what had happened whilst he'd been away. 'At least those men are no longer watching the house,' she said casually.

'They shouldn't have been here in the first place, the damned cheek!' Peter muttered. When that thug appeared here - in *his* house, alleging Martin was causing problems and then having the audacity to manhandle him, he should have called the police immediately. And he would have, had it not been for Fiona insisting it would put Martin at risk. Yet, surprise surprise, Martin had been in no danger at all.

His son had let him down by getting so drunk to leave the Range Rover keys lying about for some thief to steal, yet the boy didn't possess the courage to return home and face the music? Preferring to stay away with that girlfriend of his? Who, Peter might add, would be his girlfriend no longer after this. Certainly not after seeing with his own eyes how much of a lunatic her mother was.

Talking of which...

'I hope you've had nothing further to do with that crazy woman.' Peter arched an eyebrow at his wife. 'There's nothing else to say to Shirley.'

'Mmm,' Fiona mumbled non-committedly, pretending to thumb through the latest copy of *House and Garden*. She'd thought it best not to mention that she'd remained in close contact with Shirley and intended to continue doing so.

Skye's mother disbelieved Martin's story as much as she did and what with the visitor from the past Shirley had received and her general hatred towards Skye's father - whoever that was, it was fast heading to where Fiona had no choice but to go to London herself and see exactly what was happening.

It was Shirley who'd involved Martin in the crazy goose chase to locate Skye after she'd snuck off in pursuit of the father she'd never known, so more than anyone, Shirley knew what that might entail. The problem was that the woman had divulged little.

Shirley may have been vague with the facts and offered little information, but Fiona wasn't waiting forever. She was fairly certain that Skye's father was either Zane Morelli or someone known to the man. Martin had mentioned that name, or something similar, before in relation to Skye's father. But she didn't know anything for certain.

That these Morelli characters appeared to be the opposite side of the law didn't help her underlying worry over this whole troublesome situation. And being as Martin was involved with them to a certain degree, she'd go on the search herself and deduce exactly what he was doing in under the guise of being in love with Skye Wilson.

But she wouldn't tell Peter. He'd only stop her again.

Fiona's lips pursed with determination. She had to find out what was going on and deal with it accordingly. Her son was too important not to.

• • • •

'THAT JUST SHOWS how similarly we think,' Skye gushed, her eyes shining with excitement. She looked between Zane and Erin. 'I'm glad you brought up the subject of the Starbright. Aside from going crazy about having nothing to do, I've been thinking about those women who had to be temporarily housed at Mr Solenzo's practice. It's a great idea to move them back to the Starbright refuge now the danger has passed. You opening that centre to help women was an amazing thing to do, Zane.'

Erin frowned. 'The danger you speak of as passing is only for now.' She glanced at Zane, surprised at his suggestion. 'Is it not slightly premature to move the women back when they might need evacuating again at any given time?'

'We can't put everything on hold indefinitely based on what my brother may or may not do.' Zane steepled his fingers under his chin. 'I still have plenty of guards stationed at the Starbright. Hazel did a great job of getting the place up and running and I don't want that progress wasted.'

'Even though she shafted you...' Skye sniped.

Erin's head shot up. She was not convinced Hazel had done any such thing. The unlikely friendship forged between them told her that Hazel would not have signed a statement to get the charges against Marco - the *true* accusations regarding sex trafficking and murder at Luna Film Studios, dropped.

Hazel wouldn't have lied to her or Zane *or* sided with Marco behind their backs. She'd been desperate to divorce Marco and couldn't wait until she was free and safe from him after he'd been sent to jail. She wouldn't have signed that paperwork, she just wouldn't.

Zane may have eventually reluctantly believed that Hazel had betrayed him, like the rest also seemed to, but Erin didn't. However, proving otherwise was difficult.

'So...' Drumming her fingers on the kitchen table, Skye looked at Zane hopefully. 'What do you think about me running the Starbright?'

'*You*?' Erin spluttered.

'Why not?' Skye pouted. 'I want to be of use and Zane said himself there's no danger at the moment.' *And nor would there be...* 'I was doing well there until... until that dreadful thing happened to Hazel.' She cleared fake emotion from her throat. 'So, can I?'

Zane sat back in the chair. 'I don't know... I hadn't considered you running the place.'

'Why not?' Skye pushed on a look of hurt. 'Hazel showed me how everything there runs and I believe I could do it.'

'Okay,' Zane smiled. 'Go for it then. Only on a trial basis though.'

'Zane, perhaps you...' Erin trailed off. There was nothing she could say without exposing the one thing she didn't want to voice. Whatever her personal feelings about Skye, she had to make the effort for Zane's sake.

Since Skye's admission and apology for her behaviour and the manipulative lies she'd told over the past few weeks which had all but trashed her and Zane's relationship, not to mention having people believe she was losing her mind with 'wild and undeserved' theories and the unforgivable lies spouted about Tiger, Erin couldn't deny that Skye had since behaved like the model daughter. And her becoming a stepdaughter - which is what Skye would be after she and Zane married, the relationship between them had to be rebuilt.

On the surface it seemed feasible. Since Skye admitted her resentment over Zane's absence in her life was behind the illogical hate campaign designed to ruin everyone around her, she'd gone out of her way to put things right. Much to everyone's surprise – Erin's especially, Skye had been nothing but pleasant, helpful and everything she should have been in the first place. But, as much as she wished it wasn't seated within her brain, prodding and nudging every nerve ending she possessed, there was something about Skye Wilson which didn't sit right.

No matter how more palatable and less stressful it would be to start over like she'd agreed, Erin couldn't rid herself of the deep-seated mistrust of the seventeen-year-old who was such an important part of Zane's life.

The worst part now Hazel was dead was not having anyone to discuss her worries with. She couldn't say anything about it to Zane because it would break his heart if he knew she still mistrusted Skye.

There wasn't a specific reason either, just *something...* Something that made its presence known deep down. If there was a way to stop these feelings or work out exactly where they stemmed from, Erin didn't know how, so there was nothing else to do but keep up the act and hope she was proved wrong.

'So, it's agreed?' Skye clapped her hands in excitement. 'Brilliant! I'll get started there tomorrow.'

'There's just one condition.' Zane looked from his daughter to Erin.

Skye raised her eyebrows. 'What's that?'

'Erin helps you to run the Starbright. You can do it together.'

'What?' Erin gasped. *Spending all day with Skye was the last thing she wanted.*

'It will be good for you both,' Zane said, pleased with his decision. 'It will blow away the cobwebs of the past. Plus, you'll both be somewhere with heavy security which will give me peace of mind. I've got a lot coming up over the next few days at the canning works, so I need the Starbright running like clockwork with minimal input from me.'

'It's a fantastic idea!' Skye beamed, not meaning a word of it. 'Just think, Erin. This way we can build a *real* relationship. I promised I'd make up for everything I've done in the past and this is the perfect way to prove that to you.'

And although she didn't want the suspicious bitch hanging around and watching her like a hawk, the Starbright had just revealed itself as being the perfect cover for getting things together for Marco. It wouldn't be difficult to keep Erin distracted. There was so much to do at the Starbright there wouldn't be time to bat an eyelid at what *she* was up to.

Skye smiled widely. 'This will be so good!' And the sooner she got things in motion meant the sooner she'd be out of this dump, away from Zane, Erin and Martin and living in the penthouse with her *real* father.

FIVE

WAITING FOR SKYE to come down the hallway, Zane kissed Erin, wishing he could remain here rather than going out. When Skye reached him, he turned and kissed the top of her head. 'Good luck today, both of you.' He then looked to Leo. 'After you've dropped them at the Starbright, you're picking up the women from Solenzo's?'

'Yeah,' Leo nodded. 'I've already spoken to the Starbright's morning shift and one of the men will drive the second van so we can return the women in one go.'

Zane frowned. 'Hang on, if you're doing that, who's watching the penthouse?'

Pausing at the door, Leo waited until Skye and Erin had clambered into his van. 'Tiger.'

'*Tiger*?' Zane's face broke into a wide grin. 'He's back? That's great! He didn't say! We were supposed to talk but I haven't apologised yet or...'

'He's not back per se,' Leo shrugged. 'I met up with him yesterday and he's doing this as a favour for me. He knew I couldn't deal with the women *and* watch the penthouse. It's only for today though, but he'll talk to you soon. No offence, but you need to get a guard doing stuff like this rather than me.'

Zane's elation at Tiger's possible return disintegrated. He wanted his man back in the fold for good so that the unpleasantness Skye's fake allegations had caused could be put to one side, but he'd wait as long as he had to.

And yes, he did need a guard on watch rather than tying up the only experienced man he officially had left in his inner circle. 'I'll get someone else on it tomorrow but please tell Tiger I appreciate him stepping in.'

After Leo left, Zane shut the door and walked down the hallway hoping Erin embraced the chance to build a proper relationship with Skye. It was all he wanted – to provide the family Skye had never had and be with Erin - the woman he loved.

Entering the kitchen, he was surprised to see Martin at the table. 'You're up early!'

Martin smiled nervously. 'I was hoping to catch you before you went out.'

Zane glanced at his watch. 'I'm strapped for time, but if it's quick then, yes, go on.'

'Well, I... erm... I was wondering if you had any… erm... work I could do?'

Zane paused with one arm in his leather jacket. 'Work for me? I presumed you'd be heading home now you and Skye have sorted things out. She mentioned you're going to university in September.'

'That's the thing,' Martin grinned sheepishly. 'I've decided not to. Some things are more important.' He took a deep breath. 'I love Skye and want to be with her. These last few weeks have underlined just how much and I… erm… I want to marry her.'

'*Marry* her?' Zane cried. 'What does Skye think about this?'

Martin's cheeks glowed red. 'I haven't asked her yet. I wanted to speak to you first. I'm planning on renting a flat too but to do that I need money and well… I thought I'd ask if you had anything I could do...'

Zane frowned, unsure whether he liked the sound of this.

They were both so young, but then again, he couldn't say Martin wouldn't do his all in looking after Skye. *But there was another issue.* 'I'm not sure whether my line of work is suitable…'

Martin laughed, relieved to not be immediately turned down. 'I know what you do, Mr Morelli, and let's face it - I've experienced what that involves to a certain extent...' He gestured to his healing facial injuries, courtesy of Damon Sandler. 'I'd be willing to learn whatever you need.'

Folding his arms, Zane nodded. *That was true.* It was also true that living here these past few days, Martin had been exposed to discussions surrounding the firm. Not directly, but he'd overheard plenty. There was little point placing the lad out of earshot, considering what he'd been involved in during his pursuit to find Skye. And as the lad loved Skye, it wasn't like he was untrustworthy.

That Martin wanted to take responsibility and provide a home for Skye earned an additional tick in Zane's box too. He wouldn't lie - with both Skye and Martin now in the house it was getting somewhat cramped - certainly not something to be endured on a permanent basis and if Martin and Skye had a flat close by, then Skye would remain near. 'Okay, let me think about it. I might have something for you.' He pulled on the other half of his jacket. 'I have to get on now. Oh, and call me Zane.'

'Great! Thanks!' Martin beamed. 'I appreciate it.' But what he *didn't* appreciate was that he couldn't put off talking to his parents any longer. Especially with the advent of his decision. Not taking up his place at the renowned university he'd had his heart set on for so long wouldn't be happily received, but his mind was made up. Skye was his world, his life and his future and no one could make him think otherwise.

He stopped Zane halfway through the door. 'There's just one more favour… Can I borrow a car?'

• • • •

GLANCING AT HER PHONE, Skye shoved it back into her

handbag. She didn't have time for texts now.

She'd already received details from Marco with the names of the men he wanted located. Luckily, Erin hadn't asked who the text was from when it came through on the way here. Skye had purposefully angled the phone away so Erin couldn't see. The nosy bitch would have presumed it was Martin. It usually was...

But she needed to get things sorted to justify ducking out later to go to the place Marco mentioned and see if she could find those men. The quicker things were in the pipeline, the better.

'That's right, ladies,' Skye said, welcoming the women clambering out of the vans through the front door of the Starbright Centre, her confidence belying her seventeen years. 'It's great to have you back!' She beamed, honestly not caring if they were here or not. These craggy tarts could stay under Mr Solenzo's protection within the special area reserved for 'Morelli clients' forever. But them being here at least brought more comings and goings which would help with doing what Marco needed. The more distractions to keep Erin's nosy beak out of her business, the better.

Damn Zane for throwing the spanner of Erin in the works, Skye thought. But she could hardly kick up a fuss. Not if her alleged wish of becoming 'great friends' with that cow was to be believed.

'Friends my arse,' Skye muttered under her breath. That was something that would never happen and the quicker that woman joined Hazel in hell, the happier she'd be. 'If you can make your way up to your old rooms,' she continued, her face already aching with the strain of being so bloody nice.

Feeling a tug on her jacket, Skye turned to find a woman's bony fingers clutching her sleeve. 'Yes? What is it?'

'Where is the Hazel lady?' a woman asked, the deep lines of stress and overwork making her appear older than she was.

'Hazel's no longer here,' Skye explained carefully. 'A family problem.' *That was the story they'd agreed on.* Erin's insistence not to upset the women with details of a murder occurring under their noses was apparently important.

'Oh! That is big shame,' the woman said, her Polish accent thick. 'We like Hazel. She very kind.'

'Yeah, but I'm in charge now.' Skye stared at the hand still clutching her sleeve. *If this tramp didn't remove her fingers, then she'd...* 'So, if you could go and get settled back in your room?' Turning away, the buzz of another text coming from the direction of her handbag melted the fixed smile on her beautiful face into a scowl.

Unable to stand the irritation, she snatched out her phone and brought the screen to life.

[2 text messages]

Rolling her eyes, she opened one.

Hope things are going well?
Might have some good news but will be late back 2nite.
Love u x

Was the good news anything to do with Martin going home and cease clinging to her like a thistle? If only...

Skye moved to the next text:

When r we going to meet up? It's been ages and I want to hear the goss x

Skye frowned, wishing beyond anything that she hadn't been so stupid to give Alyson her new phone number.

Previously trashing her old phone to get rid of the evidence Erin had on her was the perfect reason not to put up with Alyson ever again. But thinking the connection may still come in useful, she'd given her 'friend' the number of the spangly new phone Zane had furnished her with. Now Alyson kept texting,

texting and texting, Skye wished she hadn't.

Alyson Read was a stuck up, silly cow - someone she'd only been friends with through school and beyond because the girl's parents had the best cars and poshest house. It made her look better associating with people who flaunted their money. Plus, being as Alyson was so big on the concept of 'best friends' she was willing to do and say anything required. It used to be things like backing up Skye's story that they had a study day, when really, they skived off school to go to the shops. Not that Alyson quit moaning the whole time, but these days she came in handy for alibis such as sleepovers and family holidays in Scotland... After all, that was how Skye had got away with looking for her father without her mother getting wind in the first place.

Alyson being so desperate to please was useful, but she was boring as hell. It wasn't like Skye could say what she was *really* doing. Alyson would have a fit of conscience and blow everything. She might even tell Shirley!

And that's how Skye saw her mother - as 'Shirley', not *mother*. Mothers weren't lunatics; they didn't dress like tramps or spend years hiding the truth from their children. They didn't do any of that. Even if Shirley had a personality transplant it was too late to make up for everything.

A sneer crept onto Skye's face. She had no need of Alyson or Martin anymore. She'd seen the collection of swanky cars in Marco's underground car park. Then there was the penthouse itself... Once this plan pulled off, she'd have her pick of cars, plus she'd be living somewhere flash overlooking the Thames!

Becoming aggravated that women were still hanging around, Skye gritted her teeth. 'Get a move on!'

For all she cared, these skanky bitches could stay in their rooms for eternity because she had better things to do. And one of those very things was to get Erin to make herself useful.

Six

WITH A TREMBLING HAND, Shirley slammed the telephone receiver back into the cradle and stared at it for a few seconds before hefting down her bulk to pull the cable from the phone socket. Doing this was to be on the safe side in case Zane attempted to ring back straightaway.

After he'd had the audacity to turn up here the other week, why would Zane Morelli phone her? She'd made it clear that she didn't want to see his face nor hear his voice ever again?

Shirley stumbled across the room to take back residence in the armchair, the cushioned upholstery compressing her body and reducing the violent trembling coursing through her.

Even though she'd disconnected the phone, her eyes tracked back to it, expecting it to ring. It remained silent. For now… But she'd have to plug it back in soon in case Skye tried to get in touch.

She swiped away the perspiration on her brow with pudgy fingers. She'd been on tenterhooks since Zane appeared on her doorstep pretending that he cared and that he was concerned about Skye. After that incident, it had taken *ages* to stop being frightened to breathe in case doing so summoned him back to the door. But Zane hadn't come and Shirley had begun to think that he'd taken her feelings on board.

But now he'd phoned she knew it would never stop.

Shirley didn't want to see, hear or talk to Zane or *any* of them. Ever.

Fighting to keep the rising tears under control she picked up her cup of coffee on automatic pilot and stared at it, wondering why it was in her hand. *She didn't like coffee, did she?*

She no longer knew what she wanted or what she liked and hadn't done for seventeen years. Existing had been the name of the game. Ploughing her worthless existence in looking after her daughter was the sole reason why she dragged air into her lungs.

It would have been preferable to slowly expire from lack of oxygen than continue in a world which ripped her soul from her body, but she had to remain doing what was needed. It had been that way from the start. Looking after Skye was the only thing keeping Shirley alive. If she'd succumbed to the urge and walked away from this eternal torture, then she'd have lost her daughter.

There was no choice but to remain alive after Skye was born or her parents would have farmed her new baby out for adoption quicker than she could blink. It was what they wanted and what they'd tried to do *countless* times since the second her mother walked in as she dressed, seeing with her own eyes the unmistakable shape of the six-month pregnancy Shirley had alternated between denying and trying to hide.

It was then that the horror and shame of her parents had been complete. Her father especially, had not let her forget the day Guiseppe Morelli had paid them a visit, forcing them to leave London. This became triplicated by the horrible truth that the wanton, promiscuous behaviour of their only daughter had resulted in a bastard.

A bastard that she was too far pregnant to remove. A bastard sired by *that* family.

Yes, Shirley had slept with Zane Morelli. He was her first

and she'd loved him. *Believed he loved her...*

Shirley closed her eyes in despair as unwanted memories pushed into her mind. She didn't want to think of it. It never went away, but now it was amplified. As for the terror of losing her daughter all those years ago, it looked like her worst fears had happened otherwise Skye would be here with her now.

Even after all of this time, tears pricked the back of her eyes. The unnecessary resurfacing of memories that usually hovered in a safe place just underneath the surface, where most of the time they remained, had flooded back. And it was all because Zane wouldn't allow her a tiny bit of respite.

After everything, he couldn't even let her go through the motions of what allegedly passed as a life without making things worse. Why couldn't he leave her alone and let her continue wading through the tatters of existence he and his family had left her with?

She'd managed for so long but now it had all been for nothing.

Believing that Zane: that animal, that filthy, violent psycho had loved her and wanted to marry her was the epitome of pure immature insanity.

If Zane had decided he wanted to be with the Sicilian woman promised to him rather than her, then she'd have preferred it if he'd broken her heart that way, rather than sending his brother to ruin her. There were less destructive ways to impress her unsuitability and give him the perfect excuse to pave the way for his preferred and *real* fiancée. But Zane had *chosen* to engineer the worst and cruellest way possible. And for that, she despised him.

Every single day since, Shirley had been forced to look around her - firstly at the immense home her parents purchased with the ill-gotten blood money and secondly, after they'd died, embarrassed by their disappointing daughter until the very end, having to bear the home she now lived in.

This one. One thing of many purchased with the payoff that had stolen her life.

Shirley blankly glanced around the huge lounge of her detached house. She didn't hate it. She didn't like it either. She felt nothing. Not anymore.

Every single possession she owned had been purchased one way or another with the money the Morellis supplied in exchange for the family leaving the city. The only good thing that filthy cash had bought was putting Skye through the best education and lavishing her with everything she wanted. But money couldn't heal *Shirley* - nothing could do that.

At least she'd ensured her daughter was raised and nurtured in a way so that there was not one drop of Morelli blood inside her.

Despite having her own valid reasons, removing any links to *that* family hadn't been a purely personal one. A long time ago – even before the baby which swelled the young Shirley's slim figure into the unmistakable shape highlighting her fall from grace, was born, she'd decided her child would not suffer because of how it had come to exist. It wasn't her baby's fault.

And Skye had not suffered - even after her looks began to resemble the family she should never have been part of. Shirley loved her child unconditionally and she'd believed she'd succeeded in keeping the Morelli genes inside Skye dormant.

Until the girl took off in pursuit of her father...

Not that Skye knew what the man had done. *No one* knew. That was something Shirley had vowed never to speak of. Not because she feared repercussions. The Morellis had already killed her. She remained silent for Skye's sake.

People could draw their own conclusions and think what they wanted, but there was one additional caveat that she'd promised herself: the Morelli's would never get within ten miles of her daughter.

Yet now they were and it was the worst feeling.

Skye was with *them*. And that nudged the final part of any will to live out of Shirley's heart.

If she couldn't get Skye back before those bastards destroyed and infected her beyond redemption, then there really was no reason to continue this hollow existence. Unless Zane called or turned up to return Skye to her rightful place, he needed to stay the hell away.

The only person she wanted to see less than Zane was her rapist.

But that Zane knew what Marco had done - *arranged* for him to defile her and then stood back whilst she and her family were driven out of town was in some ways worse.

• • • •

'THEY SEEM GLAD TO BE BACK,' Erin said, watching the last of the women disappear up the stairs. 'After everything they've been through, being uprooted again wasn't ideal so I'm pleased they've been able to return.'

'Yes,' Skye muttered, forcing herself to agree with Erin's holier-than-thou niceness towards these hookers.

Marco had the right idea. What better way to rake money in than by getting sluts to do what they did best – earning money on their backs and getting filmed in the process? Having the initiative to bring them into the country in a container didn't warrant criminal proceedings! The world was full of fucking do-gooders. It was downright wrong attempting to slap a criminal tag on a lucrative business decision. Marco had given those women a place to stay and a job - a whole lot more than what they'd had in whatever tinpot country they'd originated.

Skye was only glad that she'd aided in getting the ridiculous charges against Marco dropped.

Now, onto phase two...

'Oh no!' Skye stopped stock still in the corridor outside the room which had been Hazel's office.

Erin frowned. 'What's wrong?'

'I-I'm not sure whether I can bear using this room as my office,' Skye whispered, her eyes brimming with tears like they were so adept at doing when the need arose. 'I know I said I'd run things and I'd need all of Hazel's files but... but I can't face going in there.' She turned to Erin, her eyes haunted. 'It's pathetic, but even seeing that desk where she sat, rigid… her mouth full of money and... Oh God!' Heaving, she dry-retched.

'It's okay.' Erin placed her arm around Skye's trembling shoulders. She didn't blame the girl for being upset. What had happened to Hazel was bloody horrific. It would be difficult for Skye using the room where she'd discovered the grisly corpse. It wouldn't be easy for *anyone* knowing the history those four walls held.

She shuddered. An unwanted image of her friend choked with a throat-full of money filtered into Erin's mind. She hadn't seen the sight herself and didn't know whether how she envisaged it was worse or better than it actually had been, but either way it haunted her.

'Why don't you do what I planned on doing? Settle the women in upstairs and chat about what therapies they want to resume over the coming weeks,' Erin suggested, steering Skye away from Hazel's office. 'I'll box up the files in here and then one of the guys can remove the furniture. In the meantime, pick another room to use and I'll order new furniture. Zane won't mind.'

'Are you sure?' Skye clutched Erin's arm. 'Thank you. I didn't expect it to affect me so badly.'

'I think anyone would feel the same,' Erin smiled sadly. 'It's fine, you go on and I'll sort this.'

'The documentation I need is in the filing cabinets on the left and I suppose Hazel's personal stuff can be binned.' Skye looked down sadly. 'It's not like she needs it now.'

Neither did Hazel need all of that money crammed into her throat. Skye knew she could have used a lot less to get the job done and it irritated her that if she'd put a bit more thought into what she was doing she could have pocketed half herself. Still, it had achieved what was needed.

Trudging up the stairs, she kept up her distraught act until she was out of sight. A smile then crept back onto her lips. Erin could do her back in lugging around those bloody files. Meanwhile, she'd sit down and give Alyson a call to test the water.

Her idea was good and one that would suitably impress Marco. After that, she'd get on with picking out decent furniture for her new office.

SEVEN

ON ROUTE TO THE Thames Canning Works, Zane decided to take a quick detour. He hadn't been to the headquarters he'd recently set up using one of his father's old property purchases for a while. Marco was out, but he was on the bones of his arse with no one to scout the territories he'd previously had control over, so the man wasn't an immediate threat.

A smile flickered over Zane's lips. Regardless of Sandler still not yet being six feet under, most of the territories Marco had filched were now safely back in *his* hands. And things would only continue that way. It wasn't like Sandler could jump out of his ICU bed and "leg" it down to any of the territories to demand them back, was it?

Chuckling to himself as he pulled his bike into the cemetery on Swains Lane, Zane removed his crash helmet and wandered over to his father's grave. The last time he'd visited was when he'd first glimpsed Skye after finding the flowers she'd left. This, followed by her frequently following him had spawned the theory that the striking woman in the silver car was a possible enemy.

How things had changed.

Were he not in a graveyard, Zane would laugh.

The young woman's presence and unknown identity which had them all up in arms couldn't have turned out more differently.

Dropping to his haunches at the side of his father's headstone, Zane flicked a leaf off the meticulously tended grave. 'Hi Dad. Sorry I haven't been for a while,' he said, his voice low. 'I thought I'd let you know the business is going well and that Marco's plan didn't succeed. I also have other news...' His lips curled into a smile. 'You're a grandfather. Her name's Skye, she's seventeen, beautiful and you'd love her!'

How Zane wished his father had lived to see Skye, certain she'd be the apple of his eye.

'I've only just found out about her... It's a long story. We've had a few ups and downs, but it will be all right.' He traced his finger over the raised lettering of his father's name. 'I just need to sort things out with the girl's mother. You may remember her - Shirley Wilson? Being how important family was to you, I know you'd want me to deal with this situation properly, so regardless of her hiding my daughter from me all of these years, I'll see Shirley right.'

And he would. Now he knew what Skye had insinuated wasn't true, things were different: Skye wasn't raised in a hovel by an uncaring mother, nor was she surrounded by drunk, lecherous men. Shirley had looked after Skye well and clearly cared a lot about her, so he'd make sure the woman got the help she needed.

But doing that was proving harder than he'd thought. Although his initial visit to see Shirley a couple of weeks ago hadn't gone well, he'd thought the shock of seeing him again may have passed and now she'd be more receptive to talking for their daughter's sake.

Martin had previously confirmed he'd told his mother to pass onto Shirley the news of Skye's safe return to the house so her mind would be at rest over that. But after getting the phone slammed down on him again this morning, Zane had to accept getting any further with the woman wouldn't be plain sailing.

Shirley was clearly mentally disturbed, but he was determined to make peace and dissect why she loathed him so much, therefore he would arrange whatever help she needed to become well. That way he could get the answers he craved.

Zane brushed a few more twigs from around the grave. He didn't feel stupid talking aloud to his father. It was the closest he'd get to a conversation with the man he'd idolised and who he'd always strived to make proud. But although he told himself he wouldn't allow it to get to him, Zane couldn't prevent his eyes from moving to the inscription on the gravestone which had done nothing but plague him since first seeing it:

GUISEPPE ALPHONSE MORELLI
4th March 1928 – 15th February 1996

Father, husband and hero
Your legacy will live on in your only son

Zane's teeth clenched. He must get the stonemason to change the inscription Marco had instructed. Yeah, he knew it was a dig - another ploy to rub salt in the wound as if missing the funeral in the first place hadn't been enough, but it still grated.

Guiseppe Morelli had *two* sons, not one. And one of them didn't have the right to use the Morelli name.

Zane rose to his feet, reminding himself that it wasn't *him* who had nothing. The business was running well, he had a beautiful fiancée who loved him and a gorgeous, intelligent daughter.

What did Marco have? A penthouse that wasn't even his and a bunch of men who no longer worked for him?

A soft chuckle escaped from the back of Zane's throat.

Marco had failed. He'd achieved nothing and lost *everything*. He might have succeeded in deleting any mention of his existence from their father's headstone, but that would be rectified.

'I'm off now, Dad.' Zane traced his finger along the top of the headstone. 'I won't leave it so long next time.' For now though, he'd better get on with everything else.

And one of those things was to break the news to Leo about Damon Sandler.

• • • •

ERIN STARED AT THE BOXES of files taken from the filing cabinets in Hazel's office. It would have been easier to get the cabinets moved to a different room, but she'd promised Skye new furniture, so that was what would happen.

She glanced around the room again, each time sending a shiver of unease rippling through her. It was almost like the dying figure of Hazel might materialise in front of her, her face twisted in the grotesque expression she'd heard recounted so many times.

Taking a deep breath, she stepped behind Hazel's desk armed with another large empty box. This was the bit she'd been putting off - clearing Hazel's personal items. Thankfully there was only three drawers to sift through so it shouldn't take long.

Pulling open the first drawer, Erin picked out a handful of pens and pencils, a ruler and some Tippex. She turned a yellow pencil around in her hand, fingering the slight indentations at the end. A lump formed in her throat picturing Hazel sitting in this very seat with her notebook in hand, her brow furrowed, thinking of ideas to help the women housed in this refuge and for those yet to come. The pencil would be between her teeth as she concentrated, her long nails tapping on the desk before scribbling down her ideas.

Erin pulled open the second narrow drawer, revealing a packet of white envelopes, a book of stamps and a hardback diary. Tentatively pulling out the diary, she opened the page marked with blue ribbon.

The day Hazel died...

Biting her lip, Erin stared at Hazel's writing. It was like the woman herself: elaborate with flounces but distinctly clear.

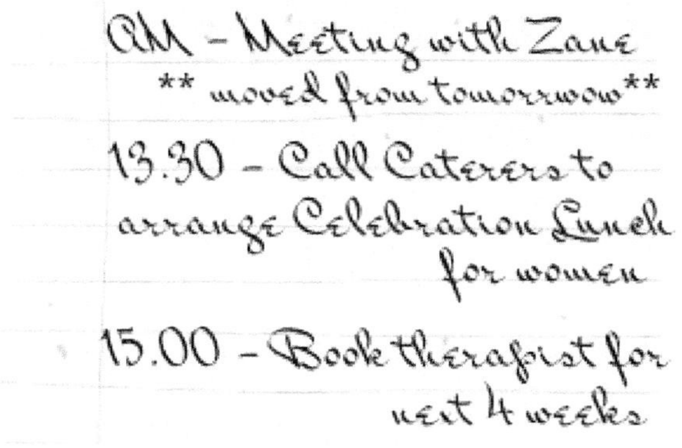
AM - Meeting with Zane
** moved from tomorrow **
13.30 - Call Caterers to
arrange Celebration Lunch
for women
15.00 - Book therapist for
next 4 weeks

Erin scanned the previous day, seeing the same sort of entries. She wasn't sure what she'd expected. It wasn't like there would be an entry saying: *"appointment with my murderer"*, was it?

About to close the diary, she flicked to the week afterwards - the week Hazel never got to see. More ideas and arrangements for the women.

And a Post-it note...

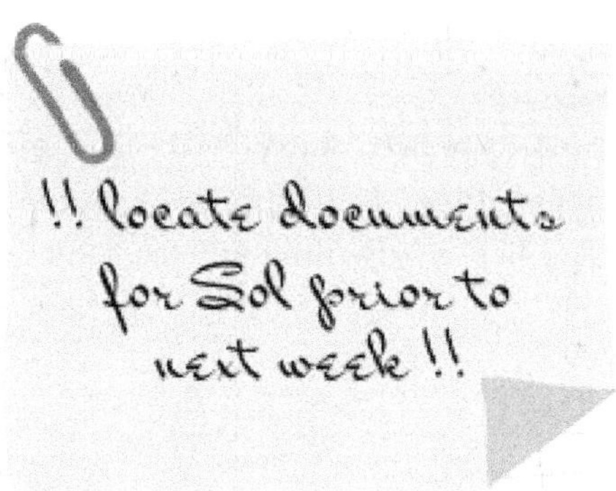
!! Locate documents
for Sol prior to
next week !!

Erin frowned. *Sol Prior? Who was he?*

Lifting the sticky note to reveal the date underneath, the vague note now made more sense.

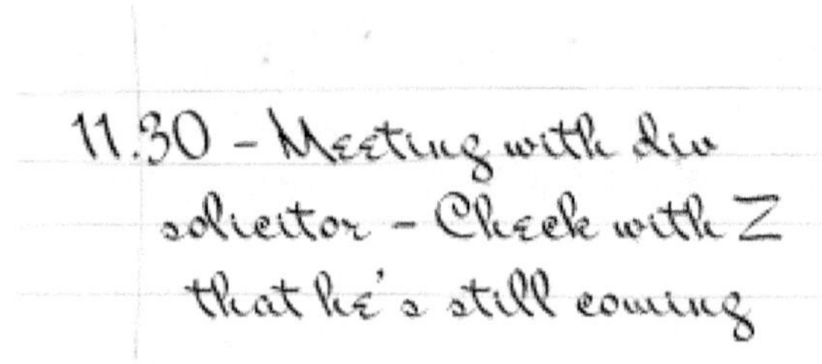

Erin sighed dejectedly. That must have been the meeting Zane had arranged for Hazel with that solicitor regarding her divorce.

Her eyebrows knitted. Another reason why it made no sense for Hazel to sign the statement guaranteeing Marco's release. Unless it was like Zane thought and a smokescreen designed to throw everyone off the scent.

Pulling the Post-it note from the page, Erin stared at it again: *locate documents*.

If Hazel's aim was to distract everyone by arranging a meeting with a divorce solicitor, why would there be a note reminding her to find the paperwork? It wasn't like her diary would be seen by anyone else, which could only mean the paperwork had gone missing.

Missing or misplaced?

Tugging open the deep bottom drawer of the desk separated into partitioned runner files, Erin flipped between them, scanning Hazel's familiar handwriting on the tabs of each divider:

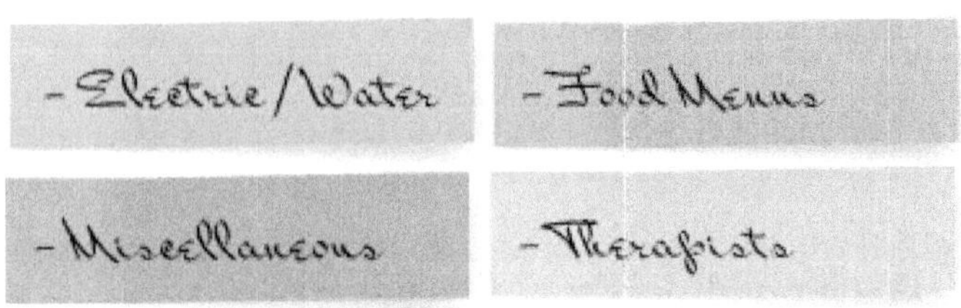

This related to the refuge rather than personal stuff, so wouldn't Skye require this too?

Apart from perhaps this one...

Erin pulled out a file labelled *'Pers p/work'* and peered inside. Short of a letter and an envelope marked 'Wedding docs' it was empty.

Unfolding the letter, Erin quickly scanned it. It was from the solicitor requesting that the 'enclosed form' was filled out and returned with the SAE and to have the original copy of her wedding certificate with her for their meeting.

There was no form or self-addressed envelope present so Erin could only guess Hazel must have completed and returned it as requested. But peering into the wedding documents envelope showed it to be empty. No wedding certificate in here.

Erin quickly thumbed through the other partitions, none of which held the missing documents. Her lips pursed. There was nothing else in the drawer either. It must be in the desk *somewhere*, but she'd already been through it.

Her heart began thumping. She'd go through the desk and the boxes she'd just filled with paperwork from the cabinets once more just to double check the documentation wasn't in there and if it wasn't, did that mean someone had taken it?

Damon Sandler perhaps?

But why? Hazel wouldn't need a divorce once she was dead, so why take the paperwork?

Erin frowned.

Why would *anyone* take it?

Suddenly, an idea glimmered. Had the documents been taken because they held Hazel's signature? A signature which could be copied onto the statement by someone who then handed it to the police.

EIGHT

'YOU KNOW THAT DOCUMENT found on the floor in Hazel's office the day she died? The statement which ensured Marco's release?' Erin said, checking she had Zane's attention.

'What of it?' Only half concentrating, Zane swigged from a bottle of beer.

Breaking the news this afternoon to Leo that yesterday, the mission to rid the world of Sandler had failed, his anger and rising obsession to finish what he'd started had taken pole position. He felt like a failure - a complete and utter fucking failure and although Leo promised to think of a way to get the job done, Zane couldn't see how the prospect of waiting an indeterminable length of time until Sandler was well enough to be released from hospital would be something he could bear. The need to permanently ruin that bastard was overriding all logical thought and he knew that was bad news for his sanity, as well as the ability to think clearly.

Now Erin was banging on about that business with Hazel again. Like he needed another reminder of how he'd let emotions cloud his ability to adequately judge someone's real intentions.

How could he forget that bloody statement? He'd made it

clear he didn't want to dwell on Hazel's betrayal. It changed nothing, just rubbed his face in how the woman he'd thought so highly of had let him down.

'I think her signature was forged...'

The bottle of beer paused halfway to Zane's mouth. He felt like launching it against the wall. 'The statement on the floor was unsigned, Erin. Hazel must have had a copy and that was the spare.'

'But I've just told you about the note in her diary reminding her to find the missing paperwork before the solicitor's meeting,' Erin pushed. 'What if someone took the documents and used them to copy her signature? Sandler could have killed Hazel because she refused to sign the statement and *then* stolen the documents so that *he* could forge them.'

'Sandler didn't forge her signature. I asked him,' Zane snarled, wishing Erin hadn't mentioned that bastard's name. He didn't want to think about the fuck up in that hospital room yesterday.

'And you believed him?'

'People tend to speak the truth when a knife is about to get wedged in their fucking neck, so yes, I believed him. Plus, you're forgetting that statement was dated two days prior to all the shit happening.'

'Then he must have done it beforehand! Sandler must have previously broken into the Starbright, stolen the documents and then...'

'For Christ's sake! When will you accept how it is?' Standing up, Zane slammed his bottle down on the table. 'I don't like what Hazel did any more than you do, but the fact remains the same - she's the only one who could have done it. And we - including *you*, have to live with that.'

Erin turned away, her mind churning. No, she wouldn't live with it because she didn't believe it. There was something else not being considered here, but it was ridiculous, wasn't it?

Hearing a text notification, Zane snatched up his phone and brought the screen to life. Any deflection from this conversation was a bonus.

[Leo]

Bit of a long shot but I may have a way to successfully remove Problem A

Despite his festering bad mood, Zane felt the corners of his mouth turn upwards. *Problem A...*

This time the reference, albeit a code for Sandler, didn't trigger the usual wave of resentment. Whether Leo had thought of a feasible plan to bypass the unacceptable length of time before there was a repeat opportunity to deal with Sandler or not, Zane didn't know, but if anyone could come up with a workable solution, short of himself or Tiger, then it was Leo. And that alone considerably brightened his outlook.

'Is Skye still not back?' Erin asked, eager to change the atmosphere. 'She left early to pop into town, but I wouldn't have thought she'd be so long. Was that her on the text?'

'No, it was Leo.' Zane shrugged. 'But Skye might as well take some freedom while she can. We don't know when that will change.'

Erin pursed her lips. It was true that the situation with Marco could turn on its head at any time, so surely it wasn't sensible for anyone to push their luck. 'Even Martin's disappeared.'

'He's borrowed one of the vans. He said he had a few things to tie up, but he'd best be back in time for tomorrow,' Zane muttered. 'He's got a job to start.'

'A job?' Erin's eyes widened. 'Working for you? You can't be serious! Martin won't cope with that kind of stuff!'

'Relax!' Zane laughed, his mood brightening. 'He asked for work. I was going to think about it, but then I realised I needed someone to watch the penthouse. That isn't a hands-on thing, so I thought, why not! That's all he'll be doing. I can't waste experienced men on watching doors!'

'Yes, but I didn't think Martin staying around here would

be a long-term thing.' Erin gestured around the small sitting room. 'We're not exactly overrun with space.'

'Why do you think I'm giving the kid work? He wants to rent a flat for him and Skye.' Zane raised his eyebrows. 'He's planning on marrying her…'

'Oh!' Erin was slightly bemused. That was good - in as much that Skye would no longer be living here, but she'd still be in the *vicinity*. And with the thoughts that she hadn't yet voiced to Zane still in her mind, she wanted Skye around even less than before.

'I don't want Skye made aware that Martin's working for me,' Zane continued, oblivious of Erin's inner turmoil. 'She'll only worry, so if he wants a job then the first thing he needs to learn is to speak of what he's doing to no one - his missus included!'

'But you tell *me* everything.' Erin wrapped her arms around Zane. 'At least you do *now*, I think...'

'Ah, but that's different. *You're* different!' Grabbing Erin's wrists, Zane pulled her onto his lap. 'Let's pick up where we were this morning before we got rudely interrupted!'

With the feel of Zane's hands, Erin found she could bypass the nagging thoughts crowding her mind for a short while.

• • • •

DOUBLE CHECKING this was the place Marco had sent her, Skye entered the Black Bear and glanced around the nicotine-stained walls.

Her nose wrinkled in distaste. This wasn't the sort of place she'd choose to spend her time but if being here meant she got what she wanted, then so be it.

And she *would* get what she wanted because it should have been hers in the first place! If Shirley hadn't been such a useless bitch, the opulent lifestyle Marco offered would have been hers from the start. She'd have been born into it. Instead, she was sharing a home with the brother who had stolen Marco's birthright not once but twice. It was sickening.

Skye shuddered, not understanding how Marco was so controlled about it. He'd been transparent with her from the start. The first time they'd met he'd explained how Zane had stolen the firm from him. Marco's father – *her* grandfather, had wanted Marco to run the empire after his death, not Zane, yet Zane had somehow elbowed his way in and Skye couldn't understand how.

In fact, she'd been astounded and couldn't blame Marco for getting Zane locked up. She'd have done the same and for Marco to spend years rebuilding what had been stolen from him and ruined, only to have it snatched again the second Zane was released from jail was a further twist of the knife.

Disgusting.

Zane Morelli deserved everything that was coming to him, yet Skye could see how people might be fooled into believing him the wronged party. That man had the gift of masquerading as someone who might even be classed as 'pleasant' with his fake pretence at maintaining a moral high ground when he felt like it. Oh, how he loved to spout how *he'd* got turned over, when in reality it was the other way around.

A shudder ran through Skye knowing she could have fallen for the lies herself had she not known differently. She was just lucky Marco had told her the real story before she became another of Zane's statistics.

And Shirley was no better...

Just thinking about Shirley made Skye's blood boil. Being such a slut to bed both brothers, her mother should have had the sense to marry one of them. And the *right* one - her real father - *Marco.*

That was why it had been so easy to agree to Marco's plan. They were like two halves of the same coin. Listening to her father was like having a conversation with herself. She'd realised from that very first moment that they were so similar she'd agree without hesitation to whatever he suggested. Besides, it was her duty and her right. The Morelli empire was *hers* to inherit and no one was usurping that.

Skye moved to the bar, careful not to place her handbag in the pool of spilt beer on the chipped bar top. 'White wine, please,' she said confidently. 'Large.' It was unlikely she'd get questioned over her age. She was only a few months short of eighteen. Besides, this place didn't like look like it cared either way.

As the barman deposited her wine on one of the few beer mats, Skye wondered whether to ask if he knew of the men Marco had outlined, but then thought better of it.

'Are you lost, love?' The barman eyed Skye appreciatively. 'This don't look like the kind of place a girl like you would drink in.'

Skye smiled coldly. 'I have broad horizons…' Turning her back, she moved away from the bar. She hadn't time to listen to corny chat up lines.

Now, were there any men matching the details here? If not, then she'd have no choice but to ask Pervo behind the bar if he knew them.

Pulling her phone from her bag, Skye retrieved Marco's earlier text:

Baz - tall with big nose

Red - ugly fucker - missing finger - ginger

Dylan - skinny & speaks funny

Wow, what a great collection, Skye thought acidly as she scanned the room.

Ah, there was a ginger bloke over there, but did he have missing fingers? Nothing for it but to go and look.

Picking up her drink, she stalked in the direction of the ginger man at a table with another man. Deciding as she neared them that there was no point beating around the bush, she stared at the man's hand. He certainly had what looked like a missing finger. He was also ugly as fuck. 'Are you Red?'

The ginger man looked Skye up and down. 'Who wants to know?'

'I wouldn't question this chick too much, Red. You never get offers as good as this!'

Skye glared coldly at the man's companion who had unwittingly confirmed his mate's name. 'I can assure you that I'm not on offer. Do you know Marco Morelli?'

Red's whole poise changed. He glanced over his shoulder. 'Why?'

'Stop pissing about!' Skye snapped. 'I've been sent by Marco to speak to you.'

The second man stared at Skye suspiciously before turning to Red. 'Marco wouldn't send a bird. It's a set up.'

Skye sighed. She'd expected a reaction, but this was proving more tiresome than she'd warranted. There wasn't time to mess about, but it was impossible to explain who she was or why she was here without going against Marco's orders.

No one could know she was his daughter. Not yet. Zane might hear about it and he couldn't be any the wiser until the time was right. 'Marco wants you to work for him, starting *now*. He wants total allegiance and full compliance. Whether you want to take up the offer or not is your choice, but if you're interested, name your price.'

Red sat forward, his mouth hanging open in surprise. 'Marco's been released? I thought th…'

'Leave thinking to people capable of it,' Skye interrupted. 'Your mate's confirmed you're Red…' Turning to the second man, she looked him up and down. 'Therefore, you must be Baz.'

Glancing at Red, Baz nodded. 'Correct, but...'

'Where's the other one? I have details of a...' Skye pulled out her phone once more. 'A skinny bloke who speaks funny. Is he one of yours?'

Red laughed. 'That'll be Dylan. Hey Baz, this chick must be on the level. Marco always had a dig at Dyl about his voice.'

Skye inwardly breathed a sigh of relief. She'd located the right men, however, there was one issue which had to be nipped in the bud before going any further. 'Let's get one thing straight.

I ain't no "chick", "darlin'" or "babe". You take orders and explain yourself only to me. For the time being, Marco will not be involved. Is that understood?'

Spotting the shared glance of amusement between the two men her eyes narrowed. She'd call their bluff and hope her instincts were good. 'If something's funny about that or you feel unable to take orders from a woman, then say so now. I've told you before you can name your price. There will also be bonuses for good work and whoever I deem capable enough I will inform Marco to choose as his new second, so the choice is yours, gentleman. Are you taking me seriously or shall I look elsewhere?'

NINE

'MARTIN?' Seeing who was on the doorstep, Fiona thought she must be hallucinating. She'd expected the postman or a window company, but not Martin - not her *son*!

A wave of pure elation rippled through her and she leant against the door jamb for support before an almighty squeal of joy escaped from between her lips. She threw herself at Martin and covered his cheeks with kisses. 'Oh my God! You're back! I can't believe it!'

'Steady on!' Martin laughed, equally pleased to see his mother. 'You'll give yourself a coronary!'

'What on earth is going on out h… Martin?' Peter stopped in between the lounge doorway and the hallway.

'Hi, Dad,' Martin said awkwardly.

Reining in his initial shock, Peter's eyes narrowed. 'Finally decided to return? How did you get here? It isn't like you had the use of my Range Rover!' He peered around the side of Martin. 'Where's that girlfriend of yours? You know, the one who caused all of this trouble in the first place!'

'Peter!' Fiona scolded. 'Martin hasn't even got inside the house yet!' Stepping aside, she turned back to her son. 'Take no notice of him, darling, and come inside. Where are your bags?

And Skye? Where is…'

'It's just me. It's only a fleeting visit,' Martin said brightly, knowing this wouldn't be easy. His dad immediately jumping on the bandwagon about the car showed exactly what an uphill battle this would be. And that was without the bombshell he was about to drop regarding university. He glanced behind him at the driveway as an afterthought. 'As for getting here, I borrowed a van.'

'A van?' Peter cried. 'You came in a bloody *van*? Why not hitch a lift on the back of a skip lorry or perhaps one of those trucks that delivers workmen's toilets? Something else the neighbours can point their finger at!'

'Peter!' Fiona hissed. 'Surely it matters little how Martin got here. That he's back is what's important.' She led her son into the living room as though he'd never been in the house before. 'Can I get you a drink? What about your favourite? A Shandy Bass?'

'You said a fleeting visit?' Peter stared at his son like he had just descended from another planet. 'What's that supposed to mean?'

Fiona found herself getting agitated. She'd heard Martin say about a fleeting visit too but preferred to gloss over that, suspecting, by her son's face that the answer would be something she'd rather not hear.

'I've decided to stay in London for a while,' Martin winced, thinking it was better to just come out with it.

'You're… you're not back to stay?' Fiona whimpered, her bottom lip trembling.

'Well, I'm about to start a job and I...'

'A job?' Peter scoffed. 'What for? It's the end of June! There's only eight weeks before you start at St Andrews. There's prep work to do and things to organise, so how can you do any of that ready for university if you're living and working in London? And living where? It's preposterous!'

Martin could almost sense the hole appearing ready to swallow him up and transport him to the centre of the earth. A horrible feeling that he'd made things worse instead of better, crushed him. 'Erm… I've decided I'm not going to St Andrews in September,' he said, his confidence sounding genuine when it was anything but. 'I'm staying in London. Me and Skye are getting married.' *Not that he'd asked her yet, but she'd say yes because she loved him.*

Peter laughed - a big booming laugh. This continued until he realised Martin was serious and then his mirth abruptly tailed away. 'Married? To that girl?' His eyes formed slits. 'Over my dead body!' He got to his feet, his face reddening. 'There's no way you're marrying into that family of mentally ill, lunatic...'

'PETER!' Fiona screeched. 'Be quiet!' She turned to Martin. 'Is that what you really want, darling?'

'More than anything,' Martin beamed. 'I thought by getting a job I could rent a flat and...'

'Rent?' Peter boomed. 'Renting is for paupers and people with no prospects! Martin, you are *not* giving up university and you're *not* renting a flat! After all the years we've paid to put you through the very best education, you are not throwing it away for a dead-end job and a woman with a dubious family! I won't allow it!'

Fiona remained silent, her mind churning. She needed time alone with Martin to find out what was really going on before Peter drove him away. Only then would she decide whether she could bear for her only child to give up his dreams.

• • • •

MARCO PACED AROUND the penthouse, the additional lines of cocaine he'd shovelled up his nose this past hour accomplishing nothing but diminishing his stash.

What would he do if it ran out? All the dealers he'd employed had jumped ship and he could hardly place a casual call in to the Delgados – his big suppliers. Not at the moment, anyway.

Snatching up a bottle of whisky, he swigged from it, hoping to get relief from the burn. *He didn't.*

For all he knew, there could be an invoice outstanding with the men he'd had an arrangement with - those who bought in cocaine from abroad by the container-load and who had guaranteed his ability to supply half of London. But he'd hazard a guess that in the scant few weeks he'd been forced out of the picture, that wanker, Sandler, hadn't kept on top of the supply. Unsurprisingly, the next level in the chain had looked elsewhere to keep their customers happy. It was also likely that Sandler hadn't weighed in any outstanding payments, which was not good. Marco had bagged a rare deal with the Delgados, but they were people even *he* didn't want to get the wrong side of, therefore aside from everything else, he dare not show his face until he knew the score. Red and Baz should have heard what the situation was on the street, so he needed to hear what they had to say.

Marco's thick, dark brows bunched together. How was he supposed to make money trapped in the penthouse?

Sandler was to blame for all of this, the idiotic fuck. He should have offed the twat when he had the chance. Now he'd have to wait until it was safe to leave these four walls and in the position to steam back into everything.

For fuck's sake - his studios were still closed because the police were dragging their feet in giving him the green light to resume filming. Even then, the council would probably play their face and revoke his licence.

He had to regain his clout and do it fast.

Marco stared at his phone, his jaw clenching. There was nothing from Skye yet and she should have located the men he needed by now. It came to something relying on a slip of a girl to run his business, but then she was his daughter.

She'd done alright so far - aside from killing Hazel. Skye had overstepped the mark on that one, mainly because he'd wanted to do it himself. But Skye's mother was a different story… Shirley had a shed load of cash and this was a fact because he vividly recalled what had happened at the time.

Marco's lips twitched into a smirk, an idea sparking in the

recesses of his wired brain. He knew there was a reason why he'd taken that notebook from Skye's bag. When the opportunity presented itself, he hadn't been sure why he'd done it, but inevitably everything had a reason, even it wasn't obvious at the time.

And now it was.

His seventeen-year-old daughter hadn't yet quite lost the habit of writing her name and address in the front of diaries like a child. And that was good because now he had Shirley Wilson's address.

Perhaps it was time he paid her a visit? If he'd known she'd produced his child, then he'd have called in his share of the cash ages ago, but the greedy bitch had kept schtum. Something else she'd be explaining.

Marco drummed his thick fingers on the table. He might get away with booking a taxi from here to where that worthless slut now lived. It would cost a few quid, yes, and if needs be he could do it under the cover of darkness. But who would see him walking the ten yards from the complex entrance to jump in a taxi parked on the fucking road outside?

No one.

But first, he'd book that slut from yesterday.

Stabbing the relevant digits into his mobile, he raised it to his ear, smiling to hear Callie's dull voice. 'Get your arse over here within the hour... What do you mean, you can't?' Marco chuckled nastily. 'I think you'll find you can! Cancel your plans. There's something else I want you to do for me… Yeah, that's right... I'll make it worth your while.'

TEN

FEELING MARTIN'S ERECTION against her lower back, Skye squirmed out of his embrace and got out of bed.

'What's the rush?' Martin frowned. 'You don't have to get up yet!'

'I need to get started early.' Skye moved to the dressing table and retrieved some clean clothes. 'I'm really busy. Now I'm entrusted with running the Starbright I don't want to let anyone down.' And she needed to get things in place to ensure Erin didn't walk into the meeting she'd arranged with those men either. There was also the call she had to make to Marco before anyone could eavesdrop.

Having Martin share her room was not what she wanted. He was now superfluous to requirements and his clinginess was sickening. However, she could hardly say she didn't want him anywhere near her - not when she was supposed to be desperately in love with him and giving things another go.

Still, if things worked out the way she planned, she wouldn't have to put up with this ridiculous charade much longer. And her plans had worked out pretty bloody well so far.

Martin swallowed down his disappointment at Skye's eminent departure and swung himself out of bed. Approaching her from behind, he wrapped his arms around her waist. 'You're not in a bad mood because I didn't come back until late last night, are you?'

'Of course not! Why would I be?' Skye smiled, inwardly bristling with Martin draping himself around her yet again. She brushed him off under the pretence of opening the wardrobe. *Why couldn't he just fuck off and leave her alone?*

'It's just that when you're not with me, it's like half of me is missing and I can barely breathe,' Martin whispered, the urge to tell Skye of his plans teetering on the edge of his tongue. How he wanted to surprise her about getting a flat, his job - and best of all, that they would be married. *With* her father's blessing!

But he couldn't. Keeping the surprise until everything was lined up was an altogether better solution. Frustratingly hard, but also easier now he had to keep his new job a secret. What better way to justify not telling Skye the truth about what he was doing for work than because of a surprise proposal? She'd be over the moon when the time came to reveal all.

How did he get this lucky?

And yes, his parents - especially his father's reaction, wasn't the best, but they'd come around. Especially once they realised how happy he and Skye were.

Skye hadn't asked why he hadn't returned until well past midnight, but then she was so nice, she wouldn't pry. She trusted him, but he had to say *something* in case he was late back again tonight. He had no idea how long this apartment watching thing would go on for. 'I start a job myself today,' he announced proudly, turning Skye to press his lips on the end of her nose.

Rather than scowling in disgust at Martin's closeness, Skye feigned interest. 'Oh? Where are you working?'

'Just a petrol station.' Martin shrugged. 'I thought I should earn a bit of coin.'

'Good idea,' Skye said. 'You'll need it for when you go to St Andrews.' The prospect of another few weeks of Martin attached to her like a limpet was bad but at least the end was in sight.

Martin swallowed uncomfortably. He hated lying, but the second part of the surprise - that he wasn't going to university anymore and they could be together forever as from *now*, could only be revealed as the ultimate bonus once the first part was in place.

'I'd better go,' Skye said. 'I'll see you later.' *Or better still, never again...*

• • • •

'BUT THEY CAN'T stay in London!' Shirley gasped, the hem of her green A-Line skirt threatening to unravel from her habit of picking at the stitching. She always did that when she was nervous. And she was nervous a lot of the time. Usually, most of it.

She raised her eyes to Fiona. Not expecting Martin's mother to arrive at her house, she very nearly hadn't answered the door. Now she wished she hadn't because what she'd just learnt made things worse.

'I can't say I'm happy about it either,' Fiona said glumly. 'You don't want to know how Peter reacted.'

Shirley was only partially listening as Fiona rattled away about her husband's meltdown. Her concentration was centred on the window where a butterfly was trapped between the glass and the net curtain. She watched the insect flutter pointlessly, its small brain reasoning that if it aimed towards the outside visible through the glass, then it would escape its prison.

That was how Shirley felt many years ago as her growing belly showed there was no escape. The butterfly that she had once been expired the day she realised her fate: the man she'd loved and who she'd believed loved her, was as sick and twisted as them all.

'Shirley?' Fiona leant forward, her face a picture of concern. 'Are you listening? If you know the people my son is living with, then I have the right to know who they are.' *Because she didn't like the sound of any of this.*

When recounting what he was doing and where he was staying, Martin had been uncharacteristically vague – a trait usually reserved for speaking to his father. From this alone, Fiona deduced that her son wasn't being truthful. Him hiding facts could only mean that he was involved in something that she wouldn't like. 'This Zane Morelli person they're living with… Is he Skye's father?'

Shirley dropped the hem of her skirt back into her lap. 'Skye is living with Zane? He told me she'd gone missing, not that she was *living* with him! He's still lying then, I see? I knew he knew where Skye was and that it was all a pretence! But why is she living with *him*? Still keeping it in the family!' Her eyes narrowed as she spat the word, 'family'. 'He phoned me again yesterday. Did you know that? I knew it was him the second I picked up the phone. I could smell his lies down the telephone by just looking at it! They should all rot in hell!'

Fiona sighed with frustration that Shirley still hadn't answered the question. 'I already told you Martin said Skye had returned. He asked me specifically to let you know.'

'Did you?' Shirley frowned. 'Well, I don't care. This is Zane and his games. You don't want your son near *any* of that family, Fiona. They're all cursed. They taint everything they touch.'

'But who are they?' Fiona cried. 'No one will actually tell me! Are they criminals? Are they part of a London gang? Is it Skye's father? Tell me!'

Shirley stared at the wall, her mouth moving with silent words.

'Shirley? For God's sake! This is important!' Fiona barked. 'Have the decency to tell me what you know! This is my son!'

'The Morellis are whoever they want to be,' Shirley muttered, her eyes glazed. 'Liars, lovers, cheats, violent psychopaths... But at least one of them is dead – their evil bastard of a father and...'

'Wait! Whose father is dead? Skye's father? Is Skye's father a Morelli?'

'Unfortunately, Skye's father is not dead. And she's NOT a Morelli!' Shirley swung towards Fiona, her eyes blazing. 'She'll *never* be a Morelli! Money can only buy so much! They need to leave my daughter alone. But now she's just like him... like them... like the dead one... I'm glad he's dead.'

As Shirley began humming a high-pitched tune consisting of the same few notes, Fiona wanted to slap sense into her. *She'd get nowhere at this rate.* 'I'll phone and speak to them,' she suggested. 'Perhaps I can get an idea of wh...'

'Do not call any of those filthy creatures!' Shirley heaved her heavy frame out of the chair with surprising speed. She pointed at Fiona, the flabby undersides of her arm wobbling. 'Stay away from them and accept that your son has gone forever!'

A shiver of cold thundered through Fiona. She knew Shirley was slightly unhinged, but there was something behind her eyes that showed there was more at play here than eccentricity - or as Peter put it - *craziness*.

Shirley wasn't crazy, but *something* was wrong. Exactly what, Fiona didn't know, but whatever it was, it bothered the woman to an alarming degree. By the looks of it, this 'something' which had haunted her for many years, hinged solely around these Morelli people.

That alone was disturbing enough, but for Martin to be staying at one of these people's houses, was worse. Whether Zane Morelli was Skye's father or not, she still didn't know for certain. It sounded like he might be and it would explain Shirley's attitude if the man had abandoned her, but she couldn't speculate. She *mustn't*.

But one thing this *did* underline was that she needed to get Martin *and* Skye away from wherever they were as soon as possible. It was clear no good could come of it.

Fiona's hand moved to rest on her handbag where she'd hidden the slip of paper Martin handed her last night for her 'peace of mind'. *The address where he was presently staying.*

Perspiration broke out over her back and dampened her

white blouse. She'd been given that address on the proviso that a) she didn't go there and b) didn't tell Peter.

Fiona had agreed. Of course she had. She'd do anything for her son, but she had to speak to him and find out if what Shirley said was true.

If it was and Martin was staying at the house of a criminal, then she was starting to feel like she would need to break the promise she'd made him.

ELEVEN

'IF ANYONE COMES IN unannounced, pretend you're guards.' Skye looked between each of the men in turn.

'I was wondering why you'd insisted on us wearing this.' Baz glanced disparagingly at his black work issue trousers and nondescript shirt. 'I thought there must be some sort of weird dress code to get in here!'

Skye scowled. 'Don't be fly. I just don't want you drawing attention.'

'Who is it you're expecting to turn up? You said *you* ran this gaff.' Red glanced around the room with its fancy glass desk and sleek black cabinets.

'There's a nosy blonde bitch by the name of Erin. She doesn't know enough to realise you lot don't work here, but I don't want her sniffing around.' Skye pulled a leatherbound organiser from the drawer and placed it on the polished glass surface of her brand-new desk.

She'd gone all out with the new furniture. This stuff was bang on trend. Expensive, yeah, but Zane wouldn't mind. He hadn't had much choice about it anyway because she'd already charged the whole lot to his card. Paying for same day delivery and for the items to be assembled on site hadn't come cheap either, but they wanted this place run properly, didn't they? Sitting in an office filled with Hazel's crap charity shop junk didn't ooze professionalism. Besides, she didn't want anything that whore who had tried and failed to stiff Marco, had touched.

Looking up, she met eyes with the three men the other side of the desk in the equally new matching leather chairs. 'Some of the guards might question you but just tell them you're new. They won't say much, neither will they have the guts to mention you to anyone who matters, but the only times we can meet here is when *he* or his cronies aren't on site and I know for a fact that won't happen today.'

Red frowned. 'He? Who's he? What is this place, anyhow?'

Skye rolled her eyes. 'It's a heavily guarded women's refuge, hence why I dressed you to blend in as guards.' Did she have to spell *everything* out for these morons? Marco said they were decent, so when were any of them going to grow a brain? 'And "he" is Marco's brother, who, if he sees you, will realise that you don't belong here.'

Dylan almost toppled off the padded leather chair. 'You're telling me that you've brought us to a gaff owned and run by *Zane Morelli*?' The owl-like head that looked too big for his body swivelled on his spindly neck towards Red and Baz. 'Did you know about this? Fuck! We can't be anywhere Zane Morelli could turn up!'

'Marco wasn't wrong when he said you speak funny, was he?' Skye snapped. The man had the weirdest, high-pitched voice which sounded like broken glass running along a xylophone. 'Your screeching is giving me a headache. Furthermore, Zane does not run this place, *I* do.' She glared at the three men. 'Because I run this place, I know whether Zane is here or not. I know what I'm doing, so quit whining!'

She picked the leather organiser back up whilst keeping a close eye on Dylan. He was a candidate whom she would not put forward to Marco for having second-in-command potential. It was pushing it for him to even pass as a guard - there was more meat on a twiglet! 'What is your usual role, Dylan?' Skye folded her arms across her chest and stared at the skinny man. 'Why did Marco list *you* as one of the specifically requested men?'

'Dyl took over after Marco's other tech guy got killed. He's a dab hand with computers, phones and all that,' Red explained.

'Hmm, that explains everything, as well as why he can't cope with answering the question himself!' Skye sneered. 'Now, before we discuss the finer points of your first job, have you heard anything on the grapevine about the dealers in Marco's territories? Anything at all?'

Red exchanged an uncomfortable glance with Baz and Dylan. As far as any of them were aware, Marco no longer had *any* territories that hadn't been lifted by Zane. There were other things muttered about that anyone in the know had been made party to as well.

He stuck his finger in the collar of the over-starched shirt he'd been made to wear, realising by the others' silence that he would be the one breaking the unfavourable news.

'I'm waiting...' Skye hissed.

'Well, it's common knowledge that Marco is not supplying coke anymore. His previous dealers weren't happy to be left in the lurch with no supply. As you're probably aware when that happens, it has a knock-on effect'. Red cleared his throat, not wishing to be the harbinger of this next part. 'I don't know how true it is, but I've heard that the whole arrangement with the Delgado firm has been taken over by someone else.'

Skye's irritation grew with the injustice of what her father was being put through. She knew Marco had trusted that tosser Sandler to keep on top of things in his absence. Bad mistake, that was. 'Who is this new party?'

Red shrugged. 'That I don't know,' he lied. He wasn't taking responsibility for confirming *that*. If Marco couldn't work out the most likely contender of taking over the city's main drug supply in relation to the loss of his territories, then it wasn't something he'd put his neck on the chopping block for.

Skye watched Red carefully. She also watched the other

two men. The fucker was lying. They knew, along with *everybody* it seemed. And just as she'd expected, it was down to the traitor whose roof she currently resided under.

Marco would be even less happy to have this latest theft from Zane confirmed. Still, there was nothing to be done about that new arrangement right now, so the one vital task that *could* be done, needed to be ironed out. Once that was complete, Zane would be one step closer to total annihilation anyway.

Forcing herself to smile at the three men, Skye clasped her hands together. 'Okay, so let's get on with what we're here to discuss. I don't want you here any longer than needs be.'

• • • •

NOT WANTING TO CHANGE the habit of a lifetime by acknowledging anyone he deemed below him unless he had to, Marco strolled past the concierge in the penthouse reception.

'Your taxi is waiting outside, sir,' the nervous looking man at the front desk said as Marco sauntered past amid a cloud of aftershave.

'I know that!' Marco barked. 'Why else would I bother coming down here?' Snorting in derision at the man's stupidity, he yanked open the double glass doors and quickly checked outside before setting foot on the short path to the road. Fuck waiting until nightfall. He wasn't wasting time anymore.

The way was clear, as expected.

A low chuckle escaped his throat. Zane hadn't got men to spare to watch the place he'd once lived in. From what Skye said, Zane only had one experienced man left on his payroll - the rest were newbies. Now Skye had kicked off her recruitment drive, it wouldn't be long before he had the numbers, therefore he and Zane would be equally matched.

Approaching the taxi, Marco pulled open a door and clambered in. 'Guildford,' he muttered. No point mentioning East Horsley just yet. Looking at the thick fuck behind the wheel, it was unlikely the cunt even knew much English, let alone where East Horsley was. Not that he was familiar with it either, but it was close to Guildford, so he'd get there first and then tell this twat to find the fucking place.

Marco pulled out Shirley's address, along with his silver bullet holding a couple of grams of cocaine. He snorted a loaded level from the attached tiny spoon and dragged his hand underneath his nose.

Taking his phone out of his pocket, he tapped out a text. It was best not to call Skye in case the dickhead driving understood more than he gave him credit for.

Where r u? Have u organised wot u said?

Pressing send, Marco smiled at his choice of words. Skye would know *exactly* what he meant. It was best to be vague. Being released without charge was one thing, but he didn't trust those fuckers in the police not to tap his phone. They'd kept hold of it the majority of the time he'd been locked in that cell which gave adequate time to place a bug. He wasn't giving those bastards an inch to pin more shit on him.

Providing Skye pulled this off and that slapper from last night did her duty and obeyed his instructions, there was no reason why he couldn't get this show on the road and pull in some brass to keep the kitty topped up.

After Callie had fulfilled his 'other' needs, he'd told her what else he was looking for. The tart may have been miffed to not receive more of his drug stash, nor anything to numb the pain when he'd tried out some other things he fancied, but then her comfort was not what he paid for. Plus, he needed her alert in order to remember his instructions.

Marco's grin widened. The smack around the face he'd given the slut as he'd shot his load had driven the message home. He expected results and if the bitch didn't want her plastic looks melted, then she'd do everything he'd asked for.

He didn't need much to get the filming running again. The penthouse was a cracking backdrop and the order he'd put in for replacement camera kit should arrive later today. It was an expense he could do without, especially as he had everything required at the Luna studios, but it was best to leave that well alone for now.

Scowling through the grimy taxi window at the growing traffic out of London, Marco glared at his mobile. Why had Skye not responded? He expected a faster turnaround to his texts than this. He hoped she'd pulled in that tight little mate of hers that she'd mentioned.

If she'd failed, then Callie would have to round up some of her hooker pals instead. But the first option was a real money-spinner and what he wanted, so Skye had best deliver.

As if governed by the power of thought, a text notification pinged and Marco quickly opened the message.

`Hvg meetg with your men at mo.`

Right? And so she should be. That Skye had located those three men was good, but it wasn't fucking hard!

He scowled, hoping she wouldn't disappoint his expectations. Questioning her because she wasn't volunteering the required information was getting on his nerves.

`Any word about wot we discussed?`

This time the response was quicker.

`New owner. U can guess who.`

Marco accidentally bit his tongue as his jaw clamped shut. So, he was right that Sandler had fucked up and the Delgados had gone elsewhere. And he shouldn't be surprised that the deal had been awarded to his cunt of a brother.

Fury buzzed through Marco's veins. He'd get back on top shortly and then hell would be a holiday destination for that bastard.

Containing his seething, he stabbed out another text,

imagining the harsh prodding of the phone's buttons were Zane's eyeballs.

```
And ur mate? Did you talk to her about the idea?
```

Marco was gratified by the almost immediate response. Skye was learning to not delay. It was what he expected and anything less would not do.

```
Yes I phoned her yday + she's interested.
```

Marco's face squished into a grimace. *Interested?* What, like the snotty bitch thought she had a choice? From what Skye said, her friend was perfect - posh and inexperienced. But whoever the little slag was, she was mental if she believed she had a say on *anything* once his sights were set. And it was up to Skye to ensure he got what he wanted, otherwise they'd fall out.

Marco drummed his thick fingers on the plastic of the inner car door. He didn't want ructions with his daughter - she was proving useful, but she was young and if she didn't yet know there was no room for sentiment in this life, then she soon would.

He smacked the back of the driver's seat. 'When you reach Guildford, continue to East Horsley.' He watched the driver's eyes move to meet his in the rearview mirror.

'Where's that?'

'Fuck knows, but you're the fucking driver, so it's up to you to find it!' Marco barked. 'And get a move on. I haven't got all bloody day!'

Nor had he got time to waste in topping-up his funds. He hoped for Shirley's sake that she'd had enough sense not to blow all of the money his father had paid her and her stinking family to fuck off out of London.

TWELVE

ERIN WAS PUTTING her shoes on in the hallway when the doorbell rang.

Zane came out of the kitchen, followed by Martin. 'Can you get that?'

Opening the front door, Erin's face broke into a wide smile to see Tiger. 'Hey! Come in. Zane! Tiger's here!'

As Tiger entered the house, Erin felt it the perfect time to leave and give Tiger and Zane the privacy to talk. She'd been wondering whether Skye's rush to leave this morning had underlying motives, but perhaps the girl was aware Tiger was due and couldn't face the man whose reputation she'd almost destroyed. Whatever the reason, it was best all-round if Skye wasn't here. The added awkwardness wouldn't aid Zane in getting his trusted man back into the fold.

Hastening up the hallway, Zane extended his hand and shook Tiger's. 'Come through, mate. This is Martin, by the way. He's just on his way out.' He nodded to Martin standing awkwardly behind him. 'Martin, this is Tiger.'

'Pleased to meet you,' Martin mumbled, the sheer size of the man grunting acknowledgement and dwarfing him, serving as a stark reminder of who and what he was involved with.

Zane pulled a set of keys from his pocket, handed them to Martin and spoke under his breath. 'There's one of my vans parked two roads up. It's a white Transit. Take that. You know the rest. Call me with any developments.'

Nodding, Martin dutifully took the keys and squeezed past Erin.

'I'll see you later.' Erin kissed Zane on the lips. 'Good to see you again, Tiger,' she called as she followed Martin out of the house.

'Can I give you a lift?' Martin asked as he and Erin walked up the road.

'But you're going to Battersea.'

'That's okay.' Martin shrugged. 'The detour won't take long.' *Zane told him that Marco rarely surfaced before lunchtime, so it wasn't like he'd miss anything.* 'I'd have taken Skye too, but she left extra early this morning.' Reaching the van, he opened the door for Erin.

Erin sat quietly as Martin pulled away up the road, wondering why Skye felt the need to go in so early. She'd promised she wouldn't look for reasons to suspect the girl, but it was difficult. That note in Hazel's desk haunted her and no matter how much Zane denied the signature had been forged, she couldn't shake it from her head that Skye was somehow responsible. But her forging the signature made no sense, especially with her turn around in attitude. Skye hadn't put a foot wrong; neither was there a plausible reason behind what would be gained by it. Nevertheless, the suspicion remained embedded.

'Did Skye say why she needed to go in so early?' Erin asked. 'I've seen today's agenda and there's nothing planned to warrant such an early start.'

Martin shrugged. 'Just that she's busy. I do know she's desperate not to let you guys down and wants to make things a success.'

Erin couldn't deny that Skye wasn't giving it her all. She'd worked like a trojan yesterday with settling the returning women back into the centre. Skye had strong leadership qualities, just like her father, so perhaps it wasn't fair to hold onto this incessant threat of expecting things to unravel. By cynically suspecting ulterior motives, she wasn't honouring her promise to wipe the slate clean. Maybe Zane was right and it was time she accepted that Hazel had betrayed them and remained on side with Marco. If that *was* the case, then perhaps her gruesome death had been a blessing.

Erin shuddered. Thinking such a thing heightened the disappointment with herself.

'Are you all right?' Martin frowned. 'You've gone pale.'

Erin smiled weakly. 'I'm just tired.' Pulling herself together, she forced brightness into her voice. 'I hear the plan about the flat and marriage is a secret. Is that right?'

Martin grinned bashfully as he negotiated the traffic. 'I want to line everything up before I propose and tell Skye about the flat. Having you guys on side and Zane giving me work means a lot.'

Further guilt flashed through Erin. Support wasn't the reason she was behind Martin. It was the impending relief of not having Skye under the same roof and that was uncharitable.

'I wish my parents were as supportive,' Martin added glumly. 'My mum took it better, but my dad... well, he's not impressed about me jacking off university.'

'Have you... erm... told them exactly what it is you're doing? Or who you're working for?' Erin suspected she already knew the answer to this one.

'No, I know not to mention anything,' Martin muttered. His mother only knew Skye's father was involved because he'd stupidly told her some stuff in panic when he'd been kept prisoner, but that was about it. He hadn't elaborated and what he was doing now she would deem far from palatable. He hadn't said a bean to his father and nor by the looks of it, had his mother and Martin dearly hoped it remained that way.

Worry also prickled about giving his mother the Dalston address, but she'd promised not to turn up and he trusted her. 'I don't think anything I say will make my parents forgive me for binning off my studies.'

'I'm sure they'll come around,' Erin smiled, not sure whether that would be the case at all. Martin was wasting his opportunity of going to one of the best universities only for the high chance of Skye turning around and dumping him.

See? She was doing it again! She wanted to give the girl some credit, she really did, but the hard truth was, after what Skye had done, Erin would never trust her.

'Here we are,' Martin said as they turned into the Starbright Centre's road.

'Thanks,' Erin smiled. 'If you could just drop me... Oh!' Looking ahead, the centre's entrance was blocked by a van. 'I tell you what, just drop me here. I'll walk the rest of the way.'

'Don't be daft. It's raining. I'll turn around at the end of the road. The van should have finished delivering by then.'

Passing the stationary white Transit, Martin looked in his rearview mirror at the men getting into the van and the unmistakable figure of Skye talking to the driver. 'Who are those guys?'

'I've no idea.' Erin watched the spectacle in the wing mirror.

'If Skye's out there with them it must be a delivery,' Martin reasoned, doing a three-point turn at the end of the road.

'Yeah,' Erin said brightly, not believing a word. All deliveries went around the back and no one *ever* parked across the drive. Skye knew that being as *she'd* been the one to enforce Hazel's rules.

Retracing their tracks towards the Starbright, Erin watched the van pull away. Skye had already vanished, presumably back inside. She'd say nothing to Martin, but what she *would* do was see if anyone mentioned a delivery or the presence of a Transit with men that Skye appeared to know inside it.

If the girl was hiding things, it would soon be obvious.

• • • •

LIKE MOST DAYS, Shirley wasn't sure what time it was or even certain which day of the week. What did it matter when every day, week, month and year was filled with a pointless mix of nothingness?

There was little benefit in watching the television either. It was only ever on for company – a voice other than the ones droning incessantly in her head as her mind span from one thought to another in the endless cacophony of chaos.

At first, she remained unmoving; the staccato rapping translating as part of whatever dross was coming from the television speaker.

Was it even morning? Had she been to bed?

Shrugging, Shirley accepted those to be more questions that she had no answers to and reverted to staring blankly at the moving screen where a pretty, slim woman glided around her sparkling kitchen preparing a recipe for her equally perfect husband and cherished children. The woman's melodious voice explained how to prepare the next part of the recipe, her excited attitude probably infectious to those possessing the wish to be part of life.

Which Shirley did not.

It was only as the rapping continued, did she wonder whether there was another possibility for the noise, other than from within her mind. Suddenly realising it was the door, she sat bolt upright.

Fiona! How could she have forgotten? Fiona had mentioned something about returning later, hadn't she? Or was that a different day?

Shirley wasn't sure but busied herself with bumbling down the hallway. Perhaps Martin had been in touch again? There could be news.

Pushing away the threat of that news being bad, Shirley removed the many bolts and chains from over the door and tugged it open. 'Did y…'

The breath flew out of her lungs as she found herself thrown to the floor, hitting the side of a small rectangular table on the way down. Gasping for breath, she blinked into the bright glare of the pendant lampshade now directly above her and tried to make sense of what had happened. *Had she lost her footing? Passed out? Had a funny turn?*

'Jesus H Christ! I'd never have recognised you in a million years!' The light above became eclipsed as Marco moved over Shirley's prone figure. 'I've heard of people letting themselves go, but this is taking the piss!'

A clamouring, ringing combination of jingling bells and clashing metal saucepan lids clanged in Shirley's brain at the voice from above her. The last time she'd heard that voice was when it growled threats into her ear whilst her face was pressed into the dusty concrete of an industrial warehouse. It wasn't something she would forget but God knows she'd tried.

Vomit rushed up from her stomach like a tap on full force as a mixture of fear and unbridled panic avalanched.

All these years she lived in fear of this day: the moment when Marco Morelli turned up on her doorstep or she bumped into him in the street. The latter was unlikely because she rarely ventured out for that very reason, but as the years passed with no word, no mention, no threats or sightings of any of that godforsaken family, she'd begun to think - dared to hope during her lucid moments that maybe, just *maybe* it wouldn't happen.

It not happening was of vital importance - not just for what was left of her own sanity, but for Skye's well-being. If Marco found out that the night he'd forced himself on her had resulted in a child - *his* child, then it was possible, no – it was *guaranteed* he'd want his offspring.

And being as her daughter was his heir, it was worse. Marco would see Skye as his God's given right to take. Another possession…

And Skye had gone searching for this nightmare?

Suddenly aware that Marco was talking, or rather shouting and still looking down on her like a succubus, Shirley forced herself to look up at the man who, along with the rest of his family, had ruined her life.

Well, he wasn't ruining Skye's.

'You're not having her!' she spat, unearthing a show of courage from the depths of her soul - a remnant of the girl who once upon a time fought for what she believed in.

Since the night 'it' had happened, Shirley believed in nothing apart from her daughter and she'd die to protect that girl from these monsters in the guise of human form. 'Stay away from h…'

Shirley's words abruptly ended as Marco snatched a fistful of her hair and yanked her from the floor. 'You're telling me to stay away from my own flesh and blood?' He twisted his fingers in the tangled hair and pulled Shirley's head down at an angle. Still holding tightly, he shoved her up against the wall, his forearm against her throat. 'Skye is mine,' he spat. 'Mine! She is no longer your concern.'

'I-I'll never let that happen!' Shirley spluttered, gasping for breath. 'I... I'll...'

'You'll what? Take me on? You and whose army?' Marco looked Shirley and down in disgust. 'Oxfam?'

Shirley wanted to pull Marco's hand from her hair; push his arm off her throat. She couldn't breathe. Her eyes watered from the searing burning in her scalp, but she couldn't move. Skye had chosen to remain in London. Skye had chosen this... this man over her.

NO!

Lucidity stormed her brain. '*You're* the one forcing Skye to stay in London. 'You and your...' She could barely bring herself to think of Zane, '...your brother.'

'Ah, yes... Him...' Marco unexpectedly dropped his grip. He stared at the fingers which had been wrapped in Shirley's hair, then wiped them down his trousers. 'My dear brother had a lucky escape by not marrying you. Look what he'd have ended up having to fuck!'

Rubbing her throat, Shirley sagged against the wall. 'Let Skye go. She's no use to you. She's just a young girl, who…'

'That's where you're wrong.' Marco wandered casually

down the hallway into the sitting room.

Shirley scrambled to follow, finding Marco picking up a framed photo of Skye taken when she was three years old. It was Shirley's favourite picture of her daughter. 'Put that down! Skye is nothing to do with you. My daughter is nothing like you.'

Marco swung around. 'She's *everything* to do with me!' Removing the photograph from the frame, he shoved the picture into the pocket of his jacket. 'She's very much *like* me. A carbon copy, actually and she's already been useful.'

Shirley blinked. *No!* Skye was nothing like Marco. She wasn't like *any* of the Morellis. Skye had been brought up well; she had nice friends; a nice boyfriend. Skye was pretty, kind, sweet. She was *all* of those things. None of the brash evil coursing through the veins of the Morellis. Through Marco; through Zane; through...

Marco glanced around the neat living room with the expensive furniture. 'You've deprived me of my rights concerning my daughter for years, yet by the looks of it, you did okay out of it. Nice drum you've got here. You see, you sold any ownership or opinion about what happens to my daughter the second your greedy cunt parents cashed my father's cheque.' His eyes narrowed into menacing slits. 'I don't remember any mention of impending children at the time, which surprises me. I'm sure my father would have paid double had he known.'

Shirley's hand clamped over her mouth as vomit rushed north. She'd never sell her child. Not to them. Not to *anyone*.

'Where are your parents anyway? Dead, I hope,' Marco sneered, then shrugged. 'They're not important, so let's just cut to the chase. From what I'm guessing, you got a double payout. You inherited your parents' gaff when they dropped off the twig and in turn, you bought this one.' Moving forward, he jabbed his finger into the fatty folds of Shirley's chin. 'I've got my daughter, but you owe me for not telling me she existed. So, to start with in making amends, I want half of the cut you got paid to fuck off out of town, you fat, greedy bitch. Plus interest.'

'What? You th...'

'Listen, you riffy cow. I'll speak slowly and try to be patient, but don't push me. Take stock and remember that if it wasn't for me, you wouldn't even have a kid, so it's time you showed me some appreciation, as well as giving me a long overdue apology for not telling me about Skye.'

A strange, swirling mist descended on Shirley. *Marco wanted her to thank him and apologise?* A loud, screechy cackle escaped her lips. It could have been laughter. Or hysteria. It might have even been an unknown reaction to the most insulting thing she'd ever heard.

If she'd been concentrating, she'd have spotted the flash of shock and confusion akin to slight embarrassment her reaction caused passing over Marco's face before it was rapidly replaced with rage. She should know that Marco Morelli's nemesis was being laughed at or not taken seriously, but nothing was further from her mind until she felt one of her breasts being twisted, followed by a flash of pain in her face. Now she was on the floor with Marco's knee pressing into her stomach and his hand back around her throat.

'Begging for my cock again, Shirley?' Marco spat, his cold eyes drilling into hers. 'That's a shame, because I wouldn't screw you again even if my life depended on it! But I *could* use this!' Leaning across, he pulled the chair at Shirley's side towards him and with brute force, snapped off the leg. 'How about *this* gives you a good time? I'm sure you don't care about a few splinters! After that, I'll keep it for when I get back and see if any of my men fancy using it on the daughter you think isn't worth thanking me for.'

Shirley squeaked in horror as Marco pushed apart her heavy thighs using his other knee. There was little he could do that would destroy her further, but not Skye. Not her daughter...

Seeing Shirley wavering, Marco grinned. 'Say it... I'm waiting...'

'T-Thank you,' Shirley whimpered, her mind zoning to

blankness.

'What? I didn't quite catch that.' Marco ran the splintered end of the chair leg along the mottled skin of Shirley's inner thigh.

'THANK YOU!' Shirley yelled. If it meant Skye was safe, then she'd live with thanking this beast, this foul creature, this...

'Much better, but isn't there something else you need to say?' Marco snarled.

This time Shirley wouldn't wait until she was forced. The words stuck in her throat, but they would be worth it. 'I... I'm sorry.'

Jumping up, Marco casually dropped the chair leg onto Shirley's stomach. 'That wasn't difficult, was it? I'm not sure a measly apology and thanking me makes up for everything you've done, but I'll mull it over whilst you write me that cheque.'

THIRTEEN

'YOU SURE SHE DIDN'T mention anything about a delivery? I definitely saw her outside speaking to men in a Transit just before I came in.'

The guard shrugged. 'They must have been who she had a meeting with.'

'Meeting? What meeting?'

'What are you doing in here, Taylor?' Skye flounced into the room, avoiding glaring in Erin's direction. *Sticking her beak in already, was she? Now this idiot had opened his trap.* 'Get back to your post.'

She waited until the man hurried out of the room, making a mental note to find more reasons why there was no longer a job here for him. 'What was that all about? I hope he isn't causing trouble. He's not very good that particular one,' she lied.

'No, no trouble. I was just asking him about a delivery.' Erin watched for a reaction on Skye's face but found none. 'When Martin dropped me off, I saw you talking to men in a van.'

'There was no delivery,' Skye snapped, containing her irritation. Erin shouldn't have even been here for another half an hour, but Martin had ballsed things up by giving her a bloody lift, the stupid, moronic fucking idi…

'The guard mentioned a meeting,' Erin probed. 'There was nothing in the diary. I would have been there had I known.'

'It was a last-minute thing. Not something I expected either.' Skye busied herself with picking paperwork up from the desk so she could hide the scowl creeping over her face.

'A last-minute thing?'

'Yeah, I felt we could do with a couple more guards.' Skye turned around, confident she'd found a plausible reason. Lowering her voice, she jerked her head in the direction of the door. 'Like I said, I've noticed some of them here aren't the best and… well, let's put it this way, when I was speaking to the women yesterday when you were sorting out the office, it seems that some guards in particular are making the women uncomfortable.'

Erin frowned. 'Are you saying they've been acting out of turn?' Zane wouldn't take on anyone who wasn't personally recommended to him by a trusted source. He'd be horrified if anyone had behaved in such a way.

'I'm not saying anything for definite. You know that many of the women's English isn't great, so I could have misread it, but it's also a feeling I've picked up on.' Skye shrugged. 'Aside from that, there's a few guards who just aren't switched on. They're lazy and we haven't got time for that. Taylor is a prime example. Anyway, a guard who's been nothing but brilliant put forward a couple of names, so I interviewed them with a view to giving them a trial. That doesn't hurt, does it?'

Erin's frown deepened. 'Which guard recommended these men?'

Skye's face hardened. 'Look Erin, I know we've had our differences and that we're jointly running this, but if I have to explain and outline every single thing and run each idea past you, then we'll not get much done, will we?'

'No, but...'

'If you wish, we can pick up on this later.' Skye moved to the door. 'Interview the men yourself if you like, but I've got to go. I've arranged a meeting with a linen company. Having a contract in washing towels and bedding will be economical in the long run, but rather than being resourceful, I guess I should have sought permission about that from *you* first!'

Leaving Erin standing at the desk, Skye left the office and hurried up the corridor. *Fuck.* All she could hope for was that Erin didn't push for a further interview or continue the conversation over which guard had made the non-existent recommendation. Just as she'd expected, Erin was watching her like a hawk whilst playing the game of 'we're friends now', so getting the bitch off the scene quick was vital. As for Martin, being as he was becoming even more of a liability, he'd have to exit stage left sooner than planned too.

Remembering something else, Skye pulled her mobile from her pocket. Judging by her father's silence after the last text she'd sent about Alyson's interest in his 'project', she'd give the girl a nudge. She didn't want Marco thinking she wasn't up to the job, therefore it was prudent that as much as possible was delivered before schedule.

Only that would prove she deserved the inheritance Marco could offer.

• • • •

PULLING UP EXACTLY where Zane specified, Martin killed the engine and stared in awe at the exclusive penthouse complex. He squinted through the sun, his mouth falling open at the size of the uppermost apartment - the most elite of them all. There were several balconies up there and those were just ones he could see!

His parents were well off - that was no secret, but *this* place... and on the banks of the Thames too? Bloody hell, it must have cost millions!

And it belonged to Zane.

He shuddered. Or it *had*, until Zane's brother took possession.

Martin hadn't asked about the ins and outs of what had gone

on between Zane and Marco, neither had it been offered. To be honest, he didn't want to know. It only underlined that the Morellis were into heavy duty stuff to pull in the sort of money to own places like this. And this reignited the nervousness deep within his bones at his own involvement in it. But then, Zane was Skye's father; Martin loved Skye and if he wanted to be in her life, which he did more than anything, then he needed to get his head around that this was how it was. Besides, soon he'd officially be part of the family.

Martin was so engrossed with his thoughts and at staring at the upper penthouse that he didn't register the taxi pulling up in front of the manicured pathway at first.

It was only when he heard a car door slamming, did he remind himself what he was actually here for. Rapidly moving his gaze to ground level, he was just in time to see a taxi depart. His eyes darted to the shiny double doors of the complex, only to see a flash of the sun reflecting off the glass as the door closed behind whoever had just entered the building.

Martin tensed, his heart pounding. *Shit.* Someone had just gone inside and he'd missed it?

Shit, shit, shit!

His eyes darted around as if retracing his vision would rewind the last few seconds and replay what he'd missed.

Was it Marco?

Martin squinted harder against the bright reflective glass in the distance. It could have been anyone - even the postman.

Yes, it probably was. There must be plenty of deliveries to a place like this. But then, if it was the postman, wouldn't he have come out again by now?

None of this meant it was Marco though. Zane said that the man never moved in the morning, so it couldn't be him. And if Marco didn't surface until late, then it wouldn't be anyone summoned to see him either.

Picking up his phone, Martin stared at it. Should he call Zane? He'd made it clear he wanted to be immediately informed of any developments.

He sagged against the bench seat of the Transit. That was just it - he had no developments to speak to Zane about. He hadn't seen who'd entered the building and no one had come out.

Martin expelled a juddery breath. He must stop panicking. He'd already ruled out the plausibility of it being anyone of interest and he hoped that was the case. But as Zane was trusting him to undertake this work, the very least he could do was get it right.

No. He was panicking. It wasn't anyone of note. It was fine.

Martin went to place his phone back on the seat, deciding that from now on he wouldn't take his eyes off that entrance, when his mobile rang.

'Mum? What is it? Are you all right? Skye's father? Well… erm, it's not really up to me to… Yes, okay, Zane is her…' Listening to the frantic babbling, an increasing wave of nausea rolled over Martin. 'What do you mean? Who said that? No... no, listen, Zane's fine. He's been fine with me, anyway... I... What?'

Sweat broke out along his neck. 'I... erm... no, I'm working at... No...' He hated lying. Especially to his mother, but he couldn't tell her the truth. Even less so after what he'd just heard. 'Skye's father is fine, Mum. You know Shirley isn't all there and... What? No! You can't! You promised! You... Mum?'

Martin stared at his mobile, the screen blank where his mother had cut the call.

He clenched his teeth, nausea moving into full blown sickness. She'd promised him, yet now because of Shirley's mad wittering about Zane being cursed or some other rubbish, she was threatening to come and see for herself.

She couldn't!

If Zane discovered he'd given out the address of the house in Dalston to anyone, yet alone Martin's father who would immediately run to the police, then his dreams of marrying Skye were out of the window. Zane would not take this lapse in trust well.

Martin brushed his floppy fringe out of his eyes before it stuck to the sweat on his brow. Why had he been so stupid? He thought he'd allayed any fears his mother may have had about him staying in London. He also thought she'd believed him after explaining that his frantic calls and messages about being kidnapped, held prisoner and that loads of people wanted to kill him as being a mistake. Yet now he'd made things worse. He'd all but confirmed Zane was Skye's father. He'd thought his mother already knew; sure he'd blurted that out when he'd phoned her from inside the cupboard. But now Shirley had gone off on one again and infected his mother with worry, his future with Skye hung in the balance.

Snatching his phone up again, he dialled his mother back. He had to stop this madness in its tracks before she and his bloody father turned up at Zane's house and ruined the chance of him ever being happy. If they turned up, then a life having anything to do with Skye, Zane or *anyone* ever again would be down the toilet.

FOURTEEN

BASED ON THE deferential acknowledgment of his men overseeing the Thames Canning Works, Zane was assured that Tiger would experience no resistance to issued orders.

Tiger Shoreham's reputation was elite in the enforcing world and Zane was only relieved that Skye's ridiculous antics and his own bad behaviour in falling for his daughter's lies had remained safely within the four walls of where it occurred. The guards present that day had made the sensible decision to obey instructions not to breathe a word about the 'crossed wires' that had unfortunately followed. If Skye's fake allegations had got out and rumours circulated on the grapevine, Tiger would not have agreed to come back to work.

Zane knew he was lucky that Tiger had accepted his apology at all. The man didn't have to and he wouldn't blame him if he hadn't.

His irrationality that day taught Zane that regardless of what the situation involved, he must weigh everything up. But doing that was easier said than done when the subject involved Skye - the daughter who had overtaken Erin in importance. The love and pride he felt for Skye blew his mind and outshined everything else, but for Zane and like his father before him, family was everything.

Family also meant more than just blood. It included those close to him of whom he would defend with his life. People like Tiger – the man, much to his shame, he'd let down. But no more. Now Tiger had given him the chance to rectify his gross misjudgement, Zane was determined that wouldn't be a mistake he'd make again.

Walking into the expanse of the rear warehouse, Tiger inspected the racks containing metal vaults holding the remains of their cocaine supply. 'The next shipment is to be stored here?'

Zane nodded. 'It's due next week. It's a big one - the biggest yet!'

Tiger moved between the empty racks; the space created to make room for the vast amounts of gear expected shortly for weighing, cutting and bagging ready for distribution. 'Marco has royally fucked up by losing the contract for this lot that's due!'

'Yep, but his loss is our gain,' Zane grinned. 'I've got men ready to do the grunt work and the dealers are on standby, but you're happy to oversee it as agreed?'

'Yes, I'm good with that,' Tiger said, making mental notes of how many kilos would pack on each rack.

Zane watched, his relief palpable. He'd been unsure whether Tiger would accept running the warehouses. He knew this man like being in on the action, but this killed two birds with one stone: Tiger would not have to cross paths with Skye, such was his caveat for returning and an experienced hand was needed to oversee this operation. Only himself, Leo or Tiger could do that. These people he was dealing with in this arrangement were hard-core, big players – possibly the biggest. So big, it made *them* look like boy scouts.

Regardless, Zane hoped that eventually Tiger's resentment toward Skye would mellow enough for him to work wherever he wanted, but for now, him being back where he belonged - within the inner circle, was something that a scant few weeks ago he hadn't expected to be possible. Things were still a little strained, but that was expected. Besides, he'd accept whatever the man he'd let down so badly felt able to offer.

'Any headway with the girl's mother?'

Tiger's question caught Zane off guard. Out of courtesy he'd gone out of his way not to mention Skye, or anything linked to her. The question also brought the nagging worry about Shirley back to the forefront. The busy day had so far been a balm by diverting his attention away from that subject, but now it was back.

He rubbed his hand over his chin and sighed. 'I tried calling her again this morning, but she hung up when I got as far as "Hello Sh…". In a nutshell, that's as far as I am with it.'

Tiger grinned even though the situation was far from amusing. 'What will you do?'

'Get her help.' Zane shrugged. 'How I'll convince her to accept it, I don't know, but I've got to do something.' *And he still didn't know why she hated him so.*

• • • •

RED EYED HIS HALF-EATEN EGG and chips disparagingly before stubbing out his fag in the centre of one of the greenish-coloured yolks. 'I'm sure this is fucking rotten. I'll get food poisoning at this bloody rate! Whose idea was it to come into this dump?'

Baz glanced around the ropey truck stop, hoping the present clientele didn't take offence at Red's comments. Most of the men in here were bigger than them put together and looked suited to being in a zoo rather than 'Rob's Diner'.

Admittedly, the food wasn't great, but it was the only place they'd spotted to grab some nosh on the way back from Dagenham. Not that any of them were hungry. Well, *he* wasn't and by the look on Dylan's face, he wasn't the only one. It was a good job, considering this grub had a high chance of turning someone anorexic rather than risk eating it, but coming in here and going through the motions of eating was a good excuse not to discuss the subject scraping painfully against each of their brains. This, however, was a futile gesture as it was only a matter of time before one of them mentioned it. Somebody had to. Baz just didn't want to be the first and thankfully, he didn't have to be.

'I don't like it,' Dylan said as he repeatedly squeezed a crusted-up plastic tomato sauce dispenser onto a grubby napkin.

Red stared at the globs of sauce plopping from the bottle, sure it wasn't supposed to be that colour. 'I don't like it either.' He pushed his plate into the centre of the formica table. 'That's why I ain't eating any more.' His face screwed up in disgust. 'I've a good mind to demand my money back. It tastes like shit! I'll probably die of food poisoning now and...'

'You've already said that,' Dylan snapped. 'And I wasn't talking about not liking the food. I meant about this "job" we've been given. I never signed up to kill someone or...'

'Keep your bloody voice down,' Baz hissed. Dylan's squeaky voice was already gaining the attention of several gorilla-like men who had turned to stare in their direction. He leant over the table, careful to avoid putting his elbow in the mound of tomato sauce. 'I'm uncomfortable about it too.'

'We said we do it and considering where the orders have come from, I don't see what choice we've got,' Red added. 'If that's what Marco wants, then that's what will happen.' He'd make sure *his* part of it was tip top because the second-in-command role that bird banged on about had his name on it. 'Let's just get on with it.'

'But I've never heard of this woman. Who is she anyway?' Dylan whined.

Red shrugged. He hadn't heard of a chick called Erin Langley either, but that was by the by.

'Are we *certain* this is an order from Marco? The target works at the Starbright place. She's the one Skye said was nosy, so what's that got to do with Marco? Why does he want her gone?'

Red gritted his teeth. All the years he'd known Dylan, yet

the man's voice still set his fucking hair on edge. 'An order from Marco or from Skye is the same difference at the moment, remember? We're being paid to do what's asked, whatever that may be.'

'Yeah, but murder? I track people and bug fucking phones. I ain't no killer!' Dylan squawked.

Baz didn't have the excuse of being the tech guy and had got his hands dirty more than once for Marco Morelli, but he suspected this particular order was a little more complex than previous ones. It could have a far-reached and detrimental fallout if it went tits-up or it was ever discovered they were behind it.

That was the reason behind his reticence. He folded his arms across his chest. 'Whether I like it or not, if we don't want Marco on our case, then we've just got to get on with it,' he sighed. 'But for the record, I don't like it.' His eyes met the other two men in turn. 'The reason I don't like it is because I think, as I reckon you two have already worked out, that the bird to be offed - this Erin Langley woman, is Zane Morelli's missus.'

Seeing the shock on Red and Dylan's faces, Baz reached the depressing conclusion that the men he was stuck working with hadn't had a clue and that made him question even harder about how the hell he'd got himself involved in this accident waiting to happen.

FIFTEEN

ZANE SNATCHED A PIECE of toast from the stack on the plate in the centre of the table and winked at Skye. He then gave Martin a glance which read that he wanted to have a catch-up.

Martin had given no hint last night whether anything had been seen at the penthouse, so Zane took that to mean there was nothing to report, but the boy must learn that regardless of whether there was or not, he expected to be kept informed. But Martin had walked in late last night with the look of a hunted animal. He wore the same face this morning, so if the kid couldn't handle the late nights or the stress of keeping his manoeuvres to himself and away from Skye, then perhaps Erin was right - the lad wasn't up to even doing a basic hands-off surveillance task.

Zane would have taken Martin to one side last night for an update had Skye not insisted on hanging around. She was doing the same this morning, so the lad would have to make the effort to bring him up to speed one way or another.

About to broach the question of when Erin and Skye were leaving for the Starbright, Zane noticed the frown on Erin's face. 'What's up?'

'I was just trying to call back a number that I had a missed call from.' Erin lowered her mobile away from her ear and stared at the screen. She then flicked through the call log. 'Whoever it was called at 7 AM.'

'That's early.' Zane slung a mug of boiling hot tea into his mouth. 'Who was it?' Aside from with each other, they all kept their mobile numbers under wraps. It had been the same since replacing their phones after Marco and his cronies learnt of their old numbers. No one wanted bugs or trackers.

'I've no idea,' Erin mused. 'But whoever it was isn't answering now.'

Suspecting she knew *exactly* who had called, Skye deflected from her unease by pouring herself a glass of orange juice. When she'd handed Marco's three goons this address and phone number yesterday, she'd presumed they possessed the sense not to blatantly call. Doing that risked trashing the whole plan before it got off the ground.

The thick bastards. Why Marco wanted those three involved, she wasn't sure. They didn't possess a brain between them. Turning to Erin, she smiled brightly. 'It's probably one of those computer-generated, cold call things.'

'But where would they have got my number from? Very few people have it.'

'Phone networks are always selling on their lists and then crappy firms ring around active mobile numbers.' Skye didn't know whether that was true or not, but it sounded feasible.

'You shouldn't have returned the call,' Zane said, shrugging his jacket on. 'Don't risk that again. It could be anyone.' He then turned to Skye. 'Are you not going to the Starbright today?'

'Of course. I'm ready whenever Erin is.' Pretending she wanted to accompany Erin to work was ridiculous, but she had to keep up the act. It didn't help that she had to check whether Alyson was still heading to London today but would call the dopy bitch the second she got a free minute without anyone breathing down her neck.

Erin shoved her phone back into her handbag. She hated not

knowing who'd tried to reach her, but for once, Skye was probably right about it being a random cold call. Still, with so many enemies, it was difficult not to look for threats everywhere.

But there was also something she needed to speak to Zane about and she needed to do that as soon as possible.

Seeing Zane finish doing up his boots, she took the opportunity to wrap her arms around his neck and pressed her lips against his ear. 'I need a quick word,' she whispered, aware Skye was watching her every move.

A shadow of a frown flitted over Zane's face. 'I'll see everyone later.' Taking Erin's hand, he led her into the hallway. 'What's the problem?' he asked, his voice low.

'Skye's hiring new guards and said one of yours recommended someone, but...'

'I thought something major had happened!' Zane sighed. 'Can this not wait? I've got a shed load of things to do this morning and...'

'But she's already conducted an interview without mentioning it to me! Apparently, some guards who are making the women at the refuge uncomfortable, but I haven't noticed anyth...'

'I'm sure Skye knows what she's doing and if one of my men have recommended th...' Zane stopped talking when Skye moved into the hallway followed by Martin.

'I thought you'd left without me!' Skye said brightly, her cold eyes fixed on Erin.

'I was just saying goodbye to your father.' Erin's heart sank. She couldn't say anything else now. *Perfect timing, as usual.*

'We'll continue this later if needs be, Erin. I'll see both you girls later.' Zane then jerked his head at Martin lurking in the doorway. 'A quick word?'

Kissing Erin again, he steered Martin back into the kitchen and waited for the front door to close behind the two women.

He didn't like the sound of what had been said about guards

upsetting women, but as for the rest - Skye had the same mindset as him when it came to getting a job done, so he was confident whatever was going on, she'd got it in hand. Erin must stop breathing down the girl's neck and give her trust. She'd promised a fresh start and he wasn't convinced that was happening, but right now, finding out updates about the penthouse was of prime importance.

Leaning against the kitchen door, Zane blocked any opportunity for Martin to decide he didn't want to be confined in the room. He fixed his eyes on the young man who looked like he'd shrunk at least two inches during the night. 'What's to report? Judging by your face, there's something.'

• • • •

ALYSON STARED from the train window, concentrating on anything other than the excitement buzzing through her. It would be great to see Skye again. To think she'd spent ages worrying about whether the girl she'd known since *forever* was okay after going in search of her father. She should have known Skye was fine and that she'd been worrying over nothing.

Pretending to Shirley that she had no idea where Skye had gone was awful - especially as Shirley kept calling up in a state about it. But that was what friends did, wasn't it? Having each other's backs was what it was all about.

Admittedly, Alyson had begun to feel uncomfortable when Shirley rattled on about 'danger' and 'criminals', but it hadn't taken long to put things into perspective. She was well aware that Shirely wasn't quite the ticket. Besides, everyone had the right to know who their parents were and it was wrong of Shirley to keep that from her daughter.

It was no wonder Skye was a bit extreme sometimes, but then, being the quieter one out of the two, being around Skye brought Alyson out of her shell and she needed that. Alyson didn't want to be boring her entire life and now she had the chance to experience something exciting, she intended to do just that. That's why she'd accepted Skye's invitation to come to London. There was also a part of her which was intrigued to meet the man that Skye's mother had been so desperate to hide.

Skye had sounded really excited talking about her previously unknown father. She said he was great and this made it all the stranger why Shirley was so against her ever having anything to do with the man.

Alyson inwardly shrugged. It was most likely because the man had dumped Shirley her nose was out of joint. But did that give her the right to cut off access for all these years? Not telling that poor man he was a father was inexcusable!

It wasn't fair of Shirley to make her daughter pay for her own personal resentment. The woman wasn't right in the bloody head!

Ignoring the bespectacled man on the opposite seat who hadn't stop staring at her since she'd got on the train, Alyson wiped her clammy hands down her jeans and pulled her phone from her handbag, determined not to let anything unnerve her.

She'd never been great at dealing with attention from the opposite sex. 'Crippled with nervousness', her mother always said - the very opposite of Skye Wilson…

Skye revelled in attention and was good at dealing with it too. She soaked up compliments and knew exactly how to play things. But then, it was easy being so pretty and Alyson wasn't a patch on her friend when it came to looks. Or personality, for that matter.

In fact, she felt as dull as ditchwater compared to Skye and even though Skye had always tried to convince her that she was equally as beautiful, Alyson knew Skye was just being kind.

But now, with this trip to London - with the sights and bright lights, maybe this was her time to shine?

A smile edged onto Alyson's mouth. What Skye said on the phone sounded brilliant! Her father was loaded and living in one of those executive penthouses! A whole fleet of fancy cars at his disposal too. It was like a fairy story.

Alyson shivered with excitement. It wasn't like she'd gone without. Her parents owned a sprawling house with massive grounds, they had loads of cars and a helicopter took her to a birthday party once, but this... this was different. *London* was different. London was where the excitement lay and where all the bright young things and everyone who was *anyone* resided.

Skye's father sounded both trendy and fashionable. He even had a cool name:

Marco.

How cool was that? It wasn't like Edward or Ralph. Or Robert.

As the crackly voice through the train speakers announced the next stop, Alyson brought her phone to life. *Not long to go now*, she thought, scrolling to Marco's address and the message Skye had texted.

Thames Heights, Battersea
It's on the banks of the Thames. Get the Victoria Line to Vauxhall and then a taxi. They'll no where 2 go. Everyone's heard of these apartments. When u reach the complex tell the concierge who u are and he'll give u a code for the penthouse floor. You're expected, so there won't be probs.
See u soon
xx

Alyson chewed her lip. She'd hoped Skye would meet her off the train. She'd never gone to a random place alone before, but Skye insisted she couldn't meet her from the station because she was coming in the opposite direction from work.

Skye had a job too - and a manager's job at that!

Why couldn't things like that – exciting things – happen to *her*?

Alyson made a conscious effort to relax. This was half of her problem – she was always on edge and worried about everything so no wonder nothing interesting ever happened. Besides, it wasn't like she'd be on her own in the penthouse because Skye would be there too. At least she hoped that would still be the case…

She excitedly tapped out a text:

`I'm almost there. About to get off the train. Are you on your way to ur dad's place? xx`

The reply came within seconds.

`I won't b long. Leaving work now. Will meet u there. Can't wait to c u xx`

A wide smile broke over Alyson's face. This trip would be fab.

• • • •

'MY PERSONAL FEELINGS aside, I have to say that I agree with what you're saying,' Tiger said, his forehead knotting into a frown. 'However, there's not a lot I can do about it, being as I'm giving Skye and anywhere she is, a wide berth...' Sitting on a tea chest, he wedged one foot onto another opposite. 'No, it's fine. I understand why you're asking.'

Looking up as the door to the large storage room in the Thames Canning Works opened, Tiger acknowledged Leo's arrival and continued listening to what Erin was saying. Her apology for bringing up the night Skye pulled that shitty stunt on him which almost cost him his chosen family and whole career, not to mention a tooth, wasn't fine. The less he thought about that night, Skye Wilson and anything surrounding her, the better, but he was damned if he was letting that little bitch rule his temper.

He took a deep breath. 'No, I didn't see her go near it, although that's not to say she didn't before I got in there... Yeah, that's right - it was on the floor... Okay... no problem.'

Ending the call, Tiger stared at his phone, his frown

deepening.

'Problems?' Leo asked, his eyes scanning the cutting desks waiting to be populated with people to bag up the coke the minute the delivery arrived.

'No and yes. I'm not sure.' Tiger remained thoughtful, staring at his blank phone. 'That was Erin. She wanted to know a couple of things - my opinion about some of the guards for one. Taylor in particular.'

'Why? From what I know of the guards at the Starbright they seem all right.'

'Skye's adamant some of them are lazy and aren't doing their job. She's also made insinuations about some making the women uncomfortable. On top of that, she's taken it upon herself to interview some new guards.'

Leo raised an eyebrow 'Does Zane know about this? All his guards come personally recommended from men he *does* know. Who are these new people?'

'No idea.' Tiger shrugged. 'Zane dismissed Erin's concerns, apparently. He wants Skye's judgement to be trusted.'

Leo snorted loudly. 'Trust Skye? Yeah, right! And casting aspersions over the men's motives... Ring any bells?'

'I'm hardly likely to forget what she did to me, am I?' Tiger spat. 'That's why I'm here overseeing this, rather than anywhere else.' He swept his arm around the expanse of the room, his eyes burning brightly.

'Sorry, mate.' Leo raised his hand in submission. 'I didn't mean to downplay the shit you went through.'

Tiger nodded, placated. 'Erin also wanted to know whether I saw Skye near Hazel's desk that particular night. I didn't, but she's convinced Hazel was not behind signing that statement.'

'Like we all are,' Leo added.

'Erin reckons Sandler got in beforehand, but I can't see how.'

'Nor can I.' Leo shook his head. 'No one breached defences before that day.' Even the mention of Sandler's name riled his temper. 'So, Erin thinks Miss You-Know-Who has something to do with it? If she does, it wouldn't surprise me.'

Tiger cracked his knuckles. 'As much as none of us want to believe that Hazel stabbed us in the back, I'd rather that for Zane's sake.'

Leo nodded. Skye engineering that betrayal would finish the man. Regardless of what anyone thought of the girl, Zane was besotted with his daughter, but try as he might, Leo couldn't fathom what possible gain she'd get by shafting Zane. She stood only to gain by Zane's *success*, not lose.

Unanswered questions aside, Leo had his own plan to put into motion - one to remove some stress from Zane. He'd promised to think of something and he had. And that was happening today.

Hoisting himself off the tea crate he was perched on, Leo got to his feet. 'All we can do is keep our ears open and our eyes peeled where that little Madam is concerned. Talking of two-faced, slimy pieces of shit, I've got an appointment with our friend, Mr Sandler, soon.'

And he was looking forward to it even if it meant he had to make himself look like a cunt.

Sixteen

HEART THUMPING, Fiona held her breath as Peter swung the car around on the large driveway. She waited as he drove to the bottom, the crunching of the gravel under the tyres taunting her.

'Hurry up,' she muttered, half-expecting Peter to change his mind, saying he wouldn't bother getting a paper after all. It would go something along the lines of, '*I don't know why I bother reading this. They only print nonsense about the Foot and Mouth thing, the Middle East or Milosevic's trial at the Hague.*'

Whether Peter knew why he bothered or not, it never stopped him reading the bloody paper like clockwork every day though, did it? Moaning that the paper boy had twice omitted to deliver the blasted thing this week was his latest gripe.

Seeing the car disappear from the end of the driveway, Fiona dashed to the phone.

She didn't have long. Best case scenario, Peter would be fifteen minutes and relied on him stopping to chat to the newsagent about golf, like usual. If he didn't, then there was even *less* time.

Snatching up the receiver, Fiona stabbed in Shirley's number. She'd dialled it so many times recently she knew it off by heart. This window of Peter being out of the house was the only chance she had because if he caught her calling Shirley against his strict instructions to have nothing to do with the woman, he'd go mad.

But after what Shirley said yesterday about the people Skye and Martin were living with, she had to get to the bottom of things. Martin saying the opposite about this Morelli person didn't make sense. And him calling her back, begging her again not to ever 'turn up' at the address he'd given her, along with the distinct feeling that he was hiding something, only heightened Fiona's resolve to get the full picture before taking it upon herself to interfere and break her promise.

Shirley could provide that information and this time Fiona was adamant she'd succeed in getting it. If the woman would only answer the bloody phone!

Slamming the receiver down, Fiona immediately snatched it back up and redialled. *Why wasn't Shirley answering? Come on!*

The call rang out again and then again. On the fourth attempt, a horrible thought slithered into her head.

What if those men had returned? What if the Morelli person who'd previously appeared at Shirley's door had come back and done something awful? Shirley was clearly frightened of him and that he should keep calling and not leaving her alone was worrying.

Panic bubbled. *What should she do?* Was there time to get to Shirley's and make sure she was all right before Peter returned?

Fiona shook her head in desperation. *No.* There was no way she'd get there and back in time. But she had to get to the bottom of this - both for Shirley's welfare and the truth of who Martin was involved with. She'd just have to wait until Peter returned with his paper and then think of an excuse why she had to go out. But how could she bear waiting any longer when...

With the sudden frantic banging of the front door, blood dropped down Fiona's veins to pool within her feet.

Was this that thug who had previously come here looking for Martin? He was connected with this so-called Morelli gang.

Oh God...

Knowing she had little choice but to answer the door whilst the frenzied knocking continued, Fiona stumbled along the hallway and with shaking fingers, turned the knob.

• • • •

AS MUCH AS MARTIN was nervous about being here again, it was better than getting the Spanish Inquisition.

His eyes remained focused on the entrance to the penthouse complex, determined that this time he wouldn't mess up. Whatever happened, he wouldn't take his eyes off this place. Not even to blink!

That he'd got a second chance and avoided admitting his screw-up to Zane about missing who had entered here yesterday, was lucky. And the way Zane grilled him this morning was enough to ensure he wouldn't mess up again. And being as he clearly wore his feeling like a billboard, he also had to work on his poker face.

Martin squinted against the glare of the sunlight bouncing off the glass double doors of the building. *Christ, he'd go blind at this rate.*

It was slowly sinking in that there were many facets to this kind of work that he hadn't bargained for and he wasn't sure how good he was at it. But he'd better rapidly improve because he'd already had more than enough hints at what might befall him if he crossed lines.

Zane might be acting pleasant and accommodating at the moment, but Martin wasn't deluded. He knew he'd be in the shit if he let any of these people down.

And 'shit' didn't adequately cover the result of what could happen should that occur.

A shudder passed through his rigid body in the van's uncomfortable driving seat. If Zane discovered he hadn't been honest when he'd had every opportunity...

Martin sighed - his breath expelling in juddery gasps. It was clear when Zane collared him earlier that he knew something was up. Martin could have admitted that he'd missed information yesterday and if he had, Zane would have probably taken it better than later discovering he'd emitted chunks.

Why had he kept quiet. Panic perhaps? Or because he'd been put on the spot? He didn't know, but he'd done it now and there was no turning back. The only positive thing was that whoever he'd missed wasn't anyone important and that was the main thing.

But Martin had admitted *something* and Zane hadn't been happy to hear that Shirley was saying all of this stuff to his mother.

Yes, Martin knew he'd previously been adamant that his mum believed his story. He'd insisted that she'd accepted everything was fine and that the stuff he'd spouted about being abducted, threatened and hidden in cupboards, was a misunderstanding. But that was before Shirley convinced her that Zane was a psychotic, animalistic criminal - not safe to be around under any circumstances.

Martin had blurted this out, explaining that his mother had had a bit of a wobble, but it would be okay. He'd made it clear that things were fine and Shirley was wrong.

He swallowed dryly. As well as being the opposite of happy, Zane wasn't convinced, but under the circumstances, Martin thought he'd done a pretty impressive job of assuaging Zane's concerns.

That wouldn't be the case had he admitted that he'd made another 'small error' by handing his mother Zane's address...

For God's sake, he'd only given it to her for her peace of mind. He hadn't expected her to start talking about showing up!

It was okay. She wouldn't come to Dalston. For a start, she didn't drive and secondly Martin reckoned she now believed him. It was obvious when he'd immediately called back just to reiterate that there was absolutely no need for her to come to the house.

Martin breathed slowly in and out to quell his rising panic.

His mum would honour what she promised. Her knowledge that Shirley wasn't all there, helped. But now he'd told Zane *two* lies and this didn't sit comfortably within his head.

Martin's eyes moved to where he gripped the edge of the dashboard like if he let go then he'd tumble into an abyss.

He must look at things rationally. He hadn't actually *lied.* Not offering up information that hadn't been specifically asked wasn't lying, was it?

Just concentrate on what you've been told to do, Martin silently repeated as he shifted his gaze back to the apartment complex entrance.

Wait! Who was that?

Sitting forward, Martin blinked to lubricate his dry eyes. *It wasn't Marco Morelli - not unless he'd taken to wearing women's jeans and high heels.*

He watched the woman continue up the pathway to the entrance, wondering why if she lived there, did she keep looking up at the expanse of the building like she'd never seen it before?

She had a large holdall too.

Martin frowned. Perhaps she was one a mobile hairdresser or something?

Anyway, it wasn't Marco. Neither was it anyone who could be classed as an 'enforcer' or 'someone of note', so... *Hang on!*

As the woman reached the doors she glanced nervously over her shoulder, allowing Martin a glimpse of her face.

Was that...?

Although he was some distance away, Martin was convinced that the woman looked like...

It was!

Lurching forward further, Martin focused harder to double check his eyes weren't playing tricks. As the woman disappeared inside, Martin sank back into the seat.

What was Skye's friend doing here? As far as he knew, Alyson Read never came to London, so why was she going into that building?

Martin grabbed his mobile off the seat. Skye would know what Alyson was doing in London because those two were close.

Keeping his eye on the building, Martin pulled up Skye's number, but with his finger on the call button, stopped.

How could he tell Skye he'd seen Alyson here without breaking his promise to Zane?

He'd pushed his luck by not volunteering the additional information as well as omitting other 'select' points as it was. Blatantly going against the crystal-clear instructions to keep schtum about his work and keeping Skye unaware of it would not be one of his best ideas.

Frowning, he placed the phone back on the seat. Although that woman had *looked* like Alyson, maybe it wasn't? It had been a while since he'd last seen her, so he couldn't be sure. She might just be someone who *resembled* Alyson.

Plus, look how far away he was parked. From here, it would be easy to get confused with someone similar looking. He didn't know Alyson all that well, so how could he be certain it was her, based on a few similarities?

Yes, that was most likely it.

Marco and anyone who might be working for him was the task here, not flapping over someone resembling one of his girlfriend's mates!

Martin's lips thinned. The trouble was, whatever he told himself and against all of his plausible arguments, he *knew* it was Alyson Read.

It was okay. So, he couldn't ask Skye whether she knew Alyson was in town, but he *could* tell Zane about it later and then it was up to him whether he wanted to speak to Skye about it. In order to do his job diligently, Martin would concentrate only on the task in hand. He'd just clock the exact time Alyson left. After all, she might have a relative who lived in one of those apartments and therefore her presence in Battersea would make total sense.

• • • •

'I-I DIDN'T KNOW WHERE else to go,' Shirley babbled, her fingers gripping the door jamb like claws. 'I wasn't going to come... I told myself not to. I... I sat all night waiting for him to come back... I couldn't risk leaving the house but then I realised I *had* to. I-I had to see you and tell you th...'

'Oh my God! What on earth has happened?' Fiona shrieked, finding her voice after being rendered speechless finding Shirley in such a pitiful state on her doorstep.

For the second time, her eyes darted over the deep scratches on Shirley's face; at the vivid bruising around her eyes and nose and her swollen jaw. Her eyes were haunted with a look even more intense than the last time Fiona had seen her. But this was different... this was... 'Come in quickly!' Grabbing Shirley's arm, she prised her off the door frame. 'My God, you're shaking!'

As Fiona led Shirley into the lounge, she realised 'shaking' didn't adequately describe the violent juddering coursing through Shirley's body. Taking a glance out of the window, on edge about Peter's impending return, she helped Shirley into an armchair, then poured a small brandy from the selection in the drinks cabinet.

Wrapping Shirley's trembling fingers around the wide bowl of the glass, Fiona could only hope she didn't spill it on the rug. She'd never explain *that* to Peter.

Shirley stared at the glass in her hands. 'I-I don't drink.'

Fiona sat in the nearest armchair and reached to gently lay a hand on Shirley's arm. 'You're in shock. Drink that brandy and tell me what happened.' She looked once again at Shirley's obvious injuries, noting a fresh bald patch in the woman's knotted hair. Her panic dissolved and instead anger brewed. 'Who did this to you?'

She tried to be patient whilst Shirley jerkily raised the brandy to her mouth and took a large gulp. The woman was vague and spoke in riddles with answers she'd provided before, but Fiona wasn't accepted that this time. This wasn't a random attack on the way to the shops – this was *personal*. Plus, Shirley had mentioned 'him'.

Fiona's eyes narrowed. 'This was that man you told me about it, wasn't it? The one who keeps phoning you and turning up? It was that Morelli person - the one Martin is now staying with.'

'No!' Shirley cried, her eyes wide. 'It w…'

'Stop fobbing me off!' Fiona yelled. 'Tell me the truth. My son is involved with this! What has that man done to you?'

Shirley blinked several times, knowing the minute she spoke the words out loud there was no turning back. 'That's why I'm here. I know I have to tell you.' Her hands wrung tight knots in the stained material of her skirt. 'After everything he did… what his family did, he blames *me*. He… he wanted money… made me write him a cheque. I-I had no choice because… because he threatened me... T-Threatened to rape me, like before. He had a stick… He was going to...'

Fiona stared in horror as Shirley's eyes filled with tears. 'He... he raped you? Last night, he raped you? Oh my God!'

'No!' Shirley's head shook frantically. 'No, he threatened to, but before... He did it before.'

'I don't understand,' Fiona gasped. 'What do you mean, "before"? Please don't lose track of reality, Shirley. If Zane Morelli raped you however many years ago, then we *must* go to the police.' Taking the empty brandy glass from Shirley, she clutched her hand. 'You've got scratches and bruises everywhere. That's evidence the police can use to arrest that man and...'

'It wasn't Zane!' Shirley cried. 'Yes, Zane destroyed my life, but he never laid a hand on me that I didn't want. Instead, he arranged it so his *brother* did. It was Marco who came last night and Marco who raped me all those years ago. *Marco* is Skye's father.'

Fiona's head swam, unsure how to process this information, but she had to. She snatched up the phone.

'No!' Shirley wailed, flailing to grab the receiver. 'Don't phone the police! He'll take it out on Skye. He'll…'

'I'm not calling the police!' Fiona gained back control of the telephone. 'I don't know what to do about what you've just said, but what I *can* do and what I'm doing right now, is stopping that animal cashing the bloody cheque he forced you to write!'

SEVENTEEN

PULLING INTO THE LAYBY in a back road running parallel with the hospital, Leo pulled on a thin blue top and beige jacket. He looked like a prize cunt but ticked the boxes of someone who worked for social services, rather than a right-hand-man for one of London's infamous criminal organisations.

He'd dress as a turnip if it meant he could cut Zane some slack and give the guy much needed relief from the shit on his back.

Pulling out a pair of black-framed glasses from his pocket, he slipped them on and gave himself a quick once over in the rear-view mirror.

With these specs, the wig and the clothes, he barely recognised himself! It was amazing what could be picked up from a charity shop for a few quid!

Okay, so the jacket pulled over his broad shoulders and the wig itched like fuck, but it wasn't like a bunch of nurses in a busy intensive care unit would pay much attention to what *he* looked like. Not when they had high dependency patients coming out of their ears to run around after.

Besides, it wasn't like he was attempting to sneak into an operating theatre and masquerade as a surgeon. This would either work or it wouldn't. Either way, it was worth a punt.

Leaving the van in the layby, Leo hurried up the road, confident there was still a shortcut through the wooded verge which led straight to the hospital.

No one had seen him leave the van or walk the short distance down the road before darting into the trees because this back road, used mainly for hospital deliveries, was deserted. At this time of day, the majority of van and lorry drivers were at burger vans or McDonalds. It would be quieter in the hospital during lunch hour too and neither was it visiting time. He'd timed it perfectly.

Leo had specced this out to ensure the optimal chances of success. Providing Sandler was back on the ward and well enough after the latest 'unfortunate incident', courtesy of Zane, there was a good chance this would work.

Clearing the shortcut, Leo upped his pace into the hospital grounds towards the building housing that toerag, Damon Sandler.

Although he'd previously promising Zane that he'd think of a way to speed up Sandler's demise, rather than waiting for him to be discharged, it wasn't Leo's responsibility to take this on. But, in all honesty, Sandler had been a thorn in his *own* side for far too fucking long. On several occasions already he'd been forced to stand to one side, biding his time and letting the prat continue to draw breath. That never ceased to antagonise him.

Patience wasn't one of Leo's virtues, so it wasn't an unpleasant prospect jumping on this particular task without set orders. He was doing himself, Zane and *everyone* a favour.

Grinding his cigarette end into the ground, Leo yanked open the hospital doors and adopted the stance of someone who knew exactly where he was going.

He just hoped he could pull it off.

• • • •

DAMON LAY UNMOVING in bed and stared at the wall. It was all he'd done since Zane Morelli's recent visit removed the last remaining chink of wanting to cling to life.

There had been mutterings within his earshot of 'showing signs of depression' and 'short term antidepressant use may be warranted', bandied around more than once and Damon could only presume that was in relation to him.

Something else he'd come to realise during this impromptu hospital stay was that patients were discussed like they were deaf, mad and blind, regardless of whether they were or not, but he cared little.

How exactly would a few weeks' worth of antidepressants make a difference to never walking again; losing everything and having a whole host of psychos biding their time until they offloaded him? Zane Morelli almost succeeding in doing just that in this very room said it all. Why didn't the nurses just kill him themselves? They might as well.

And so, no, he wasn't depressed - he was just utterly pissed off that his life's work was reduced to *this*.

Damon glanced down at how the bedsheet sunk to nothingness where the lower halves of his legs used to be.

The nurses and doctors coming into his room with their condescending, shit-eating grins, speaking with tones reserved for shy, unwilling kids at crap holiday parks when trying to coax the little retarded bastards into 'joining in' and 'making the effort', was pointless.

What the medical staff here and the long list of do-gooder therapists with their ridiculous, supercilious plans of getting him 'back on his feet' again, didn't realise was that their ideas meant jack shit. For a start, he no longer had any fucking feet and secondly, even if he did, he was fucked.

There was no way out. No means of come back. *Ever*.

One way or another, whether that be today, next month or next year, those Morelli fuckers would descend and flick off his light.

It was just a case of when...

Damon's hands clenched into fists underneath the greying sheet, the injustice suffocating him.

What really fucked him off was that bitch nurse from before allowing Zane in. The slut *must* have realised he was an enemy, rather than a brother. Who would he get next? Marco proffering to be his long-lost mother?

For fuck's sake. It was ridiculous. So no, he didn't want to see anyone and neither was he interested in any 'therapies' on offer.

Exactly where would that get him?

Even if he did finally get discharged from this dump, it wasn't like he had a life, was it?

Damon ignored the tap on the door, knowing it made no difference what he did because whoever was the other side would enter regardless.

'We need to have a chat about your next steps, Mr Sandler.' The nurse's voice grated as Damon clenched his jaws harder. He didn't turn his head to see who entered. *Next steps?* Why was there always a fucking dig about walking, running - doing *anything* with the things he no longer had?

Stupid whore. He wouldn't give her the satisfaction of reacting, the silly bitch.

Instead, he kept his gaze fixed on the familiar yellow-faced clock, convinced it hadn't moved in the last twenty-four hours.

'The doctors are pleased with how your injuries are healing,' the nurse trilled as she pulled back the sheet.

'Really?' Damon muttered sarcastically, half-wondering being as this thick tart was rummaging under his bedsheet whether she'd mind giving him a hand job.

On second thoughts, his dick probably no longer worked either.

Despite her small frame, the nurse shifted Damon to an upright position even though he made it as awkward as possible by pushing himself into the bed. Regardless, he found himself manoeuvred to the edge of it.

'You've done so well, given your little setback,' the nurse continued as she pulled a wheelchair parallel with the bed.

Damon inwardly raged. *Little set back?* Morelli not only

gouged open his fucking stumps but planned on letting him bleed to death. Call that a 'little setback'?

He was about to voice his displeasure when he clocked the wheelchair. His face crumpled into a grimace. If she thought he was getting into *that* to be paraded around like a bastard cripple, then she had rocks in her head!

'Mr Chantry has come to speak to you about rehabilitation. Things like arranging an adapted flat?' The nurse transferred Damon from the bed into the wheelchair before he'd even clocked it was happening.

It was at this point Damon abandoned the plan to remain unresponsive and silent. He twisted around as far as he could in the metal monstrosity he found himself in. 'Wait a minute! I don't wa...'

'Mr Chantry will take you for a walk around the grounds while you chat,' the nurse smiled. 'It will be good to get some fresh air.'

Damon's newly unleashed panic hit an all-time high. This could be Marco, for all he knew. He contorted further to try and get a view of the alleged Mr Chantry.

'Hello, Mr Sandler. I'm Greg Chantry. We'll soon think of a plan to get you back on your feet.'

As he found himself being wheeled out of the room and along the shiny corridor Damon only managed a quick glimpse of a tall, bespectacled bloke, but that was enough to allay his fears. This wasn't Marco Morelli *or* Zane. But it hadn't escaped his notice about yet another tactless dig - this time about feet.

He had no intention of chatting to this prick about walk-in baths or bed hoists. If he was going into the hospital garden, he was having a fag. He was absolutely choking for a smoke.

• • • •

WHEN THE LIFT DOORS OPENED to the private floor of the penthouse, Alyson nervously stepped into the plush corridor and headed to the ornate and only door on the level.

Imagine a whole floor all to yourself, she thought, her hand hovering over the doorbell.

She hoped Skye was already here. She'd sent another text whilst in the taxi but hadn't received a reply. If Skye hadn't arrived, wouldn't it be best to wait until she did? What if she didn't know what to say to Skye's father? Wouldn't it be awkward?

But then, Skye may already be inside and just missed the text. If so, then she'd be hanging around in the corridor for ages for nothing.

This was silly. She'd ring the bell and go in to introduce herself. Wasn't she going to be more headstrong and enjoy herself?

As Alyson pulled on her reserve of courage to ring the bell, the matter was taken out of her hands when the door suddenly swung open.

'Ah! You must be Alyson. Please come in.'

As she stared at the man in the doorway, Alyson wasn't sure whether her mouth actually fell open or whether it just felt that way.

Unable to stop herself, her gaze trailed over Marco's naked torso, his broad chest and tantalisingly distinct abs, down to the thick white towel wrapped low around his hips - low enough to reveal that 'V' leading to...

Blushing with thoughts she seldom experienced, Alyson willed her voice box to work, but to her horror found that she only managed a strangulated squeak.

Skye hadn't mentioned that her father was drop dead gorgeous! Neither had she mentioned he might answer the door in only a towel!

Christ! What did she do now?

Knowing her cheeks were furiously burning, Alyson moved her gaze upwards to find Marco's eyes piercing through her very soul, sending shockwaves through her body.

Come on! She had to say something. *Anything*!

'I... I must be early,' she stuttered, using the edge of the door frame to steady herself. *She'd turn around and head back towards the lift.* 'I-I'm sorry to interrupt. I... I'll wait downstairs until you... you've...'

Marco's hand shot out to grip Alyson's wrist, cutting off her words as well as halting her retreat. 'I was in the jacuzzi.' He raised an eyebrow. 'You're more than welcome to join me...'

'I... erm...' Alyson tore her eyes away from Marco's muscled frame and glanced over her shoulder. *Where was Skye?*

Marco studied the girl on his doorstep and swallowed his brewing chuckle. She was definitely inexperienced. It was obvious by her reaction. Skye was bang on with her description too. From what he could see, this friend of hers was spot on and just what he was looking for.

But he must slow down. This one was a green as it got, so she'd need putting at ease. Now he'd seen exactly what he was dealing with, loading her with coke wasn't the best idea. Something else he had would work much better. 'Won't you come in?' he drawled, his eyes twinkling. 'Have a drink or two and relax.'

Alyson found herself steered into an immense hallway. With her heels clicking on thick marble tiles and her wrist searing from Marco's electric touch, she couldn't stop staring in awe, especially when she was led into an open-plan living area bigger than the entire ground floor of her parents' house - and their house was massive!

And that view... Wow!

'This place!' she gasped. 'It's... it's amazing!'

'Hard work enables nice things in life.' Marco was already mentally lining up how this girl would fare with his plans. She was prettier than he'd expected - *much* prettier. Skye hadn't given this chick enough credit. And with the new cameras that arrived yesterday now rigged up and ready to roll, there was no time to lose. Pulling money in and getting back on top of everything, including this bird, was the name of the game.

• • • •

'YOU MANAGED TO get your paper then?' Fiona's voice sounded unnaturally bright, but Peter wouldn't notice. She couldn't remember the last time he noticed anything about her, except when she didn't agree with his opinion.

She glanced out of the window at Shirley stumbling down the driveway. She must keep Peter talking because if he turned around and saw... 'You were quite a while, Peter.' *But not long enough by any stretch of the imagination.*

'Bloody temporary roadworks are at both ends of the road! Three-way ones too.' Peter scowled. 'And where were the workmen? I'll tell you where they were – clustered on the grass and nowhere near the damned road. Chaos it was! Ridiculous!'

'Right…' Fiona didn't give a jot about the roadworks, traffic lights or *any* of it. It had been a close enough call as it was hearing Peter's car crunch up the drive. She'd always hated that gravel – the sound set her teeth on edge, but today it warned her of his impending arrival. And although it was difficult dragging Shirley from the lounge to the kitchen and out the back door before Peter came in through the front, she'd managed it.

She'd got Shirley out just in time, but it was close. The to-ing and fro-ing on the phone with Shirley's bank had taken far too long, but she'd eventually got the cheque Shirley had written, stopped. Being as she'd written it out for cash, if it had been processed there was no turning back, but thankfully no one had attempted to cash it yet. Now they couldn't.

After finishing with the bank, Fiona had tried to call Martin to tell him to get out of that house and London immediately, but there was no answer. There was no other option but to go down to London right now.

Before Shirley's revelation, it was a case of finding out what was happening. Now, it was no longer a fact-finding mission - it was *vital*.

With what she now knew, it was a case of life or death.

Fiona stole another glance at Peter still pacing up and down the lounge, ranting about his inconvenience. She felt dreadful ejecting Shirley so hastily. The woman was in no fit state to be alone, but what choice did she have? If Peter had found Shirley sitting there, especially the state she was in, then all hell would have broken loose. He'd have called the police quicker than she could have taken a breath. Now she knew the facts and for the record - *believed*, then calling the police was the one thing that couldn't happen. Not whilst Martin was in the house of one of these animals and unable to be reached by phone.

Although she hadn't quite managed to get the whole story from Shirley before Peter appeared, she'd got enough to...

'Have you been drinking?'

Fiona swung around to face her husband. 'What?' She'd hidden the brandy glass Shirley had used behind the sofa. Had it rolled into view? She scanned the carpet, then chanced another glance out of the window. Shirley had cleared the driveway and gone. *Good.* 'What do you mean, "drinking"? Of course I haven't been drinking. It's not even ten in the morning!'

'I can smell it!' Peter's forehead crumpled with a deep frown. 'It smells like brandy.' He moved to the drinks cabinet and peered at the bottle of Remy Martin.

'It wasn't me!' *At least that was true.* 'I did give the sideboard a polish while you were gone. Maybe that's what you can smell?'

'Perhaps...' Peter frowned.

'I hope you're not going mad in your old age!' Fiona's laugh was a little high pitched to appear natural, but she continued regardless. This had to work because there was no other way. 'I hope you haven't forgotten about the frozen meals I've prepared for you.'

Paper in hand, Peter paused halfway to sitting in the armchair. 'Frozen meals? What do you mean?'

'Oh my God! You *have* forgotten, haven't you?' Fiona huffed dramatically. 'It's today! My trip with Janet and Margorie. You knew it was today!'

'What bloody trip?' Peter barked. 'Whatever are you talking about?'

'This proves that you take absolutely no notice of anything I say!' Fiona flounced across the other side of the room. 'I've had this planned for ages, Peter! It's that two-day craft workshop – the one in Oxford!'

Peter finally dropped into the seat and scratched his thinning hair. 'I don't recall you mentioning that.'

'Probably because it's of no interest to you! But I'm going and I'm leaving shortly,' Fiona said, injecting a relevant amount of bitterness into her voice, which wasn't difficult.

Peter frowned. 'Maybe I remember you mentioning something, but is it wise swanning off on a nonsensical whimsy now Martin's playing silly devils with university? I'd have thought you'd be more bothered with sorting that out and getting him to see sense, rather th...'

'Whimsy?' Fiona shrieked, genuinely put out, even though she'd dreamt up the whole thing. 'According to you, everything I do - everything I've *ever* done is pointless!' She blinked away the film of forming tears. 'I deserve a break with friends after the stress I've been through lately!'

Immediately contrite, knowing he'd get hours of grief for this faux pas, Peter resentfully got to his feet. 'I suppose it won't make any difference about Martin's decision at the moment.'

'No, it won't!' Fiona snapped. 'We're better off discussing it with him again in a few days when everything has settled down and he's had chance to think about what he's considering giving up.' She glared at her husband. 'I'm going to Oxford and quite frankly, Peter, I don't care if you don't like it. Neither do I care if you're too forgetful to remember where the freezer is when it comes to your dinner either!'

With that, she flounced from the lounge, slamming the door behind her. It was only after she'd stomped up the stairs and shut the bedroom door, did she expel a large lung full of air.

That had worked better than expected.

Reaching underneath the bed, Fiona pulled out her leather weekend bag ready to pack a few days clothes.

She was going to London.

Now Shirley had given her the whole story - at least *most* of it, she had to deal with it. But deal with it in a way that would jeopardise no one else.

She would go to where Martin was presently staying.

Fresh perspiration erupted down Fiona's back, not having the first clue how to broach it. Zane Morelli was party to Shirley's horrific rape as a teenager and Skye was the product.

It was nauseous even comprehending that fact.

These people weren't of this planet and she had to get her son away from them. Despite Skye's innocent involvement in this, there was no way Martin could marry into such a despicable family. That poor girl would have to shoulder the fallout of her father's behaviour.

As for Zane Morelli, well he could stay out of her son's life as well.

Shoving the last items of clothing and toiletries in her weekend bag, Fiona made one last attempt to dial Martin's number, but the line rang out yet again.

With no further time to waste, she zipped up her bag and hastened down the stairs. She had to get to Dalston fast. But before she did that, she'd go to Shirley's house and hope the woman agreed to accompany her.

Because Shirley was the only one who could prove this.

EIGHTEEN

HIS GRIP STILL FIRM around Alyson's wrist, Marco backed her towards one of the deep leather armchairs so deftly that she had no choice but to sit down. He leaned closely over her. *Far too closely*... 'Let me get you a drink.'

Looking up into the piercing blue eyes of this beautiful specimen of a man, his breath hot on her cheek, Alyson wanted to faint.

Why did she feel like this? Marco was Skye's father, for God's sake. He was... *old*. About forty or something! Positively ancient! How was it possible to feel this kind of intensity?

Feeling the distinct loss as Marco finally dropped his grip of her wrist and stood back up to his full height, Alyson watched him move across the massive space to the glass drinks cabinet against the wall, entranced by his pure masculine form.

Shoving the uncomfortable thoughts steadily gaining pace to one side, she cleared her throat and watched him expertly pour amber liquid into two crystal tumblers. The sunlight from the floor-to-ceiling window spanned the length of the wall and gave a panoramic view of the Thames and London. It also scattered a myriad of rainbows reflecting from the facets of the expensive crystal glasses in Marco's hand.

What drink was that? She didn't recognise the bottle, but then she had little experience. She rarely drank - it was one of Skye's standing jokes that she was the most well-behaved person ever. Alyson was tired of being well-behaved, but also nervous. What if drinking sent her funny or she threw up? That would be embarrassing.

But Skye was right – she needed to let her hair down. She was seventeen now, not seven! But where was Skye? She said she was on her way but that was ages ago and there still was no sign of her.

Pulling her eyes from Marco's fine physique, she looked for her handbag. She'd text Skye again and see how much longer she'd be.

Hang on. Where was her bag?

Alyson peered over the padded arms of the chair. It wasn't there. She was sure she hadn't left her handbag and holdall in the hallway, but what with the unexpected sight of Skye's father, her brain was all over the place.

Suddenly startled to find Marco in front of her, the hint of a bulge visible underneath the towel, colour rushed to her cheeks. 'Oh, erm… thanks,' she mumbled, taking the glass he held out.

Desperate to focus as her fingers brushed his, Alyson raised the thick crystal tumbler to her lips and took a gulp, praying she'd concealed her grimace when fiery liquid hit the back of her throat. She couldn't have anyone thinking she was immature - that would be mortifying.

Marco watched Alyson intently. He'd tread carefully and then he'd be home and dry. But he wasn't waiting *forever.*

'Did... did Skye say how long she'd be?' Alyson asked. 'I can't wait to see her.'

'She'll be here soon,' Marco drawled. *She should have been here long ago.* He'd made it clear what time he expected her and didn't appreciate tardiness. Plus, that cheque from Shirley was waiting to be cashed and that needed to be done as soon as possible.

It was only because he'd had such a successful day yesterday by getting his dues from that grotesque, withered old bitch that he hadn't yet lost his rag over Skye's lateness. His daughter not being here in a timely fashion to allay her friend's anxieties could have gone horribly wrong. Thankfully, he was a man of many talents and had put Alyson at ease.

Marco smiled widely, mainly to show off his straight white teeth. 'The good side of Skye running late is that there's time to get to know you. It's great to meet my daughter's good friend. Skye's told me so much about you.'

Alyson glowed with pleasure. 'She has? Well, we've been friends since forever, so...'

'I've missed out on so much of her life already, so it's nice to meet someone who's been close to her for so much of it.' Marco's gaze homed in on Alyson. 'I presume Skye told you that I wasn't aware of her existence until recently?' He allowed his eyes to drop, pulling enough disappointment onto his face to make it look realistic.

Alyson swallowed dryly. *The poor man.* He may be gorgeous and not what she'd expected, but she could almost taste the pain and injustice flowing from him in waves. Shirley had a lot to answer for. 'Yes, Skye told me. You must be happy she's here now though?'

'Oh yes.' Marco raised his eyes. 'I wouldn't be without her.' *Because she was vital for the end result.*

Sensing someone on the stairs from the upper floor, Alyson glanced behind. *Skye?* She went to get out of the chair to greet her friend until she realised it wasn't Skye, but an unknown woman. She watched the blonde, who was almost as undressed as Marco, descend from the galleried landing, her infinitely long, shapely legs towering for miles before reaching the edge of the matching white towel she was wrapped in before turning to Marco in confusion.

'Ah, yes… Alyson - meet Callie. Callie, this is Alyson - my daughter's best friend. I mentioned she was coming today.' Marco gave Callie a knowing look. This slut best not forget the orders, nor to give the subtle sign of what particular method would be used. She'd best not screw it up either. He'd been through things with her several times, but she was already two minutes over the timeslot he'd allotted. He'd paid this cunt enough cash, so she'd be sensible not to fuck it up.

Callie glided barefoot over the beige rug towards Alyson. 'Pleased to meet you.'

'Callie is... a good friend of mine,' Marco said.

Quickly necking the remains of whatever filled her glass, Alyson took Callie's outstretched hand, not wanting to quantify the pang of disappointment that Marco had a girlfriend.

Of course he had a girlfriend. A man such as Marco wouldn't struggle with *that*.

She studied Callie as they politely shook hands. She was undoubtedly beautiful, but her eyes... they looked a little... not right. Tired? Spaced?

As she released Callie's slightly clammy hand, Alyson felt a sharp scratch in the centre of her palm. She didn't want to be rude by yelping or pulling away. The woman must have a jagged nail. It hurt, but not enough to make a big deal.

'Are you joining us in the jacuzzi, Alyson?' Carrie drawled, her long legs making quick work of reaching Marco where she proceeded to drape herself over him.

'Give the girl a chance to get settled in, Cal,' Marco said, his voice calm, when really he wanted to punch her in the face. He'd said not to rush things, but from the slight wince he clocked on Alyson's face, Callie had got the ball rolling.

'Perhaps we should wait until Skye arrives?' Alyson suggested, sure she'd just seen a flash of annoyance on Marco's face, but she must have imagined it. 'Out of interest, where is the jacuzzi?'

'It's on one of my roof terraces,' Marco winked. 'Now, how about another drink?' Extracting Callie from his lap, he stood up.

'Maybe I shouldn't. I feel a bit...' Alyson suddenly experienced the strangest urge to laugh. It was so weird. It was like hot lava flowed through her body, undulating in rippling waves. She felt... felt...

She didn't know *how* she felt.

'Are you all right?' Marco asked with fake concern as he watched Alyson's eyes become glazed as the drug kicked in. Knowing the time was almost here, the throbbing of his cock began in earnest.

Alyson clutched the armchair as it moved. Except it wasn't moving. *What was happening?*

She should be panicking, but instead she felt good. *Really* good. Hot and dizzy, but good, nevertheless.

All she could do when Callie's towel dropped to fall around her ankles revealing her nakedness, was to dreamily stare as the woman with the stunning body walked towards her.

• • • •

'WHAT WERE YOU THINKING?' Skye barked. If looks could kill, then Red would certainly die. He was receiving the brunt of her wrath, mainly because he was so ugly he made her stomach turn and therefore deserved it. 'Did it not cross your mind that phoning Erin was a stupid thing to do?'

Snatching her long dark hair into a ponytail away from her neck, Skye scowled. She was hot, tired and irritable and these idiots were not helping her overall foul mood.

She should be at the penthouse by now. She only had a small window of time to justify her absence from the Starbright before that nosy bitch got on her high horse, yet now she was wasting time dealing with these mugwops.

'I only called because I needed at least one definite handshake to set up a remote tracker,' Dylan explained. 'It was only the once. I didn't expect her to phone back!'

'Well, she did!' Skye sniped. 'And being as the "mystery phone call" was the subject discussed around the bloody breakfast table this morning, Zane's now aware of it and therefore suspicious.'

Standing up, she then promptly sat back down. There was

nowhere to move in here. Confined to this stupid table right in the corner of the pub was ridiculous. She'd thought she'd seen the last of this dump.

'Nothing has been compromised. We'll stake out the address you gave us as planned today,' Red said, not missing Skye's venomous glare was aimed mainly at him. 'We would be there by now had you not pulled us in for this impromptu meeting.'

'Are you questioning my orders?' Skye spat. Now these three dolts might have ballsed up her plans to clear that bitch out of the way, she despised them almost as much she despised Erin. *Red especially.*

'I'm questioning nothing.' Red folded his arms across his chest. 'But I *was* wondering why we're meeting in the Black Bear again. I was under the impression the Starbright was the new venue from now on.'

'That's changed,' Skye muttered. 'Your presence didn't go as low key as planned because the nosy cow is suspicious.'

After Erin's big song and dance about clocking these three at the Starbright, there was no choice but to ditch the place as the rendezvous point. It would have been ideal had that cow not bloody ruined things again.

Skye knew Erin was suspicious. She'd clocked the bitch filling Zane in about it in the hallway this morning. That woman had as much intention of a 'fresh start' as *she* did. She turned back to the three men. 'I want her gone as top priority.'

She then glanced at her watch. 'I've got to go. There's somewhere I have to be, so get on with what you're doing and...' She eyed the men pointedly. 'Keep a low profile. I want no one spotting you, but I need this finished ASAP. Do you understand?'

Satisfied with the nods she received, Skye snatched up her handbag and left the Black Bear. It was only about ten minutes to the penthouse so hopefully she wouldn't have missed too much of Alyson's humiliation and accompanying descent into despair.

A sly sneer slid onto her face. She was looking forward to that supercilious cow getting ruined. It was things like this that made her glad to be alive.

• • • •

OPENING HIS THROTTLE, Zane's bike churned up the loose gravel on the Bolts' pristine driveway, not caring if bits flicked up and smashed a window.

When he'd pulled into this road, he'd spotted a car turning out of the Bolt's driveway straightaway. Even at a distance, there was only one occupant - a male, so he'd had high hopes of having a sensible conversation with Fiona Bolt. Martin said she was the level-headed one out of his parents, so it wasn't a negative to miss out on meeting the father.

But the visit hadn't worked out as he'd hoped. Finding the house empty was disappointing. Zane was aware Fiona didn't drive and wasn't in the car that had left, but there was no answer from the four times he'd rung the bell. Having no choice but to give it up as a bad job, he'd sped back down the road and made good progress towards his next stop.

East Horsley wasn't far.

Zane's lips curled into a snarl behind the visor of his crash helmet. He hadn't wanted to go to Shirley's again - not after how she'd freaked out last time. The gouges she'd clawed down his face had only just fully healed, so the last thing he wanted was a repeat performance for either of their sakes. And what with her attitude towards him when he'd phoned - hanging up the second he'd spoken, he hadn't high hopes in succeeding in getting any sense out of her.

The Bolt woman was the key. She was more likely to tell him what nonsense Shirley was spouting – that's if he got as far as convincing Fiona that he wasn't the 'psychotic, animalistic criminal' that Shirley said he was.

Well, not as a rule anyway.

In all truth, he felt like wringing Shirley's neck for this latest set of problems. By God, he knew the woman needed help and despite purposefully cutting him out of his daughter's life and despising him for reasons only known to her, he was determined to get her the treatment she needed - if she accepted it, that was.

That aside, whilst she was going around bad-mouthing him to others, she was a liability.

Making out to the mother of the lad Skye was set to marry, who was living in his home, not to mention now involved in his business, that he was untrustworthy and psychotic, even in a small way, was not conducive to anything.

From what Martin said, Fiona wasn't irrational, but if Shirley had done a good enough job of scaring the woman half to death with what could befall her son and spouted enough insane stuff of what he'd allegedly done as she hallucinated her way through life, then what sane mother would ignore that?

Under those circumstances and knowing Martin was living in the same house as someone she'd been told was a 'danger to society', she could easily call the police. And that Zane couldn't risk, however big or small the chance was.

Martin said no problems would stem from it, but Zane couldn't be sure. Too much was going on for any flies in the ointment by means of police involvement.

But Fiona Bolt not being home changed things. He had to sort this, so there was no choice but to give Shirley another try.

Entering the quaint little town of East Horsley, Zane's Yamaha thundered through the street, attracting unwelcoming stares from people outside the row of black and white shops on the Ockham Road. Gritting his teeth, he ignored the glares and continued to the house he'd visited once and once only.

And once had been enough...

Pulling onto Shirley's driveway, Zane yanked his bike onto the centre stand and quickly dismounted. He could do with a smoke but couldn't justify spending one second longer from finding out what the fuck Shirley was trying to achieve.

Hating him for reasons only known to herself was one thing, but screwing up the Bolts' trust in the family their son was marrying into, was another. Nor would he stand by and allow Shirley to screw up his firm with lies that could drag the Old Bill into it. Especially not with a huge delivery of coke due to drop next week.

Whatever Shirley thought of him, a good chunk of the profit gleaned from that coke would make its way into Skye's inheritance fund. It would benefit *their* daughter, so she wasn't doing anyone any favours.

Leaving his crash helmet hooked on his handlebars, Zane knocked on Shirley's front door.

And waited.

Knocking again, this time louder, his impatience threatened to spill over. Instead of booting the door down out of frustration, he bent to peer through the letterbox.

No sign of movement.

'Shirley? Are you there?' Zane called through the stiff gold opening.

Receiving no response, he straightened up and paced around the front of the house. There was definitely no movement from inside. Surely she couldn't have gone out? Shirley *never* went out.

Tugging his cigarettes out of his pocket, Zane lit one and inhaled deeply.

A quick wander around the perimeter of the large house gained nothing either. There was no one home. A wasted afternoon that he didn't have time for.

So now what? If she wasn't in, she wasn't in.

Fuck.

About to bang on Shirley's door one final time, Zane stopped with the buzzing of his mobile. Fumbling to extract it from one of his jacket's inside pockets, he answered. 'Leo?'

A thin smile formed on Zane's face. 'You have? Fucking brilliant! No, I can't at the moment... Yeah, take him there. In fact, take him there and leave him to stew. I'll deal with him either later on or in the morning. Great job, mate!'

Ending the call, Zane grinned. *Leo had done it, the star!*

That Damon Sandler was at this very moment trussed up in the back of Leo's Transit considerably brightened Zane's mood. He may have spent a fruitless afternoon fighting the latest fire Shirley Wilson had lit, but now there was a deserving volunteer waiting to unload his irritation on.

And after what he'd done, Sandler deserved that more than most.

NINETEEN

WHIPPING HIS FIXED GAZE away from the penthouse entrance, Martin glanced at his phone hoping it wouldn't ring again. Three times now his mother had called and he hadn't dared answer it, well aware how not being focused yesterday had cost him. Missing further comings and goings was not something he was willing to chance. Especially since he'd seen no sign of Alyson Read leaving.

His brow furrowed. She'd been in there over an hour. Surely she couldn't stay all day, unless she was staying overnight with whoever she'd gone to see...

But who could it be?

The chances of Skye's friend knowing someone living in the very same building he'd been tasked to watch was uncanny. It was a classic case of causality - an interesting topic he'd covered once at college.

Martin's thoughts returned to the missed calls and tendrils of worry grew. Had something happened? What if his mother had taken ill? Or maybe his father had been in a car crash…

Oh God...

Maybe he should phone back? If it turned out something *had* happened and he'd ignored the calls, he didn't think he'd ever forgive himself. Things were fraught enough as it was.

With his eyes still trained on the double doors, Martin's hand inched towards his phone. Surely he could justify a quick call? It wouldn't take long to confirm everything was all right. As long as he made it clear that he was at work and unable to talk, then his concentration would not suffer.

Wouldn't it?

His plans of doing exactly that dissolved as a taxi pulled up in front of the apartments. Stiffening, his attention fully focused, he abandoned thoughts of doing anything other than seeing who had arrived.

Scarcely able to breathe with the anticipation of reporting back to Zane that he'd witnessed a possible contender for Marco's workforce arriving, Martin primed himself to remember every last detail so that his description of the man would be one hundred per cent percent accurate. Doing that was vital to...

What the hell?

Martin physically jolted as shock ricocheted through him. He didn't need to concentrate to get *this* particular description because he knew every single millimetre and tiny detail off by heart. It was ingrained deep in his soul.

His fingers moved to the handle of the car door as Skye got out of the taxi and turned to pay the driver. There was no confusion as to the certainty of who he was looking at.

Martin's pulse rate soared higher. What was *she* doing here?

His fingers twitched and tightened around the door handle as the urge to run over to Skye intensified. *But he couldn't.*

Martin swiped the sheen of forming sweat on his brow away with the back of his hand. However strong his need to rush over was, he must remain still. If he approached Skye, then how did he explain his presence? He'd have to tell her exactly why he was here and what was tasked with doing - the very opposite of Zane's instructions.

Under no circumstances was Skye to learn of what he was

doing. *Rule one of the job*, Zane had said.

Furthermore, Martin had already lied to her about working in the garage, so revealing that he'd been untruthful wouldn't look good. But why was she here of all places? She was supposed to be at the Starbright in Dagenham, not in Battersea.

Panic mounted as Skye walked up to the entrance doors and disappeared inside. Then as quickly as it had appeared, the panic dissolved.

Sinking back into the seat, Martin no longer cared how stiff his back had become during the many hours he'd sat unmoving in the Transit. A loud chuckle burst from his mouth. How had he been so silly not to work it out? It was bloody obvious!

Skye was only here because *Alyson* was! Why had he panicked?

Alyson had come to visit friends or relatives in this complex and must have texted Skye to say she was in London. It made sense now.

Martin grinned, imagining how pleased Skye must be at seeing her very best friend. It was ages since they'd met up so it must have been a brilliant surprise. Skye must have only found out about Alyson coming today otherwise she'd have mentioned it.

His brows then knitted as worry resurfaced. Should he phone Zane and tell him that Skye was at the same premises he was watching?

She had no idea of the danger, in the form of Marco, also residing in that building and Zane would rightly not want her being anywhere near that man.

But if Skye received a call from Zane, telling her to immediately leave it would break her heart. She hadn't seen Alyson for so long.

Martin's hands wrung together. *Think about this logically*, he told himself. Marco is confined to one particular apartment and dare not step foot anywhere else, even within the complex for fear of reprisals - that was why he was attempting to build up his men. Because of that, Skye being in the same building meant little. It was a huge place and with the security they had in those sort of buildings there was no way Marco could move on her even if he got the chance.

Anyway, Skye wouldn't be there for long - not while she had the Starbright to deal with.

Martin nodded to himself, pleased with his decision. Spoiling Skye's joy was unnecessary. She'd tell him about Alyson's surprise visit when he saw her tonight. And only if Alyson was planning on staying around would he have to think of a suitable reason for Skye not to return. But he'd worry about that if the time came.

There was no need to inform Zane about this either. No point in stressing the man out for nothing. With these decisions made, Martin forgot all about the intention to return his mother's calls.

• • • •

'I DIDN'T PLAN on being late,' Skye protested, affronted at Marco's attitude. 'I needed to urgently speak to the three goons you enlisted to work for you. Surely you had better choices than them? One of them only went an...'

'When do you have the experience to question my judgement?' Marco snarled, his temper igniting. 'You reckon you've got so much knowledge about how things work in this business to insinuate that I've made bad choices or that I'm that so much on the bones of my fucking arse and desperate to hire "goons", as you so succinctly put it, that I don't know what I'm talking about?'

Skye stepped back in shock at Marco's unexpected outburst. Apart from a couple of instances when he'd been a little brusque, he'd been nothing but friendly. The times he'd snapped at her were during phone calls when he'd been stressed. That was understandable, given the situation at the time. Not many people would be in the best of moods with charges hanging over their heads like he'd been facing. But he was out now and things were going well - he'd said so himself, so why the sudden change of attitude?

Skye stared at Marco - his face twisted with barely controlled rage and noticed, not for the first time, that his pupils were like pinpricks. She knew him to be party to the odd line of coke, but from what he'd said that was in the past. Even then, he'd said he'd only done it during crazy parties.

But today he was hyper - almost manic in his rage. Regardless of her instinct to argue the toss, she had to keep things on a level pegging. There was no way she was losing her place. 'I... erm... I didn't mean it to come across like that. Of *course* you know what you're doing! You're more qualified than anyone,' she pandered. 'I was just surprised that Red, Baz and...'

'You'll get used to them.' Marco flapped his hand, placated. 'But you know I have little patience for tardiness.'

Skye nodded contritely. 'I'm sorry. It won't happen again.' If Marco didn't want to know that his three chosen idiots could have already vanquished this operation, then so be it. It would have to be just *her* keeping them in line and ensuring they didn't screw her plans of removing Erin Langley before they moved on to anything Marco wanted doing.

'Anyway...' Marco gestured for Skye to follow. 'You interrupted the filming.' *Or rather his viewing of it.* Thankfully, the camera was still rolling but he wasn't happy about missing even a second.

'You're filming already?' Skye raised her eyebrows. 'I thought it would take a while to convince Alyson.'

Marco laughed as he made his way through the living area and up the stairs. 'There's little I've failed to convince a woman or *anyone* yet and I'm used to getting my way. It's especially easy if you have the correct "ingredients" to hand.'

Skye followed when Marco beckoned her into the large guest room - the one she'd earmarked to be hers once she moved in here. But then Marco continued up a metal staircase to the roof.

Careful she didn't catch her heels in the filigree metalwork of the stair treads, Skye followed. She hadn't ventured up to the roof terrace before.

Rounding the last corner of the spiral steps, she was greeted firstly with the bright blue sky; the sun rendering her temporarily blind from its glaring rays. Blinking, the familiar London skyline came into focus above a metal balustrade and then a collection of rattan furniture, a corner bar with further seating, an immense glass-top table and a wind-out canopy came into view.

She stared in awe at the sight whilst Marco dashed in the direction of a large camera perched on a tripod to peer through the viewfinder. It was only then did she take in the sunken jacuzzi surrounded by sun loungers, as well as...

Skye gawped at the scene in front of her: Alyson spreadeagled naked at the side of the jacuzzi. Her feet dangled into the foaming water below and she would have been fully exposed with her widely spread legs had her most intimate areas not been blocked from view by a blonde head.

The way Alyson's back arched and her hips bucked as the blonde sucked and licked, it seemed she was enjoying it!

How could this be?

Skye's eyes narrowed. She'd set this up to ruin the privileged little princess, not for her to have a good time!

And who was the blonde?

Skye's eyes darted to Marco only to find him watching the scene with fascination and couldn't avoid noticing the obvious tenting beneath the towel wrapped around his hips.

Quickly looking away, she found her eyes moving back to Alyson. It wasn't Marco being aroused that bothered her. What bothered Skye was that Alyson was relishing a strange woman going down on her. Judging by the urgent and growing intensity of moaning coming from Alyson's mouth and the way her hands grasped the blonde's head encouraging her to work her mouth faster made it impossible to form any other conclusion.

Alyson was a virgin. Ever the butt of jokes for never letting a man get his *hands* in her knickers, let alone anything else because she was determined to save herself for the 'right person'. Alyson took the digs as good-natured, but they weren't. Skye meant every single one of the barbed jibes she'd delivered to her 'friend' over the years.

Her eyes narrowed. Alyson was a pathetic, immature little girl, sickening everyone around her with the pathetic fantasies of knights in shining armour and Prince Charming, yet here she was, legs akimbo, being munched on by a random blonde bird!

Did Alyson prefer women? Was that it?

No, she was too holier-than-thou to warrant anyone of either sex to touch her, so why...?

Skye found herself edging closer to Marco. 'How did you convince her to be up for this?' she whispered. 'And who is...'

'Shhh!' Marco hissed. 'I'm fucking filming!' He nodded to the whirring camera. 'Keep an eye on it and make sure it stays rolling. Now Callie's got your mate warmed up, it's my turn.'

'What?' Skye gasped. 'You're going to...'

'You think I'm not having *my* go?' Marco winked. 'You failed to mention how fucking gorgeous your mate is.'

Skye had no time to protest before Marco strutted towards the jacuzzi, his towel dropping to the floor, revealing possibly the largest erection she'd ever seen.

Moving into the jacuzzi, Marco grabbed Callie's hair and yanked her off Alyson. Skye watched with a strange sense of detached fascination as he dragged Alyson into the jacuzzi by her feet, not fazed that her body and face submerged under the steaming water before finally pulling her upright.

It was then Skye realised that Alyson was completely off her head - her eyes spaced with a blank, glazed expression. *Alyson didn't even drink, the boring bitch, so what on earth had she taken?*

Unable to pull her eyes away from the spectacle, Skye watched Marco wrap Alyson's legs around his waist. Impaling her, he began thrusting at a manic speed. But it was when, after mere seconds, that Alyson's mouth opened in a silent 'O', her back arching further and her body jerking in a rhythmic overload of orgasm, did Skye realise that her confusion and surprise over this situation had morphed into something else.

Something she never thought was feasible regarding anything Alyson ever did.

She was jealous that Alyson had captured Marco's attention. *How could she be jealous of Alyson?*

Her hands began to tremble. Had she slipped into second place? Because if she had and this little nobody had overtaken what Marco deemed as 'priority', then she'd didn't like it one little bit.

TWENTY

'SHE WON'T LIKE THIS,' Baz muttered as Red accelerated away from the small, terraced house in Dalston.

'What exactly did you expect?' Red snapped, blaring his horn at an elderly lady who looked like she might use the Pelican crossing. 'Christ! Did that old bat want to get run over?'

He didn't have time to factor in pedestrians. *He* paid road tax, they didn't. Well, he did sometimes, but they never did, so he was buggered if anyone thought about interfering with putting as much distance between himself and Zane bloody Morelli as possible. 'Anyway, we said we'd case the place and watch for Erin Langley's movements. We didn't agree to gun her down in broad daylight the first time we got a bloody sighting. We need a strategy – one which doesn't include being subsequently dispatched!'

'That woman was definitely inside the house,' Dylan said from the back seat as he resumed staring at the unintelligible information scrolling over the screen of his handheld scanner. 'Or at least, her phone was.'

'I still think that if Morelli hadn't returned, we had the prime opportunity to storm the place and do the job,' Baz griped. 'I want it over with as soon as possible.'

Red gritted his teeth. So did he, but what just happened showed that if they'd acted on Baz's plan of killing Erin Langley in her own home, then Zane would have returned in the middle of it. *That* wouldn't have ended well for anyone. *There had to be a better way.* 'What do you suggest?'

'We need a schedule of Zane's movements. Find out when he's somewhere that's extremely unlikely he'll turn back from.' Baz pulled his mobile from his pocket. 'Skye can provide that. She lives with the man and once we know his movements we can act.'

'I really don't like this,' Dylan whined, his squeaky voice higher pitched than usual. 'There's something not quite the ticket here. I can't keep feeling this is solely Skye's request and not Marco's.'

Red's fingers tightened on the steering wheel. He couldn't say he disagreed with that, but Dylan's grating voice was making it difficult to think about anything clearly. 'Wherever the order came from, the brief is to get the job done. Once we get word of a clean run, then maybe we should do it somewhere other than in that house? Doing it there gives too many opportunities to leave clues and give the wrong people advantages.'

Baz chewed his lip and glanced sideways at Red, now booting the motor at well over the 30 miles an hour limit. They could do without a tug. The back of his heel pushed the gun stashed under his seat further back, like it made a difference. But Red had a point. As much as he wanted this task over and done with, there was sense in the man's suggestion.

If they got Langley into their possession rather than offloading her in situ, then anything they did after that was away from prying eyes, nosy neighbours or safe from leaving clues to help Zane Morelli and his merry men to uncover their identities. He also suspected Skye was guilty of using their services for her own personal gain rather than anything to put them in favour with the man who mattered. Perhaps delivering the Langley woman to Marco was a better option?

He wouldn't suggest that now - everyone was stressed out enough as it was, but either way, there was one thing which had been overlooked. He glanced around the interior of his cramped Vauxhall Nova. 'If we're considering taking Langley and completing the job elsewhere, we'll need a van. This heap of shit won't do. In the meantime, let's get that schedule of Zane's whereabouts.'

• • • •

BUSY FRYING a pan of sausages for dinner, Erin was startled to hear the front door shut. 'Skye? Is that you?'

Earlier, after Skye returned to the Starbright hours after leaving to undertake a 'short' errand, she'd been in the foulest mood. Locking herself away in the office, she'd blanked all attempts of conversation and Erin had been left none the wiser where the girl had been. Then later she'd refused Erin's offer of accompanying her home, stating that she was 'too busy'.

In all truth, Erin was glad to put distance between them and didn't relish the uncomfortable atmosphere beginning again now Skye was back home.

When the kitchen door opened, Erin braced herself for another confrontation, but the figure in the doorway was Zane. 'Oh! It's you!'

'That's charming, that is!' Zane pulled Erin away from the hob and into his arms. 'There was me thinking you'd be pleased to see me!'

'Oh, but I am!' Erin melted into Zane's arms. She'd never *ever* tire of this man. 'I didn't expect you. I thought you'd be late back. How did things go?'

'Well...' Zane planted a line of kisses along Erin's neck. 'A fruitless day, as far as Shirley was concerned. No one was home at hers or at the Bolt's place.'

Erin frowned. She knew the possibility of Fiona Bolt bringing the police into the equation was playing on Zane's mind. 'Then why the good mood?'

'The shit outlook changed because we've got Sandler!'

'Sandler?' Erin cried. 'You haven't brought him here, have you? Or have you already killed h…'

Zane silenced Erin with a kiss. 'Sandler's not here and believe you me, I *was* planning on finishing him tonight. I've been waiting a very long time to pay that cunt back for trying to kill you, as well as everything else, but I decided I'd be generous. I've left him to sweat until the morning.'

'Then wh…'

'He's at the Canning Works and he'll remain there until tomorrow,' Zane grinned, his eyes twinkling. '*Then* I'll kill him.'

'But how did you get him out of the hospital?' Erin asked, caught up in the excitement of Zane's contagious good mood.

'Leo,' Zane grinned. 'That man's a fucking legend! Tiger's guarding Sandler until morning and then...'

'Am I interrupting something?' Skye failed to hide her distaste at Zane and Erin wrapped in each other's arms. She'd had a dreadful day. No, *more* than a dreadful day and walking in to see these two all over each other just rubbed her face in it. 'I'll give you some privacy, shall I?'

Concern washed over Zane's previously jubilant expression. 'Don't be silly. It's as much your house as it is ours.'

Erin kept her smile in place when really, she wanted to slap Skye's snotty expression away. 'Did you finish everything you needed to do at the Starbright? I'd have waited for you. I...'

'Oh, what's this? Another dig? I'm not good enough again, is that it?' Skye failed dismally to keep her anger in check.

The entire way back from Marco's in the taxi she'd gradually become angrier and angrier until she thought she may combust. She hadn't gone to all of this trouble; done all of this groundwork or put up with shit, only to be replaced in favour by the likes of Alyson fucking Read! Or that two-bit hooker, Callie, or whatever she was called. The blond tart was definitely a hooker because the doped-up bitch even admitted it.

Marco should not be granting kudos or time on anyone

except *her*. She didn't care if the man wanted a shag. After all the time and effort she'd put into this, he *owed* her and she didn't expect to be insulted by a mealy-mouthed little girl like Alyson getting the attention. It wasn't acceptable.

'Are you all right?' Zane lightly rested his hand on Skye's shoulder, frowning as she moved from his touch to bang around the cupboard for a glass.

Erin spoke to Zane quietly in the hope Skye wouldn't hear. 'She's been like this since she returned from the...'

'I can hear you!' Skye snapped and then visibly sagged, finally remembering she had a game to continue upholding. 'I'm sorry. I know I've been touchy today. I've got a lot on my mind.'

'With work?' Zane frowned. 'Has something happened at the Starbright that I should know about?'

'If you must know or before anyone jumps to conclusions, I went to finalise the laundry contract with that linen company, only to find that they've moved the goalposts.' Skye looked down despondently. 'They've changed the price, which means it's not viable any longer.' She met Erin's eyes, challenging a reaction. 'Something else I've failed at in your eyes, no doubt?'

Erin shot a quick glance at Zane. 'I wasn't thinking that. I...'

'No one was thinking that, Skye,' Zane interjected. 'We both know how much work you've put in at the Starbright and for that, you should be proud. These things happen. There will always be suppliers who take the piss when they think a deal is set in stone.' He smiled. 'You've done the right thing by pulling the plug.'

'It doesn't feel like that,' Skye sighed. 'If you don't mind, I'm going to bed, I'm not hungry.'

Erin and Zane exchanged glances as Skye yanked open the kitchen door and walked down the hallway. She barged into Martin on his way in through the front door but completely blanked him.

'Skye? I...'

'Not now, Martin.'

Martin glanced in confusion after Skye as she flounced off without another word. He then moved into the kitchen. 'Was it something I said?'

Zane shook his head. 'She's had a long meeting with a laundry company this afternoon and she's pulled the agreement.' He shrugged his large shoulders. 'She's disappointed but she'll be okay. Don't take it personally. Anyway, what's the news from the penthouse?'

Martin glanced over his shoulder in the direction Skye had left and tried to formulate an answer. Why had Skye said she was with a laundry company when she'd been elsewhere? Why wouldn't she mention that she'd met up with her old friend?

Furthermore, where did this leave him in answering Zane's question?

Twenty One

GETTING UP AT the crack of dawn, Fiona padded across the worn carpet to the dubious-looking tea and coffee making facilities. Her nose wrinkled up at the layer of collected dust on the small UHT milk cartons and wondered how many months, or even years, they'd been there.

Opening one, she tentatively sniffed it and then flicked the kettle on. She'd risk it – her mouth was as dry as a bone. Enough time had already been wasted.

Arriving at Shirley's last night, it had taken longer than expected to convince the woman to accompany her to London. Okay, so it was a big ask expecting Shirley to join her in facing the man who was part of ruining her life, but unfortunately it was necessary.

Finally getting through to Shirley during a gap in her hysterical bawling that doing this was the only way to protect both Skye and Martin, she'd bundled her into a taxi. It had cost a bloody fortune, but it was impossible to go on the train. What if Shirley had run off or started gibbering to other passengers about was going on? It was the sort of thing she'd do during a blind panic and Fiona couldn't run that risk.

Besides, it wasn't like Peter's credit card couldn't take the hit. The chunk of money Fiona also withdrew off it from the cashpoint had come in handy too.

Hearing a strange grunt from the other bed, Fiona turned. At least Shirley had stopped talking. Half the night she'd been kept awake from Shirley babbling and shouting in her sleep. Consequently, she was exhausted, but it wasn't like she'd have got much rest anyway.

She eyed the thick crust of limescale around the kettle spout as it finished boiling. *Maybe she should just have a glass of water?*

Fiona pursed her lips. It hadn't been the plan to spend the night in a crummy hotel - or *any* hotel. She'd have preferred to head straight for the address Martin had given her, but a further meltdown from Shirley when they'd been dropped in Dalston put paid to that. Drawing attention from the crowds, Fiona accepted there was little choice but to go elsewhere for the night and deal with things fresh-faced in the morning.

Even if she'd succeeded in stabilising Shirley's spinning brain it would have been too late to attempt a visit. On the upside, there was more chance of catching Zane Morelli at home in the morning. Didn't people like that do their dirty deals and illegal activities under the cover of darkness?

The only issue was, thanks to the terrible night's sleep she'd had, Fiona felt as opposite to 'fresh-faced' as humanly possible. She felt like she'd been hit by a truck.

The twenty-seven ignored calls from Peter didn't help either. For God's sake, she was at a craft workshop for a couple of days in Oxford as far as he was concerned!

She frowned, supposing she should at least let him know she'd arrived safely. Reluctantly pulling out her mobile, she sent a quick text:

You don't need to keep phoning. I am here and really enjoying it. Janet and Marg say hi.

See you soon.

F

x

That should do it.

Fiona glanced at the bedside clock, hoping the time was correct. *Now, onto Shirley...*

Moving to the bed, Fiona gently shook Shirley's shoulders. Getting no response, she applied more force. 'Wakey wakey! Time to get up!'

With a groan, Shirley gradually opened her eyes and blinked before confusion followed by panic set in. 'Oh God! I thought I'd dreamt it, but we're here, aren't we? We're in London! I can't... I just can't do it!'

Fiona sat on the edge of the bed and grasped Shirley's arm. 'Yes, you can. We can *both* do it and we'll be just fine.'

'But...'

Fiona took a deep breath. *No more excuses. This was happening. It had to.* 'I know you don't want to, but we're doing this, Shirley. We're seeing Zane and facing him head on. Then we're retrieving our children from his and his disgusting family's clutches. Okay?'

Blinking like a startled rabbit, Shirley swallowed dryly, her fingers twisting over and over in the powder-blue bedspread. 'I... I...'

'*Okay*?' Fiona repeated, her tone sharp. She didn't enjoy shoehorning people into things they didn't want. The dreadful experience Shirley had been put through made it even harder, but their children's welfare overrode any guilt. She must save them and this was the only way.

She smiled at the trembling woman in the bed. 'I'll make you a nice cup of tea whilst you get yourself up and dressed. We need to go over there as quickly as possible so we can see Zane before he leaves for the day to screw up someone else's life.'

Shirley suddenly lurched from the bed and ran into the en-suite shower room. The loud retching noises which followed brought home what a difficult day this looked likely to be.

• • • •

'WHY ARE YOU staring at me?' Skye snapped, glaring at Martin in the mirror's reflection. He made her skin crawl. Thankfully, he'd made no attempt to touch her last night *or* this morning which was good as far as she was concerned, but it also meant there was something bugging him. And she didn't know what it was.

Not that she particularly cared. There were more important things to think about: like making sure that two-faced bitch, Alyson, didn't overtake her in Marco's favour. It was *her* money he was sitting on, not Alyson's. But Martin staring at her like she'd been diagnosed with a highly contagious disease was getting on her nerves. Neither did it help the raging turmoil and bad mood she'd been in since yesterday afternoon. 'Stop looking at me!' she yelled, turning from the mirror to face him. 'What's the matter with you?'

Martin faltered. He didn't like upsetting Skye, but after lying awake half of the night with the creeping sense of something being far from right, the worry wouldn't go away. 'It… it's just that you don't seem like yourself...'

Slamming her mascara down onto the dressing table, Skye rolled her eyes. 'Who else am I, then? Hillary Clinton?'

'Of course not!' Martin spluttered. 'I... I'm just worried about you, that's all. You were upset last night and... and... well, I hope it's nothing to do with me...'

Skye's irritation bubbled past the point of salvage. Normally, the sight of Martin was the cause of any bad moods, the fawning, stupid bastard. But for once he had nothing to do with her stress, apart from bloody well adding to it. 'I'm allowed to be in a bad mood occasionally, am I not?'

'Yes, of course you are.' Martin refrained from touching Skye's arm in a placating gesture. 'I... erm... I just thought you'd have been happy after seeing... erm...' *Shit! He couldn't say that!*

'After seeing what?' Skye's skin prickled. *Did Martin know something? No. How could he?* 'Seeing what? Seeing who? What are you getting at, Martin?'

'I… I just meant after what you said the other day about the upcoming contract with the laundry, I thought that...' Martin blustered, his voice tailing off.

'Didn't you hear what was said last night when you came in?' Skye barked, her eyes narrowing. 'The contract with the laundry fell through. How exactly am I supposed to be in a good mood about that? Do you not pay attention to anything?' *See? Stupid to the fucking core.*

Wait a minute... He said 'previously'. She'd said nothing previously to Martin about this fictional laundry contract, so how would he know? Suspicion brewed.

'I just thought... I... erm...' *Wasn't Skye going to mention seeing Alyson?* 'So, nothing else happened? What I mean is, well, you didn't... erm... didn't see anyone else? I thought that perhaps y...'

'You think a lot, don't you, Martin? Are you going as nuts as my mother?' Skye yelled, moving from the dressing table. 'You clearly have too much time on your hands with this brain-dead garage job of yours!'

Hurt washed over Martin. He was doing a job for them - for their future and Skye was sniping about it? Not that he worked in a garage, but it wasn't like he could tell her what he was *really* doing. But why had she not said where she'd been?

Folding her arms over her chest, Skye glared at Martin. 'I'm not sure what's going on in that head of yours, but I don't like being interrogated.' Snatching up her handbag she moved towards the bedroom door. 'I'm heading to work.'

'But it's too early!' Martin gasped. 'Why are you going in so early? It's only...'

Turning back, Skye snarled, 'Because I don't want to be around *you* right now. I don't exactly know what you're insinuating, but I *do* know that I don't appreciate it. In fact, if this is how it's going to be with you in the future, then maybe we don't have one!'

As the door slammed behind Skye, Martin slumped against the bed, his head in his hands. Raw dread snowballed. Skye couldn't leave him - he couldn't bear it. He loved her more than it was possible to love *anyone*. If she left him, how could he live without her?

It was then the base facts tapped Martin on the shoulder. Raising his head, he dragged his fingers through his floppy hair. Whether he wanted to acknowledge the burning question clamouring or not, he had little choice.

This wasn't the first time Skye had lied. Nor was it the second. The untruths she'd told about him stalking her; about abusing and threatening her; about not leaving her alone... How she'd made out he'd behaved had almost cost him his life on more than one occasion since coming to London. And he'd only come here in the first place to search for the girl he loved and who he'd believed to be in danger.

Nor was Skye innocent of all the other lies she'd told, along with her fabricated back story.

But they'd put that behind them, hadn't they?

Loving her so much made that the only option. But why would Skye conceal being in the penthouse complex yesterday? Why would she lie and not tell him she'd seen Alyson? It didn't make sense.

Worry constricted Martin's heart as the final and most important question clawed a steady hold within him that was difficult to shift. It kept pushing for attention over and over within his mind: *Did he really know Skye at all?*

• • • •

'HE'S HIDING SOMETHING.' Zane slugged down his scalding tea like it was water. Seeing Erin's expression, he glanced over his shoulder, double-checking they were alone in the kitchen. 'Martin - he's not levelling with me.'

Pausing from filling her mug, Erin frowned. 'About the penthouse? What makes you think that? You said there was nothing to report.'

'*Martin* said there was nothing to report, but two days with no one going in or out, apart from a postman seems unlikely.' Zane stared into his almost empty mug. 'It's more than that... I reckon he *has* seen someone but won't say. Coupled with the shit his mother could cause, I'm thinking perhaps I should get rid of him.'

Erin gasped. 'Oh, Zane! You can't! Not with him and Skye being together and...'

'Not like that!' Zane laughed despite his concern. 'I mean, moving him out of here. I'm not opposed to "requesting" that he distances himself from Skye either.' His brows knitted. 'She's my daughter and I don't want fallout landing on her.'

Erin nodded, quietly thinking that Skye would handle herself whatever the circumstances. 'I get the impression things may be naturally petering out between them anyway. Skye doesn't seem happy. Perhaps she's found out about Martin working for you?'

Zane absentmindedly fingered the scar running down his right cheekbone. 'If she has, then it's only because *he's* told her. If he has, then at least that would give me the excuse to get rid of him and solve the problem!'

Unless the problem stems from Skye, Erin thought. 'Did you get to the bottom of what's going on with the guards at the Starbright? I haven't seen those new ones Skye hired since.'

Zane frowned. 'What with all this shit going on with Shirley and Sandler, that's fallen by the wayside, but I will find out. Which reminds me...' He got to his feet. 'I must go and deal with Sandler. At least that's something to look forward to and one less wanker to keep tabs on.'

'I can't help but feel resentful that I won't be party to his demise,' Erin said.

Zane grinned – that half-smile that never failed to melt Erin's heart. 'You know I need you at the Starbright rather than anywhere else at the moment. I'll be sure to give Sandler a very clear message from you, though.'

Erin nodded. 'Then unless you have an issue with it, I'll do some digging myself on the Starbright guards.'

'Fine by me,' Zane said. 'One less thing for me to do.' He leant in for a lingering kiss. 'I shouldn't be late tonight.'

'What about Shirley, Fiona Bolt and the concerns you have surrounding Martin? What are your plans with them?'

'I'm not sure, but that's something we'll discuss whilst celebrating tonight. Because we *will* be celebrating!' Zane winked. 'Sandler's passing cannot possibly go unmarked.'

Erin couldn't help but smile. The subject was macabre and realistically she should be uncomfortable with what Zane may have planned for Damon Sandler, but instead she wished she could witness it. Was she twisted or sick in the head? By others' standards, possibly, but then other people hadn't witnessed what Sandler had been behind or had orchestrated, had they?

Now that disgusting man would pay the long overdue and ultimate price Not only for attempting to kill her, but for murdering Hazel in such a despicable manner. On top of that, helping Marco's evil pursuits was enough of a reason alone to rid the world of the scum.

Erin watched Zane disappear through the front door and with the familiar sound of his motorbike engine, unease overshadowed her. She'd do digging on the guards at the Starbright as planned. After speaking to Tiger the other day she'd hoped to hear something by now, but she hadn't, which just left her to do it. She just had to ensure it was out of Skye's earshot.

Aside from not causing further ruckus, Erin still couldn't shake the stubborn concept that things were not as they seemed. The nagging insistence that Skye was somehow connected to the forged documents leading to Marco's release wouldn't go away, despite there being no justifiable reason for her to be behind it. And the weird atmosphere accelerating between Skye and Martin; Fiona Bolt's threat of bringing on their downfall and Shirley having disappeared, only propelled the endless prodding that something else - something she couldn't quite put her finger on, was working in the shadows; waiting for the right time to blow everything they'd all tried so hard to sort, out of the water.

And no matter how hard Erin tried to shrug off or analyse the known facts - even *theories*, she couldn't reach a conclusion that made sense. It felt like the speed of something unknown was increasing and they were blindly walking into a trap, yet she didn't know what to do or where to look to stop it.

Or furthermore, pinpoint exactly where it was coming from.

Twenty-Two

WHEN ALYSON FINALLY WOKE, she struggled to get her bearings. The excruciating banging in her temples and the arid dryness of her throat overtook logical thought. Not that she had much of that. It felt as if someone had stuffed every possible space inside her skull with cotton wool. Her stomach hurt and...

Oh!

She gingerly moved her hand down within the bedsheets, immediately realising she was naked.

What on earth?

Wincing, she gently touched her sorest area, unable to pinpoint exactly where the gnawing throbbing somewhere deep inside her, originated. A flicker of panic unfurled. Everything - including parts she hadn't previously realised existed, hurt.

How...?

Forcing her aching body upright, she withdrew her hand from under the sheet and squinted at her fingers. They felt sticky and wet. Her heart lurched seeing through her blurred vision that they were covered in blood.

She wasn't on her period - that was two weeks ago!

'I'm bleeding! Oh God! I'm bleeding! Skye? Are you there? Where are you? What happened? I feel...'

'I hope you haven't made too much of a mess on the bed,' a voice drawled. 'Those are silk sheets, you realise?'

Alyson turned her head, a crescendo of pain ricocheting through it a split second later. She cringed at the wave of agony before focusing on who owned that voice. *Who was it and what did he mean by 'mess'? Had she been bleeding all night? Was it even morning?* 'I...'

'You were fantastic night last night,' the voice continued, followed by pressure on the bed.

Alyson turned in the opposite direction, noticing that the huge circular mattress stretched out far behind her as well as in front. 'Where am I? Wh…' She abruptly stopped as her vision fine-tuned the blurred shape in front of her. She sucked in her breath, her heart skipping a beat. 'Oh! I...'

'Skye wasn't exaggerating when she said you were perfect,' Marco said, slipping both hands around Alyson from behind to cup her breasts. 'You're exactly what she said, except *better...*'

Alyson's panic spiralled. She tried to swerve from the man's grip, but she couldn't. He was touching her - touching her *breasts*! She'd never let...

Snippets of memory then filtered into Alyson's brain. Oh God! Marco! Skye's father! What had she done? She hadn't... hadn't... done that with Skye's *father*, had she? She couldn't have. She'd never... never have done *that.*

Tears brimmed as the concept of what must have happened seeped into her brain. She'd lost her virginity to Skye's father? Oh no... Oh God! Skye would never speak to her again after this. She'd never speak to *herself* again.

All her life she'd resolved to give that very special part of herself to someone because he was the one - her husband, so what could have made her relinquish something important?

'Hey!' Marco gently turned Alyson to look deep into her eyes. 'Why are you upset?' *Who gives a fuck if you're upset?* He glanced past her to the camera set to roll again. 'Don't be upset, beautiful,' he murmured, tracing his thick finger down her cheek to rub across her bottom lip. 'It was amazing. *You* were amazing. Callie thought so too.'

'I...' Alyson pulled her eyes away from the hypnotic ice-blue ones of the man, spotting the strange woman lying at the foot of the huge bed. *She'd done things with a woman too?*

Scrabbling to make sense of this deluge of unparalleled information, staring at the blonde triggered the full return of Alyson's senses. She remembered how she'd immediately been struck with how gorgeous Marco was. Then her surprise at the feelings the sight of him engendered. After that, the blonde woman coming down the stairs and then there was nothing but bliss and the urge to touch both those people... and to be touched by *them*. It was all consuming.

Amazing, actually.

She remembered now… The jacuzzi…The way Marco pulled her into the water... And then...

'Oh!' she gasped, scarcely able to believe that she - mousy little Alyson - the one always on the sidelines – had partook in carnal activities. *And* enjoyed them.

Because she *had* enjoyed them. It had made her feel... *He'd* made her feel like…

Her eyes moved back to Marco's piercing gaze which squeezed her very soul. Sidetracked by how the feelings this man sparked contrasted so sharply with what was important of how to believe and what she wanted from life - what she *thought* she'd wanted from life, Alyson barely noticed the scratch to her arm. Before there was time to process anything, a rush of unfathomable bliss, similar to last night hurtled through her.

Marco took a further glimpse at the camera, pleased to see the red light indicated it was working.

Callie had done well - this gear was good shit.

Allowing the syringe to drop to the floor, he flipped Alyson over. He was done with niceties - there was no need for them. Nor was there any need for Callie any longer.

Pulling Alyson into position beneath him, he extended his leg. It didn't take much to shunt Callie off the bed to land with a thump on the marble floor.

Alyson heard the thud, she'd even seen the flash of irritation in Marco's eyes, but now nothing short of him and the electric sensations of her nerve endings buzzing, mattered.

Something pushed against the sore area between her legs. It hurt but that was okay. The pulsing within her had started and all she knew was that soon she would achieve that state of ecstasy where her body didn't belong to her. She would experience that sense of detachment as the building crescendo within her reached its limit and blew, sending her into freefall.

Nothing else mattered. And this man, this gorgeous man, was the one teaching her how to experience that joy.

• • • •

IT WAS STRANGE how Damon jolted from not giving a toss whether he lived or died, to having the attitude of being determined to cling to the slippery edges of life in whatever format offered.

He'd lost his legs for a reason. Wasn't that what people told themselves when faced with shit luck or lumbered with horrific options? A test of faith; God's will; everything would become clear in the end... *'Things that test us only make us stronger...'*

Damon clenched his jaw. He'd heard it all before, but he'd bypass all that 'pushed to the limits of endurance' stuff if he had a choice.

He may not have suddenly experienced an epiphany or seen the Holy Grail, but he *had* changed his mind about his life being pointless.

Fuck whatever he had to do in order to live. He wasn't lying down and dying however much Marco demanded it. Or Zane. Or *any* of those fuckers.

Getting blamed was nothing new, but he wasn't getting offloaded for something he hadn't done. And he hadn't done whatever he was being accused of to deserve being in this situation.

Probably not, anyway...

Well, okay, he had tried to kill the Langley bitch, he'd hold his hands up to that one, but that was because she was a lying whore who'd taken the piss and dropped him in the shit. But he hadn't killed Hazel. Nor any of the other stuff he'd been blamed for.

For fuck's sake, hadn't he suffered enough? What did any of these people think he'd achieve from a hospital bed? Sod all, but they couldn't leave it, could they?

Damon wanted to clench his hands into fists but that was impossible considering he'd been tied to a chair the entire night.

Again, he wasn't sure what method it was thought he might employ to use as an escape tactic after that wanker had chucked his wheelchair into the fucking stream.

A strangulated groan of frustration came from Damon's mouth. How could he not have recognised Leo-bastard-Holland?

Granted, he hadn't expected someone to go to the trouble of dressing up like Clark Kent to pass as a social worker. Plus, he hadn't got much of a look at who wheeled him off down the corridor towards the hospital grounds either. That it hadn't been Marco or Zane was enough. His only priority after that had been smoking a fag.

Stupid, stupid, STUPID.

He should have known. He really should have bloody known!

Damon glared at the unmoving figure of Tiger Shoreham in a chair. If the man had moved even an inch since arriving here, then he hadn't seen it. Perhaps the overgrown bastard was dead?

Maybe they all were - including *him* and he'd gone and missed it?

Damon expelled a pent-up lungful of air. It wouldn't surprise him. He'd missed just about everything else these past few months.

And my, how he'd paid for it.

'Are you aware that you're pissing yourself?'

Damon's surprise at the voice coming from the man-statue was more shocking than having pissed himself.

Even though he didn't want to grant anyone the satisfaction of gleaning a reaction, he was unable to stop himself from glancing down in the dim light to see the large wet patch on his jeans. He inwardly shrugged. *What else did they expect?*

'I offer my sincere apologies if I've contaminated your premises,' he muttered, immediately regretting his smart-arse comment when the force of Tiger's massive fist connected with his already bruised cheekbone. Damon came to the conclusion that being as he'd decided he wanted to live after all, perhaps he should button it.

The hideous truth dawned yesterday as the path of his wheelchair diverted from the outermost circuit around the perimeter of the hospital garden into a random wooded copse-like area. It was then he'd realised that, aside from the first initial seconds of confusion, the 'social worker' was something to do with Marco or Zane.

And then when he was unceremoniously propelled from the contraption onto the ground amid a pile of take-out cartons and clumps of dubious-looking tissues and glimpsed the back end of a white Transit, he knew without doubt that he wouldn't return to hospital.

This might have been good until the 'social worker' ripped his glasses and wig off, revealing himself to be none other than that bastard, Holland.

Damon knew then that it was the exact opposite of good.

Over the past few weeks, he'd cycled through every emotion known to man: blind fury, resentment, self-pity, jealousy, hopelessness, raw regret and numbness. And as the journey in the Transit commenced, throwing him from side to side, his barely healed wounds smashing against the metal bulkheads, Damon experienced every single one of those emotions again, one after another in startling clarity.

He'd fully expected to meet his maker within the hour, the last journey likely to have taken him to his final destination, but short of getting a few slaps and being tied to a chair, nothing had happened.

He'd waited and waited and still nothing...

Now it was a new day and he was still breathing. And this outlined something relevant.

The ghost of a smile inched its way onto Damon's battered face.

It was obvious. Zane and his band of bastards had no intention of killing him. Because they *needed* him.

Zane Morelli had finally got his facts right and learned that the posh Surrey kid was the one behind Hazel's murder, not *him*. Zane must also have come to the conclusion that the attempt on Langley's life was down to instructions from above and he'd finally reached the verdict that *he* was the ideal contender to help push Marco off the precipice he was teetering on.

Damon's chest puffed out with a surge of self-importance. Zane's backward mind had eventually deduced that *he* held the key; the one who knew of Marco's plans and no longer had a problem speaking of them.

This made sense because it wasn't a secret that Marco had royally turned over his one-time second-in-command - or should he say, the person who had *deserved* to be the second-in-command. Therefore, the sensible thing to do was utilise that font of knowledge.

Him.

He would tell Zane everything in order to prise away the last finger Marco dangled from.

Damon quietly smiled. Once it was done and things were back on an even keel, he'd find a way to live with his change in circumstances and reduced mobility. Perhaps he'd study for something? The Open University did courses and stuff like that, so he might give that a try.

TWENTY THREE

SKYE IGNORED the impatient tuts from the queue behind her which had grown considerably longer in the time spent waiting whilst this bloody idiot moved at the speed of a tortoise.

Hearing yet another, 'for God's sake', she looked over her shoulder and delivered a withering glare at the woman she presumed the noises originated from.

Pleased to see the woman immediately avert her eyes, Skye smirked. The stupid bitch's hair was so tight it clearly affected her judgement. Refraining from suggesting that she demand compensation from whomever had made her resemble a microphone, Skye instead turned back to the counter and ploughed her irritation towards the gormless-looking bank teller.

Weren't qualifications required to work in banks? This one must have slipped through the net because she didn't have a clue.

Skye's jaw tightened. She didn't have time for this. It was a simple transaction for God's sake! How difficult was it to cash a bloody cheque? It was standard practice.

She made a big point of pulling up the sleeve of her jacket to stare at her watch, her eyes returning to the cashier to burn a hole into the centre of the woman's forehead. *Come on!*

It had taken ages to get to East Ham this morning thanks to a problem on the tube. She'd probably gone overboard going to a bank so far away, but she couldn't risk anything local. It was best to be somewhere different. But if she didn't get this wrapped up quickly, then Erin, the nosy bitch, would be on the warpath again with endless rounds of questions when she finally returned to the Starbright.

Opening her handbag, Skye pulled out the canvas bag she'd brought to hold the money as an additional hint that she'd been waiting for far too long.

The cashier looked up. 'What did you say your name was again, miss?'

Skye frowned. 'Name? I wasn't asked. Look, will this take much longer? I need to be back at work and...'

'As this cheque is for a large amount of money, can I ask what it's in relation to?'

'What the hell has that got to do with you? The cheque is made out for cash and I want the money!' Skye's face screwed into a grimace. 'That's what you do here, isn't it? This is a bank?' She waved her arms across the glass fronted cashier units. 'Yep, it looks like one to me and so therefore can you do what you're supposed to because I'm busy! You're dragging this out for no reason.'

The woman waited patiently for Skye to finish ranting before speaking. 'We require notice for this amount of withdrawal. We don't hold this kind of money in the vaults on site, so...'

'You're telling me you don't have money in a *bank*?' Skye screeched, aware everyone's focus was now centred on her. 'That's ridiculous!'

Worry then prickled. Did they suspect something untoward? If she didn't get this cheque cashed or brought the police digging around, Marco would go spare. Okay, so £750K wasn't a tenner, but a bank was a bank and it wasn't like Marco had done anything wrong. There was nothing illegal about that cheque - it was rightly *his*.

Even if there had been a thousand other people volunteering to cash the cheque for Marco, Skye wanted to be the one doing it out of principle. That sneaky cow of a crazy mother of hers had never given one inkling that she'd been sitting on *that* sort of cash all these years. Why the fuck did the old cow wear such shit clothes?

It served Shirley right for Marco to expect back what she'd borrowed. That Marco cared enough to lend Shirley the money in the first place, only for her to disappear and then hide his daughter from him, said it all. It also fired Skye's urge to make her mother pay in *every* way, the lying, sneaky piece of shit.

Marco was within his rights to request the money back after what Shirley had done to him. And to *her*.

Skye's brows knitted. That crazy cunt with the cheek to call herself 'mother' knew what she was doing when she took the money and disappeared. Shirley knew she'd behaved like a cowardly money-grabbing slag, otherwise she wouldn't have written this cheque for Marco in the first place - she'd have run to the police. That she hadn't, highlighted her guilt.

Another reason to hate the withered old tramp.

But none of that changed the fact that this ugly dimwit was dragging her feet.

Skye glared at the woman tapping away at the keyboard on her desk. 'Get me my money,' she spat. And it was her money. Or it *would* be. *Every penny of it would be hers eventually.*

'If you could bear with me just a moment. I have to check a few things.' Taking the cheque, the woman's cheeks vibrated as she rose from her chair and glanced at Skye with detectable suspicion.

'Hey! Where are you going with that?' Skye's question remained ignored as the woman disappeared into a back office. She caught a glimpse of a man in a pinstripe suit before the closing door blocked the view.

She glanced at the unhappy customers behind, her uncomfortableness rising. That cow had taken the cheque!

She'd taken it to show that man in the room - a man who looked like the bank manager…

Shit.

Did that mean there was a problem? Did they suspect she was dodgy?

Fuck.

Skye's eyes darted to the wall behind the counter, the blinking eye of the CCTV showing she was being filmed. A cold sweat broke out down her back.

The cheque was above board and returning the money to its rightful owner, but if the bank thought it wasn't... If they thought extortion was involved, they'd bring in the police.

Nausea brewed. They might be calling them right now…

If the police went to the penthouse and saw the cameras - saw Alyson...

Marco had only just been released from the fit-up to jail him over extortion and women. His film studios were still closed, which meant he was being watched closely. Any slight trip-ups and he'd be hauled back in and she couldn't let that happen. She'd only just found him and wanted what he could offer.

Skye's eyes moved back to the blinking red light of the camera, then swung around, her usually composed face drenched with worry. This time the irritated people in the queue didn't register.

Should she get away before the police turned up?

But if she did that, would she not look more suspicious? They'd got her on camera too...

Shit. SHIT.

Skye's head span as she weighed up her options, her sweaty hands fumbling as she shoved the canvas bag back inside her handbag. Then the door of the back office opened and out of it emerged both the woman and the man.

Skye's feet remain rooted to the floor. *She was too late. She should have gone. She should have...*

Reaching the counter, the man peered over his glasses, his beady eyes scrutinising Skye. 'I'm afraid we can't cash this cheque, miss.'

'Oh... I...' Skye stared at the cheque in the man's hand. 'Why not? I mean, wh…'

'It appears to have been stopped by the drawer's bank.'

Skye's heart thudded so hard it felt it may burst through her rib cage. 'Stopped?'

'Yes, miss,' the man continued. 'Come through to my office and I'll make further enquiries and see exactly what the problem is.'

'No, no,' Skye gabbled. 'I'm late for work as it is. I'll have to come back later.'

'But miss, if you...'

Skye had already pushed through the queue towards the door. Her only driving force was to get away. She knew what they'd do. They'd hold her in that room until the police arrived. It was obvious.

Barging through the doors, she skittered along the pavement, it taking her full concentration not to break into a run back to the tube, but she settled for a brisk walk.

It was only after a few minutes of walking steadily, but quickly in the opposite direction without hearing sirens did her thrashing heart begin to calm.

She was overreacting, surely? Cheques got stopped all the time, didn't they? That ugly cow realised the cheque had been stopped and went to see the manager because she didn't have the balls to break the news herself. It didn't mean they were suspicious.

She'd panicked for nothing.

Aggravated for jumping off the deep end, Skye's pace slowed to a sedate stroll. *How stupid.* The bank had nothing on her. Even if they did have suspicions, what could they prove? They didn't have the cheque as evidence because she'd got it back.

Marco wouldn't be happy, but he'd have to sort it out with Shirley. Her eyes narrowed. *Stopping the cheque?* She might have known her mother would pull another bitchy stunt, but...

Oh fuck!

Stopping dead in the middle of the pavement, ignoring the abuse from people almost crashing into her, Skye scrabbled in her bag.

Fuck! She'd left the cheque. She'd left it in the bank manager's hand!

All the colour drained from her face. She'd left the evidence. Marco would go berserk.

• • • •

'I REALISE THIS might put you in an awkward position, Taylor, but I'm trying to ensure things run smoothly.' Erin knew she could hardly come out and say to one of the Starbright guards that this wasn't so much to do with 'smooth running', but the urge to get information - *anything* to give her theory about Skye credence. Either that or accept that she really *was* wrong and her suspicions were down to a personal grudge.

She was fairly sure this was instinct rather than a grudge, but without something concrete it looked like she had a personal vendetta against the girl. It was no secret there was no love lost between them.

She studied the burly guard. Taylor had been known to Zane for years, therefore she found it unlikely the man should be a problem, both in work effectiveness and unprofessionalism towards the resident women at the Starbright. But Skye had specifically named this man out of all of the guards, so for what reason could she have something against him?

In Erin's opinion, the man looked weary and unsure, rather than guilty or defensive. 'I promise you that anything said here will not be freely spoken of.' Sensing reticence, she pressed on using a different angle. 'In your opinion, how are the women upstairs settling in?'

'In all fairness, Miss Langley, I couldn't tell you. Those areas are not on my rounds.'

Erin frowned. 'You don't see the women?'

'No. I deal with the offices, storerooms and front hallway.

The only time I see any women is when they arrive.' Taylor said. 'The guard to speak about upstairs areas is...'

'Oh! For some reason I thought you were on that route,' Erin said, her interest piqued. How could Skye insinuate Taylor made the women uncomfortable when he had no contact with them? 'How are you finding your hours?'

'It's been crazy the last few weeks with these eighteen-hour shifts, but I'm happy to earn my money.' Taylor's brow creased. 'Have I done something wrong?'

'No. You've done nothing wrong.' *That was obvious.* Erin then faltered, unsure whether to ask the question burning on her lips. Deciding she had little to lose, she continued. 'There's no issue, but I'm wondering... have you had any run-ins with anyone? Anyone here, I mean?'

Sensing Taylor's confusion, Erin realised she may as well get straight to the point. 'By "anyone", I'm talking about Skye.'

Taylor stiffened, his jaw working.

'As I said, whatever you say will go no further,' Erin repeated.

'Let's just say that she doesn't like me.' Taylor shrugged. 'I guess you saw that yourself when she balled me out in front of you a couple of days ago, but I don't want to speak out of turn.'

Erin perched on the edge of the desk. 'Please continue - I need full honesty.'

'Well, there's been a few times where my rota's been changed last minute and I haven't been told,' Taylor admitted. 'Luckily, I doublecheck everything, otherwise I'd have missed shifts. I haven't got proof that it was Skye, but...'

'But you think it was?'

'Yes, I do. There's been other things too. She asked me to take things up to the women's floor, but, like I said, there's a set rota for access. Hazel made it clear that only those on that shift must be there. It was done as a means of safeguarding, so I'm sticking to her rules.'

Erin nodded. *And good rules they were.* That way,

discrepancies could be narrowed down to specific people. If Taylor had done what Skye had asked, it would have given proof of her allegations, however untrue. But what had been said begged one question in particular. 'Is there any reason why Skye might have taken a dislike to you?'

Taylor hesitated once more, but Erin waited patiently, knowing the heavy silence would eventually prompt him to speak. He knew something and she was going nowhere until she *also* knew what that was.

'There's one thing that may be behind it...' Taylor muttered. 'Skye was friendly to me before - towards all of us, but afterwards… the way she spoke and looked at me changed, yet she's still nice as pie to everyone else. It started the day that man showed up at the window.'

Erin fought the urge to hurry Taylor along. That day was when Martin located Skye and she accused him of being an ex stalking her. That was what had almost got him killed, as well as giving Sandler the opportunity to murder Hazel a couple of days later. *That's if it was Sandler...*

'The thing is, and I'm not sure whether Hazel mentioned it, but I told her about something I'd noticed.'

Erin's senses shot to high alert. 'What did you tell her?'

Taylor rubbed his hand over his bristly chin. 'Seeing that bloke at the window sent Skye crazy. She was freaking out, but before she did, I saw her face and she *smirked* before the screaming panic started.'

'Smirked?' Erin frowned.

'Yeah, like a sneer. She looked straight at the bloke and sneered. I saw her. Only then did she freak out. My gut told me her show was for *my* benefit. Anyway, I told Hazel about it and I think Skye discovered what I'd said. Either that or she worked out that I'd clocked her act. Ever since then she's been trying to get rid of me by making out I'm shit at my job. And I'm not!'

'Far from it,' Erin muttered. This explained Skye's vendetta towards this guard, but what else did it mean? 'Did you notice anything else between this event and when Hazel was murdered? Or afterwards?'

Taylor shook his head. 'Not really. It was chaos in the days following. Actually, there was something...' He glanced over his shoulder as if Skye might catch him discussing her red-handed. 'After Skye's change in attitude towards me, my instinct told me to watch my back. Once I'd seen how good she was at playing different characters, I wondered how far she'd go to get rid of me, so I kept an eye on her as much as possible.'

Erin inwardly seethed, personally able to vouch that no matter the cost to others, Skye *did* go to whatever lengths necessary to get what she wanted. Look what had happened to her and Tiger. But she wouldn't mention to Taylor about Skye's thinly-veiled insinuations about him in relation to the women upstairs. Not yet, anyway.

'The day before Hazel died, I saw Skye coming out of the group therapy room. She'd been talking to Hazel - I've no idea what about, but she wasn't happy. Anyway, I followed her and she let herself into Hazel's office.'

Erin sat up. 'Without Hazel there? What was she doing?'

'I don't know.' Taylor shrugged. 'She wasn't in there long, but from where I was standing along the corridor, I saw her leave and it looked like she'd got some paperwork.'

Erin's heart began crashing. *The stolen documentation?* 'What paperwork?'

'I don't know but whatever it was, she shoved it down her top as she left.' Taylor looked down at his large feet. 'I was planning on telling Hazel about it, but, well, I never got the chance...'

Erin nodded. No, because Hazel was murdered not long afterwards. Was what Skye took from Hazel's office used to forge the signature which got Marco released? 'Okay, thanks Taylor,' she smiled, her mind spinning. 'Now I'm aware of this I'll be alert for anything Skye might say involving you. I'll make sure that whatever her grievances are with you, it won't cost you your job.'

Taylor nodded. 'Appreciated.'

As Taylor moved to leave, Erin remembered one other thing. She hadn't had any updates from Tiger on the subject, but this man being on the actual job was perfect to ask. 'Before you go, how are the new guards getting on?'

Taylor paused halfway to the door. 'What new guards?'

'Skye interviewed guards two days ago. As far as I know, they started straight away.'

'Not here they didn't,' Taylor said. 'We haven't had new guards start for weeks.'

'Are you sure? They came in a white Transit.'

'Oh, them? Yeah, one of the other guards asked Skye about that and I made sure to listen,' Taylor explained. 'She said they were people from the canning works bringing equipment Zane wanted. I don't know who they were.' He shrugged his large shoulders. 'But then, us guards here don't know any of that lot from Battersea.'

'I must have got mixed up,' Erin said. 'Thanks for the info today.'

Her expression remained passive until Taylor left the room before it morphed into a scowl. *So, Skye had lied again?* Those 'guards' weren't guards at all. It was impossible they were men from the canning works because Zane, Tiger or Leo knew all the men there and would know if any were transferring locations.

So, who were they?

And the other stuff Taylor said about seeing Skye with some paperwork. Did that mean Skye was behind the forgery? Without the documents, there was no proof, but if it *was* Skye, then unless the documents had been destroyed, they would still be around. And judging by her previous endeavours, there was a chance the paperwork could be somewhere in her bedroom.

Erin glanced at her watch. She had no clue where Skye was. Martin said she'd left for the Starbright early, but no one had seen her.

There might be time to nip back to the house and see if she could locate anything in Skye's room. If the documents were there, then Zane would have to accept his daughter *was* involved with the betrayal everyone laid at Hazel's door.

As it stood, the truth of what really happened had been buried along with Hazel's body.

But had it?

• • • •

'IT'S CORRECT SO FAR, I'll give her that,' Baz muttered, alert for unexpected arrivals turning into the road.

'Yes, it seems so.' Red's eyes remained trained on the door of the house just in view from where they'd parked. Thankfully, he'd squashed their van in front of a Luton, otherwise this would have been pointless from the outset.

He glanced at the list of Zane's movements that Skye had texted over first thing. Admittedly, no one was overjoyed to be informed their watch commenced at 6 AM, but Red needed to see for himself that Skye's schedule was spot on, give or take five minutes. That had to be done before they could spec out how to do this job safely, but so far so good – Skye was almost *exact* with both Zane and Erin's estimated departure times.

Baz shifted in the seat and glanced at Red. 'Okay, so we accept the schedule of movements could work, but we also know that no one's in the house. We saw everyone leave and not expected to return for hours, so what's the point remaining sitting here watching if we're not going to strike? My arse went to sleep hours ago and I'm bored fucking shitless!'

'But that's just it,' Red muttered. '*Expect* is the key word. We can't expect, we have to *guarantee* things before moving forward. We need to know how likely or frequently the chance of changes are.'

'For fuck's sake, how long is a piece of string?' Baz snatched a half-eaten packet of Minstrels off the dashboard and crammed a few more into his mouth. He was bloody starving and it was only mid-morning. 'We could case their movements for *weeks* and still things could change at any given time with Morelli or his goons rolling up. Our only option is to act and hope that doesn't happen.'

'I appreciate that, but we have to at least have one or two days as tests to see how many deviations there are from the estimates.' Red stared longingly as Baz tipped the remaining Minstrels into his mouth, the selfish, greedy bastard.

'I know I've said it before, but if we're doing this then I want it over and done with. Sitting outside a psycho's house all day isn't something I'm enjoying.'

'I get that,' Red agreed. This wasn't comfortable for anyone, but he intended on landing that second-in-command position and would do whatever it took to get things right, even if Baz would rather cut corners. 'We're still stuck with the orders th...'

'I'm getting a signal!'

Red and Baz jumped, both having forgotten Dylan's presence even though he was sat between them on the bench seat. It was easy enough done when the man's grating voice was silent. Aside from that 'feature', Dylan was one of those people that no one paid any attention to, apart from when he had something like *this* to say.

'It's the target,' Dylan continued, glued to the screen of his tracker.

'Langley's here? This is our chance!' Baz yelled, reaching under the seat for his gun. 'Let's do her now!'

'Don't be fucking stupid!' Red snarled. 'Do you listen to nothing I say? If she's back, then Morelli could be on the way too, therefore we wait.'

'Where is the bitch? I can't see her.' Baz craned his neck to stare out of the window.

'Get down both of you!' Dylan's voice scraped through everyone's eardrums. 'She'll draw level with the van any second.'

Making the rare call to act on Dylan's words, both Baz and Red slunk down in the seat and froze, watching carefully as, just as predicted, Erin walked past the Transit towards the house.

Red's breath caught in his throat as she reached the short

path to the house and stopped to turn in their direction.

'Fuck!' Baz hissed. 'She's spotted us.'

'No, she hasn't,' Red whispered. 'She's checking the road, not looking at us but she could have been. *That* underlines why when we *do* make a move, it has to be done carefully.'

In silence they watched Erin walk up the path and into the house. It was only when the door shut behind her, did anyone breathe.

'So now what?' Baz asked.

'We wait and see if Morelli arrives or if Langley goes back out.'

Baz's mind ticked over. 'Why haven't we got a tracker on Morelli? If we had, then this would be easy.'

'That's a very good point' Red turned to glare at Dylan. 'Why haven't we got that?'

'I tried,' Dylan whined. 'I couldn't get the signal to handshake.'

Red exhaled through his teeth, the hissing sound almost as aggravating as Dylan's voice. 'Then you need to try again.'

'I… erm... I think I might have taken Zane's number that Skye gave me down incorrectly.'

Baz and Red exchanged frustrated glances. 'We can't ask for the number again - it will make us look like right cunts, so we'll have to gauge it on what we've got.' Baz sat upright in the seat. 'Look, if Morelli's on his way back, then we'll know soon enough. I can't imagine that he'd... Hang on! Who are they?' Learning further forward, he peered through the smeared windscreen.

Following Baz's gaze, Red homed in on two figures coming down the road towards the target house in the opposite direction. Two women - a strange pair. One looked well-to-do and she had a short, fat, rather dishevelled looking woman gripped by the arm, almost frogmarching her along. 'It might be one of those care in the community things. They take out th...' His voice trailed off as the women diverted up the pathway to the target's house. 'They're going to Morelli's!'

'Who the hell are they?' Baz cried. 'Jehovah's?'

'I doubt it, but shut up and watch,' Red hissed. Were these people the reason Langley had returned? It didn't seem likely. 'No one's answering the door.'

'Langley's still inside,' Dylan said. 'The back alley for these terraces leads to the front from two doors down so we'd have spotted her either way, even if she left via the back door.'

'Then we wait longer.'

TWENTY FOUR

ZANE DISMOUNTED his bike around the side of the Thames Canning Works. His pleasure at the prospect of completing a chapter which had been the bane of his life for what seemed like centuries, fell away the second he saw the text from Leo.

The thoughts of an evening with Erin in his bed celebrating Sandler's demise with a bottle or three of champagne turned into the white anger that Sandler invariably sparked. Knowing that creature's very presence here now risked screwing up the vital next step in his plan was typical. It was the worst possible timing.

He stared at the phone screen once more to make sure he hadn't hallucinated, but the words were still there.

`Delivery early. Lorry due anytime this morn.`

Zane rushed into the canning works, his heart thundering. The drop wasn't supposed to happen for four more days, so why had no one been made aware of this change until now?

It had taken some wangling to convince the Delgado firm that he should replace Marco in their arrangement. That family was a notable one in the trade and their supply network was immense. They were involved with virtually *all* drug exports from South America and therefore, anyone in the game, wherever in the world, dealt with them at some level in the supply chain.

But it was unusual to deal *directly* with the Delgados themselves. How exactly Marco had achieved this was something Zane was curious about. And then for him suddenly to be sidelined by the notorious firm was even more intriguing.

But Zane, having successfully swung it that *he* would take over where his brother left off, if it was discovered there was unrest in the ranks in the form of a half-mutilated man located where the high price Class-A powder would be stored would not act as a favourable first impression of a deal he hoped to continue. *Needed* to continue.

On the ride over here he'd convinced himself not to allow his base hatred for Sandler to overtake necessity. Rather than infect his sensibilities, he would remain methodical, calm, measured and effective in the dispatch of the man.

But faced with that fucker screwing up yet more of his life, Zane saw only red.

Slamming through the warehouse doors, his rage spiked further at Sandler's pitiful figure. Secured in a chair, the pointless remains of the man's legs looked ridiculous. Raw fury bolted through Zane's as he was then bombarded with the crap spouting from Sandler's mouth.

Things were precarious enough without hearing that this cock actually believed there to be a glimmer of hope for his situation. Zane wondered whether Sandler's ill-perceived notion of somehow being 'useful' meant he'd lost his effect on people who previously quaked in their boots?

Leo clocked Zane's expression. 'I take it you got my text?'

Giving a sharp nod, Zane stalked towards Sandler, his nose wrinkling at the strong stench of piss from the floor underneath the chair. He zoned the man's droning voice from his brain. He must remain controlled. This bastard could not be dispatched here now. Not when men from the Delgado firm could arrive at any time. 'Shut the fuck up, Sandler. I ain't interested!'

'You'll get little sense from him. I've listened to his fucking bullshit all night!' Tiger said.

'We need to get him out of here and fast,' Zane muttered, scouring his brain for an alternative location to hold Sandler during the coke drop.

'You have to listen!' Damon croaked. 'If you bring me on side, I could help you get revenge on Marco.' His eyes sparkled amongst the swollen bruises of his face. 'I'd be an asset! I know how Marco works. I'm one step ahead. I can help. I won't let you down.'

Fighting to keep himself on the leash, Zane turned away, his fists clenched and his jaw working overtime. *Wouldn't let him down? As if Sandler knew more about Marco than he did!* Ignoring Sandler, he spoke to his men. 'Leo, put this fucker in the van and keep him there until you hear otherwise and Tiger, remain here with me for the handover.'

Leo grabbing the van keys set Damon off again. 'I'm not going in a van!' he squawked. 'Are you so pussywhipped that you can't tell a good thing when it's offered? I knew that silly bitch would play you as well! If only my shot had killed her like it was supposed to, you'd be thanking me by now! It won't be long before you work out she's a poisonous slut.' Just the thought of Erin sent Damon into a tailspin – so much so that he failed to spot the murderous rage in Zane's eyes.

'Ignore him,' Leo muttered, moving to the door. 'I'll bring the van into position.'

'She won't stop, you know!' Damon continued, his eyes wild. 'She'd have fucked me if I'd allowed it. After lying her way into Lunar Films, she threw herself at me every day. She'd screw anyone if it got her where she wanted, the whore!'

Tiger stepped forward. 'I'd shut the fuck up, if I were you!'

'No, I won't!' Damon yelled. 'Zane needs someone to tell him the truth, rather than agreeing and nodding like you two fucking puppets! I bet Langley killed Hazel. Thought about that, have you? She wanted Hazel's place! Being with Zane is only to get closer to Marco. It's *him* she wants, yet you're all licking her arse and fawning over her like silly cunts?'

Both Tiger and Leo attempted to stop Zane as he flew at Sandler, but they didn't stand a chance in halting his wrath now it was unleashed.

• • • •

FIONA'S ARM ACHED from holding Shirley securely as she knocked on the door of the small house.

This was definitely the address Martin had given her, but the neat little building in a row of terraces didn't look the sort of place an underground gang leader and psychotic criminal would live or use as a base. But maybe that was the point? A normal dwelling would arouse no suspicion from anyone nearby. There could be a thousand dismembered corpses underneath the patio or in the flower bed for all she knew.

Her eyes tracked nervously to the tiny patch of earth peppered with flowers underneath the front window. *There wasn't room there to bury a body, was there?*

Pulling her focus back together as Shirley attempted to jerk out of her grasp once again, Fiona wanted to scream. The only abnormal thing in this road was Shirley. The woman was so raddled with nerves it was infectious, but it was imperative she handled this. 'Please calm down, Shirley,' she whispered. 'You know we have to do this, but I promise that I won't let anything happen to you.'

Fiona couldn't promise any such thing. They could both be bludgeoned to death if what Shirley said about these people was true. But she also had to put faith into what Martin said about this man. There was no alternative - not if she wanted to get him away from here.

Having received no response from her knocking, Fiona tried again - this time using the loud brass knocker. 'He must be here,' she muttered and dearly hoped they weren't too late and Zane hadn't already left for the day.

Getting here had taken longer than it should have. Shirley

had three wobbles on route which slowed them up. Even extracting her from the hotel had taken almost an hour. But it now being mid-morning didn't mean Zane had started *his* kind of day.

Fiona banged on the door again, her stress levels rising. She didn't even know what she would say to this Zane person: Ask nicely for Martin to be allowed to come home? Explain what Marco did to Shirley two days ago and hope the man possessed a spark of morals and finally realise that beloved brother of his was out of order? Perhaps, if Zane didn't relinquish his clutches over Martin she should threaten to go to the police and report Marco's rape of Shirley eighteen years ago, along with Zane's part in arranging it?

Which way should she play it?

She had didn't know but hoped that everything would become clear when faced with the man himself.

Whatever happened, she wasn't giving up. Even the churning mess of nervous energy crawling through her body making her light-headed with fear wasn't enough to deter her off the task.

Taking a deep breath, Fiona raised her hand to give the knocker another hammering when the door opened.

TWENTY FIVE

ERIN HAD PLANNED on ignoring the knocking of the door. Going through Skye's room was important, not dealing with cold calls or religious zealots! But the knocking hadn't stopped, so whoever was doing it wasn't going away. But after the initial shock of realising who was actually on the doorstep, she'd never been so grateful to have answered it.

She hadn't expected Martin's mother to turn up and she *definitely* hadn't expected Shirley Wilson.

Compared with this, even locating proof of Hazel's wedding certificate in Skye's belongings paled into insignificance.

Quickly pulling herself together, Erin cleared her throat to speak, but Fiona Bolt beat her to it.

'I apologise for arriving unannounced, but we must speak to Zane.' Fiona glanced at Shirley's trembling figure next to her. 'It's urgent.'

'He's not here,' Erin said. 'I'm Erin. Perhaps Martin mentioned me? Maybe I can help?' She stood to one side. 'Please come in.' Heart thudding, she avoided focusing on Shirley's physical appearance and ushered the two women into the small sitting room.

She indicated for them to take a seat. *What the hell did she do now?* Call Zane? Tell him Shirley and Fiona were here? But what if Fiona had already done what Zane dreaded and involved the police?

'Zane came to see both of you yesterday,' Erin said, dismayed to hear the slight waver in her voice. 'Unfortunately, neither of you were in.' She reached for her phone. 'I'll see if I can get hold of him now and let him know you're here.'

Dialling Zane's number, Erin subtly eyed Shirley perched uncomfortably at the very edge of an armchair. The woman had not uttered a word since the normal-looking woman out of the two, who looked equally as shocked to find *her* answering the door, had introduced herself as Fiona Bolt.

That either of these women were here at all was unexpected, but it was Shirley who rendered Erin speechless. She wasn't sure what she'd expected Zane's first proper girlfriend to look like. It was in her head that the woman Zane had unknowingly produced a child with would bear a resemblance to their stunningly beautiful daughter. But Shirely was as far removed from possessing any shared characteristics with Skye as humanely possible.

Erin cut the unanswered call and smiled weakly. 'I'll try again.' She redialled, praying Zane would pick up. *But how could he? He was busy dealing with Sandler. Shit.*

Erin believed that Zane had exaggerated when he'd said he'd hardly recognised Shirley. She'd presumed he'd played things down so not to fuel her insecurities over the situation. Despite almost twenty years having passed, Erin had expected Shirley to be drop dead gorgeous and worried Zane would be tempted down the road he'd already travelled, but...

Against her will, Erin's eyes fell back to Shirley's overweight frame, her chins wobbling as her full body tremoring showed no signs of abating. The mismatch of ill-fitting, stained and unflattering clothes, along with the lank hair plastered around her pudgy face just wasn't what she'd imagined.

But one thing was certain - Zane wasn't kidding when he'd said Shirley had a problem and her darting eyes, twitching and inability to remain still underlined that.

Realising that she'd been worrying over nothing all this time, guilt prodded. Erin classed herself as non-judgmental and not the sort to harbour cruel thoughts over someone's looks, yet she was doing that very thing. She should concentrate on the *other* very obvious things about Shirley Wilson.

As well as looking unhinged and terrified, Shirley's face was covered in scratches and bruises. What had happened to her?

Erin ended the second call. 'I'm afraid it's just ringing out. I know Zane's in a meeting this morning, but...'

'When will he be back?' Fiona's eyes held a hard, cool expression that Erin didn't expect to find so unnerving. 'I don't know.' She then smiled kindly at Shirley. 'It's nice to finally meet you, Shirley. Zane's spoken a lot about you, so if there's anything I can help either of you with in his absence, then…'

'Get yourself away from Zane Morelli while you still can!'

Shirley's voice came from nowhere - the loudness and conviction of her words sending shivers down Erin's spine. She tried not to let this strange outburst unsettle her, but it did. 'Look, I know you were reluctant for Skye to come here, bu...'

'Shirley's right,' Fiona interrupted. 'The man you're with is dangerous. I'm here to collect Martin. He cannot stay here a moment longer!'

Erin blinked in confusion, then glanced at Shirley before turning back to Fiona. 'Martin told us that Mrs Wilson has been saying things to you about Zane that she's... erm... got the wrong idea about. Zane told me what happened.'

'Ha!' Fiona scoffed. 'I very much doubt the man you're living with has told you *everything...*' Her eyes hardened further. 'Then again, maybe he has…' She tugged her arm away from Shirley's clutching fingers. 'No, Shirley, I'm telling her. This woman's either part of it or she's not. And if she's not, then she deserves to know the truth!'

For the first time since opening the door to these two women, fear overtook Erin's surprise. Her pulse raced. *Was Fiona quite as rational as Martin made out?* 'I don't know what this is about, but I can assure you that Zane has done his utmost to get in contact with you, Shirley. He has a right to see his own daughter.' Was this the opportunity to get the answers from Shirley that Zane had been after for so long? 'He doesn't understand why you didn't tell him about Skye.'

Fiona suddenly jumped to her feet, pulling Shirley with her. 'This is pointless, Shirley. It's clear this woman is in on it, so we're wasting our time.'

Getting the first spark of irritation, Erin also got to her feet. 'Hold on a minute! I had no idea Zane had a daughter and nor did he until...'

'What?' Fiona laughed. 'Why do you keep talking about Skye as if she's *Zane's* responsibility? His daughter? Are you trying to insult Shirley even further?'

'Fiona, don't... I...' Shirley didn't want to be here. *She didn't want to discuss this. It was all too close. All too painful.*

'What the hell is going on?' Erin barked. Bringing her mobile back to life, she tried Zane once more. 'You're both insane!'

'Don't pretend you don't know anything! You've made it obvious by jumping to your boyfriend's defence! And there was me thinking perhaps you deserved to know what he's capable of!' Fiona shook her head, her eyes cold. 'You disgust me! You know Marco is Skye's father and you also know exactly how that came to pass. You know Zane arranged for Marco to rape Shirley and you're also aware that his revolting family paid her family off and forced them to move out of London!' she spat, her composure blown. 'Or did Zane omit that particular part of his repulsive life? Yet you're happy living with him? What does that say about you? Maybe it was *your* idea for Marco to visit Shirley two days ago, threaten to rape her for the second time and give her a beating, as well as forcing her to write a cheque for a considerable amount of money? Getting a percentage, are you? Christ! You make me sick!'

'Marco? He...' Erin stood rigid, sure she was hearing things. *Marco? Marco raped Shirley and was Skye's father?*

It was then that she noticed the red-raw bald patches on Shirley's scalp and the fresh tears rolling down the woman's pudgy cheeks. *Could there possibly be truth in this?*

'Don't pretend you had no knowledge of it!' Fiona spat.

Erin's mouth moved but nothing came out. Normally the first to fight her corner in antagonistic situations, instead she found herself leaning against the wall for support.

Knowledge of it? Of course she had no knowledge of it! Neither did Zane.

Did he?

No. No, he didn't. He couldn't have. But if this was true and Skye wasn't Zane's daughter, it would kill him.

'Now I'm packing Martin's things and getting him away from you animals!' Fiona yelled, pulling Shirley out of the room. 'I'll find his bedroom myself.'

Coming back to life, Erin moved to follow Fiona and Shirley as they thumped up the staircase and then stopped. Let them pack Martin's things - there was only one thing *she* could do.

Snatching up her mobile, her shaking fingers dialled Zane's number again only for it to ring out. Busy dealing with Sandler or not, she had to tell him what had happened and tell him *now*.

Bolting to the front door, she dashed down the path. She'd get a taxi and go to the canning works herself. Fiona and Shirley could do whatever they liked in her house, but she must find Zane.

• • • •

IT HAD TAKEN a long time for the last trace of life to ebb from Damon Sandler. A lot longer than Zane gave the man credit for. But then again, he'd purposely dragged out the torment of the man for as long as possible before his willpower gave up and he'd finished the job.

Ignoring the ringing of his mobile for the umpteenth time, he slumped against a tea crate in the corner of the warehouse and sucked in deep measured breaths to still his ever-raging fury.

From the shadows, Leo eyed Zane dragging his bloodied fingers through his hair and then moved his gaze to the hideous remnants of the vicious assault. He then glanced at Tiger, knowing they shared the same thoughts. The second Zane struck the first blow they both knew it was too late to postpone the inevitable.

Sure, Sandler had it coming, but Leo didn't think he'd seen Zane lose it to this level for a long time - if ever. This killing was definitely personal, but it being personal didn't change that a lorry load of coke and people from the Delgado firm accompanying the shipment could descend at any given time - perhaps an hour from now or maybe a minute. Zane had promised the storage facility to be a safe and blemish-free environment - untouched by rival factions or retaliation issues, yet here it was - knee deep in blood and the butchered remains of Marco's second-in-command scattered across the concrete. 'I think we can safely surmise that Sandler is no longer,' he muttered.

'We'd best get this shit cleaned up,' Tiger said. Pulling up his sleeves, he unrolled a tarpaulin and placed it on the floor.

Snapping out of his hypnotic state, Zane jumped to his feet. 'We can't store a body here. These people might insist on inspecting the building, so we need to get it out of here.'

Tiger and Leo exchanged glances. It wouldn't be easy moving a body whose entrails were hanging out and various other parts weren't securely attached. Leo edged his boot out of the way of an eyeball on the floor - the first part of Sandler's anatomy to be removed.

'We can't transport a blood-soaked tarpaulin in one of our vans either,' Zane said, his voice hollow and distracted. 'Moving it like this will trail blood everywhere, including outside so we can't... Ah, hang on!'

Striding to a storeroom, Zane disappeared inside, emerging seconds later with a large bag.

Tiger stared at the black canvas bag. Okay so it was oversized, but not *Sandler-sized*. 'He ain't gonna fit in there.'

'He will.' Zane dragged Sandler's remains off the concrete onto the tarpaulin. 'Tiger, start cleaning up the floor and me and Leo will make this cunt fit in the bag.'

Grimacing, Leo rolled his sleeves up, not looking forward to what he may get caked in. He'd seen a lot of things in his life. He'd orchestrated plenty of them himself, but despite everything, there was always one in particular which had the power to make him queasy and this particular job was it.

'Hold the other end,' Zane muttered, getting a grip of the bottom of Sandler's right stump.

With Leo pushing the broken torso against the concrete, Zane shoved the remains of Sandler's leg at a right angle, the sickening crunch as it dislocated, loud.

'Fuck's sake,' Leo hissed, bile rising.

'Look on the bright side.' Zane moved to the second leg. 'At least we haven't got to break and fold the *bottom* half of his legs.'

Tiger moved around the area scooping up bits of flesh, including the rogue eyeball and the main part of Sandler's tongue, while Zane and Leo worked in silence, breaking and folding the rest of Sandler's limbs.

With sweat pouring down his brow, Zane manipulated the body into a third of its usual size and secured it with rope. They both rolled the tarpaulin up and dragged it over to the bag and with a final burst of effort, the zip closed.

'I'll wash the floor now that's gone,' Tiger said. He'd bleach it later. The smell of chemicals would be a giveaway to visitors, so removing the stain was the key part for now.

Zane sluiced blood off his hands and face under the tap. His dark clothes hid the stains and that would do for the time being.

Leo jerked his head at the stuffed holdall on the floor. 'Where shall I ditch it?'

Zane finished drying his face on his T-shirt and frowned, the possibility of Fiona Bolt or even Shirley speaking to the police never far from his mind. 'For now, it needs to be stored somewhere not linked to us or anywhere that could be searched. We can't leave it in a van or dump it. It could be stumbled across. Have a word with the crushers.'

The man running that place did nothing for free and although Zane didn't want any favours outstanding, there were limited options available.

Nodding, Leo reluctantly hefted the heavy holdall onto his shoulder and made his way out of the warehouse to his van.

It was only when Zane heard Leo's engine fade into the distance did he allow himself to take a much-needed full breath. But it wasn't over yet. Not by a long shot.

Grabbing a bucket, he set to work in helping to bring the concrete floor back to its pre-killing appearance. He was lucky the lorry and the Delgado firm representatives hadn't yet arrived, but he had to be ready for when they did. Then and only then would it sink in that Damon Sandler was permanently out of the picture.

• • • •

'FINALLY!' Slamming the door once Skye stepped through, Marco stalked back down the hallway.

Skye's face was flushed from rushing, but now she was finally here the dread returned with a vengeance. She'd had it all planned how to explain what had happened at the bank with the cheque, but now she was actually *here*, coupled with Marco's less than enthusiastic welcome, her well-rehearsed explanation had disappeared.

Instead, she found herself following Marco and hovering uncomfortably inside the open-plan lounge. *What was the matter with her?* Why had her trademark confidence deserted her? By God, she was acting like a timid child! She was acting like Alyson-bloody-Read!

Talking of which...

Skye scanned the room, pleased to see no trace of that pathetic little bitch remained. A wave of satisfaction overshadowed the dread. She'd worried unnecessarily over that silly cow having any clout and should have possessed more faith. It was obvious that on sobering up from whatever Alyson had been stupid enough to take, the sad little cow had realised her plans of remaining virginial were smashed to smithereens. And worse – they'd shortly be viewed by perverts too fucking ugly to get any themselves and who resorted to getting their rocks off by subscribing to Marco's new adult channel. Again, another idea she'd come up with to help replenish the money Zane had stolen from him.

'Well?' Marco's harsh voice jolted Skye from her self-indulgent praise. 'I ain't got all day! I'm in the middle of something.'

Skye's face fell, noticing now she was no longer panicking, that all Marco wore was a hastily pulled on pair of lounge pants. She glanced around again. 'Please don't tell me that vapid hooker is still hanging around? Haven't you tired of Callie yet?'

Going against her forte of downplaying her reactions, Skye knew she'd flinched in response to the vicious snarl appearing on Marco's face as he stormed towards her.

'Who I entertain is of no business of yours!' Marco spat. *And no, Callie was no longer in the picture – not that he would be explaining that to Skye.* 'Now, where's the fucking money that you collected?'

Stepping back, Skye searched for the correct words. Her usual reaction to an attitude such as this would be to cut the perpetrator off with a perfectly delivered, doubly harsh retort. But for once, she was unsure how to handle it. *Marco was so angry. Look at his face.* She hadn't even given him the bad news yet.

Her mouth opened in what she hoped would be a suitable response when she was halted by a familiar voice.

'Skye!'

Skye turned to see Alyson descending the stairs from the

galleried landing. She moved fluidly, like her limbs were made from rubber on overstretched cords. And... she was stark naked. *What the...?*

'Babe!' Alyson gushed, throwing her arms around Skye's neck and covering her cheeks with wet kisses. 'Why haven't you already been to see us?'

Us? Skye extricated herself from Alyson's claustrophobic embrace, the scent of chemicals stinging her nose.

'You look fantastic!' Alyson continued, oblivious. 'Doesn't she look great, Marco? Amazing! How are things, babe? You should stay and have drinks, shouldn't she, Marco?'

Skye couldn't rationalise the wittering verbal diarrhoea flowing out of Alyson's mouth and the relaxed confidence this usually micro-mouse of a pointless girl exhibited. Plus, she was standing here butt naked – not a care in the world, her pert breasts bouncing as she jiggled up and down with boundless energy and what seemed like... *joy*.

She studied Alyson's face when the girl stood still long enough for her to focus on it. It was flushed, with glazed, dilated eyes. 'Alyson, what are you on?'

'On?' Alyson chirped, giggling coquettishly. 'I was on a couple of weeks ago, but not now. Although, you should have seen the mess that I...'

'You've taken something again, haven't you? Like you did yesterday.' Skye glanced at Marco. He hadn't mentioned Alyson would stay longer than it took to do the filming.

Alyson draped herself back over Skye. 'You were here yesterday? Are you sure? I would have remembered if you had been here.'

'I was here yesterday, believe you me.' Skye found herself edging away from the bare nipples rubbing against her own through her white blouse.

'You never said your father was so gorgeous,' Alyson slurred, lurching onto a different tangent. 'How could you not warn me that I'd be face to face with the most beautiful man in the world?' Raising her hands above her head, she span around and stumbled into the glass coffee table. It was like she was pass-out drunk - except she wasn't drunk at all.

Marco pulled Alyson into his arms and lowered her onto the coffee table. He pushed two fingers inside her, pressing his thumb against her most sensitive area. 'Why don't you go upstairs and wait for me there?'

Alyson moaned loudly and robotically spread her legs wide, her hand reaching for Marco's engorged cock straining against the thin material of his lounge pants.

Watching in speechless horror as Alyson functioned like a programmed sex doll, Skye was about to question what the hell was going on when Marco pulled Alyson to her feet.

'Off you go. I'll be up in two minutes.' After giving Alyson a long, lingering kiss, the smile Marco wore as she dutifully disappeared upstairs, fell from his face.

'What the fuck is this?' Skye gasped. 'Why is she still here? What have you been giving her?'

'Don't stick your nose into my business, just answer my question. Where. Is. My. Fucking. Money?' Marco growled.

Despite her shock and unease at what she'd witnessed in the last few minutes, Skye knew she must tell Marco about the bank. 'They wouldn't cash the cheque. It's been stopped.'

Marco's face crumpled into the ugliest scowl. 'Stopped? What do you mean, fucking stopped?'

'Something you need to take up with my bitch of a mother!' Skye rolled her eyes flippantly. 'It looks like she's turned you over again.' She huffed petulantly, unwisely missing the change in Marco's eyes. 'I waited ages, only for the bank manager to explain the cheque had been stopped by the issuing bank. Don't worry, they know it was nothing to do with us.'

'And then you left, did you?'

'Yeah, I didn't run off or anything.' Skye found herself grinning despite the situation. 'I did think about it for a split second, but then I realised it was Shirley's doing.' She laughed. 'I was getting paranoid about the CCTV and forgot to get the cheque back, but that's no biggie. Shirley can just write you another one - preferably one that won't get stopped!'

Marco stared coldly at his daughter. 'You left the cheque at the bank? You were on their CCTV; you left the evidence with them and then you then came straight here? Is that what you're telling me?'

'Like I said, they don't suspect anything untoward. Besides, it's not like it isn't *your* money – Shirley owes you! Anyway, I'd have been here sooner to tell you what happened, but I went to a bank in East Ham rather than…'

'You came straight here?' Marco repeated.

'Yes, I just said that and...'

Skye didn't even see the punch smashing into her right eye to knock her clean off her feet coming until she was flat on her back with searing pain ricocheting through her face. She gasped in shock.

'You stupid little cunt!' Marco roared, looming over Skye. 'You could have led to the police here! And never question or make comments who I have in my house ever again!'

This time Skye didn't miss the hatred rolling off Marco as he stalked upstairs, his hands already undoing the tie cord of his lounge pants.

Marco leant over the banister of the galleried landing and glared at his daughter on the floor. 'Get out of my apartment and don't show your fucking face again until you've got the money and something useful to say.'

TWENTY SIX

'LOOK!' Baz nudged Red in the ribs.

Red paused from seething about the Spurs latest defeat in the paper to glare at Baz. Then he saw why Baz had elbowed him. 'Fuck! It's her!' He watched their target move down the path from the terraced house. 'Where's she going?'

'I don't know, but for God's sake, let's take this chance whilst we've got it!' Baz threw his seat belt to one side. 'There's no sign of Morelli and it's been over half an hour since Langley returned to the house. We have to do it now.'

Red hesitated. It *had* been half an hour and if Morelli was going to show up it was likely he'd have done so by now. He squinted through the glass as Erin heading up the road in the opposite direction. She looked like she was on a mission.

'Come on!' Baz yelled. 'What the fuck are we waiting for? We don't know if we'll get another opening like this. We must take it!'

Against his prior insistence of several days' reconnaissance, Red found himself agreeing with Baz's urge to move now. Would they get another chance without Zane or his henchmen in the vicinity?

Making his mind up, Red fired the van's engine, sweat

already running between his shoulder blades. 'I'll draw level, you two jump out and wang her in the back. You'll need to remain in there with her but be fucking rapid about it because we're in broad daylight.'

'What?' Dylan rasped. 'You want *me* to help drag a woman off the street? That isn't what I do. I...'

'It is now,' Baz snarled, gripping Dylan's arm. 'Get ready to go and don't say a word. Your voice is very, shall we say, memorable.'

There wasn't far for Red to travel to overtake Erin. Pulling over a short distance ahead, Baz jumped from the van, dragging Dylan with him and they raced around the front of the vehicle, meeting Erin head on.

Erin was taking her phone from her pocket to call Zane, Leo, Tiger - *any* of them, when two men appeared. She knew immediately that this wasn't good.

She opened her mouth to scream and put them off, but the hand clamping over her mouth scuppered that. Her feet scuffed pointlessly against the pavement as she was dragged backwards. 'MMMPH!' she squawked against the foul-smelling hand.

'Open the fucking back!' Baz cried.

It wasn't a voice Erin recognised, but that hardly mattered. She was being dragged off the street in broad daylight. It had to be something to do with Marco.

Heart pounding, she flailed around to dislodge the vice-like grip on her arm as well as the hand over her mouth. Feeling her elbow connect with a body, she repeated the manoeuvre, this time harder.

'Jesus! She's breaking my ribs!'

This voice was different. It was a distinctive, scratchy voice - a horrible sound that sent goosebumps prickling over her body.

Catching a glimpse of a rather frightened looking man in a white van's doorway amid a flurry of blurring shapes, a flash of green and the noise of metal doors, Erin found herself pulled inside. The whole process took seconds.

With the clanging of metal ringing in her ears, she was plummeted into darkness. Erin blinked but her eyes wouldn't adjust from the glaring sunlight she'd been plucked from.

'Where are we taking her?' the scratchy voice asked.

'Shut it! Everything's in hand.'

A fist banged on the inside wall of the van and with a lurch, the van moved away, Erin struggled to remain sitting upright on the grimy metal floor. She hoped she hadn't lost her phone. Not that she had the first clue how she could alert Zane about what was happening, but she had to pray an opportunity presented itself. If it didn't, she had a strong suspicion that she wouldn't escape from this unscathed, if alive at all.

Her hand traced the outline of her phone in her pocket, trying to gauge which way up it was. She jabbed at it, hoping she'd pressed the buttons correctly.

If she'd done this right and a call connected, then out of the limited contacts on her phone she just had to hope she hadn't picked Skye's number, or the one belonging to Hazel that she couldn't bring herself to delete.

• • • •

MARTIN WASN'T IN THE FRAME of mind to do this today. He doubted whether he'd ever be in a state to do anything ever again. Even breathing unaided felt unsurmountable - a task too complicated and exhausting to fathom.

He stared at the penthouse entrance half-heartedly, the same way he'd done for three days, wishing he'd never volunteered for this. Had he not asked Zane for work then he wouldn't have seen what he'd seen. He wouldn't be left with unanswerable questions or a sick feeling deep in his belly. Neither would he question things he didn't have answers for. More to the point, didn't *want* answers for.

But he'd seen it - he'd seen all of these things and now he couldn't unsee them.

Skye had been in this building, as had Alyson. But Skye not

telling him about it and blatantly lying about where she'd been, coupled with her treating him like he was someone she'd just met, made creeping tendrils of doubt about the girl he'd been determined to marry, ramp up tenfold.

Everything that had happened since Skye lied about going to Scotland with Alyson had accelerated. It had been weeks since she'd disappeared to reinvent herself in London with a built-in story, including lies about how *he* fitted into her life. Then there was all the other lies she'd told - not just about him, but about everyone.

And now *this...*

But what Martin really dreaded and what made it all the worse, was the inability to find reasons, excuses or slight obscurities that could explain the host of inconsistencies anymore. The only thing now repeating in his head was that Skye wasn't who he thought she was. She wasn't who *anyone* thought she was...

And if she wasn't who any of them thought she was or who he'd believed her to be since first knowing her, then who exactly was she? What was she attempting to achieve?

Martin wanted to rest his head against the steering wheel and not look up ever again. He wanted to remain asleep until all of this was confirmed to be a bad dream. He'd stay mercifully oblivious until his life stopped rapidly descending into tatters. Whichever way he looked at it, everything that was happening - everything he'd been doing for Skye's benefit, was in actuality making *him* out to be untrustworthy and a liar to everyone - himself included.

He reluctantly raised his eyes back to the point he'd been instructed to watch, scared in case something else happened that he didn't want to take on board. He couldn't cope.

He'd missed half the morning anyway. Countless people could have gone in and out and he wouldn't have a clue. Something else he'd failed at. But for the first time Martin was no longer just worried for himself, but for everyone.

He pulled out his mobile. He'd give his mum a quick call.

He always felt better hearing her voice.

But then the flash of sunlight rebounding as the complex doors opened made him look up. His heart lurched and sank at the same time seeing Skye hurry from the building holding her hand to her face and looking uncharacteristically upset.

Martin remained motionless - the thought of rushing to her aid not gaining traction. It was an unfamiliar feeling. Skye was injured and upset, yet he felt nothing but confusion.

The only certainty was that Skye was not who she said she was. Martin didn't know her and, as far as he could ascertain, neither did anyone else.

Twenty Seven

LEO SCOWLED at the mounting traffic. It was always the same around the Barbican, but given the time of day, this route was probably the least offensive if any routes around central London passed as being that.

At least he'd crossed the Thames, so providing the traffic eased once he'd got through this bit it shouldn't be too bad heading out through Shoreditch to the car crushers in the arse end of Cambridge Heath. He'd grab something to eat once he'd dropped the cargo off. Not that he was particularly hungry.

That was a rarity in itself, but not wholly surprising.

Leo shuddered, still hearing that puke-inducing noise of snapping bones. Ever since he could remember that particular sound made his mouth go inside out and nothing had changed.

He kept a steady watch in his wing mirrors as he continued crawling towards the junction of Long Lane and the A1. Nobody was on his tail. *Good.*

Hearing his mobile come to life, Leo felt around on the bench seat for it, hoping it wasn't Zane telling him the shit had hit the fan over the coke drop. He could do without turning back with a bag of body bits in the rear.

Balancing his mobile on his knee, he turned left onto the

A1 and frowned as he glanced at the screen. *Erin?* Answering, he flicked the call to loudspeaker. 'Hel…?'

He stopped almost immediately on hearing a voice that was definitely not Erin's. It was a man's voice - a deep, gruff voice. Along with the voice, there was also loud background noise which sounded like it was coming from inside a dustbin on a roundabout.

Leo's hackles immediately went up. Ignoring the presence of a half-dismembered corpse in the back of his van, he pulled to the side of the road. Turning off the engine to hear as much as possible through the tinny speakers of the phone, he ploughed his full concentration into his mobile.

Erin might have accidentally dialled his number from her pocket - the sound was muffled. Or was she speaking to guards at the Starbright? It wasn't like he'd recognise any of their voices.

But Leo prided himself on his instinct and his instinct screamed that something bad was happening.

Frowning, his forehead bunched as he picked out voices over the unmistakable vehicle noise. He was right about something being wrong.

Erin's voice was clearer than the man's. She was sarcastic, bitter: *challenging*.

'Where exactly are you taking me in this shit-heap of, I can only presume, a Transit? And what's with the green bits on the side?'

'Listen to the little tart's observation skills!' the gruff voice mocked. 'Prefer to only travel in Ferraris, do you? I apologise… As for where we're going, well, you'd probably rather not know.'

'I don't reckon on Marco being in Dalston at the moment, so I guess we're heading to Battersea?' Erin continued.

Leo bristled. *This was to do with Marco? Shit!*

His fingers reached for the ignition. How long would it take to head back to Battersea? It would take ages to return to where he'd just come from. And how far towards Battersea was this vehicle?

A 'Transit' wasn't much of a lead to go on either. And what was that part about the 'green bits'?

The unknown man's reply cut into Leo's frantic thoughts.

'Paranoid, aren't you? Why presume this is to do with Marco?'

'But you've confirmed that it *is* to do with him because otherwise you wouldn't know who I was referring to.'

Leo almost smiled. Even in the midst of being in the back of what Erin thought *might* be a Transit, with people unknown, her wit knew no bounds. That girl had bottle, that was for sure.

But it wasn't funny. Marco had got some goons to take Erin. Zane would go tits. But all the anger in the world wouldn't make up for something happening to her.

As he wracked his brain, he felt sick. He had to call Zane, but being as he was already on the road, he'd try and head this Transit off, wherever it was.

Leo started the engine, still straining to pick up the conversation through the phone speakers. The tinny noise was breaking up more and more frequently so they must be in a dodgy signal area.

Stay on the line, Erin, Leo willed. If he could keep her there and she kept talking, he might get more info on her location. She'd been asking the right questions, but Leo needed more, otherwise it was like looking for a needle in a haystack.

Still at the side of the road with the engine idling, he knew he had to make the decision to drive, but which fucking way? There was little but crackling coming through the speakers now.

Fuck.

Hang on! Erin said she couldn't see Marco being in Dalston, which meant these wankers must have got to her there. But wasn't Erin at the Starbright in Dagenham?

Leo's mind raced. It was stabbing in the dark but if that van had taken Erin from Dalston and was heading to Battersea, then...

Leo screeched back onto the A1, taking a right into Old

Street. If he was correct, from the few threads he possessed, and the Transit *had* left Dalston, then depending how far it had travelled, they'd have either already passed him and he was heading the wrong way, or they'd probably take the route down the Queensbridge Road to join the Hackney Road, which he would shortly reach.

But if he was wrong...

Leo gritted his teeth as the tone from his mobile signified that the call had completely dropped. He dared not call back.

Stamping his foot on the accelerator, he expertly weaved in and out of the traffic. If he got a tug with a corpse in the back then he was fucked, but then so was Erin if he didn't do his utmost to pinpoint a Transit that ticked the right boxes.

In the meantime, he'd keep trying to get through to Zane.

• • • •

SKYE STORMED THROUGH the Starbright reception as quickly as possible, ignoring the guards. She held her phone so tightly she'd be happy if it snapped in two if she wasn't using it as a prop to concentrate on, rather than looking up.

Reaching her office, she hurried inside, making sure to lock the door behind her. Only then did she place the phone on the desk and sink into her leather chair.

Raising her hand, she gently prodded the skin around her eye, not needing a mirror to confirm that it would shortly be as black as Newgate's knocker. Judging by the swollen flesh she could feel underneath her fingertips, it was halfway there already.

How would she explain this? Walked into a door? Martin lost his temper?

Exhaling loudly, she put her head in her hands. Neither of those excuses were suitable. She couldn't blame Martin for this one. She'd left before him this morning and no doubt he could prove he'd been at his stupid, poxy garage job, so what the hell should she say?

What about somebody attempting to mug her?

That might work. Zane would go Godzilla about it, wanting to hunt the perpetrator down, but being as she hadn't got a 'good look' at her attacker, then where would he start? It could be anyone...

Except it wasn't anyone...

Opening the bottom drawer of her desk, Skye fished out the small bottle of vodka she'd bought the other day to christen her new office. She had no idea why she'd bought it because she didn't like vodka much but now she was grateful for it.

Dismayed to see her fingers shaking, she unscrewed the bottle and took a swig, wincing as the spirit stung her throat.

Yeah, she'd say some tosser tried to pinch her handbag. That would do.

As the adrenaline began to recede, the real facts returned with a heavy thump. And those she wasn't quite ready to accept.

How could she accept that Marco - her own flesh and blood - her own father and the one who she was doing *everything* in her power to put right the wrongs committed against him, had hit her?

He'd threatened her, spoke to her like dirt and punched her in the face.

Angry tears, along with a desperation that felt unnatural, encased Skye in a glutinous, nasty shroud.

Marco had been so nice: it was him and her against the world - two halves of the same coin. Yet it was like he'd suddenly been replaced by someone she didn't know.

She'd done everything he'd asked. She was on his side - his, not Zane's or Shirley's - *his*.

So why?

Skye wasn't sure whether the hot tears rolling down her sore cheek were from rage or betrayal. Maybe both.

Did Marco not want her anymore? Did he regret having a daughter? Did he wish she didn't exist? If so, what had changed when he'd previously been so pleased to have her in his life?

Everything was perfect until she'd brought Alyson onto the scene.

Swiping the snot from under her nose with the back of her hand, Skye's eyes hardened. *This was Alyson's fault.*

Alyson wasn't the pure, innocent little rich girl she'd made herself out to be. Alyson had turned Marco against her. It had probably been *her* plying Marco with drugs to make him act out of character.

A fresh wave of desolation crashed over Skye as she considered whether it was possible she'd weighed up Marco incorrectly in the first place.

She couldn't have.

All the poison that bastard, Zane, spouted about his brother was wrong. *Marco* was the victim in this, not Zane and she refused to allow anything else to seep into her brain and make her question her allegiance.

Now Alyson was trying to elbow her out?

Well, she wasn't having it.

Skye snatched her phone off the desk and quickly stabbed out a text.

`I want an update.`

`Now.`

Pressing send, she took another swig of the vodka then sat back and pursed her lips. If Red and his two fool mates hadn't moved further forward with the plans for Erin, then she'd...

A slight smile then tugged at the corner of Skye's mouth. She bypassed that, for the time being, she hadn't received an immediate response from that ginger-haired twat and tapped out a further text.

`Where the fuck r u now? We need a meet at the usual place ASAP.`

`B there at 3.`

Sitting back in the chair, Skye smugly waited for a reply. Red wouldn't dare ignore her. He knew better and whatever they were doing or not doing with Erin, they now had another job to do.

Removing Alyson was their next assignment. That way, if she was right and her alleged 'friend' was the instigator behind Marco's personality transparent, then removing her would also remove the problem and things would return to normal.

Alternatively, on the slim chance that Alyson *wasn't* anything to do with Marco morphing into Jekyll and Hyde, then at least she wouldn't have to put up with the boring bitch texting her again.

Twenty Eight

ZANE MASKED HIS MIXTURE of happiness and relief as the last crate of cocaine was lifted out of the arctic and a forklift manoeuvred it into position on the end rack in the specially vacated warehouse.

It wasn't the done thing to act pleased - even over the closure of multimillion pound deals. Maintaining a stoic 'ten a penny' attitude like this sort of thing happened all the time was the accepted face to wear. But inside, Zane was jumping up and down with joy.

As he'd headed towards the pinnacle of his father's firm, these type of deals were commonplace. But that was before his life was turned upside down by being incarcerated for six years. But since being released and having to start from scratch, this sort of arrangement no longer happened. *Until now...*

And this was the first of many more lucrative deals and arrangements yet to come. It had gone without a hitch, which showed that he'd now achieved a strong foothold. The only way was up from here on in. Once word spread that he worked with the Delgados, firms would queue up for association with him and more offers would follow.

All the frustrations and angst from the past were gradually

cancelling out. Only one remained - and that particular one in the shape of Marco – was not of immediate importance, being as the man was drowning quietly somewhere in a pit of doom of his own making.

The buzzing of Zane's mobile threatened to spoil his mood. Buttoning the call, he flicked the volume from vibrate to silent. It was Leo again. The second time now. What the bloody hell was the man thinking? Leo knew he'd still be knee deep with the Delgados, so why phone?

For God's sake, Leo was more than capable of dealing with whatever that greedy bastard at the car crushers wanted in return for dealing with Sandler, so he needed to just get on with it. Leo didn't need approval, he should know that. Especially during the middle of *this*.

Removing the annoyance as rapidly as it appeared, Zane smiled brightly and extended his hand. He hadn't expected the head honcho of the Delgados firm to accompany the drop, but it was a good sign. 'It's been a pleasure doing business with you, Mr Delgado. It's good to meet the main man.'

'Likewise, Mr Morelli,' Diego Delgado grinned, exposing a mixture of shiny white teeth interspersed with gold ones. 'I'm sure you understand I needed to see with my own eyes who I've agreed to work with after the, how do you say it… debacle with your brother.'

'Ah, yes, but "brother" isn't a term I use any longer where he is concerned. We parted ways a long time ago, as I'm sure you're aware. I do, however, understand your initial reticence to continue dealing with the same family. However, I'm very glad you decided to.'

'I can see well enough that you are not like him, Mr Morelli. For a start, you have no interest in my wife.' Diego Delgado smiled but it was cold and loaded. 'Here's to our relationship continuing.' With a final nod, Diego Delgado clicked his fingers to summon his accompanying posse of guards and left the warehouse.

After the door closed behind Delgado and his entourage,

Zane lit a cigarette and leant back against the worktop. That went well, short of the strange comment about his wife, which was odd.

Zane shrugged. Foreigners had different takes on humour. Either that, or Marco had made a play at some point for the man's wife. It wouldn't surprise him and would explain why the association was so bluntly cut off.

Still, nothing to do with *him.* Zane had the coke and the Delgados wanted to do further business, so everything was falling nicely into place. At least on *this* front…

Zane trailed his finger along the nearest set of tightly packed bags of cocaine. He'd pull in a fortune with this - the start of many good things to come.

A wide grin cracked his face. A double celebration tonight was now definitely in order. He couldn't wait to tell Erin the good news: the deal was done and Sandler was gone.

Now to get the people on standby in here first thing tomorrow to start weighing and cutting this lot up. In fact, he'd get Tiger onto arranging that now.

Where was Tiger, anyway? He hadn't seen him since he'd stayed in the other room whilst the last part of the deal was wrapped up.

About to go and search the door opened and Tiger stepped through. 'Ah, I was just coming to find you,' Zane beamed. His face then fell at Tiger's expression. 'What's happened?'

'Leo's just called.'

'Yeah, he called me a couple of times as well, but I was dealing with...'

'Someone's got Erin...'

At the words he dreaded hearing, Zane's good mood shrank to a tiny white dot.

• • • •

LEO RACED UP THE Hackney Road heading in a direction he thought the van holding Erin most likely to take.

Sweat poured from his brow. What if the van had already

passed and therefore he was now going in completely the opposite direction?

He didn't dare think about what that could mean.

Damn Zane for not answering his mobile. Not that it made a difference. Even with a motorbike, Zane wouldn't be any quicker. Not now. But he hoped Tiger had relayed the message.

He scanned the road for a white Transit sporting a green stripe, green writing... green *something*.

That's if he'd heard correctly?

What sort of cunt used a van with distinguishable markings for something like this? It was unlikely, but what else did he have to go on?

Spotting a Transit travelling the other way, Leo squinted against the glare. It was white, but *'Geoff's Plastering Services'* was emblazoned on the side. And there was no green.

Fuck! Come on!

Taking a left onto the Queensbridge Road, Leo knew time was running out. If he couldn't locate the van, then God only knew where this would end up. Where Erin could end up...

Leo's mobile suddenly broke the rhythm of his laboured breathing. 'Zane! Yeah... I'm looking now. I'm on the Queensbridge Road... I don't know... I think they're heading to Battersea, but I can't be sure... Yeah, that's right... A white Transit with possible green signage – maybe a stripe. Yeah... Okay.'

Cutting the call, Leo threw his mobile back on the seat. Zane was on his way and Tiger was heading in the other direction. Surely between them, they would find the...

Wait! Was... was that it?

Leo strained to focus on a vehicle in the distance. It was a white van, but did it have any green? Should he even be looking for green? That part could be completely wrong.

What should his deciding factor to give chase be? If he picked the wrong vehicle, then it would be a disaster, but if he didn't make the call on one which *did* turn out to be the correct one, then what?

Putting his foot down, Leo crossed the bridge over the London canal, pulling slightly to the right to get a better look at the approaching van. He hoped he wouldn't get stopped for driving erratically, but he had to chance this. If he could just see part of the side of that Transit, then...

Fuck!

Changing down a gear, Leo took a sharp left turn off the Queensbridge Road mirroring the target Transit. The van left the road at the last minute. It also had the remnants of a peeling green logo on the back left-hand side…

That was the one. It *had* to be.

Why else would it suddenly veer off? The driver must be suspicious from the way he'd shifted across the lanes and reacted accordingly.

Leo gritted his teeth. He had to keep on its tail. Closing the distance, he negotiated the road, keeping track of where he passed. Zane wouldn't locate him unless he had markers.

He'd turned off Queensbridge onto Scriven Street then hung a left on Lee Street onto Clarissa Road. *Fuck, he'd never remember this...*

Riding his brakes inches from the bumper of the other Transit, Leo gripped the wheel. He passed Lovelace Street, Pamela Street, Samuel Street…

Where the fuck was this van going?

And then he saw it.

The London canal was at the end of this road… Like just *there…*

Slamming on the brakes, Leo yanked the steering wheel onto full lock. His tyres screamed as he cleared the left-hand turn, narrowly avoiding overshooting into the murky water.

The target Transit was ahead and this road was a dead end.

He'd fucking got them!

• • • •

FIONA PACED HOPELESSLY back and forth in Zane Morelli's sitting room and stared at Shirley still sobbing in the chair. It was impossible to think straight with her wailing and muttering. It had been over half an hour since she'd heard the door slam and Erin leave. And she hadn't yet returned.

For Erin to run off spoke volumes about the woman's guilt. Fiona's lips pursed. It looked like she'd been right with her conclusions.

It was strange though. Martin had spoken highly of Erin and Fiona was prepared to give her the benefit of the doubt. After all, Erin Langley wouldn't be the first woman to be duped by a sly man's lies.

Fiona had felt almost responsible for what the repercussions would be about warning the poor cow what the man she thought she loved was *really* like and what he'd been party to in the past. Leopards never changed their spots...

But it was Erin jumping to Zane's defence that tipped Fiona off balance. In fact, aside from with Peter, especially when he'd dragged his feet when Martin's safety was on the line, she didn't think she'd ever felt so bitter towards another person. She hadn't felt the same level of hatred even towards that thug who had burst into their house looking for Martin. Angry, scared and worried for her son, yes, but hatred - not quite.

Yet seeing the pure misery on Shirley's face and knowing what she'd been put through at the hands of these people, starting all those years ago when Zane arranged for his brother to defile her, enraged Fiona to an extent that she hadn't realised she possessed. Even though Erin seemed genuinely shocked to learn the home truths, the surprising affinity Fiona felt for Shirley outweighed everything.

'You... you shouldn't have said anything,' Shirley said, her voice hollow.

Fiona inwardly sighed. Shirley had said the same thing every minute or so since she'd repeated the facts to Erin.

'You knew I didn't want to discuss it. You said you wouldn't talk about it.' Shirley twisted the hem of her skirt around in her hands. *Twist, twist, twist.* 'I don't like thinking about it, yet I do nothing *but* think about it. I don't want anyone knowing. I...'

'Erin Langley knew everything. It was obvious.' Fiona justified herself for what felt like the hundredth time.

'You don't know that! Not for certain! It's not your place to tell anyone and...'

'Someone had to do *something*!' Fiona barked. 'I'm sorry if you don't like it, Shirley, and I know it's difficult for you, but these people must be stopped!'

'You don't know what they're like.' Shirley looked up, her big blue eyes haunted. 'You shouldn't have said anything. I don't want anyone to know.'

Fiona turned her back, unable to bear the same thing yet again. She glanced at the open packet of cigarettes on the table. This was enough to make her start smoking!

'I don't want to be here,' Shirley continued. 'Not in his house. I don't want to be near him or *any* of them! Don't you understand?'

Fiona nodded. 'I know.' And she *did* understand. Well, thankfully not completely, but doing this would help Shirley as well as keep both of their children safe.

But what Shirley hadn't yet taken on board was that Fiona would be saying exactly the same things she'd said to Erin, to Zane and Shirley needed to back her up on it. Zane must put a stop to his brother's threats and extortion and if he didn't, then she'd involve the police. It was the least Zane Morelli could do considering what he'd engineered to get himself off the hook in the first place.

Everything had consequences and it was about time the man realised that.

'When is that woman coming back?' Shirley asked. 'I don't want to stay in this house - *his* house, any longer.'

'I don't know when Erin's coming back,' Fiona muttered. *Or where she'd gone...*

Another explanation of Erin's disappearance, if it wasn't to do with guilt and shame, was to fetch the boyfriend to deal with it instead.

A flicker of nervousness filtered through Fiona's anger. She hadn't forgotten that the Morellis were head of a feared gang. She could be killed for this. They *both* could. As could Martin by association...

That thought alone made her blood run cold.

But Shirley had a point. They couldn't remain in a stranger's house indefinitely. What if no one came back? Peter had backed off from texting and phoning, but she'd said she would only be at the craft workshop for two days, so if she wasn't back home by tomorrow then he'd want to know why.

Fiona swallowed uncomfortably. There was no way of remaining in London longer without explaining to Peter what was really going on. And that would be a disaster.

She stared at the three holdalls that she'd packed full of Martin's belongings. She had his stuff, so now she just needed *him*.

For God's sake! What was she doing? As Martin's life was on the line here, was it really her place to fight Shirley's battles? Wasn't the point of coming to London in the first place to get Martin out of the clutches of these people?

It was, yet she'd become sidetracked.

Her eyes moved to the gibbering mess of Shirley still perched on the armchair. 'Maybe you're right,' Fiona said, unzipping her handbag. 'I know you're struggling by being here, so once I've got Martin we'll leave, okay? I'll phone him right now.'

TWENTY NINE

'WHAT THE HELL IS HE DOING?' Dylan screeched, breaking the long silence he'd kept up since getting in the van.

'Oih! Take it easy up front, dickhead!' Baz banged his fist against the metal wall. 'I was just getting somewhere with this slut.' His hand returned to continue fumbling with the button of Erin's trousers. 'Now where was I?'

'You were about to get the fuck off me,' Erin snarled, pushing Baz's hand away for the third time. She'd no idea that the other frightened looking man was capable of speaking before now, yet it was clear why he'd chosen to remain silent. *That voice!* It made her feel almost as sick as the constant pawing by this other bastard. 'Nobody has explained what this is all about yet.'

'If you can't work that out love, then you must be thick!' Baz sneered, his hand groping around to reach between Erin's thighs. 'Why don't you just concentrate on what you're best at, eh?'

As the van lurched to one side again, Erin clawed at the filthy floor in the hope of grabbing onto something, yet to her horror, found herself on top of the man with the gruff voice and wandering hands.

Her eyes had slightly adjusted to the pitch-black interior, but still only the vague outlines of two people were present. As the man ripped at her top, fear knotted in the base of her stomach.

'There was me thinking I'd never risk touching a bird belonging to a Morelli, but it's not like it matters now.'

Hot foetid breath clouded Erin's face as she twisted and wriggled away from the hands squeezing her breasts. 'Get off me, you filthy bastard!' she screeched, her legs kicking into space rather than connecting with anything.

Had she got through to anyone on that call she'd tried to make? She could have sworn she'd heard a voice - albeit for a split second and not long enough to deduce whose voice it was. But whoever it was, had they heard anything? Had they heard enough to realise she was in trouble?

Erin's fear heightened. What if they hadn't seen her name on the screen and thought it a prank call or wrong number? What if she was mistaken and it hadn't connected at all?

'Jesus Christ!' the man with the ear-splitting voice yelled loud enough to reinstate the profoundly deaf of hearing as the van lurched violently to one side.

Erin's head connected with the van wall and she yelped, finding herself now wedged between both men. Her fingers raced to do up her trousers and pull her top down. But before she could she was thrown across the opposite side by yet another violent swerve.

'Pack it in, Red!' Baz roared, banging the wall yet again.

Then there was the unmistakable screeching of tyres. It felt like they were travelling sideways.

Flailing in the darkness, Erin found herself flying through empty space amid the deafening sound of crunching metal.

• • • •

AFTER THE IMPACT, it took Leo a second or two to pull his brain into working order. He blinked in confusion at the steam hissing from the front of his van.

What the fuck happened?

He clenched his teeth, finding them still present and then wiped a trickle of blood away from his eye. Nothing was broken; he could see and he could still think. He was okay, but why was he looking at the world from this strange angle? Everything was on the tilt.

That other van...

Erin!

He instinctively reached for his gun underneath the seat, only for a horrible creaking noise to assail his ears as the horizon tipped again.

Leo froze. The van was moving like a bastard seesaw. From his position with one arm half under the seat, he moved only his eyes to look in his wing mirror. He couldn't see the back half of his van but *could* see that where it should be there was only water.

Holy fuck! The back end of the van was hanging over the canal. Shit!

He had to get out of here.

Where was the other van? Was it just him who'd crashed?

Leo's mind replayed turning onto Dunston Road which ran parallel with the London canal. He'd got the other van cornered, but then it veered across his path and he'd hit it side on. But was it still here, in the canal or had it driven away?

Hardly daring to take a breath in case he tipped the balance, Leo gingerly reached for his gun and painstakingly sat upright. The van remained balanced on its perch, but he had to be quick. He was no good to Erin lying at the bottom of the canal.

Inching his phone nearer, he dialled Zane and left only a short message. 'Off Dunstan Road. Crashed.'

Cutting the call, he left the same message on Tiger's mobile before opening the van door. Relief surged seeing the edge of the canal was behind him and he could step onto the concrete. Clambering out, the van remained in place, but the back wheels were off the road and definitely hanging over the cut. Leo also saw the rear doors had flown open and was just time to see the last trace of the bag containing Sandler's corpse glug underneath the surface of the canal.

Shit! Still, no time to waste.

Dashing around the front, it was obvious the other van had not made a getaway because it was stuck in the middle of the road, the back crumpled.

Find Erin or deal with the men?

It had to be the men. If he got shot dead, he couldn't help her at all.

Racing to the other van's cab, Leo saw the driver trapped inside. No one else was there so Erin must be in the back. But what if this wasn't anything to do with her? What if he'd misread the situation?

Leo scowled. Fuck it. This cunt was dodgy, so it had to be them. 'Where is she?' he roared at the ginger-haired man half-trapped behind the steering column.

Red's relief faded at seeing a rescuer when the barrel of Leo's gun came into focus through the broken glass. 'No! Wait!'

At point blank range, Leo pulled the trigger, splattering the contents of the man's head over the inside of the windscreen. He then glanced around. The area was deserted, but someone must have seen the crash. Or at the very least, heard the shot?

Maybe not. Hopefully no one took notice of stuff like this around here. But something was now definite - he'd not only lost one body to the canal but gained another one.

Wiping sweat from his brow with his forearm, Leo raced around the back of the Transit and pulled on the double doors. It was difficult with the majority of the van mangled but he had the brute force required. He cocked his gun, knowing it likely more of these wankers were inside.

With a final tug, Leo freed the mangled door and heaved it open, the grinding noise fraying what was left of his nerves. He peered into the cavernous interior.

It was empty. How could it be empty? Had he been sitting disorientated in his own van for so long that they'd made a run for it?

The concept of having misjudged the situation filtered back into Leo's throbbing mind once again, but then at the far end against the bulkhead, he spotted bodies in the gloom. 'Jesus,' he hissed, his stomach lurching at the tell-tale shock of blonde hair amongst the pile. 'Erin?'

There was no movement – only silence.

Without further hesitation, he clambered into the back and with considerable effort, pulled the crumpled body of a large man off the smaller figure underneath. The head hanging at a strange angle and the blank vacant eyes showed that this one was dead.

Chucking the body to one side, Leo dropped to his knees next to the figure beneath who was undoubtedly Erin Langley.

'Shit,' he croaked, taking in the deep gash to Erin's forehead. God knows what damage there was underneath. 'Erin?' His thick fingers searched for bare skin on her neck to detect a pulse. *Please let her be alive.*

This was the second time in a few short months that he'd faced discovering whether this woman still had her life or not. Once had been enough, yet here he was again. 'Erin? Can you hear me?'

No answer.

Fuck. FUCK!

Wait! Was that a pulse?

Leo's fingers slipped on the blood covering Erin's skin and felt around again, his own heart hammering.

It was a pulse. Not a strong one, but a pulse all the same.

Screw the shooting in the cab, screw Sandler in the cut. All that was important now was getting Erin help. He was damned if he'd let her die. 'Stay with me,' he muttered. Placing his gun down, he yanked his phone from his pocket, his shaking fingers getting as far as dialling '9' when movement stopped him.

There was another fucker!

Dropping the phone, Leo scrambled for his gun as a skinny man lurched from the far corner towards the open doors. 'Stay where you are, bastard!' he roared, taking aim.

The skinny man was half out of the doors when the gun fired. But when nothing happened, the man stumbled onto the concrete outside.

Leo fired again. And fired again.

The trigger wasn't pulling the full way down. The fucking gun was jammed!

'Fuck!' he roared as the man disappeared from view.

Leo pounded the wall of the van with the barrel of the gun. It made no difference - the bastard had got away. He could give chase, but Erin was more important.

Doing what he was about to do risked everything. He couldn't remember the last time he'd done this – if ever. This time, Erin was in too much of a state to go to Solenzo's, so there was no choice.

Retrieving his phone, Leo dialled 999 and keeping hold of Erin's hand, waited.

THIRTY

IN A STATE OF SHOCK, Martin followed Tiger's instructions. He abandoned his post outside the penthouse complex the second the van arrived containing the men from the canning works sent to take his place.

These men were armed - he wasn't. Martin's job was to be 'eyes only' and now the alert had sounded that Marco had moved - or ordered a move to be made, men with knowledge and weapons were required.

Martin couldn't say he was sorry to step down from watching that cursed penthouse, but the day that was already bad had now ramped up to a hideous level.

From what he could gather from the vague and rushed phone conversation he'd had with Tiger, Marco hadn't just ordered a move – he'd pulled one off. And Erin had been hurt in the process.

Parking down the road from the house in Dalston, he yanked on the handbrake. Skye had been injured this morning too - he'd seen the state of her eye. He had no idea who had done it or where she'd gone since. Nor did he know how badly Erin was hurt or what had happened. All he knew was that he'd been told to return here and await further information.

And as if things weren't stressful enough, his bloody mother had called six times. He hadn't answered any of the calls - there was too much swarming around his head to take on anything else.

Hurrying along the pavement, glancing over his shoulder repeatedly in case he was being followed, Martin pulled the house keys from his pocket. He didn't want to do this anymore. And as much as it pained him, he didn't think he wanted to be with Skye any longer either - not now he knew she was lying. *Again...*

But he could hardly disappear now. Not after what had just happened. It didn't stop him feeling like a sitting duck though...

Shoving the key in the lock, Martin fumbled to open the door and hastily shut it behind him. Standing in the hallway, he was halfway through releasing the pent-up stress he'd held whilst scurrying from the van to the house, when he stiffened at the noise coming from the sitting room. He could hear a faint mumbling.

Cold sweat broke out. *Who was in there? And... and was that sobbing?*

With a shaking hand, Martin grabbed the baseball bat from the umbrella stand and inched towards the sitting room. *It didn't sound like Skye.*

Taking a deep breath, he raised the bat and kicked open the door, jolting back as he was assailed by a loud scream. It was only then did he realise who the scream came from.

Shirley Wilson.

'What the…?'

'Martin!' Fiona lurched from the other side of the room. 'Thank God you're here! The woman who lives here ran away after I told her the truth about your "friend", Zane.' Grabbing his hand, she tugged him into the centre of the room. 'We have to go! You're leaving London. It's not safe. I've packed your stuff.'

Martin dropped the baseball bat onto the carpet where it rolled, coming to rest underneath the window. His mouth opened and then shut. *Leaving London? Packed bags?*

His gaze moved to the pile of holdalls stacked against the wall - *his* holdalls. He then looked at Shirley muttering and rocking backwards and forwards on the armchair, her face covered in cuts, scratches and bruises. 'W-What's happened to...' He blindly gestured to Shirley. 'Why are you here, Mum?' He turned to Fiona, his face a mask of confusion. 'You said you wouldn't come here. You said you'd never...'

'That was before I knew the truth about these people,' Fiona snapped.

'But...'

'I'm not going into details about it now, Martin.' Fiona shot a wary glance in Shirley's direction. 'I'll explain more once we're out of here. Now, hurry and grab your things. Everything's ready, so you just need to...'

'I'm not leaving.' The tone and conviction in Martin's voice shocked everyone, including himself.

Fiona controlled her surprise and folded her arms. 'Martin, you *are* leaving. It's not safe here. As I said, I'll explain everything wh…'

'I'm not leaving,' Martin repeated, equally as loudly as the first time, but perhaps with further conviction. 'I'm not leaving London.' He wanted to, Christ, he wanted to, but not now - not with everything.

'If you're concerned about Skye, then...'

'I'm *not* leaving, Mum!' Martin snatched his arm out of Fiona's grip. 'Erin's been in an accident and...'

'An accident?' Fiona cried. 'How could she have been in an accident when she was here not an hour ago!' She reached for Martin's arm again. 'Don't you see? This is their control tactics. It's lies to keep you in their clutches and...'

'Erin's badly hurt,' Martin said, his eyes cold. 'And I can assure you that it's not "lies"! She was attacked around here after leaving this house.' He wouldn't give any more details now even if he had them. His mother couldn't come here like this and start laying down the law. She'd promised that she'd never do this, yet here she was.

As much as he wanted to get away from what had fast become an utterly fucked up state of affairs and whatever relationship he thought he'd had with Skye could be nothing but over, he couldn't leave. Not yet.

Seeing Fiona's confusion, Martin continued. 'I'm not coming back home. I need to stay here. Erin's been good to me. They *all* have, despite what you may believe, so I'm not disappearing on them now.' He folded his arms. 'You shouldn't have packed my things and neither should you be here. Please go. Things are difficult enough.'

That was an understatement. Because as well as what had happened to Erin and what that may or may not mean, he had to let Zane know that Skye had been to the penthouse. And that she'd been there more than once.

Until he'd done so, plus got the answers to his *own* questions, he was going nowhere and his mother would just have to accept that.

• • • •

BEFORE THE AMBULANCE arrived and possibly the police, Leo knew he was on borrowed time and had to act fast. 'I'll be as quick as I can,' he whispered, stroking Erin's hair.

Risking sticking his head out of the back doors onto the street outside, he was relieved to see the place still deserted, short of a couple of young lads eyeing him suspiciously as they leant against the railings in front of a block of flats opposite.

The flats weren't high rise and the vans blocked out most of the view, so he should be okay with what he was about to do. Either way, he was doing it.

'Fuck off, yeah? Nothing to see here,' Leo growled, giving the two lads a flash of the gun that had let him down so badly. They weren't to know the fucking thing was now as much use as a chocolate fireguard, were they?

The hooded youths, who had been maintaining their persona of hard cases, didn't need telling twice and hastily scuttled off down the towpath under the bridge.

Leo would have chuckled had this situation been any other, but *this* was about as non-amusing as it got.

Having no choice but to leave Erin unattended, he set about dragging the large man with the broken neck out of the van. With a grunt, he heaved the heavy weight onto his shoulder and tipped him over the buckled railings his own van was embedded in, into the canal.

He waited for the body to sink under the murky water. It seemed to take forever and every second that ticked by meant more chance of someone spotting him.

Leo wiped the slick sheen of sweat from his face and turned to face the van Erin remained in.

Clambering back inside, he gingerly lifted her from the floor and edging as smoothly as possible out of the door, laid her on the road next to his van. He knew it was unwise moving anyone with a head injury, but he still had to ditch the van with the ginger bloke in it.

His head turned in the direction of the sirens which were gradually getting louder. *He had little time.*

Praying he hadn't made Erin's injuries worse, Leo raced back to the rogue Transit and stared at the mess in the cab and the remains of the ginger man's head.

Shit! He couldn't lob this body into the canal. It would leave too much of a mess on the road just getting the fucker into the water. Furthermore, even with the corpse gone, how would he explain the blood-soaked interior of the wreck or the flesh and gore peppering the driver's cab?

There was only one thing for it.

Yanking open the driver's door and trying not to meet the vacant gaze staring at him, Leo leant over the corpse. Gritting his teeth, he stuck his hand in the man's pocket and rummaged around. Everyone had a mobile these days and this prick's phone might have numbers or info on it which could give further intel on Marco's next move - that's if this was down to Marco.

Which seemed likely.

Leo's fingers closed around the plastic casing of a phone-shaped object and with relief, he extracted the mobile and stashed it in his own pocket.

It was only then that he released the handbrake.

Using the open door as a means of a grip, he ploughed his shoulder and the rest of his immense strength into shunting the Transit backwards. 'Come on!' he roared, his muscles screaming in protest. He'd ache like fuck tomorrow after this.

'Fucking move!' he yelled, sweat soaking the front of his T-shirt. Feeling the van shift, he surged forward. With one eye on Erin, still unconscious but breathing, he bounced the van nearer to the water's edge and prayed this thing and its grim contents would go over before the approaching sirens reached their destination.

Releasing his grip of the door at the last second, Leo clung to the railings, every fibre in his body burning as the Transit tipped nose first into the canal.

'Go on!' he hissed, hoping the back wheels didn't catch after the front had cleared. They didn't. The front hit the water first with a surprisingly quiet splosh and the rest followed.

Front heavy, the nose went down quickly. The door being open helped the van to fill with water. It was still taking too long, but he'd done all he could.

Except *this.*

Snatching a large, pointed stone from the bank, Leo knelt down next to his front tyre. He pulled out his flick knife and drove the blade into the wall of the rubber and as the air escaped, he used the stone to make the slash less neat.

Chucking the stone into the water, he raced back to Erin, dropped to his knees on the pavement and took her lifeless hand in his. 'The ambulance is almost here. I'll tell them I lost control and hit the railings. You hit your head on my dashboard, okay?'

He didn't know why he was saying this - it was unlikely she could hear him, but speaking the story out loud helped him get what he needed to remember straight in his own head.

He'd take the flak for the accident. It was the best thing to do. Punctured tyre equalled lost control. *Easy.*

Leo glanced towards the canal. His Transit was the only vehicle now remaining and it was just him and Erin on the scene. If the authorities had no reason to suspect anyone else was involved that was just fine by him.

• • • •

ZANE PARKED his bike as close as possible to the entrance of the hospital. He'd have ridden it straight through the fucking doors if it was half-possible, but this was close enough.

He slung his helmet on the handlebars, not bothering to secure it. Everything could get nicked if it meant he got inside quicker to find out whether Erin would live.

Racing across the tarmac, his heart thundered in his chest. *Please let her live*, he repeated to himself. *Please.*

Why had Erin left the house in the first place? More to the point, why the fuck hadn't he answered his mobile when she'd called? She'd called several times and he'd ignored every one.

Why?

Because he was busy with the Delgados, that's why. Regaining his status in this city and rubbing Marco's face in that fact was more important than anything else - more important than the woman he loved - more important than *everyone.*

It wasn't, but that's how it felt. It felt very much like that at this precise moment.

And nothing changed that he'd ignored Erin's calls. He should have answered them. Better still, he should have been with her - or at the very least, ensured someone was with her at all times, like he'd insisted upon not so long ago. He should have done the same for Skye too. But it was too late now.

Bile bubbled at the back of Zane's throat. He should never have allowed either of them freedom. Even though Marco had no clout, no men and nowhere to move, he should have presumed *nothing*. He'd misjudged everything and Marco had got to him regardless. Erin was right all along – it was unsafe to revert to normal.

Zane loped up the stairs and barged through the hospital's double entrance doors. Leo would be around somewhere, but where?

Leo's update that Erin was being blue-lighted to hospital that Zane had received on route to Dunston Road was vague. Where in the fucking hospital had they taken her? It was a big place.

Zane darted across the reception area, his head twisting in one direction and then the other. *Where should he go? A & E? Intensive Care? Where? Fucking where?*

Deciding it would take longer asking the staff on the desks than searching himself, Zane sprinted off. He had no time to waste. He had the right to know whether Erin was okay.

Leo not embellishing on Erin's condition, only that she wasn't in a good way, did not fill him with enthusiasm.

'Get out of my way,' he snarled, pushing through another set of doors only to be met by an equally stark, endless corridor. Sweating, he stopped and looked in both directions, suddenly at a loss what to do or where to go. Only that he was wasting time he did not have.

'Mate!'

Hearing Leo's familiar voice, Zane span around with relief and rushed over, his eyes betraying the fear he usually hid so well. 'Where is she? Erin - where is she?'

'They're with her now.' Leo steered Zane into a side room. 'They said to wait in here.'

'Why?' Zane resisted going inside the room. 'Why do they want us to wait in here?' He grasped at his hair. 'This means it's bad. She's dead, isn't she? Erin's fucking dead and I...'

'Stop!' Leo planted Zane into a plastic chair. 'She's not dead. I've told you that they're with her right now.' He kept his hand on Zane's shoulder and stood in front of the chair in case Zane made an attempt to dash out of the room. The truth was that Leo didn't know for sure what was going on, but truly hoped Erin wasn't dead. She was still alive when they'd reached hospital, but anything could have happened since and he didn't want to comprehend how badly Zane would take it if she'd lost the fight.

He swallowed dryly. Erin hadn't looked good. Not good at all.

Pulling tortured air into his lungs, Zane fought to keep control of his spiralling panic as another thought pushed into his already overcrowded mind.

'What are you doing?' Leo cried seeing Zane rip his mobile from his pocket.

Bringing the screen to life, Zane was unable to believe that neither he nor anyone else had failed to get *this* covered. 'Fuck! Skye's not picking up.' *Had someone been sent to take her too? No, no, no!* 'Where's Tiger?'

'I sent him to oversee the men at the penthouse, he...'

'Fuck that!' Zane stabbed more digits of his phone. 'Tiger? Yeah, it's Zane... I don't know… We're still waiting for news. Look, I need you to do something... I wouldn't normally ask, but... I need you to guard Skye… Yeah, *Skye*... It's urgent. Whilst Marco or people working for him are on the loose she's an obvious target.'

The silence down the line sent Zane spiralling further. 'Listen - she's not answering her phone. I need you to head to the Starbright immediately. Guard her with your life! Yeah, that's right…'

Ending the call, Zane stared blankly at the wall. Asking Tiger for that was a tall order considering the position Skye had put him. But this... what had happened, transcended everything.

Leo watched Zane closely. Tiger would be less than happy to go on Skye's watch, but the man was good and would push his personal opinion aside for Zane like he always did.

'Maybe I should have asked Martin to go,' Zane muttered.

'No, it has to be Tiger. Martin hasn't got the nous,' Leo said firmly. 'Did Martin spot anything at the penthouse?'

'I've heard nothing, so as far as I know – no.' Zane looked

at the door in desperation. 'For God's sake! When will they tell me what's going on?' Jumping from his seat, he took Leo off guard. 'I'll find out myself.'

'No!' Leo grabbed Zane's arm. 'Don't interfere! Let them do their job.'

'Erin's everything to me!' Zane screamed. 'I need to know if she lives! I have the fucking right to know whe…'

The door to the small side room suddenly opened, cutting Zane off mid-rant.

A doctor entered, his scrubs covered in blood. He looked in trepidation at the two men facing each other off. 'Which one of you is with Erin Langley?'

Leo gestured to Zane. 'I came in with her, but it's Zane you need to speak to.'

'I'm Zane Morelli – Erin's fiancé,' Zane barked. 'Just tell me - is she alive?

Thirty One

PULLING UP OUTSIDE the Starbright, Tiger stared at the familiar driveway. It had been some time since he'd set eyes on this place and he'd intended for it to remain that way until the event which had almost cost him more than a front tooth faded into a distant memory.

The accusations and what had followed were still too close to the surface for comfort, but he had to do this. It was the right thing to do.

Right or not, he drew the line at parking on the driveway. He'd stay on the road and walk the short distance.

He wasn't looking forward to being in the same building as Skye Wilson, but whatever that girl had done, he wouldn't let her become the next target.

Erin being the first was bad enough.

Taking a deep breath, Tiger went to get out of his car when he spotted Skye's familiar figure hurrying down the driveway. Why hadn't the stupid girl picked up her phone? If she had, then she'd know that it wasn't safe for her to go walkabout.

He grabbed the door handle ready to dart out and tell her to go back inside immediately, but paused when a taxi drew up and Skye clambered in.

The taxi sped off before Tiger could react. Pulse racing, he turned the key in the ignition so hard it was a wonder it didn't snap. Slamming the motor into gear, he hacked the car around and sped after the cab. Keeping Skye in his sights was as good as guarding her. He'd see anything unusual or untoward happened and at that point, he'd step in.

Doing it this way for as long as possible was better than being alone with her after what she'd done. This way she could accuse him of nothing.

As he tailed the cab out of Dagenham, Tiger frowned. It looked like she was heading back into the city. She certainly wasn't going to Dalston…

Perhaps Leo or Zane had got a message to her after all and she was heading to the hospital? But surely he'd have been informed if Skye had been called away from the Starbright?

He sped up, grateful the traffic was moving quickly. Changing lanes, Tiger followed the taxi onto the East India Dock Road, his confusion growing. This confusion heightened as he followed onto the slip road and then headed right into Poplar.

The taxi took lefts and rights before eventually pulling over at the side of the road in a dubious looking street. Tiger parked further back and waited.

Skye was getting out of the taxi and heading into...

His dark eyebrows pulled his forehead into a crease. *The Black Bear?*

As the taxi drove away, Tiger jumped from his car and headed up the road. Whatever Skye was doing in the Black Bear, he didn't know but intended to find out.

• • • •

'BLOODY HELL, LOVE. Who gave you the shiner?'

Skye slapped a five-pound-note on the bar and glared at the barman. 'Just give me a glass of wine. I'm not in the mood for wisecracks.'

'Okay, okay, keep your hair on!' The barman picked one of

the cleaner glasses off the shelf. 'I didn't expect to see you back here so soon.'

'What are you? A stalker?' Skye snarled, turning away to glance around the pub's gloomy interior. There was no sign of Red and his band of idiots, but they'd best show up as instructed.

This day was going from bad to worse and she didn't need this pervo behind the bar attempting witty conversation on top of everything else. Despite this, she found herself self-consciously touching the bruised flesh around her eye. She'd thought she'd done a decent job of hiding this under concealer, but clearly she hadn't if this moron felt the need to comment.

The second her wine was deposited on the bar she snatched it up and studied the cloudy-looking glass. *Was that lipstick? Urgh.*

No doubt Alyson was at this very second, sipping from cut crystal and lounging on a balcony overlooking the Thames, whilst *she* was in this shitpit waiting for the three bloody monkeys.

Skye decided to risk taking her mobile off aeroplane mode. Putting it on that setting was a habit she'd deployed after hearing that having a signal meant she could be tracked.

She refreshed her messages in case Red had sent a pathetic excuse over his lateness, but there was nothing.

With building irritation, Skye glanced at her watch: 3.05. He should be here by now, the useless bastard. That bunch of twats had better not have forgotten.

Calling Red, it went straight to voicemail.

Ignoring her, was he?

Well, she wouldn't leave a voicemail, she'd just text him. *Again...*

Skye's nails clicked against the phone buttons as she tapped out a text:

`I'm here. Y r u nowhere to be seen?`

Pressing send, Skye reached for her glass, interrupted by her phone buzzing.

That was quick, she thought, already simmering over the excuse she expected to see as to why she was standing in this dump waiting.

[Leo]

There's been an accident. Erin in hospital.

Stay at the Starbright. Tiger on way.

Skye frowned. *Was Erin dead?* That would save the hassle of further organising it herself. She then fleetingly wondered if Zane had also been involved in the accident but dismissed it. Leo would have said if that was the case. In some regards, it was unfortunate that Zane hadn't been tragically killed, but then that would ruin the big reveal Marco had in store.

Worry then flickered. After Marco's earlier behaviour she wasn't sure whether she was still involved in his plans. She'd have to calm the waters there.

Hang on!

Dread lurched along Skye's spine. *Tiger was on his way to the Starbright? For her?*

Shit! If he got there to find her missing it would send the cat amongst the pigeons. The last thing she wanted was *him* having a valid reason to pull her up over something - she was well aware he despised her.

Necking the glass of tepid wine, Skye took a further glance around the Black Bear, double checking that Red and his troupe of tossers hadn't snuck in without her noticing.

Fuck it, she'd have to return to the Starbright straight away. She tapped out a final text to Red.

Call me to rearrange

URGENTLY

Ignoring the barman's ever watchful eyes, Skye snatched

up her handbag and stalked through the pub, dialling the Starbright number as she went. 'Hi, yeah, it's Skye,' she said to the receptionist. 'I've been delayed at the bank. The bloody queues here have been dreadful, so if Zane or any of his men show up looking for me, tell them I'm fine and will be back as soon as I can. Yes, okay… Thanks. Bye.'

Shoving the mobile back in her bag, Skye should have looked where she was going. Slamming into someone she looked up. 'Sorry! I...'

'This is a strange bank, wouldn't you say?' Tiger blocked Skye's path and waited to see what her reaction would be on getting caught red-handed.

• • • •

ZANE'S EYES STRAYED back to Erin, pale-faced on the bed. The only sound, short of his own breathing which sounded unnaturally loud in the silence of the small, private room, was the bleeping monitors signifying the heart of the woman he loved remained beating.

This was good, but as for the rest of it and what made Erin, *Erin*, was absent.

He raked his fingers through his hair, the concept of Erin remaining a shell like she was at this precise moment, terrifying. Would she recover? Would she heal from the head injuries she'd sustained?

No one knew for certain. Not yet. But from what the doctor said, Erin had been sedated in order to give her body the best fighting chance to heal and they'd know more shortly.

His hands clenched into fists. Knowing more 'shortly' wasn't good enough. He wanted to know now. He *had* to know now. Waiting even one second longer to know if Erin would return to him as he knew her and not be left damaged or a different person, was unbearable.

But like it or not, wait was all he could do. *Wait, wait and fucking wait.*

Telling himself that she was alive and that was the main

thing, was wearing thin. Yes, of course he was glad she was alive, but he wanted to know for how long and in what state.

'Head injuries', the doctor said. *'Perhaps serious...'*. Yet there was no means of knowing for definite *how* serious until the scan results came back and the sedation was lifted.

Erin had already undergone several tests before he'd reached the hospital. She'd had others since - blood and other stuff he didn't understand. Those results would offer more indication of the situation.

Zane's rage continued bubbling just under the surface at a dangerously high level. How could he sit here for an indefinite period not knowing the outcome?

All of the things he'd worked for; strived to put right; fought to recapture, paled into insignificance. Apart from one...

Marco.

The sinews in Zane's neck jutted out as his teeth ground together. Marco had sanctioned this further attempt on Erin's life. How could it have been missed that he'd got people back doing his bidding? Marco had been covered from all angles.

The celebrations Zane had planned to have with Erin over the coke deal and Sandler's demise now seemed paltry and arranged a thousand years ago. And that Skye could be next on the hit list turned his blood to sludge.

But Leo said Skye was under Tiger's watch, so she was safe for now.

Gingerly reaching out to touch Erin's still hand, Zane pretended she wasn't lying lifeless at all - just asleep. If he blocked out the wires, the beeping monitors, the metal cage holding her head still and the bandage covering the gash on her forehead, she looked like she always did when sleeping: beautiful, serene and perfect.

His.

'Come back to me, you hear?' he murmured, concentrating so his voice did not crack and betray the tumult of emotions crashing within. 'We've got lot of plans to fulfil yet.'

Feeling a lump forming in his throat, Zane was glad for the

interruption of the door opening.

'There you go.' Leo placed a polystyrene cup of coffee in Zane's hand. 'Sorry I couldn't get anything stronger, but this was the lesser of the evils available in the vending machine.'

Zane nodded and sipped at the black liquid that classed as coffee on a different planet. His throat was so dry, he'd drink petrol at the moment and couldn't care less what was in the cup, providing it was wet.

Leo plonked himself down in the chair the other side of the room, his gaze moving to the figure in the bed. 'Any news in my absence?'

Zane shook his head. 'No, short of that last blood test you saw them take, there's been nothing.'

'She'll be okay,' Leo said, aware how lame it sounded. 'Erin's a fighter. She'll come through.' Out of everything, that was true. Erin Langley was the most determined chick he'd ever known, so if anyone could come back from this, *she* would.

He sipped at his own nasty looking coffee, stealing a glance at Zane from behind his cup. He wanted to ask if Zane blamed him for Erin lying in this bleak hospital bed. Whether it was right, wrong or indifferent, there was a large part which blamed himself.

Leo swallowed dryly. It was *him* who'd slammed into the side of that Transit. That it swerved into his path wasn't the point. It was still *him* behind the wheel of the vehicle ploughing into the one Erin was in. It was *him* who'd caused the impact. It was also *him* who'd moved her and could have worsened her injuries.

But he wouldn't ask. Doing that would be for his own absolution and Zane had enough on his plate without assuaging *his* guilt.

Feeling his phone vibrate, Leo slid it out of his pocket and glanced at the new message.

Tiger:

Am with Skye. We need to discuss this

Leo frowned. *Discuss? Discuss what?* Whatever it was would have to wait.

A short knock on the door prompted him to shove his phone back into his pocket and watch Zane sit up in anticipation as the doctor entered.

'You've got the test results?' Placing his coffee down, Zane scrambled to his feet. 'What are they? Will she be okay?'

The doctor motioned for Zane to sit back down. 'We've had the scans interpreted and although nothing is set in stone at this point, what we have seen looks encouraging.'

Zane exchanged glances with Leo. 'Wh-what does that mean? She's okay or not? Which?'

The doctor's neutral expression gave nothing away. 'There's a tiny degree of swelling on the brain, but...'

'Swelling?' Zane cried, his eyes darting to Erin. 'Fuck! Sorry, sorry, I meant that can't be good, can it?'

'Well, a certain amount of swelling isn't unusual after a sustained head injury. We'll monitor her closely over the next twenty-four hours and providing the swelling doesn't increase, it's less likely there will be any lasting damage.'

Zane's eyes brightened. 'That's good, then? She'll be okay?'

The doctor shook his head. 'It's far too early to say anything for definite. There's no brain bleed which is excellent, but we have to wait and see.'

'But what you're saying is that as it stands it's good news?' Leo added, hoping to steer Zane to think positive.

'At this point in time, yes,' the doctor confirmed.

'What about broken bones?' Zane asked. 'Are there any? And what about the other tests? Did you find anything?'

'No broken bones, Mr Morelli. Not on the preliminary X-rays, anyway.'

'Shouldn't you do further ones?' Zane pressed.

The doctor paused momentarily and studied Zane. 'We would normally do so, yes, but that's not advisable now.'

'Why not?' Zane felt a familiar flicker of anger. If they weren't giving Erin the best possible care he'd move her elsewhere. He'd throw all the money he had at them to ensure no stones were left unturned. Maybe he should move her to Solenzo's private practice? The place had always sorted his men out in the past.

But did Solenzo have the relevant equipment to deal with *this*?

'The reason we can't do further X-rays is because Miss Langley is pregnant. Now we know that, then non-vital X-rays are inadvisable.'

Zane blinked, unsure whether he'd heard correctly. 'Pregnant?' His eyes shot to Erin. 'She's *pregnant*?'

'The bloods we took earlier have shown that to be the case, yes.' A smile appeared on the doctor's stressed face. 'I take it you were not aware? Miss Langley isn't far along – a few weeks at most, but I can assure you that the baby is perfectly fine. So, congratulations, Mr Morelli and remember - no matter the darkness of a situation there is always a chink of light.'

THIRTY TWO

IT FELT STRANGE rebuffing Skye when she barrelled into the house seeking refuge in Martin's arms. It was a natural reaction to comfort her, but he couldn't. He just *couldn't*.

After seeing her at the penthouse *twice*, yet she'd breathed not a word about it, so he didn't know what to think. Coming to a conclusion was not getting easier. If anything, since Erin had been hurt, it was harder.

Not to mention his mother and Shirley showing up.

He hadn't expected to see his mum on the doorstep and if he was honest, he felt betrayed. She'd given him her word that she'd never come here.

With Skye's attitude and his father treating him like a muppet, perhaps by now he should be used to feeling let down, but he'd never expected it from his mother. Maybe she didn't see it that way, but betrayed was how he felt.

Despite this, guilt raged for all but throwing his mum and Shirley out of the house. It wasn't how he'd usually dream of doing things, but what else could he do? The way his mother was acting there was no choice. Her ranting about being around Zane, Erin and things being 'unsafe' underlined that Shirley had achieved the unthinkable. His mother had taken those mad ramblings over *his* word. And it hurt.

Martin's face fell. To think only a few days ago he'd believed his life was going in the right direction. He'd got Skye; he'd had Zane and Erin's approval and respect. Even his mother had accepted his decision not to take up the coveted place at St Andrew's University. She'd also supported his wish to marry Skye.

But that was before. What did he have now? A woman with a track record of lying to him and who was still doing so; a mother who went back on her word and betrayed him and, if he didn't remain with Skye, he'd no longer be part of Erin and Zane's life. *That's if Erin even had a life...*

That thought alone upset Martin more than he thought possible, but there was only so long he could sit here saying and doing nothing.

He watched Skye sobbing pitifully and then looked at Tiger who, as always, had a face chiselled from granite. That this man was here at all after what Skye had done meant things were more serious than his worst-case scenario.

Martin cleared his throat. 'I take it there's still no news about Erin?'

Tiger's head didn't move but his eyes swivelled in Martin's direction. 'I suspect we'll get an update shortly.'

'I can't believe this has happened!' Skye exclaimed, looking every inch like the devastated stepdaughter she tried so hard to be. 'Since starting again, me and Erin have got on so well and... Oh, God! Just thinking about anything happening to her is terrible!'

Yeah, right...

She waited for Martin to offer consolation, either physically or via soothing words, but there was nothing forthcoming.

Her brain ticked over silently. Something had been wrong with Martin for the past couple of days but she didn't know what it was. And that, she didn't like.

Martin was normally so transparent and malleable it was easy to convince him of anything. That's why she'd picked him in the first place! Admittedly, it had been a sickeningly long road of putting up with his fawning and boring words of love and endearment. Pretending it was mutual was especially irritating. Over a bloody year she'd shouldered that burden but she was now on the home straight and would allow nothing to stop that - not even Marco whacking her. That part was a blip. He didn't mean it.

Talking of which, neither Martin or Tiger had commented on her swollen eye. Even that dork in the Black Bear spotted it, so why hadn't either of these two?

Raising her head from the suitably bowed position which offered a break from retaining an expression of angst, Skye plastered grief back into place. It was hard pretending to give a shit about Erin and her face ached from holding the pseudo-concern. Why couldn't the stupid bitch have just died on impact, rather than dragging it out?

That attention seeking cow would do anything to cause aggro. Even putting herself in a coma...

All Skye knew was that she'd gladly shake the hand of whoever had crashed into the van. Pity they hadn't done a thorough job.

Talking of which, Red still hadn't texted back. Why hadn't he let her know they'd succeeded in nailing Erin? It had to be them behind it. That was what she'd instructed, after all.

A wisp of guilt flickered somewhere inside Skye's head. She'd been balling Red out for his lateness, when in reality he'd been busy following her orders.

Maybe his phone got damaged in the crash and that's why he hadn't contacted her? That didn't explain why the other two morons hadn't been in touch though.

Sniffing loudly again for effect, Skye decided to utilise the opportunity to vent a little of her faux distress on Tiger. The overgrown prick had nothing on her - even if he *thought* he did. Being as he despised her, she had nothing to lose, plus it would pass a bit of time pretending to wait for news.

'Can no one see how upset I am?' she snapped. 'It doesn't

help when it seems someone is trying to accuse me of things again.' She cleverly hid her sneer behind the hand covering her face, ensuring it trembled just the right amount.

'Accused?' Martin looked up. 'What do you mean? Who's accusing you?'

Skye swallowed her smugness. *Ah, so Martin did care. She shouldn't have doubted his stupidness, the fool. She still had him by the balls.* 'Oh, Tiger can explain, being as he's the one who doesn't trust me. It hurts, you know? Really hurts. I've already apologised for what I said before.' She forced a lone tear from one eye. 'You can't punish me forever, Tiger.'

Tiger's face remained blank. The conniving little bitch was playing games, but he wouldn't rise to it. He knew what she was doing – she'd been the same since he'd caught her in the pub. Instead of explaining herself, she'd flounced off pretending Erin's injuries were more important.

That was okay, he'd wait. Let her dig her own hole. Because there *was* a hole and he looked forward to witnessing her falling into it.

'With what's happened to Erin, things are upsetting enough,' Skye whined. 'Plus, I've already had my own share of unfortunate incidents today to deal with.' She gestured to her darkened swollen eye and paused to see if anyone commented. No one did. *Again...*

'It's late,' Tiger muttered, his gravelly voice taking a distinctly sharp tone. 'Perhaps you should go and get some rest. I'll remain here and wait.' He met eyes with Skye, catching the undercurrent of poison behind her contradictory long-lashed baby blue orbs that at first glance looked beguiling to the uninitiated.

He knew better. As did Leo. But he'd got this venomous little mare over a barrel and if she even *thought* about protesting it would only serve to uncover her as the devious cow that most of them had already worked her out to be.

Kicking off further about his comment, which on the surface had her best interests at heart, would make her out to be unreasonable. He knew full well that Skye relied on depicting herself as the polar opposite, but he needed her out of the room. Sharing the same air and breathing what had previously passed through her lungs made him sick to the core.

Tiger had already broken his own protocol not once but *twice* today: firstly, by agreeing to guard Skye and secondly by driving her back to the house - just him and her. But it was worth it. She might be remaining schtum for now about her presence at the pub, but she'd have to explain herself when Zane returned. Erin's accident or not, Tiger wasn't letting this one go. Skye Wilson was doing something behind their backs and this time she'd be held accountable.

Internally scowling, realising that she couldn't argue without looking like a spoilt bitch, Skye was working out how she could ramp up the bleeding-heart routine further, when everyone froze hearing the front door open.

THIRTY THREE

'THAT'S GREAT NEWS!' Tiger said, a genuine smile breaking on his face for the first in what seemed like months. 'Really promising.'

'Yes it is, I'm so pleased!' Skye gushed. 'I've been going out of my mind with worry. I was told to go to bed.' She glared pointedly at Tiger. 'But I'm glad I didn't because I'd have missed this wonderful news.' Throwing herself against Zane, she wrapped her arms around his waist for the third time since he and Leo returned to the house.

'Erin's still sedated and hasn't yet regained consciousness, but the doctor thinks she'll be okay.' Noticing the blackening swelling around Skye's eye, Zane gently extracted himself from her. 'What the fuck happened there?'

'Wh…? Oh, that's nothing.' Skye self-consciously touched the sore area on her face.

'It isn't *nothing*! Who did that do you?' Zane barked.

'No really!' Skye cried. 'A door rebounded on me. It was my own fault. I wasn't paying attention.' Based on Zane's immediate reaction, using the door excuse rather than a mugging seemed the sensible choice.

Zane studied Skye. 'Are you sure about that?'

'Absolutely!' Skye laughed. 'Don't you think I'd tell you otherwise? Now, come on. This isn't about me! I want to hear about Erin.'

Zane frowned. He'd usually push for more information but tonight he was distracted, stressed, relieved, ecstatic over the baby news and worried, all at the same time. 'Well, I...'

'Erin? She's all right?' Martin piped up, his relief visible. 'What happened? Who took her?'

'It appears Marco had people working for him after all,' Zane's voice was filled with audible rage. 'I don't know how that was missed...'

Martin fidgeted uncomfortably. 'I-I saw no men entering or leaving the penthouse. I...' *And he hadn't. Only Skye...*

'Well, Marco *did* have men and from what we can gather, they snatched Erin from outside here,' Leo said grimly.

'Here?' Skye squeaked. *Top effort, Red! He'd done something right for once.* 'W-Who are these people and where are they now? Are we in danger?'

'We've no idea who they were,' Zane admitted. 'But thanks to Leo, two of them are dead.'

'Unfortunately, one got away after I hit the van and my gun jammed. But the one that escaped was a lanky streak of piss who looked like he'd shit himself, so I don't think we should feel threatened by him. However, that doesn't mean that there aren't others…'

'*You* caused the accident?' Skye's eyes widened. 'Oh no, Leo! You must feel dreadful for injuring Erin so badly.' She ignored the heavy silence descending at her accusing words. It was a convenient deflection tactic to hide the shock that two out of the three men she'd instructed were no more. How could she complete her plan now? Sure, Erin might die without further intervention which was good, but Alyson wouldn't and that had been their next task. This was bloody inconvenient.

Zane clocked Leo's desolation. 'It was no one's fault. The van had to be stopped and this was the only way.'

Turning to hide his pain, Leo moved to the sideboard and

poured Zane and Tiger a large whisky before helping himself to one. *Skye and Martin could get their bloody own.*

'Anyway…' Zane steered the conversation back to Erin. 'A further scan result arrived when we were with the doctor and, yes, it looks like everything will be fine. We'll know for definite over the next day or two.'

'But there *is* a chance that she might not be fine?' Skye added, ignoring the daggers Leo and Tiger shot in her direction. 'I mean, I'm sure she will be but... but isn't it best not to assume until you know for definite?'

Leo bit his tongue to prevent from screaming what a vicious little bitch this one was. 'The doctor is confident of Erin's recovery.'

'I've been so upset!' Skye continued, revelling in the attention of the room. 'I've been *so* worried. I was only just saying that I couldn't cope if Erin died now we're getting on so well.'

'Erin is *not* going to die! She's a fighter!' Leo said, sensing the renewed fear rolling off Zane in waves. He'd been positive on the way back from the hospital, but now this vindictive little cow had purposefully wiped that out with one flick of her tongue.

'You know,' Skye continued, determined to achieve maximum damage. 'I would have come to the hospital myself, but I had no idea about any of it until the last minute.' She grasped Zane's hand. 'My phone must have been out of signal or I was deliberately not told. *Some* people are hell bent on excluding me...' She then faced Tiger, her eyes filling with tears. 'Like I said, I know I've caused problems in the past for you, Tiger, and I'm trying to make up for that. You really don't need to continue accusing me of causing more problems, especially at times when families should stick together.'

Zane bristled, his worry replaced with wariness. He looked suspiciously between Tiger and Skye. 'What's the problem now?'

'H-He's been making me out to be a bad person again,'

Skye sniffed. 'But it's not true.'

'What's not fucking true?' Zane barked. 'Will somebody tell me what's going on?'

Sighing, Tiger got to his feet. 'Contrary to what Skye believes, I wasn't planning on mentioning this tonight, but now she's made a big deal I've little choice.'

Clocking Skye's snide expression, Leo also got to his feet. 'This really isn't a good time to...'

'When I reached the Starbright, Skye was getting into a taxi.' Tiger folded his arms, determined not be beaten by this malicious little girl for the second time.

'Skye?' Zane frowned. 'Why were you getting in a taxi? You know the rules.'

'I...'

'I wasn't in time to stop the cab, so I followed, knowing I could react quickly enough if I had to, but I was surprised to see her getting out of the taxi and going into the Black Bear in Poplar.'

Zane paused, his lighter an inch away from his unlit cigarette. '*Poplar*?'

Skye blinked, her mouth opening but Tiger continued before she could speak.

'I went in after her. She was at the bar waiting for someone who didn't arrive. Then I heard her call the Starbright saying that if anyone asked, she was stuck at the bank...'

Creeping dread gathered inside Zane, his foreboding amplifying things to a degree that he couldn't explain. 'Who were you meeting, Skye?'

'Why does everyone assume I'm doing something I shouldn't be?' Skye's bottom lip pulled into a childish pout. 'Every time it's the same and...'

'Why lie about being at the bank when you weren't?' Zane's eyes narrowed. 'I don't need more shit, Skye! Don't you realise we've got enough to deal with without translating what you may or may not be doing?'

'If you must know, I went to meet Alyson - my friend from

back home,' Skye said, her voice small.

'Alyson?'

'Yes Alyson. Martin knows Alyson, don't you, Martin? Alyson Read. I haven't seen her for ages! When said she was in London I went to meet her, but she didn't show up. I hope she's all right.' Skye wiped away non-existent tears. 'I-I didn't say anything about it beforehand. Being as it was over in Poplar, I knew you'd worry or not let me go, but nothing happened to me. I'm fine.'

'Oh, right!' Tiger sneered. 'Alyson? You expect us to believe that?'

'How many more times do I have to apologise for what I said about you, Tiger?' Skye wailed, getting out of the chair. 'I'm sorry, okay? It doesn't mean I'm lying about everything else.' She glanced at Martin. *Why wasn't he offering moral support against this onslaught? He knew Alyson, so why didn't he tell them?*

Zane flapped his hand. 'Okay, okay, calm down. You should have just said. Surely you can understand why it doesn't look good?'

Skye nodded contritely, internally beaming that Zane was buying it. She knew he would.

Her happiness remained until Martin opened his gob…

'There's something else...' Martin piping up again surprised everyone. 'If you went to meet Alyson at that pub in Poplar, Skye, then why did you not go to the penthouse again being as you've already been twice in the last two days?'

Skye swung in Martin's direction. 'Th-the penthouse?' *Martin had seen her go into the penthouse? Oh shit. Quickly, think of something!*

'Hold on a fucking minute!' Zane roared, turning to Martin. 'You saw my daughter at the fucking *penthouse* and didn't think to mention it?'

'Why have you been following me, Martin?' Skye screeched, throwing her hands in the air. 'Does no one trust me?'

No, we don't, Tiger thought, barely able to wait to hear what excuses this little cow would think up now. *They had her bang to rights, the liar!*

'Martin wasn't following you...' Zane put his head in his hands and sighed loudly, partly out of desperation and partly from disbelief. 'I sent him there. He's been watching the place for me.'

'For… for *you*? But why?' Skye spluttered. *Fuck, fuck, fuck!*

'Because my brother is in that complex, that's why!' Zane cried. 'Jesus, Skye! *Anything* could have happened to you!'

'Hang on. Why were you going to the penthouse in the first place?' Leo frowned.

'Because...' Skye faltered. *Shit!* 'Because Alyson was there. She's been at her Uncle John's since yesterday. He has an apartment. She was going home today, hence why we arranged to meet in that pub to say goodbye. I... I didn't realise Marco lived at the same place!' she cried aghast. *This was brilliant. They were buying it, look at them.* 'I'd have never gone there had I known. Why did you lie to me, Martin? You said you worked in a garage! Why didn't you say something about those apartments to warn me?'

Collapsing into the chair, she ramped up her pitiful angst with a fresh round of loud sobs. 'No one trust me. No one! My mother was right. I'm a useless bitch. And now, along with everything else I've done to let you all down, I'm proving everybody right! Even my boyfriend would prefer me to be in danger!'

Ramping her whole body shaking up a notch, Skye threw in a couple of dry heaves for good measure. 'It will never change. I'll never be trusted and I've only got myself to blame.' She chanced a peep through her fingers to see if she was having any effect. 'I should have killed myself like I planned last year when I discovered Zane abandoned me!'

Zane tensed, the guilt that his daughter had felt so desperately low and hopeless by his lack of presence to consider ending her life, fuelled further resentment toward Shirley for not telling him of the girl's existence. He'd already lost enough and may stand to lose even more if his fears were realised and the doctor's prognosis over Erin was wrong. That alone would kill him, but hearing Skye talk of suicide pushed him over the edge. He had to rectify this dreadful situation and give his daughter something to look forward to. She must realise how important she was.

Things had been difficult with Skye, granted, but despite admitting her resentment caused her erratic behaviour, everyone was still determined to trip her up. It had to stop. It *all* had to stop.

Getting up, Zane knelt on the floor in front of Skye and enveloped her in his arms. 'We *do* trust you,' he soothed. 'But I know it may come over as otherwise.' He flashed Tiger and Leo a look to keep their traps shut. 'Come on now. Calm down. I can't have you going off the rails on me.'

Tiger's hands curled into fists seeing Zane get played like a violin. *He was buying this act? Oh, come on!*

'You know how much help you've been with the Starbright,' Zane continued, allowing Skye to burrow her face into his chest. 'I can't imagine what we'd do without you. Both me and Erin love you very much, Skye. You must believe that because it's the truth.'

'B-But everyone thinks the w-worst of me all the time,' Skye hiccupped. 'It'll always be this way. Even Martin doesn't love or trust me anymore.'

As Skye unloaded a fresh round of sobs to soak the front of Zane's T-shirt, he glanced at Leo in desperation. Then his eyes fell to Tiger. From their stony expressions, he knew he would get no backup on this one. Even Martin didn't look like he would offer any words of support. He turned back to his daughter, her body wracked with sobs and knew he had to do something. *Anything*. 'Come on, look, you...'

'I can't do this!' Skye wailed. 'What's the point? I'll always be tarred with the same brush.'

'That's not true,' Zane muttered, thinking the opposite. It certainly did seem that way.

'There's no point! None!'

'Yes there is!' Zane cried, his heart breaking. 'There's always a point and especially now because you've got a big reason to believe just that.' He glanced again at the others. 'I wasn't going to mention this until I knew for certain that Erin will be okay, but...'

'Zane...' Leo's voice held a tone of warning, suspecting he knew exactly what was about to be revealed.

'W-what is it?' Removing her hands from over her face, Skye's eyes grew wide. 'Not more bad news. I can't bear it. Do you want me to leave? Is that it? I...'

'No, I don't want you to leave!' Zane pushed Skye back into the chair she'd begun to get out of. 'You leaving is the very last thing I want. You're so important to me.'

'Then what was it?'

'Okay, well, as I said, I planned to keep this under wraps until I knew for certain Erin will be okay, but you *do* have plenty to live for.' A wide smile broke across Zane's face. 'You're going to be a big sister!'

'What?' Skye's mouth fell open. 'Really?' Squealing, she jumped from the chair into Zane's arms. 'That's amazing news!' Burrowing her face into his chest, she could now afford to scowl. Erin been pregnant was supposed to be good news, was it?

It was *not* good news. It would take the edge off what was planned if Zane had a *real* child. It would soften the blow of discovering that *she* wasn't anything to do with him.

But, Skye thought, hope glimmering. Erin wasn't out of the woods yet. Even if she did recover, a lot could happen over the course of a pregnancy, couldn't it? Imagine how much more distressing it would be for Zane if Erin lost the baby she was carrying. And discovering the truth about *her* on top of it...

Feeling there could be light at the end of the tunnel, she hugged Zane tighter. 'I'm over the moon for you both! Things look different now you've told me this. Thank you.'

Because this gave her something even better to add into the mix.

Thirty Four

THE SPIRALLING WAVES of blissful fluidity which had become commonplace, ebbed and flowed through Alyson. It left her unable to do little more than gaze in rapture between the ceiling and the face of the man who had awakened her to a completely unknown world - a world which she couldn't fathom why she'd waited so long to become part of.

But she'd probably wonder about *all* of it, if only she could think lucidly for periods of more than five seconds before spinning back off down a tunnel to a place where nothing had meaning but meant *everything* at the same time.

She reached across the bed to splay her hand over the torso of the man who entranced her, finding comfort in the hard bunch of muscles under her fingertips.

Although delighted to discover that Marco wasn't a figment of her imagination or a strange side effect of the weird dreamlike state she'd spent almost the whole time in since walking into this place, occasionally confusion reared, like it did now.

She couldn't work it out. These past couple of days she'd lacked the ability to question anything - and that was odd in itself. Always a stickler for overanalysing, Skye said. Yet now it was too difficult.

Alyson frowned. Why was it difficult? What had changed?

Not that she was complaining. It was beautiful not being held back by her mind, yet something persisted in prodding an area inside which was impossible to focus on.

But wait! There was something...

That was it! *Skye.*

Alyson sat bolt upright.

Skye had been here! When? Yesterday?

No, it couldn't have been. It was months ago, surely? Not yesterday...?

Her teeth dug into her bottom lip. *Oh God, she couldn't think. Why couldn't she think?*

Shaking her head to clear the cloud-like fur surrounding her brain, she concentrated harder, fighting the pull of the spirals which had ebbed away enough during the night to function this morning.

She was certain Skye had been here, whenever that was and... and she'd been acting weird. Or was it *her* who'd been acting weird?

Alyson didn't know that either, but the memory pushed harder into her consciousness.

Feeling suddenly nervous, Alyson stole a glance at the man asleep next to her. Her immediate reaction to touch him was strong, like always, but she refrained.

That was it! After Skye arrived, Marco sent Alyson upstairs to wait and then…then she'd heard something...

Tensing as Marco slightly shifted, Alyson remained motionless. She'd gone upstairs to wait for Marco to join her and make her feel that special rush like he always did, when she'd been drawn back to the bedroom door by voices. At first the voices sounded like a choir of angels. It was only when the angels morphed into angry voices, did she realise it was *Marco* shouting. He'd been yelling at Skye about money. *His* money. And there had been something mentioned about Shirley...

Then he'd...

'Where is she?' Alyson cried before she could stop herself. 'Skye! Where is she?'

Marco awoke with a jolt. 'What?' he mumbled, his voice thick with sleep.

'Skye! She was here yesterday!' A wave of panic rushed through Alyson as she pulled the sheet around her naked body. 'Skye was here and you... you were arguing. You… you hit her!' *She remembered now. Why hadn't she done anything to help Skye? Why hadn't she reacted?*

'Hit her?' Marco propped himself up on his elbows, his face incredulous. 'What are you talking about?'

'You hit her!' Alyson said, wide-eyed. 'You knocked her to the floor. You...'

'You must be imaging things!' Marco laughed, his one hand reaching for something on the bedside table, the other for Alyson. 'Did you have a bad dream?' *What the fuck was this?* Alyson wasn't supposed to have seen anything. The girl had been sent upstairs. He couldn't have *her* going on off on one.

'I didn't dream it!' Alyson scrambled towards the edge of the bed. 'I saw you hit Skye. Is she still here? I need to make sure she's all right.'

Marco wrapped his big hand around Alyson's wrist and pulled her away from the edge of the bed towards him. 'Babe, you must be dreaming. I wouldn't do something like that. Think about it – you were up here. You can't see through walls!' As he pulled Alyson underneath him, he deftly slipped the needle into her thigh. 'Come here and let's start the day off beautifully.'

Alyson didn't notice the needle go in as she'd scooted across the satin sheet. 'But...'

Marco must be right. She *was* upstairs and couldn't see through walls. And why would Marco hit his own daughter? *It made no sense.* 'B-But you were shouting.'

Marco slipped his hand between Alyson's legs. 'Why would I shout? I love my daughter.' He traced a line of kisses between Alyson's breasts and down across her stomach, his fingers starting to work inside her. 'As for hitting her, well, that's just crazy!'

As the rush of what she'd begun to get used to spread through her body, Alyson bucked her hips. Coupled with Marco's fingers working their magic and his thumb circling *that* place, all thoughts disappeared back into the spiralling vortex. All worry vanished and all she could centre on was the floating sensation coursing through her veins.

Skye Wilson and what Alyson had seen or not seen evaporated, along with any rationality to question what just occurred to detach her body and mind from the human race.

Seeing Alyson's pupils fully dilate, Marco quit his loving approach and roughly pushed her legs up to her chest, driving himself deep.

This proved the silly bitch required top-ups of his gear during the night to keep her in the correct state. He couldn't have her questioning anything, the stupid tart.

Upping his pace, he glanced at the blinking red eye of the recording camera. He'd have to check to make sure it hadn't captured any of the shit Alyson spouted on tape, otherwise he'd have to edit it the fuck away.

Jesus Christ. This bitch had best not become difficult otherwise she was more trouble than she was worth. As for Skye, well, she knew which side her bread was buttered. The fucking slap he'd given her wouldn't kill her - just serve to remind her that he expected his instructions followed and if she failed, then she would pay.

That the police hadn't shown up here meant he was in the clear over the fuck up at the bank, which was good, but, Marco thought with a wry smile, Skye was far from stupid. If he knew his daughter at all, she'd be busy rectifying her mistake and getting the bloody money sorted right *now*.

She'd fall over herself to put things right. She knew she'd screwed up and made him cross. She wouldn't want that because like Alyson Read here, Skye was desperate to be in his life.

....

'IT'S HIM!' Shirley muttered. 'It has to be!'

Standing in front of the tea-making facilities, what there were of them in this dreadful hotel, Fiona kept her back turned to Shirley. All night again the woman had banged on about stuff that made no sense and these ramblings made even less sense because she'd embellished on nothing. And when questioned, she had no recollection of what she'd even said! The whole thing was driving Fiona mad.

Hitting the call button again, Fiona gritted her teeth hearing the same electronic voice '…unable to take your call at the moment…'

Martin couldn't ignore her forever. She had to make him see sense.

'We need to leave!' Shirley continued, the clothes she'd slept in overnight as crumpled as her face. 'He was behind it! They all were. There's no escape.'

'What are you talking about?' Fiona snapped, her patience right on the very edge. 'Who is "he"? You're making no sense!' *As usual...*

'The Morellis.' Shirley's voice was hoarse, like the name contained shards of glass which tore her throat. 'What happened to that woman... It wasn't an accident... It was *them*!'

'Oh, for God's sake! Why would it be them?' Fiona rolled her eyes. 'Erin is part of it! She knows *exactly* what her bloody boyfriend and his brother are like! She's one of them, so they're not going to harm one of their own! They might have succeeded in brainwashing my son, but they haven't brainwashed me!'

She wasn't falling for it. Like she'd said to Martin yesterday, this was part of the Morelli control tactics - the tactics that were clearly working.

The beginning of a lump formed in Fiona's throat. She'd never witnessed a time when Martin purposely ignored her calls, let alone would consider throwing her out of the house, yet that's what he'd done and it would take time to forget that.

But first and foremost, she needed to get sense into his head and she wouldn't leave London until she'd achieved that. All she had to do was think of a plausible excuse to remain here and keep Peter's interference at bay and then she'd...

'That woman didn't know what happened.'

Pulled from her thoughts, Fiona looked at Shirley. 'What?'

'She didn't know anything about it,' Shirley repeated. 'That Erin girl - she knew nothing about what they did to me, I could tell.'

'Rubbish!' Fiona scoffed. 'That woman is as guilty as the rest!'

'No!' Shirley's chins wobbled as she shook her head. 'Did you not see her face? She believed Skye was Zane's daughter. I watched when you questioned her and also when you told her who Skye's father *really* is. She didn't know, Fiona. She really didn't. Zane has been lying to her too.' Her hands started their usual wringing marathon. 'She ran out of the house yesterday because she was upset. It's *our* fault that she's been hurt. *They* must have been waiting.'

Fiona momentarily quelled her rage and discontent to think. It was true that Erin looked dumbfounded by what she'd said yesterday. Shocked and horrified. *Could there be truth in Shirley's theory?*

'Zane has lied to her all of this time,' Shirley spat. 'It's what he's like. What they're *all* like.' She heaved her bulky body off the bed. 'We have to leave. We can't stay in London. Accept that you've lost Martin to those bastards and...'

'I'll never accept that!' Fiona barked. 'And we're not leaving. Not until we've spoken to Zane Morelli.' And something was flickering at the back of Fiona's brain which she'd never considered an option and there was a small - *very* small chance that it could be relevant. It would certainly make more sense of what Martin had said about these people.

'We cannot stay. We need to leave and leave now!' Shirley raged, for once adamant and decisive. 'They'll kill us all and...'

'Is it possible that Zane doesn't know what his brother did?'

Fiona asked. 'Is it feasible that he *does* believe Skye is his daughter? Martin's always said that Zane is Skye's father. There was never any mention of the brother.'

'What? Of course not!' Shirley yelled. 'I've told you already. Zane set the whole thing up to find a reason not to marry me!'

Fiona said nothing in response. Yes, Shirley had said that and the whole sad story made sense until she'd thought if that *was* the case and Zane *was* behind it, then why would he go out of his way to get into contact with Shirley again? Why would Skye be living with him if he didn't believe her to be his daughter? And why would Martin say Zane was her father and a decent person deep down?

Looking at it now, none of it added up and Erin's reaction yesterday only added to the discrepancy.

'Have you not understood a word of what I've told you?' Shirley cried, frustrated. 'I don't understand why you're questioning this!'

'I do understand,' Fiona said quietly. But things *had* changed and she could well be correct on what had now inched into her mind over this ghastly business. One thing was certain though and that was she wouldn't be going anywhere until she knew for certain what was true. Whether Shirley liked it or not, that did mean a conversation with Zane Morelli.

• • • •

TOUCHING ERIN'S HAND, Zane's emotions were all over the shop. With her still sedated, all he could do was listen to the beeping machines and fester in his own thoughts which swung continually from one end of the scale to the other.

His relief that Erin's condition had not worsened during the scant hours of the night were offset by frustration finding her still in a state of suspended animation. All he wanted was proof she still inhabited the body that remained the same as always.

Well, not quite the same...

His eyes strayed to Erin's stomach. It was still flat with not a hint of his child growing inside, but according to the doctors, that child was definitely present. And as far as they could deduce, was healthy and unharmed.

But he had to know that Erin would fully recover and every minute with that knowledge hanging in the balance chipped away at his sanity.

On top of this came the out-of-control hatred for his brother for orchestrating this latest attack. It surpassed even the previous rage he'd felt. Then there was the latest nightmare with Skye.

All things combined whirled around Zane's head and he felt sick to the stomach with a mix of rage, worry and despair.

These ludicrous stress levels meant he'd barely uttered two words to Tiger so far today but was grateful of the man's company. There were many things outstanding which needed Tiger's presence - including overseeing the cutting of the huge cocaine haul underway at the canning works, but even so Zane was pleased Tiger had insisted accompanying him here. He needed the presence of one of his trusted men now more than ever. 'Thanks for being here, mate,' he muttered. 'I know there's lots to do.'

'Don't worry about that. Someone is overseeing the outstanding tasks at the canning works and they're good to get on with it.' Tiger shrugged. 'I'm more concerned about her.' He nodded to Erin's still figure. 'And *you.*'

Dropping Erin's hand, Zane clawed his fingers through his hair. He could sorely use a shower but couldn't justify spending a second longer than needs be away from Erin. 'I was hoping for news or that... that perhaps she'd be conscious.'

'They're taking her off sedation soon. Besides, no change is good news, but…'

Zane waited for Tiger to finish his sentence, but nothing else was forthcoming. 'I've known you long enough to know when there's something else you want to say, so what is it?' *He suspected he knew exactly what that was...*

'What you said to Skye...' Tiger's words trailed off.

'I know you don't believe I should have said anything and I guess Leo disagrees too, but I had to do something,' Zane sighed. 'She needs a reason to carry on. Believing we're suspicious of her all of the time must be difficult. I want that to stop. It's not how things should be.'

Tiger's mouth set into a thin line. There was good reason for suspicion, but there was no point revisiting that. The same way it would achieve nothing by pointing out to Zane that the devious little cow had played him again. 'I hope then that it was the right thing to do.'

Sitting back in the plastic chair, Zane folded his arms. 'Family is everything to me. I can't and won't lose anyone else. That applies to family that isn't blood too. To me, it's the same.'

Knowing this was Zane's way of giving a compliment, an unusual red hue coloured Tiger's cheeks. Zane was family to him too and that was precisely why he didn't appreciate that daughter of his taking liberties. But it was clear the subject should not be pushed and so he had no choice but the drop his doubts. 'We should get an update from the doctors soon,' he said, steering the subject onto safer topics.

'I was thinking that maybe we should move Erin to Solenzo's once she's regained consciousness. It might make more sense,' Zane said.

The private surgeon on Harley Street who had remained on the payroll since his father's time always took care of the firm's casualties. It was a safe and secure environment - away from prying eyes and Old Bill who might be digging around.

'I don't think there's any need.' Tiger frowned and glanced at Erin once again. 'She's not likely to say anything.'

'No, I know she wouldn't. Well, *she* wouldn't, but what... what if...' Zane paused, reluctant to voice the fear which still clamoured: what if Erin wasn't Erin anymore? It was *that* which bothered him the most - not that she might inadvertently speak to the police of things best kept quiet if she was no longer herself. He'd returned to prison if needs be, providing Erin fully recovered.

Tiger understood what was bothering Zane. 'I don't think moving her will be necessary. You heard what the quacks said – her prognosis is good. Plus, it's unlikely there will digging from the Old Bill.'

Zane nodded. 'It was good of Leo taking the flack for the accident. Telling the police last night that the tyre blew tallied with the damage to the van.' No reports had come in from the public. There had been no mention of anyone else at the scene, no whispers about gunfire and no sign of any other vehicles involved either. *And with that, no reason to dredge the canal.*

For now, at least, it was an open and shut case which gave Zane the opportunity to move. And that he would be doing as soon as he got the news about Erin that he was waiting for. 'You know I'll now be dealing with Marco.'

Tiger gave a subtle nod. *He'd expected as much.* 'When?'

'As soon as I know about...' He jerked his head in Erin's direction. 'The "right" time to finish my brother doesn't apply. Not anymore.'

Leaning over, Tiger laid one hand on Zane's shoulder. 'Then you should already know that whatever you decide, you have mine and Leo's backing.'

THIRTY FIVE

SKYE EYED MARTIN buttoning yet another call. 'Who was that?'

'No one,' Martin muttered, his misery and confusion no lighter this morning than it was last night. His mother calling over and over wasn't helping. The mixture of guilt about asking her to leave, along with the resentment of her breaking her promise sat like a lead weight in his gut. And then there was Skye…

Skye desperately wanted to glare at Martin. It took all of her power not to punch him in the face. That this grovelling piece of shit possessed the audacity to lie was a surprise and it caught her off guard. But no matter how sickening it was pretending to give a flying fuck what this slimy mummy's boy thought about *anything*, she had to hold things together until the finale.

And to do that, she had to lick arse, act contrite and agree with every one of these losers. The fake concern about that bitch in hospital was possibly choking her the most. But she'd do whatever she had to do in order to reach the end.

She continued watching Martin staring at his mobile with a face like a slapped arse and gritting her teeth, she dragged her 'little girl lost' look into place. 'You know, Marty, it's really hurtful that you didn't tell me you were working for Zane,' she pouted.

Martin placed his mobile down. 'Zane said work and life must be kept separate. He didn't want to worry you.' Unable to help it, he continued. 'But if you'd actually mentioned that you were going to the *last* place you should be anywhere near, then maybe I've have had no choice but to tell you!'

Skye's mouth fell open with Martin's ability to surprise her for the second time in twenty-four hours. *He was having a dig?* 'I wasn't aware I was expected to explain every second of my life in exchange for common courtesy!' she snapped, then immediately changed direction. *She couldn't lose her hold over Martin now.*

With expert precision, her eyes filled with tears. *She should get goddamn paid for this acting.* 'I-I wasn't lying to anyone!' she whined, her bottom lip trembling. 'I... I just didn't think it was important. Like I said last night, had I realised...' Forcing herself not to shudder with revulsion, she wrapped her arms around Martin's neck and pressed against him. 'I'm really sorry.'

Expecting Martin to fold like a pack of cards, apologise, beg forgiveness and tell her how much he loved her, Skye was sorely disappointed as he extracted himself from her embrace. *This was bad. She had to get him back on side.*

It was then that she noticed that the bedroom was unusually tidy. The mound of Martin's crap usually scattered everywhere was missing. 'Where are your things? Half of your stuff is gone!' She dropped onto the bed, making sure the angle was perfect to accentuate her damaged eye. 'Are you... *leaving* me? Is that why you're being so cold?'

If he was, that was brilliant! One thing to cross off the list without extra bloody work, plus it would buy sympathy from everyone else. But she had to at least *pretend* she was devastated. 'You're dumping me because I met up with my friend without telling you? Oh, I'm so stupid! So, so stupid. I mess everything up!'

Martin tensed. *Shit! He'd forgotten about his stuff.* He'd emptied two of the holdalls containing his belongings that his mother had taken it upon herself to pack, but when everyone had unexpectedly returned to the house, he hadn't time to sort the other ones.

He willed his eyes not to stray to the wardrobe where the remaining holdalls sat and instead concentrated on Skye's tearful figure.

His heart dragged with misery. Skye had lied about so many things and he was sure she was lying about *this* too. Despite her spiel last night and how she was acting now, the rose-tinted glasses where she was concerned had lost their colour.

He wanted to be wrong about this. *Really* wanted to be wrong, but until he had concrete proof that Skye was being truthful, doubt remained lodged inside him like a parasite.

It would be easier and less hurtful to brush his fears about her under the carpet, but wasn't that what he'd always done? That wasn't something he could do any longer for his or anyone else's sake. But until he'd uncovered the truth - whether it was what he wanted to hear or not, he couldn't let on about his doubts. 'I've just been tidying up because I know how much mess bothers you.'

Skye sniffed loudly. 'So, you're not leaving me?'

'Of course not.' Martin smiled weakly. *Not yet...* But it was becoming harder to hide his mistrust.

'But you seem so cold,' she sobbed. 'So unhappy.'

Martin sighed and picked up his mobile, relieved to see no further calls from his mother. 'It's been a difficult few days, that's all. I think everyone's worried about Erin.'

'Me especially!' Skye lied. 'But it's great news about the baby, so we should concentrate on that.' Now she knew Martin was still firmly under her thumb, *that* news was exactly what she *could* concentrate on. This nugget to accelerate and double Zane's grief-filled demise was the magic ticket to get her back into Marco's good books.

• • • •

'THANKS FOR THE LIFT.' Skye kept her voice cordial when really being in this car with Leo Holland was suffocating.

At least Martin's orders were to remain at the house. Her worst nightmare would be for him to be tasked to come to the Starbright and remain with her while she worked. Having to be nice to him all day would be unbearable. It would also be impossible to get in touch with Marco and tell him the latest news about Erin and her shitty baby.

But *this* wasn't much better.

Careful not to release the pent-up relief as the car pulled to a halt, Skye went to get out of the car, then stopped as Leo also opened his door. *Oh no, no way!* 'What are you doing?'

Leo's bull-like head swivelled in Skye's direction. 'Coming in there with you! What does it look like?'

'Watching me like a hawk is unnecessary. I'm perfectly here,' Skye cried. She'd get sod all done if *he* trailed her about like a bad smell.

Leo raised an eyebrow. 'Thing is, you don't exactly have a track record of staying put and your father needs to know you're not putting yourself in danger. Inadvertently or otherwise...'

Skye stared at Leo suspiciously. *He doubted her story?* She'd half-expected him to, but this wasn't good. 'I won't make the same mistake again,' she whined. 'Alyson's gone home now and even if she hadn't, now I know that psycho is in that building, you think I'd go anywhere near?' She opened her eyes wide. 'I can't believe I was in the same place as him! It freaks me out!'

Leo would have laughed if this girl didn't infuriate him so. 'Let's just get one thing straight,' he growled. 'Your innocent act might work on your dad, but it doesn't fool me. Whether I think you deserve it or not, I'm here to ensure nothing happens to you and that's what I'm doing whether you *or* I like it or not.'

Skye's eyes narrowed. *The patronising bastard.* She was looking forward to seeing his face, along with Zane's when the truth came out. Leo-bloody-Holland would feel a prize prat recalling the instances that he'd used the term 'your father' and 'dad' to explain why she was being treated like a prisoner. *Wrong man, dickhead!*

She smiled sweetly. It was best not to ruffle his feathers too much otherwise she'd be kept completely out of the picture. 'Okay, okay, if that's what needs to happen.' She clutched Leo's arm. 'But there's something that's worrying me. This man you said escaped from the van - the skinny one... Is he who everyone's worried about? Or does Marco have more men than we know about?'

Leo moved his arm, forcing Skye to drop her grip. 'You don't need to be concerned.'

'Then why am I being guarded?' Skye threw her hands up melodramatically. 'What you've just said makes no sense.'

'Okay, look – there could be others we're not aware of.'

Skye chewed her cheek. *There wasn't - she knew that much...* 'I can't bear being shadowed like this. It makes me nervous. It was so nice being free, but being a prisoner has started again. It will be like this forever at this rate! How will Erin cope being pregnant and not being able to go anywhere? What about scans and appointments? Has anyone thought of that?'

Leo frowned. 'As said, you don't need to be concerned. *Not that I suspect you are*, he thought acidly. 'Anyway, it's not for long because things are in hand.'

Skye's mouth fell open. 'You... you mean Marco... He'll be...'

'You don't need to know the details,' Leo growled. 'Just accept it will soon be over.'

'Oh!' Skye cried. 'That's a relief!'

Leo nodded brusquely. He wholeheartedly agreed with the plan to immediately move on Marco. The prick had gone too far, too many times and no further time could pass - not now they knew he was regrouping and had managed it *despite* the surveillance and safety nets in place. 'Come on, let's get inside.'

Skye kept the mask of grateful relief fixed in place as she obediently got of the car and allowed Leo's massive frame to shield her as she walked to the Starbright entrance, but inside, her mind was turning at 100 miles an hour.

Now it was a race to get a message to Marco. Erin and her bastard child were secondary in comparison to this. From what she'd just gathered, the plan to remove Marco might happen sooner than expected. The goal posts had shifted but the time Zane planned to strike was unknown. It could be any time. Even *today*.

Cold dread barrelled through her. She had to warn Marco, but she wasn't sure how to do that with this gorilla breathing down her neck.

• • • •

CUTTING THE CALL before the first ring finished, Martin contemplated setting his mobile to silent, but he couldn't when Zane or someone else might call.

He asked God once again to stop his mother from calling. It wasn't helping.

Sinking onto the bed, he picked his nails. He'd already chewed them to the quick so there was little left, but he had to deflect his all-consuming panic growing in both size and intensity.

Not knowing what else to do, he paced the room. He'd followed this same cycle in the hour since Skye left with Leo to go to the Starbright. There was a large part of him that wished he could have gone too - not to be with Skye, but for respite from the thoughts crowding his head which wouldn't leave him alone. On and on the questions swirled, the same doubts, the same fears, the guilt and the worry. Erin being a major one of those worries.

He prayed she'd be okay. Erin had only ever been good to him and the concept of her not being around because of Marco-psycho-Morelli's sick, greedy games was so unfair. But regardless of what happened, none of these people would be part of his life for much longer because it would be *him* leaving.

Closing his eyes, Martin leant against the wall and exhaled slowly, the shuddering breath leaving his lungs summing up his life.

He looked around the small bedroom he shared with Skye. It may not be much compared with the grand place he'd been brought up in. This house and the area it sat in was a million miles away from what he'd been used to. Plus, the people now in his life were of the 'sort' his father wouldn't bother spitting on if they were on fire! Yet for Martin, despite the worrying start and the unconventional nature of what he was surrounded by, he hand on heart preferred this any day to what he'd had before.

As much as he loved his mother - even his father most of the time, these past few weeks had shown in a weird way how it felt to *really* belong to a family. Not that most of the people involved here were 'real' family, but the way they fought for each other and their loyalty transcended anything he'd ever known.

And he liked that.

What's more, he liked being *part* of it. The job of watching a building knowing he could get accosted, kidnapped or even murdered wasn't everyone's cup of tea and a gulf away from what he'd planned for by going to the renowned St Andrews University. But now... now what he'd thought so important, wasn't. The prospect of returning and somehow picking up the pieces of what he'd once been no longer held much value.

He'd almost been accepted by these people.

Almost accepted and before long he'd be *fully* accepted into the fold. He wanted nothing more, but it was all ruined. The life and the future that he'd enjoyed mere days ago now lay in shreds.

Martin stared at his watch, knowing he was putting off the inevitable. People could return at any time - even Skye and if he didn't do this now, he may never get the chance.

His focus returned to the wardrobe and he willed his legs to move, but his heart was in control and playing for time.

Taking a deep breath, despite it going against every fibre of what he wanted, he dragged his brain into centre stage and his legs reluctantly moved.

Walking stiffly to the wardrobe, he crouched down and pulled the two remaining holdalls from the back of the wardrobe. Struggling to fend off the prickling tears, he hoisted the bags onto the bed, unzipped one and then the other and began pulling out the contents.

To an observer, he was merely unpacking his bags and putting everything back where it belonged, but Martin knew this was a temporary measure to outwardly appear that things were 'normal'.

It was dreadful. The invisible blockage sticking painfully in the back of his throat was from the knowledge that he'd shortly be packing everything again. But *that* time he'd be leaving the life he believed was his to have and returning to an existence which felt hollow and pointless.

Martin mechanically unloaded bundles of clothes and items his mother had packed, paying little attention to the mishmash of underwear, tops, socks, paperwork and bits and pieces in there.

She must have scooped up drawer loads of anything and everything and haphazardly shoved it into bags.

It mattered little because his mind was elsewhere, praying for an epiphany that he, along with everyone else, were wrong about Skye. It would be realised that a misunderstanding had caused this snowballing of doubt and if that happened, things would work out fine. Everyone would realise their fears were unfounded and Skye *was* being truthful; she'd lied about nothing. Everything she'd said and done: the untruths she'd spouted when he first arrived here was a one-off and she was now completely on the level.

That she'd hidden her visits to Alyson at the penthouse, the early starts for no reason, the mystery meetings, all had plausible explanations. There was nothing else to it. His building suspicions and Erin, Leo and Tiger's doubts that had run for longer than his own, were unnecessary.

He'd been worrying for nothing - they all had.

Zane would turn out to be correct. After all, he should know! Skye was his own flesh and blood, for God's sake! It was merely bad timing that things had begun to come to a head when Skye arrived on the scene. After all, she'd been the first to admit her original lies were down to her resentment and that her behaviour caused her to become everyone's prime suspect. It didn't mean that she was, did it?

And if that *was* the case, there was no need to leave at all!

Feeling slightly brighter, Martin began putting away the contents of the bags. Working methodically and with renewed purpose, he chuckled to himself as he pulled out one of Skye's hairbrushes and a furry pencil case, wondering how his mother reached the conclusion they belonged to him!

'Nothing changes, Mum, does it?' he laughed, feeling the distinct possibility that this whole sorry state of affairs could be resolved. 'She'd tidy anything, that woman!'

Pulling out the next few items, Martin paused. *This wasn't his either. Or that!*

The bunch of black socks which *did* belong to him fell to the carpet, leaving only a necklace box and an envelope. Wasn't this the necklace that he'd bought Skye for their one-month anniversary?

Putting the envelope to one side, Martin sat on the bed and gently opened the box.

His dad had moaned incessantly about the two-carat diamond on a white gold chain: *'A ridiculous amount to be spending on a girl you've only known for one month'.*

Martin hadn't cared. He'd known from the start that Skye was who he wanted to be with.

Refusing to allow sadness to encase him again, he placed the necklace back in the box and put it where it belonged - on the dressing table next to Skye's makeup bag.

Oh, and there was that envelope.

He tried his best to smooth out the creases of the brown A4 envelope that being shoved in the bag had caused, hoping there was nothing sentimental or important inside.

Opening a dressing table drawer that Skye used for bits and pieces, Martin slipped the envelope inside when he stopped.

Was that...?

Frowning, he peered at the writing on front of the envelope.

That wasn't Skye's writing.

Knowing he shouldn't, but unable to stop himself, Martin retrieved the envelope and peered inside. Heart thumping, sure he must be mistaken, he tugged the paperwork out.

How he wished he hadn't...

'What the...?'

Why would Skye have *this*?

Martin stared in confusion at Hazel Grimes' wedding certificate, it taking only a few more seconds before crushing dread descended, aided by the accompanying piece of paper with multiple signatures on.

All Hazel's…

Or *attempts* at Hazel's signature which gradually improved the further they progressed down the page.

And no matter how much Martin wanted to find an explanation for this, he failed. It meant one thing and one thing only.

THIRTY SIX

'Yes, okay. Bye.' Skye ended the call to Marco and opened the toilet cubicle door. She then froze. 'Do I get no privacy whatsoever?'

Leaning against the door to the corridor outside, Leo jerked his head at the mobile in Skye's hand as she stalked to the sinks to wash her hands. 'Who was that on the phone?'

'If you must know, it was Alyson. I wanted to check she got home safely last night,' Skye snapped. *Fuck, fuck, fuck!*

'Why come in here to do that?' Leo studied Skye's reflection in the mirror. *The bitch was lying.*

Swinging around, Skye snatched a handful of paper towels from the dispenser, showering Leo with water off her hands as she did so. 'Because I knew I'd get the Spanish Inquisition if I phoned anyone in front of *you*, so I decided to do it whilst I went to the loo because I *thought* I'd get some peace! Christ! What's the problem?'

'The problem is *you*!' Leo glared at the splashes of water down the front of his T-shirt, then snatched Skye's phone up from the side of the sink.

'What the hell are you doing?' Skye shrieked. 'You have no right to help yourself to my things!'

Ignoring Skye's protests, Leo quickly opened the call log before the phone locked and looked for the last dialled number.

Skye watched Leo, hiding her sneer at the split-second flash of disappointment visible on his face. *He'd find nothing. She wasn't that stupid.*

Eternally grateful that she'd had the sense to dial Alyson before ringing Marco, she commended her foresight. She hadn't bothered waiting to see if Alyson answered. She had no wish to speak to the two-faced slut who was probably still living it up at the penthouse.

Deleting Marco's number immediately after speaking to him was another habit she'd employed. She couldn't afford any more fuck ups. Not with this lot determined to catch her out. *But they'd have a long wait...* 'Happy now?' she sniffed. 'Alyson's number, right? Will you *ever* give me a break?'

Grinding his teeth, Leo slammed the phone down on the sink. 'Quit acting cloak and dagger and you might get a break!' Steaming with frustration, he yanked open the door and jerked his head for Skye to leave.

Skye strutted up the corridor back to her office, glad Leo was walking behind so she didn't have to conceal her jubilance at getting one over on him. Thought he was clever, didn't he? They all did. Well, they weren't as clever as *her*. 'I reckon it's got to be illegal for men to follow women into toilets...' She glanced over her shoulder, further delight spreading through her at Leo's furious expression. 'Yes, I suspect doing things like that could get a man into trouble. Especially in a place like a women's refuge...'

'You'd know all about that, wouldn't you?' Leo snarled, steering Skye back into the office.

Skye sat down, no longer bothering to hide her smug smile. There was nothing more to say. She wouldn't give this moron the satisfaction of retaliating to the cheap dig about her and Tiger. If the best Leo could do was throw old shit at her, that was *his* problem.

Pulling her diary from the desk drawer, Skye nonchalantly

flicked through the schedule for the women's therapy groups for the next week. 'I'll get on with my job now unless you have a problem with that too? Some of us have *useful* work to do, other than babysitting grown women!'

A nerve in Leo's jaw twitched as he stared at Skye's raven-haired head bent over the diary. *The bitch!* He was sure she'd been up to something, but she was loving that he'd failed to find anything.

Taking a deep breath to distract him from smashing the contents of Skye's expensive new office furniture to smithereens, Leo wondered what to do. Watching this silly cow flick through a diary, pretending she gave a toss about the women upstairs wasn't top of his priorities. There were lists of important things he *could* be doing.

He pulled his phone from his pocket and contemplated calling Zane or Tiger. They'd been at the hospital for a couple of hours now, so there must be an update on Erin's progress by now.

He hesitated before pressing the call button. Surely one of them would have phoned if there was news, so maybe he should leave it. They could be in with the doctor.

Leo stared blankly at his mobile. *Bloody phones!*

It was then that he remembered something.

He'd still got the phone he'd taken from the guy he'd shot in the van. *Fuck!* He'd meant to look through that long before now, but what with everything else...

Seeing Skye still busy with the diary, giving it her all to blatantly ignore him, Leo inwardly grinned. That suited him just fine.

Retrieving the stranger's phone from his other pocket, he hoped it had charge remaining. Relieved as the phone sprang to life, Leo checked the battery level: 20%. Not much, but enough to see what was on the fucking thing.

His large fingers fumbled with the small buttons of the cheap mobile.

There was a missed call not long before the fucker got shot.

No mention of names - just a number. It wasn't Marco's number, he knew that, but then that fucker must have changed it by now.

Bollocks.

Leo then moved to the text messages. There were messages from the same number as the missed call...

Heart ramping up a notch, he opened the last text message:

`I'm here. Y r u nowhere 2 b seen?`

Frowning, Leo moved to the next:

`Call me to rearrange`
`URGENTLY`

Then he moved to the one before that:

`I want an update.`
`Now.`

Leo checked the date and time. Yesterday - the day Erin was snatched. Again, received not long before he gunned that bastard down...

These must be from Marco or at the very least, someone working for him. Someone who was aware of the instructions to take Erin.

Leo hastily scrolled to the next text, taking another quick glance at Skye. She wasn't looking at him. *Good.*

`Where the fuck r u now? We need a meet at the usual place ASAP.`
`B there at 3.`

Leo's brain scoured through what he knew. *Meet at the usual place? 3?*

What was the usual place?

This tosser couldn't turn up because he was dead. Or shortly would have been.

Leo clenched and unclenched his free hand and chewed the inside of his cheek. Come on, there must be a correlation between this and...

Wait a fucking minute...

His eyes darted back to Skye. Tiger had followed her to a pub and, from what he remembered, that was around 3 o'clock: the same time *he'd* been giving chase to the bastards in the van and the unfortunate owner of this mobile.

His brow furrowed as suspicion grew.

It couldn't be *her*, could it?

It was unlikely, surely? How would she know th…

But Skye *had* been to the penthouse...

Maybe Alyson didn't exist? She certainly hadn't turned up at the pub they were allegedly meeting in.

Leo's eyes hardened as he stared at the mobile number against the texts and missed calls. If only he knew Skye's number, then he'd...

His eyes fell to Skye's mobile on the desk. There wasn't much battery left on this shitty mobile but enough to make a call...

Leo pressed call against the unknown number on the dead man's phone and waited, his eyes glued to the mobile on Skye's desk. *It was a long shot, but if his hunch was right...*

Skye's head jolted up at the shrill ringing and she reached to pick her phone up.

Leo held his breath. *It could be coincidence... Just wait...*

He watched Skye's eyes widen at the name on the screen. She clearly wasn't expecting a dead guy to call.

His proof was complete when Skye cut the call and the screen of the phone in his own hand read, '*Call ended*'.

Leo met eyes with Skye, her panic obvious as she registered the two mobiles in his hands. A satisfied smile spread across his face. 'I'd say you're a bit fucked, wouldn't you?'

THIRTY SEVEN

BLINKING, BUT FINDING the movement did nothing to raise her eyelids, Erin scrambled to make sense of her jumbled thoughts. *Was it the middle of the night?*

It felt like somebody had poured the thickest molasses into her head and weighted her body down with bricks. From what she could remember, she hadn't been drinking. Besides, it had been *ages* since she'd got so utterly drunk to feel like this

But this wasn't a hangover. It felt different; *strange.*

Then again, what had she been doing last night?

His sluggish brain struggled with the question. It was like wading through a vat of insulation lagging.

The first prickles of worry sprinkled as Erin reached the half-formed conclusion that she was unsure if she remembered anything at all.

'Erin? ERIN!' Zane jumped from his seat, pure elation on his face. He swung to Tiger. 'Mate! Look! She's coming round!' He grabbed Erin's hand. 'Babe! It's me, Zane. Can you hear me?'

At Zane's voice, Erin's panic subsided. If Zane was here, then she was all right. But what had happened? Her eyes still felt heavy - so heavy.' Z-Zane?' she croaked, her voice horse.

'Oh, thank God!' Zane hit the buzzer on the wall. 'I'll get the doctor. This is great news! Good to have you back, princess! Tiger, this is brilliant! I'm so bloody relieved! Did you hear what she said? She knows it's me!'

'I told you she'd be fine!' Tiger slapped Zane on the back, his own relief strong.

Erin ploughed her power into raising her eyelids and slowly, the blurred mix of lights and shapes gradually came into focus. 'Wh-where am ah?' she slurred. 'Waz happened?'

Zane looked at Tiger in panic. 'Why is she talking like that?' he cried. 'Does that mean that sh...?'

'Calm down. It's probably just the sedation.' Tiger eyed Zane banging the nurse's buzzer over and over. 'She's still half asleep, that's all.'

'Haff azsleep?' Erin repeated, her brain wading through the fog, a jumble of thoughts rushing in at once. 'A van. I werz inna van…'

'Shh, you're okay now,' Zane soothed. 'You're all right.' *At least he hoped she was.*

Erin closed her eyes and tried to focus, her head pounding. The van! She'd been dragged into a van outside the house by... By who? She didn't know. Why had she left the house?

Oh my God! That was it! 'Shuurley!' Erin cried. 'Shuurley an Feeona! They'se waz in house. They ad cometa seeya.'

'What?' Zane looked at Tiger. 'What did she say?'

'Shurrley an Feeona – Martin's muvver. They said… they came aabat Skye.' *That was another thing! Oh God - come on!* She had to get her mouth to work in accordance with her mind. She must tell Zane what had been said: that Marco is Skye's father! And that a guard saw Skye leaving Hazel's office hiding paperwork down her top. That's why she'd returned to the bloody house in the first place to look for that paperwork! It was then that Shirley and Fiona had turned up.

'Skye's the mole, Zine. Sheez working fer Marco. She's his dotter!' Erin clutched Zane's hand. 'They told me. Shurrley tole me. I believe her. I wuz trying… I was coming to fine you. You went ansering phone. You…'

'Slow down!' Zane cried. 'I can't understand you.' His panic intensified. He swung back to Tiger. 'I can't understand what she's saying!'

'She... she said something about Shirley and that Skye isn't...'

'Skye's notya dotter, Zane!' Erin cried, her eyes filling with tears. 'She's gonna destroy ya and...'

'Not my daughter?' Zane cried. 'Is that what you said? Oh, baby, you're confused, sweetheart. Look, you've had a bad accident.' He glared at the buzzer on the wall. 'Where the fuck is that quack?' He almost ripped a chunk of his own hair out in his panic as he grasped hold of his head. 'Shit! I knew this would happen! I just knew she'd be left with some kind of damage.'

'Lizzen! It must be in zer room. Hazel!'

'What's going on in here?' A doctor and several nurses burst into the room. The nurses rushed to Erin's side, quickly checking the monitors.

'She's conscious, doctor,' Zane gabbled. 'But she's talking shit. She thinks dead people are in my daughter's bedroom and loads of other stuff I can't understand. What's happened to her?'

'No! No, you no unnerstan! Thaz not wha I sed!' Erin squeaked, fighting against the nurse fiddling to get a new IV line into her hand. 'No, I don't wanna you doin that! NO!'

'Calm down, Miss Langley.' The doctor moved to Erin's side and wasted no time injecting another shot into the line.

'NO! I havta tell Zen about the... the…' Erin's eyes fluttered, her thrashing about becoming less frenzied. 'I need ta tell im it's imp… imp…'

Erin's voice trailed off, her eyelids fluttering again before falling back to silence.

Clocking Zane's distress, the doctor walked over. 'Do not worry, Mr Morelli. This is quite normal.'

'*Normal*?' Zane roared. 'She's talking about dead people

and weird shit! She doesn't even *sound* like her anymore! You reckon that's fucking *normal*?' He closed his eyes and raised his face to the stark whiteness of the ceiling. 'Jesus Christ! I feared the head injury would leave her with brain damage and now it's proven because...'

'This is common when suddenly regaining consciousness after sedation, Mr Morelli,' the doctor cut in. 'Your fiancée shows no signs of brain damage on the scans.'

Zane frowned. 'Then why is she...'

'When people suddenly regain consciousness after sedation, the brain goes into overdrive.' The doctor sat down on a plastic chair like this was a run-of-the-mill conversation at a café. 'It's a confusing experience. Some fare better than others.'

Handed Erin's medical charts by a nurse, the doctor scribbled a few notes down and then tapped his pen on the clipboard. 'The slurred voice is a side effect as the sedation wears off. Nothing else. You really don't need to worry.'

Zane exchanged looks with Tiger then turned back to the doctor. 'You're not just saying what you think I want to hear?'

'No, Mr Morelli,' the doctor smiled. 'I certainly am not. This is sometimes what happens. We didn't expect Miss Langley to regain consciousness at all today, so that she did of her own accord shows she will be just fine.'

Zane sighed with relief, then frowned. 'But as you've sedated her again won't this keep happening?'

The doctor shook his head. 'I've given her a much milder dose just to remove the overload of thoughts and the associated confusion. It will allow her brain to readjust and catch up at a natural pace. By this time tomorrow, she'll have come around fully, without panic or distress.'

Zane exhaled through his teeth. 'But the things she was saying. All this stuff about my daughter and other things I couldn't quite make out.'

'The mind is a strange place that we understand very little about but it's completely natural,' the doctor said. 'She'll be asleep for the rest of the day now, so you should go home and get some much-needed rest. And do so with the added knowledge that your fiancée and baby are both fine.'

Zane nodded, his relief palpable. He'd go home like the doctor suggested, but he wouldn't be resting. He'd use the time to finish off the tosser who had put Erin through this shitshow in the first place.

He exchanged glances with Tiger, knowing the man was thinking exactly the same as he was.

• • • •

'BUT I NEED YOU inside me again, Marco.' Alyson clawed Marco's arm, the concept of not touching him fuelling desperate panic. Her head was spinning at a faster pace than ever and everything had adopted a strange bluey-green aura. 'Where are you going? Don't leave!'

'Shut up!' Marco snarled. Alyson's incessant whining was distracting him. What time there was to action his backup plan was unknown and although he'd put the feelers out on certain things should something like this happen, he hadn't expected it to occur so soon.

'Stupid bloody girl!' he hissed under his breath. When had he given Skye permission to order men *he'd* employed to kill Erin Langley? And worse, for that order to take priority?

His face screwed into the most horrible grimace as he yanked open the bedside table drawer and rummaged around for the bag of emergency coke he knew was in there.

Even worse than Skye ordering his men to kill Langley as a priority was what she'd taken upon herself to instruct had succeeded in killing two out of the three of them.

Pushing Alyson's hand away as she continued pulling at his arm, Marco snorted a thick line of coke from the top of his bedside table, not caring if he sounded like a pig. He needed to clear his head and this finest Colombian would do just that.

Not that he had much left...

But that would shortly change.

Snatching up his mobile, he flicked through his contacts,

just about keeping his steadily escalating temper under wraps.

So, his brother planned to off him as soon as physically possible, did he? Didn't see the point in biding his time waiting for the right moment any longer?

At least Skye had done something right by letting him know of the change of plans.

Such was the extent of his scowl, Marco's thick eyebrows brushed the bridge of his nose. But her thinking she could gloss over the 'small' point that she'd instructed Langley's death by informing him of his impending demise, wouldn't work.

Oh, he'd clocked her trying that one all right. But there was little point berating her for that now. However, if Skye thought she'd got away with throwing her weight around using his name as collateral, then she'd soon realise that was a big mistake.

Still, first things first.

'Marco!' Alyson whined, so loudly it was almost a shriek.

Marco winced at the sound assaulting his eardrums. 'For fuck's sake! What is it?' he spat, the coke picking up a steady beat within his brain. *The girl was supposed to be zoned out, not hyperactive.* 'What are you bloody yelling about?'

If she didn't button it, then he'd be forced to end her life like he had Callie's.

His eyes tracked to the air conditioning hatch. It had been a shit shoving the bitch's dead body up there, but he'd been too wasted to be arsed to get rid of it by any other means. Something else he'd have to get round to shortly before the slag began to pong the whole place out.

Alyson patted the empty half of the bed. 'I don't like it when you're not next to me.'

A hint of a smile broke Marco's scowl. Yes, all of these bitches had a 'use-by' date, but he wouldn't mind shoving his cock back inside Alyson. He didn't know what it was about her that intrigued him so. Her innocence, perhaps? He wasn't sure, but perhaps if she played her cards right, he might allow her to remain around longer than planned. Especially if the films he'd got of her so far did well.

But she'd get nowhere by nagging. He'd had enough of that from his bitch of a wife and look what had happened to her...

Scraping the residue of white powder from under his nose, Marco got to his feet. 'I've got things to do. Something has happened which I have to deal with.'

Aside from getting rid of the cars and the cash that would bring, he should really sort out that dead hooker.

Marco frowned. It really was a shame. His memory of killing that slut was sketchy. He should have taken less gear before he'd done it. It was always such a waste not to remember every delicious detail. Things like when the bitches begged for mercy and cried before he removed the last few strands of their pointless, pathetic lives and if he'd been thinking clearly, he could have filmed it. That would have gone down a treat. *Those* films always did.

He shrugged dismissively. *Never mind. There would be others.*

'What do you need to do?' Alyson pushed herself upright against the pillows. 'You're not going out, are you?'

The glimmer of Marco's previous good mood evaporated. His cold blue eyes stared at hers, noticing her pupils weren't half as dilated as they should be. *For God's sake, he'd have to dose her up again.* If things kicked off, he didn't want her screaming blue murder.

Ignoring her protests, he turned his back and pressed call on his mobile. *It was time.*

'Sam? Yeah, it's me. That proposition we spoke of the other day? It's on. Yeah, the lot... They're all yours. Yeah, like now.' Marco frowned at the response from the other end of the line. He might have known this fucker would pull a stunt at the last moment, but then he hardly had a huge choice of where to sell the entire contents of the underground car park of top-of-the-range prestige motors at such short notice. It wasn't like the whole of London hadn't heard what had happened between him and Zane, so that anyone was prepared to buy the cars at all was a miracle.

Miracles aside, he'd already agreed a knock down price, yet now it looked like that price would fall further down into the bargain basement.

Keeping his voice convincingly amiable, Marco continued. 'Okay, seeing as it's you, my old friend, I'll knock £200K off, but on the condition I get the brass straightaway. Yes... the lot. Yep. The Ferrari too. All of them. Okay... Yeah, that's fine.'

Ending the call, Marco grinned. *Job done.*

Skye could flap all she liked about the possibility of Zane immediately descending on him with guns blazing, but thinking about the situation rationally – while that stupid blonde whore that Zane was attached to by the hip fought for life in a fucking grungy hospital, his stupid brother would be otherwise engaged. For a short while, at least. Long enough to get rid of these motors and pocket the brass, anyway.

Maybe he should stash Callie's corpse in a boot of one of the cars that Whittaker was taking? He'd pretend he had no knowledge of it if the man played his face later on.

Marco frowned. But was there time to sort that before he turned up? Plus, if he did that, Whittaker wouldn't deal with him again and he didn't know what else he might need the greedy, sly twat for in the future.

Bollocks. Oh well, he'd just have to think of something else.

Marco sat back on the bed and closed his eyes, enjoying the buzz of the cocaine swarming his brain.

Zane was making things far too easy these days.

Yep, he knew his brother too well. For Zane to be as bothered about Erin Langley as he'd already proved himself to be, shown by his reaction over Sandler's efforts to off the bitch, then she and she alone would be the only thing on his mind until he knew for certain she would live.

Maybe Skye had done him a favour by getting a hit on Erin. It supplied room to move without fear of interruption. It also underlined, being as they'd failed to finish Langley completely, that Red and Baz were shite at their job. How hard could it be? It was probably a blessing in disguise that they'd karked it. But

Skye's take on Zane being in Panic Mode Number Nine not knowing if Erin would live, die or end up a fucking vegetable, was perfect.

Ignoring Alyson staring at him like a lost puppy, Marco reached over to grab the syringe. She was getting on his wick now. He'd zoned her questions out, but being as there *were* questions – and lots of them, she needed to shut up and give him some peace.

Alyson eyed the needle in Marco's hand as it came into focus in between breaks of swirling confusion. 'What's that?' she asked. 'Does that mean you're coming back to bed?'

'Not right now, babe.' Marco couldn't help but laugh. Alyson might be irritating, but she was a welcome break from the stress. Not that there would be any of that soon.

Now money for the cars was inbound there was no rush to get Shirley's cheque reinstated. He'd get it off the crusty cunt in the end, but now he'd secured this price for Zane's immense collection of prestige motors, plus his father's rare Bentley, that poxy £750k from the old cow wasn't so pressing. Plus, there was still a big chunk of his nest egg remaining, so along with the cash coming within the hour from Sam Whitaker, he'd have enough to start from scratch - catching Zane off guard in the process.

Fuck this penthouse! Zane could have it back. He could have it back with bells on! And, he thought, a fresh brainwave forming, he'd even chuck in a free corpse. He'd leave that tart in the air con vents. Zane and his band of fucking jesters could sort that mess out.

The solution to the only loose end remaining was obvious all along!

Marco grinned, pleased he'd reached a workable decision. He knew everything would become clear in the end. As soon as the motors were picked up and he'd got the wedge in his hand, he was out of here.

Leaning over Alyson, he smiled as he pushed the needle into her thigh. He'd have to make his mind up whether or not to bother taking this one with him or whether she'd served her purpose.

Satisfied as her eyes rolled back in her head and the questions finally stopped, Marco helped himself to another line of cocaine. Taking a bottle of cold beer from his bedroom minibar, he glanced at the stairs leading up to the roof terrace.

Once Whittaker arrived, the deal had been done and he'd got his cash, then he'd go up to the terrace. There was a 360° view from there, so it was a good a place as any to wait in case Zane surprised him by arriving sooner than expected.

THIRTY EIGHT

'GOOD JOB, GUYS,' Zane said, striding through the large room at the back of the Thames Canning Works.

He glanced around the men who had been brought in to weigh, cut and bag the first batch of coke. They were progressing through the huge supply well.

Zane turned to the man Tiger placed to oversee the job. 'When do you reckon it will be ready?'

'In another four or five hours there will be enough for the first load to go out,' the man replied.

'Good,' Zane nodded. 'I'll let them know.'

'I'll do that,' Tiger offered.

Zane nodded his acknowledgement, grateful for one less thing to juggle and continued to the back to unlock the storeroom.

Tiger followed, sending the pre-agreed text as he did so. 'I've sent a text to the lead runner. It will filter through to the rest who will come to pick up their quota and deliver it to each dealer when the time comes.'

'Then let's get this show on the fucking road!' Zane unlocked one of the many cabinets at the back of the storeroom. He pulled open the metal door and perused the arsenal of weapons. It was a while since he'd had call to pull on this stash, but the time had come. It may not have been the way he'd planned the final stage of the game to go down, but there was no other option if he wanted to remain sane and firing on all cylinders. This shit had to finish and finish *now*. He wasn't bringing a baby into this shit-tip of a cat and mouse game. It was time to exterminate the vermin.

Sandler was done and now it was Marco's turn.

Zane eyed the rack of semi-automatics and shotguns. Tempting, but he didn't need heavy duty artillery to take out his brother. A pistol would suffice. Less mess, less weight and less fucking hassle.

He reached into the cabinet. 'What I'm after should be just... here.' Wrapping his hands around two Berettas, Zane put one in his waistband and chucked the other to Tiger. 'These are newly cleaned. No identification, serial numbers removed, no prior usage - nothing to link back to us.'

Not that Zane believed that would happen. He'd keep his cool when dealing with Marco. Long gone was the plan to scream and rant and drag out his brother's death. The belief that each second the fucker suffered represented a week of what *he'd* endured over the years he'd been incarcerated was old hat. The added pain he planned to inflict on top of that was for every other thing Marco had done to others Zane cared about.

But that wouldn't happen anymore. Erin's pregnancy changed everything and Zane just wanted Marco gone to ensure she would never be hurt again. Every further second that man stole oxygen from the world upped the risk. It was more important to keep those he loved safe than take revenge.

His original plan was out of date.

Tiger shoved the Beretta in his jacket, watching the emotions moving over Zane's face. 'I'll fetch the ammo.'

Tiger's voice jolted Zane from his thoughts. He shut the cabinet door and glanced at his phone. 'Looks like both Martin and Leo have called,' he said, shoving his phone back in his pocket. 'I won't call Martin back. We'll go to the house to make sure everything is okay first. I'll call Leo on route and tell him to bring Skye from the Starbright and take her to the house. Then we'll go for Marco.'

Now the time had come to move he wasn't leaving his daughter open to any other men his brother may have on board they were not yet aware of.

Tiger frowned. 'So, Leo's not going to be part of it?'

'No need.' Zane strode back through the door of the storeroom, leaving Tiger to lock it. 'Marco's death will be rapid. I've already wasted enough of my life on that bastard and he's not getting any more!'

Once this was over, they could get back to normal - whatever that was - and start preparing for the next chapter in life. One which he was now daring to look forward to.

• • • •

'I'M NOT HERE TO ARGUE,' Fiona stepped over the threshold into the terraced house in Dalston, leaving Martin to gape in dismay.

The expression on her son's face pained her. That it was so obvious he didn't want her here cut deep. Maybe Shirley was right and she'd lost him for good? Despite that, she had to try. She would do all she could for her one and only child, even if it cost her the relationship with him that she'd always treasured.

Martin struggled to free himself from the surprise and react accordingly. His resolve grew as Shirley followed his mother into the house. 'This isn't a good time. I...'

'I appreciate it probably isn't, Martin,' Fiona said calmly. 'Like I said, I'm not here to argue. I'm sorry if I overstepped the mark by coming here yesterday and packing your things or...' She hesitated, 'perhaps by coming here at all. But I must speak to Zane.'

Martin glanced at Shirley propped against the hallway wallpaper, staring up at the ceiling, her mouth moving in silent words. That alone unnerved him, but apology or not, they couldn't be here.

He'd already tried and failed to call Zane and the weight of the knowledge that his fears about Skye were real were getting impossible to shoulder. That he'd proved what he'd dreaded all along made things worse and these two being here when he needed to locate Zane, was not what he wanted.

Martin grabbed Fiona's arm. 'Please just go. I...'

'I've already said that I'm not here to cause an argument with you or with Zane, for that matter. Things have changed.' The more Fiona considered the possibility that Zane wasn't aware of his brother's actions, the more plausible it became. It could be wishful thinking. In fact, it probably was, but if she *had* jumped to the wrong conclusions and Shirley *had* incorrectly believed that Zane was party to the terrible act against her all of this time, then the least she could do was to see for herself how the man reacted on hearing the truth.

If he *genuinely* believed Skye to be his daughter, then even the most seasoned criminal and adept liar would fail to hide their shock - if only for a split second.

In her haste to explain herself, Fiona hadn't noticed Martin's behaviour and countenance. Her sole mission was to get inside the house and talk to the infamous Zane Morelli. But looking at her son now, she saw his ashen face and trembling hands. Worry overtook the quest for truth. 'Whatever is the matter? You look... I don't know... Ill? What's going on?'

'I...' Martin stumbled over his words, experiencing the sudden childlike urge to break down in sobs and seek refuge in his mother's arms.

'Oh my God! Is it that woman? Erin?' Fiona gasped, guilt slapping her around the face. 'Is she...? Has she...?'

'No, no, she's... Well, they *think* that she'll be okay,' Martin spluttered. 'At least that was the last I heard, but that could have changed because I can't get through to Zane.'

'So, he's not here again?' Fiona's heart sank. She'd resorted to what might even be loosely classed as threats in getting Shirley back here, yet the man wasn't around? It would be hard to keep Shirley here much longer before she bolted. 'When will he be back? And if it's not Erin that's troubling you, what is it?'

'I... I just...'

Fiona stared in horror as Martin crumpled to his knees, his head in his hands. Instinctively, she moved to his side. 'Please tell me what's happened?'

'See? They've got to him now!' Shirley suddenly yelled, her voice high-pitched and frantic. 'It happens to us all in the end. They get inside your head and you can't get them out!'

Her feet slapped up the hallway as she lurched towards the front door, her hands grasping for the doorknob. 'I've got to get out. Got to escape before he gets back. Before *any* of them do. See what they've done to your boy? They've stolen his soul! They steal *everyone's* soul!'

'Get away from the door!' Fiona screamed.

Martin didn't glance up as his mother leapt from the floor and bolted toward Shirley. What was the point? The thin strands of hope of a plausible explanation for Skye's behaviour disappeared with what he'd found in her room. And with that, so had what he wanted out of life.

Perhaps Shirley was right? Perhaps his soul *had* been stolen? Because he sure as hell felt like there was nothing whatsoever left to make it worth his heart to beat for.

THIRTY NINE

SKYE'S THOUGHTS flipped between disdain and the terrifying sensation of being encased in a gradually filling barrel of tar - the window left to breathe before inhaling the thick, sticky liquid to fill her lungs, becoming smaller and smaller.

She didn't need to turn her head in Leo's direction to know he was watching her out of the corner of his eye. The hatred mixed with pleasure that he'd finally stopped her in her tracks was obvious.

Skye kept her face neutral, but inside her fury grew. She hadn't expected this oversized moron to rumble her, but he had.

Digging her fingernails into the palms of her hands helped Skye offset the rage which threatened to spiral out of control. She knew Leo could hear her short, laboured breaths. *She* could hear them and didn't want him witnessing her stress, but although she could control most things, she couldn't stop herself from pulling in the oxygen needed to supply her thundering heart.

As Leo drove rapidly towards Dalston the silence within the car was deafening. *What would they do? What would Zane do?*

The plan was to be with Marco when the news to bring Zane's downfall was delivered, not trapped in the shitty house where she'd been forced to act oh-so bloody nice to everyone for God knows how long whilst waiting for punishment.

Or death...

Why couldn't Marco have let her move into the penthouse? That would have been the most sensible thing. She could have left Zane's place. She could just not have returned from the Starbright. She could have stepped out in the middle of the day. The guards were so fucking thick they'd have let her go. She'd managed it enough times, like when going to the bank. No one had stopped her then, had they?

Instead, Marco's insistence that she remain within the enemy's fold had now scuppered *both* of them.

Skye clenched her teeth so hard she was sure the enamel cracked. She was so close. They had *both* been so close, yet now although she'd informed Marco that Zane was coming for him, it was doing exactly *that* which had allowed Leo-bloody-Holland and his sneaky spying tactics to catch her. But what she *hadn't* done was let Marco know that she'd been rumbled. Now both she and him were in immediate danger.

How could she warn him?

Skye's eyes slid in Leo's direction. He still had her phone and there was no way of getting it back.

Whilst she'd been still in the Starbright she'd tried sneaking to the toilet again in a desperate bid to call to Marco. She could have insisted on using a guard's mobile, but that was impossible because this gorilla hadn't let her out of his sight.

Not that there had been much time to do anything once her connection with what had befallen Erin has been proved.

The sneaky bastard. She hadn't ever considered it plausible for Leo to be in possession of Red's phone.

And she should have.

She should have covered *all* eventualities, but she hadn't and within minutes of being exposed, she'd been bundled into the van.

And here they were...

Now it wouldn't be long before they reached Dalston.

Feeling a distinct trickle of perspiration run down between her breasts, Skye glowered with resentment. Oh, how the bastard was loving this. As for Tiger – he'd come in his pants when he found out. Erin would too. They'd all waited so long for this moment and it was a moment Skye believed wouldn't happen.

She never lost at *anything*. Yet now it seemed she had...

Despite the graveness of her position, she was unable to stop a smirk forming as Leo's attempt to call Zane for the tenth time failed. 'Still no answer? What a shame.'

There was no response from Leo. She hadn't expected one. No doubt he believed silent treatment was more detrimental and worrying than anything else.

It wasn't.

Nothing these fuckers did scared her. Well, not much...

Either way, she refused to let anyone intimidate her.

Leo's one and only attempt to bark at her, demanding to know about her involvement and working with Marco had fallen on deaf ears. She hadn't breathed a word and neither would she.

She was drowning in an inescapable situation, but whatever happened, she was adamant to cause at least *some* damage.

Okay, so they could presume she was working for Marco and that she'd betrayed them, but it wouldn't cross their tiny minds, especially poor old Zane's, that she wasn't his darling daughter at all.

Knowing she'd betrayed him - betrayed them *all*, would be bad enough, but the icing on the cake would be the double whammy of discovering she didn't belong to him but to *Marco...*

And Skye just hoped that she'd witness it.

'Ah, finally!' Leo's voice caused Skye to pull her fixed gaze away from the window.

'I've been trying to get hold of y… Yeah, she's here with me. No, we're fine, yeah, but listen, I need to tell you... What? No, wait! I…'

'Aw.' Skye's sarcastic laugh tinkled. 'Too busy to listen, was he? How disappointing. What will you do now?'

Being sarcastic was one thing, but as Leo slammed his foot further down on the accelerator, Skye was well aware her time was running out.

• • • •

'WHAT THE FUCK IS THIS?' Zane roared, the full power of his rage centred on Martin.

Shoving his mobile back in his pocket, he stormed into the living room, barely able to believe his eyes. He hadn't had chance to hear what Leo wanted to say because of this. And *this* certainly wasn't what he'd expected to see on walking into his home when he'd only come back to check on everything before continuing to the penthouse.

At the sudden bellowing, Fiona scrabbled from the floor where she'd been straddling Shirley in a bid to stop her from escaping. Flustered and with her face glowing a hot red colour, she tugged her skirt down from where it bunched around the tops of her thighs. Her gaze darted to the two men who had entered the room.

Which one of them was Zane Morelli? With a name like that, the dark-haired Hispanic-looking one seemed most likely.

Taking in the wild look on the man's face and the scar running just below his eye down his cheekbone, she came to the conclusion that nothing detracted from his dangerous, yet disturbingly good-looking features.

Fiona's colour heightened. Why was she acknowledging this man's good looks? Perhaps it was straddling Shirley Wilson on the floor of his living room with her skirt hitched up to God knows where wasn't the best first impression she wanted to give when she needed a serious conversation with the man.

'Oh my Jesus!' Shirley rolled around like a beetle on its back in an attempt to get off the floor. 'He's back!' Her eyes darted around too quickly to focus on anything. 'You should have let me go!' she screamed, her eyes finally centring on

Fiona. 'You should have let me go when I had the chance. You don't realise what you've done!'

'Zane? Zane Morelli?' Finding her voice, Fiona ignored Shirley's diatribe. She stepped forward and extended her hand, then rapidly changed her mind and instead patted down her hair which had become dislodged from its usual neat style. She was still not quite able to accept that she'd been behaving like a common fishwife when these terrifying men entered the room. *How embarrassing.* 'Erm, I'm Fiona Bolt - Martin's mother. I... I need to speak to you about...'

'This is your *mother*?' Zane lunged at Martin and grabbed him around the scruff of the neck. 'You bought Shirley and this woman to my house? What have they done? Brought the police to my door?'

'No!' Martin squawked, his fingers pulling against the iron grip at his throat. 'She hasn't. They haven't! It's...'

'Get your hands off my son!' Fiona yelled, instinctively picking up the nearest object and whacking Zane between the shoulder blades with it.

'Oh my God!' Shirley screamed, finally getting to her feet. 'The evil ones will make sure we all pay for our sins!'

If Martin's full concentration wasn't on preventing himself from being strangled, he might have died from embarrassment. 'Look... I...'

'Okay, everyone, I think we need to calm down.' Tiger swallowed the belly laugh pushing from the back of his throat and stopped a rare smile from displaying on his face. Instead, he wore his usual granite look. Grabbing hold of Fiona's arms whilst preventing Shirley from running towards the door, he then pulled Zane's hands off Martin's neck.

Leaving Martin coughing and Zane pacing around in exasperation, Tiger kicked the wooden fruit bowl Fiona had used as a weapon out of the way. He took another glance at the dishevelled figure of the woman next to Fiona Bolt. *This was Zane's first girlfriend?*

'I'm sorry...' Fiona garbled. 'I...'

'She wasn't calling the police, Zane!' Martin spluttered. 'She came here to ask me to leave, but I couldn't. I won't!'

'For fuck's sake!' Zane yelled. 'Have you any idea of what I'm dealing with here? I come back from the hospital to check there's been no untoward developments, only to find this bullshit!' He straightened his leather jacket, half-pulled from his back and glared at the mess around the room. 'Fucking sort this shitshow out, Martin and do it *now*!'

Martin blinked twice in succession. The room deathly quiet, he watched in horror as Zane made to leave the house. *Zane couldn't go! He hadn't told him what he'd found!* 'Wait! I found something in Skye's be...'

'And, Mr Morelli, what I have to ask may be rather upsetting and...'

'Are you all deaf?' Zane bellowed, swinging around. 'I've got something important to do that can't wait!'

Fiona shook her head. 'But this can't wait either and...'

'Be quiet, Mum,' Martin cried. 'Zane, I found th…'

'Fucking listen!' Zane roared, a vein in his temple bulging. 'I'll hear you out later but not now.'

'But...'

'Leo's on his way here with Skye, so do you think you could all cope with not acting like you're in a fucking zoo? This is stressful enough as it is!' With that, Zane stormed from the room with Tiger on his heels.

Shirley, Fiona and Martin stood in stunned silence long after the front door slammed shut behind the two men.

• • • •

QUITE ENJOYING the tinkling noise of the glass stirrer, Marco flipped an ice cube from the silver bucket into his Mai Tai and settled back on the sun lounger.

He'd thought twice about dragging this lounger across to the glass barrier separating him from the roof terrace's huge drop to the ground below. Cocaine always instilled an invincibility that nothing, not even death could precede. But for once he went along with the concept of forward thinking. Plus, it was a beautiful day and there was nothing lame about enjoying the rays from these lofty heights whilst keeping an eye out for 'visitors'.

But to receive no further calls from Skye when she'd said she'd shortly be in touch with updates set off alarm bells. Although the bells weren't deafening, they were gradually picking up prominence within his brain and the thought that something may have occurred which could have a detrimental effect on *him*, nagged.

And if it had, then he must be ready.

Marco took a long swig of the orangey liquid in the glass and his nose wrinkled at the taste. Never a fan of cocktails, he reserved that crap for entertaining the eager starlets falling over themselves to be in his high-ranking porn films.

The time of Luna films being at its heyday seemed like a million years ago even though it hadn't been long since the police and the stupid charges against him for that bollocks about human trafficking and sex slaves led to the enforced closure of the studios, as well as the wrongful time he'd spent banged up waiting for trial.

But that was over now and although he'd initially hankered over getting Luna Film Studios back up and running, that had now fallen down his list of things to do.

Marco eyed the holdall at his feet then returned his gaze to what remained of the drinks in his rooftop bar.

He had new plans now - ones much bigger and better, hence finishing off what was left of anything half-drinkable here. Being as he'd made the decision to generously gift the penthouse back to his dear brother, if he wasn't forced to kill him first out of self-defence that was, he was fucked if he was leaving the bastard anything to drink.

Marco's brow creased.

He didn't want to kill Zane - even if that's what Zane intended the other way around. He'd much prefer the sad fuck lived with a ripped-out heart from the news he had ready to drop.

And if Skye was correct, there wasn't long to wait.

Any day now, he'd experience the enjoyment of watching his brother spontaneously combust. Just think - all of that without raising a finger. *Superb.*

Certain he'd just heard a noise, Marco stilled. It wouldn't be Alyson. The amount of magic gear he'd pumped into her, she'd be off with the fairies for a long time yet.

But what to do about her?

There was no place for someone like Alyson in his new ventures. She would never fit into his plans now he had enough money to take a proper foothold back in London. And more importantly, that foothold would be achieved without anything belonging to his father or brother.

Now he had the readies to put a whole host of minions on his payroll, buy premises *and* somewhere new to live, everything from here on in would be of his making alone.

Money talked and he intended to speak loud and clear!

Unable to help it, Marco pulled the holdall from under his lounger and unzipped it to peer inside for the fourteenth time since Whittaker had handed it over. He eyed the bundles of fifty-pound notes, his excitement growing.

There was millions here!

Not bad for a bunch of cars that weren't even his!

Suddenly getting a wave of instinct, Marco zipped up the bag and sat forward to look over the glass barrier to the ground below.

Seeing a van pull up on the road outside the complex, Marco's pulse raced.

Was this him?

Please let it be. He was in sore need of finishing this day off in the most enjoyable way possible.

Barely daring to breathe, Marco's heart lurched in anticipation as two figures clambered from the van. One of them familiar enough to be able to identify purely by his outline.

'Hello, dear brother,' Marco muttered, the smile spreading

the entire breadth of his face. 'I'm glad you've decided to honour me with your presence, even if you have the misguided notion that you will succeed in killing me.'

He casually lit a cigarette with his solid gold lighter and exhaled slowly.

All he had to do now was stay where he was and wait. He'd allow Zane to think he'd done a flit before surprising him with the news he'd looked forward to sharing ever since discovering it himself.

Life didn't get much better than this.

FORTY

TIGER MADE A second detailed sweep of the vast main floor of what had once been Zane's penthouse. 'I don't think anyone's here.'

Having previously been inside this place countless times when Zane lived here, he knew the layout as well as his own flat. It hadn't changed, although countless other things had...

He eyed the tacky lighting and vast cinema screen on the far wall with derision, noticing Zane was also looking at what had once been furnished so tastefully with a similar amount of contempt.

'He's done a flit.' Zane nudged a pile of empty beer cans and a lacy thong with his foot. His eyes narrowed with barely suppressed rage. 'It looks like he's abandoned the place. Recently too. Possibly even within the last half hour.' His hands formed into fists. 'Someone is a mole. Someone in my firm has told Marco I was about to make a move. He got a heads-up and when I find out which fucker is responsible, I'll kill them!'

He felt like smashing the place up. The thought of not putting an end to Marco's attempts to kill the people he loved was unthinkable. That bastard had almost succeeded already on more than one occasion, therefore it was only a matter of time before he *did* succeed.

And that could not happen.

'Fuck,' he hissed through gritted teeth. He shouldn't have gone back to Dalston. He should have come straight here. He should have called Martin rather than physically going there.

What the fuck was he thinking? What had going there achieved, apart from walking into the circus of Martin Bolt's bloody mother and Shirley grappling on the floor and being clumped with a fucking fruit bowl?

'Jesus Christ!' He sighed in despair. What now? How could he keep Erin, his unborn child and Skye safe when the bastard hell bent on taking everything from him had given him the slip again.

When he found out who had leaked his whereabouts and plan, he'd go tits. But that didn't help him now.

'Who the fuck has been my eyes and ears? Someone at the canning works or what about the scrawny fucker Leo said escaped from the van?' Zane snarled, upending the glass table in the centre of the room in frustration.

Tiger winced as shattered glass scattered over the deep pile rug. 'I don't know, mate, but I'll check upstairs and make sure the place is empty.'

Tiger took the stairs to the galleried landing three at a time. Not leaving anything to chance, he booted the bedroom doors open one by one.

All empty.

He stopped and listened before opening the master bedroom door. *Wait! He could hear breathing.*

Were they wrong and Marco hadn't done a bunk after all, but was off his tits, lying face down in his fucking bed?

Drawing his gun, Tiger kicked open the door and moved inside, the barrel of the gun drawing an arc of cover across the room. Freezing in the doorway, he focused on the figure in the bed. *That wasn't Marco, that was for sure.*

Unable to assume this wasn't a setup, he checked behind the door and scanned the room again before fully entering. *It was clear*. 'Zane!' he shouted. 'Up here!'

As Zane's heavy boots thundered up the stairs, Tiger approached the bed and stared at the naked young woman.

'Shit!' Zane gasped as he entered the room. 'There's dried froth around her mouth. Is she dead?'

Leaning closer, Tiger gently placed his fingers on the woman's slender neck. 'There's a faint pulse and she's still breathing. But only just. It looks like an overdose.'

'Courtesy of my fucking brother, no doubt,' Zane growled. Suddenly spotting a jacket slung over an occasional chair, he grabbed it. 'Cover her up. We need to get her out of here.'

Taking the jacket, Tiger carefully lifted Alyson's limp body and wrapped her in the jacket, both to warm up her cold, clammy skin and to cover her modesty. It was then he spotted the camera. 'Look!'

Following Tiger's gaze, Zane moved to the camera on the tripod in the corner and eyed the pile of discs next to it. 'Marco's still up to his usual shit of drugging young girls up and filming them getting screwed then,' he spat.

'Disgusting bastard!' Tiger muttered, his hatred surpassing the levels Marco usually engendered.

'Ah, but it's such a lucrative business!'

Zane and Tiger turned at Marco's distinctive voice, both reaching for their guns at the exact same time.

• • • •

'OH MY GOD, IT'S *YOU*!' Fiona gasped as Leo frogmarched Skye into the house. She'd recognise that man's bulldog face anywhere. It had haunted her dreams, or rather her nightmares ever since he'd appeared in her kitchen to threaten her and Peter and accuse Martin of all manner of untrue things.

She turned to Martin, still unresponsive on the chair like his life had deserted him. 'This is the man who broke into our house and...'

'SKYE!' Shirley's ravaged face transformed with the joy of seeing the daughter she truly believed she'd lost forever. Her bulky form moved across the room, her arms outstretched. 'My baby girl!'

'Don't touch me, you evil old whore!' Skye spat. 'I want nothing to do with you! Why did you allow this fat bitch into the house, Martin? You know what she's done.'

Fiona stood transfixed at the viciousness spewing from the mouth of the girl she'd always deemed so sweet-natured and pleasant. It was like evil entities had overtaken the real Skye Wilson and replaced her with a stranger. Her eyes darted to Shirley standing like stone in the centre of the room, her arms still stretched wide for an embrace from her daughter that would never come.

'Martin! Are you deaf?' Skye barked. 'Is there anything you can do that doesn't ruin everything?'

Grabbing Skye's arm, Leo swung her around to face him. 'Pipe down! No one needs to hear any more of your demands and fucking lies!' He glanced around the room, refusing to waste valuable time questioning what the hell Fiona Bolt and the unhinged Shirley Wilson were doing in Zane's house. He was sure he'd find out at some point, but there were more important things to do.

He glared at the top of Martin's head. The stupid boy hadn't even looked up. *What the fuck was the matter with everybody?*

That he didn't know either and nor did he have time to find out. There was only one important thing here and that was to inform Zane that this twisted daughter of his was working for the enemy. 'Where's Zane? He's supposed to be here.'

Leo did quite well waiting for an entire three seconds before impatience overruled. 'Someone fucking speak! Martin! Wake up! Where's Zane?'

Martin slowly looked up and stared through Skye to Leo. He couldn't bear seeing her - not now he knew what she was. 'Zane went to the penthouse.'

Leo's throat dried. *Zane had gone to do Marco? What the fuck?* 'When?' Dragging Skye across the room with him, he yanked Martin's head up. 'When did he leave? I need to know.

Now!'

Fiona knew this wasn't the time to start telling another one of these men to get their hands off her son because whatever was happening here was more alarming than she'd warranted. Based on what she'd seen so far, that was saying something. However, as Martin's mouth silently flapped up and down, she knew she had to step in before this lunatic completely lost his temper. 'Zane was here with another man. We tried to speak to him, but he said he had important things to do that couldn't wait.'

'Shit!' Leo hissed. He glanced at Skye and then at the others. He couldn't leave this two-faced bitch here. Martin looked like he'd been slapped around the face with a wet fish, Fiona Bolt was too flighty not to do something stupid like call the police or rush her darling boy to A&E with the fear that he was having a breakdown and as for Shirley - Jesus Christ, she was about as compos mentis as an asylum patient.

Whatever his take was, Leo couldn't leave Skye to her own manipulative devices. God only knew what she'd achieve if he took his eyes off her. She'd have to accompany him to the penthouse. And, he thought with a flash of inspiration, there she'd have no choice but to confess her involvement with Marco when faced with Zane and the yellow-bellied cunt whose dirty orders she'd been carrying out behind their backs all of this time.

Without further delay, he pulled Skye towards the door.

'What are you doing?' Skye shrieked, the anticipation of spelling out some home truths to the slimy little boy she'd been forced to pretend she loved fading into oblivion.

'You're coming to the penthouse with me.' Leo dragged Skye along, her shoes sliding across the carpet no matter how hard she dug them in.

'NO!' Shirley fruitlessly pounded Leo's back with her fists. 'You're not taking my daughter to that psycho! She's not to go anywhere near Marco Morelli! Get away from her!'

Skye saved Leo the trouble of restraining Shirley by

pushing the flat part of her hand squarely into her mother's face. 'Get out of the way, you mad cow!' she yelled. She'd prefer to punch the bitch, but she wasn't breaking her nails - not now her prayers had been answered. Despite the raw dread during the journey here about missing out on Zane being brought to his knees, she might get to witness his destruction after all.

There was still a chance this could work in her and Marco's favour. And, she thought as Leo pulled her over the threshold towards the van, if it didn't go the right way, at least after Zane's life had been ruined, hers would end at the side of her *real* father.

....

EYEING THE BARRELS of his brother's and Tiger's guns, Marco laughed, his cold eyes glinting with malice. 'Shoot me if you wish, but there's little point.'

Zane's erratic breathing at Marco's sheer indifference to his and Tiger's presence infuriated him to the point of rendering him almost incapable of functioning. The pounding behind his temples was deafening. 'After what you've done, give me one good reason not to blow your fucking head clean off, you cunt!'

He could barely look at this man. The sight of his brother after so long was difficult. Marco looked the same as always, yet with the added difference of the long list of things that had been proved he'd orchestrated or done with his own disgusting hands.

Pulling himself back into gear, Zane reinstated his resolve of what he was here to do and the way he intended to do it back to the forefront of his mind. 'There's no reason you can give me which will change the outcome. You're done!'

'Is that so? If it was, you'd have already killed me.' Marco's huge shoulders shrugged, his ice-blue stare mirroring that of Zane's. 'But you don't have the bottle.' He grinned harder seeing the clenching of Zane's jaw.

Tiger subtly checked the room again for a sign that Marco wasn't alone, but aside from the girl on the bed, the place was empty. Marco was doing what he always did - aiming for a reaction and riling people so they walked right into his trap. And there had to be a trap because with Marco Morelli, there was *always* a trap.

He took an undetectable glance at Zane, hoping his friend kept his cool and didn't plunge headfirst into Marco's goading plans. However difficult it was, Zane was right. Deciding Marco's death should be fast was the right thing. It had to be done with minimum fuss so he could get back to Erin's side with the knowledge that she and the child would never be targeted again.

But that was easier said than done. *He* was finding it all but impossible not to rip Marco's sneering face from his head and shit down his neck. Most of those crimes hadn't even been against *him*, so he could only guess how Zane was holding it together.

But Marco *was* having an effect. Tiger could clearly see Zane's hand vibrating with building rage and adrenaline.

'It's unlike you to be so quiet,' Marco drawled, his eyes glinting in an unspoken challenge. 'I wonder how your dear fiancée is faring? Dribbling and requiring round the clock care yet, is she? Good luck with that!'

Losing restraint, Zane flew towards Marco. *Fuck this*. He wouldn't give this cunt the benefit of a quick death. He'd beat and torture the bastard as slowly as possible.

Marco's flash of fear lasted only a split second before the butt of Zane's gun smashed into his cheekbone. Losing his footing, he stumbled backwards, but ducked from the second blow closely following the first.

He and Zane spent years training how to fight. Sparring with each other was something their trainer insisted upon on a daily basis. Over and over they'd gone at each other. This had not only ensured they were evenly matched but enabled them to pre-empty the other's moves.

They'd been trained to work *together*, not at as enemies.

The trainer had screwed up there, but back in those days,

never in the Morellis or their associates' wildest dreams was it contemplated that Giuseppe's boys would be on opposite sides.

Tiger remained motionless as the two brothers crashed around the room delivering punch after debilitating punch to each other. Now Zane had made the call to go down this road rather than use the gun for a swift dispatch, he knew better than to break protocol and join in. Right now, and until anything changed, this was between the brothers.

'You always wanted to be me,' Zane snarled, driving his fist into Marco's straight white teeth. 'You couldn't bear that our father chose *me* to run the firm. He could depend on me, not you! From that point, you've done your utmost to take everything that you didn't have but wanted.'

Straddling Marco, Zane glowed with victory seeing a flash of pain behind Marco's eyes. 'You failed though, didn't you, you cunt? No matter what you've done, no matter what you've attempted, you fucking lost!'

Risking removing the hand grasping Marco's throat, Zane swept his arm around the huge bedroom that had once been his. 'You really thought you'd got one over on me by taking my apartment? It bricks and mortar, Marco. Bricks and mortar! That can be replaced but my fiancée can't. You tried to kill Erin twice, you bastard! First, getting Sandler to do your dirty work and then another bunch of no hopers, who I might add are now also dead!'

Throwing his head back, Zane laughed. Telling Marco everything he'd simmered over for years was cathartic. 'You've achieved nothing. You never could. Stupid really, because you somehow got yourself a wife. Until you killed her too.' His eyes then narrowed. 'Hazel was a good person. Maybe that's why you killed her. And I'll *never* forgive you for trying to kill Erin. Which, I should add, you also failed at.'

Taking the opportunity with Zane distracted, his throat free from the grip, Marco pulled himself upwards with the strength of an ox. His forehead smashed into the bridge of Zane's nose. 'You know fuck all!' he growled. 'You haven't a clue even when it's right in front of you!'

Eyes streaming from the stinging agony of his freshly broken nose, Zane grappled for control, knowing Marco had now gained the upper hand. Choking in the headlock he was pinned in, Zane seethed with hatred. Marco was trying to wind him up and it was working, but everything he'd said was the truth and Marco knew it.

He laughed again through the pain, his eyes blazing with rage. 'Even now you resort to drugging up young girls for your sexual kicks. You make me sick! The only saving grace is you never had children!'

'Is that right?' Marco sneered. 'Who told you that? Your *daughter*, perhaps? That reminds me… how is Shirley? She looked like utter shit when I saw her the other day.'

The mention of Skye was enough to push Zane off the precipice. 'Don't bring my daughter into this!'

'Actually, Skye belongs to me,' Marco said smugly, his missing front tooth rendering him ghoulish.

'If you ever touch my daughter, I'll...'

'I think you must have mistaken what I said, dear brother.' Marco smiled, sensing the start of his victory. 'What I mean is, Skye is *my* daughter, not yours.'

FORTY ONE

THIS TIME, as the hospital room came into focus, Erin didn't feel claustrophobic from dread and panic. She felt like she'd awoken from normal sleep. She blinked, relieved everything was crystal clear, with no trace of the muddled fog stuffing her head like before.

Unable to wait to speak to Zane, Erin turned over onto her side, a wide smile breaking over her face. She remembered his panic the last time she awoke, but it was different this time, but seeing the chair he'd last occupied empty, the smile slid from her face. *Where was he?*

'Oh!' The nurse stopped in the doorway as she entered Erin's private side room. 'You're awake! I'll get the doctor!'

'Where's Zane?' With difficulty, Erin slowly shuffled up the bed to adopt a more upright position.

'Careful!' the nurse chided, rushing to aid Erin in sitting up. 'Take things slowly.'

Slowly? There wasn't time to be slow. Erin now had full recollection of what she'd been trying to tell Zane. She also knew that thanks to the drugs she'd been pumped with, he'd barely understand her and furthermore, what he *had* understood, he'd brushed off as ramblings.

The urge to tell him this vital information - what Shirley and Fiona said and what the guard had seen, meant *everything*. Him not knowing or believing it was disastrous. 'I need to speak to Zane,' she repeated, this time urgently, worry igniting a growing torrent within her.

'Now, don't you worry about him, sweetheart.' The nurse patted Erin's hand. 'I'll get the doctor to check you over now.'

'But...'

'Your boyfriend will be back in the morning,' the nurse continued, oblivious to Erin's snowballing panic. 'The doctor sent him home earlier. No one expected you to be back with us so soon.'

Erin grabbed the nurse's hand. 'You don't understand! I...'

'I tell you, you've got a keeper there, love,' the nurse smiled. 'That man of yours hardly left your side. We thought we'd have to surgically detach him from you the way things were going, but the doctor finally got him to go home and get some rest.' The nurse then frowned at Erin's worry. 'I tell you what - as soon as you've seen the doctor, I'll give your man a ring and tell him you've woken up. He can then get a proper sleep tonight, free from worry and be back to see you bright and early in the morning.'

Erin knew she should be grateful for the nurse's kindness, but instead found herself torn between bursting into tears from pure frustration or pushing the nurse to the floor, ripping the lines out of her arms and discharging herself. She had to tell Zane what happened before he walked into a trap.

That girl... Skye...

That little bitch was lying all along, just like she'd thought. God only knew what else she was involved in. She'd been party to everything and had the knowledge needed to outstep Zane at every turn. 'Please! I have to see Zane now. There's stuff I haven't told him and it's vital that he knows! I should have told him days ago. Oh God! How long have I been here? How long was I unconscious? Erin's eyes grew wider, panic overtaking her. 'I *have* to tell him!'

The nurse busied herself pouring Erin a glass of fresh water out of the plastic jug on the side table. 'You mustn't worry about that either, duck.' She placed the glass in Erin's trembling hands. 'He already knows.'

Erin blinked. 'What?' Had she been talking in her sleep? Speaking aloud of the things crowding her mind and all the knowledge trapped inside her whilst her body lay useless. 'H-How does he...'

'The doctor told him.' The nurse squeezed Erin's hand reassuringly. 'He had to tell him because at one point you gave us all quite a scare.'

'T-The doctor?' Erin couldn't make sense of this. *Was she going mad?*

'Hey, don't fret your pretty head. Your fella is over the moon!' the nurse beamed. 'I don't think I've ever seen a man so happy to learn he's going to be a father.'

'A father? He's already got a...' Erin stopped as the implication hit home.

From Erin's expression, the nurse fast realised she'd made an error. Her hands flew to her mouth. 'Oh no!' she mumbled, mortified. 'You weren't talking about that, were you? I... I'm so sorry! You... you didn't know?'

Erin could only pointlessly shake her head, her mind reeling. She cleared her throat, forcing her voice box back to action. 'I... I'm pregnant?'

The nurse nodded. 'But don't panic. Your baby's perfectly fine and unharmed from that dreadful accident.'

Erin nodded automatically, her mind swarming with a thousand questions that she couldn't comprehend. Pregnant? She was *pregnant*?

• • • •

SCREECHING UP TO THE kerb directly outside the penthouse apartment, Leo grabbed his gun from under the seat and dragged Skye across the bench seat to pull her through the driver's door.

'Hey! What the hell are y...?'

'Shut it, bitch!' Leo snarled, all but carrying Skye up the pathway to the entrance doors. 'I haven't got time for your whining.'

And he hadn't. Zane might have something to say about him roughly manhandling his daughter, but he'd risk the onslaught. It was better than this hellcat getting the chance to disappear.

He wasn't giving this sly, manipulative liar a second's grace. He'd resented doing so before, but now he knew she was behind Erin's abduction and the one informing Marco of Zane's and everyone else's movements there was no contest.

Finding out Skye had betrayed him to Marco would crucify Zane and rip out his soul, but that's exactly what she'd done.

The question was, why?

Barging through the reception, shooting a glare in the direction of the concierge, Leo pounded his fist on the lift button. There was no chance that man on reception calling the police. No one was that stupid. Everyone in this building knew who the penthouse belonged to and what that meant.

Relieved that for once the lift doors opened within seconds, Leo pulled Skye into the gold, mirrored enclosure and held her against the wall with his forearm.

'It's not like I'm going anywhere,' Skye muttered, shooting Leo a death stare. *His time would come - possibly within the next few minutes. And she could barely wait.*

Leo stared at the lift wall, the ascent to the top floor taking an excruciatingly long time. He avoided looking at Skye, but despite his efforts he could see her in the shiny gold reflection. His lungs constricted further. That slight sneer on her face only fuelled his rage. Instead of being terrified of what would become of her, the girl looked like she was *enjoying* this whole thing.

She'd get a short, sharp shock when the truth sank in that Zane had done what was needed and Marco was dead. And, father or not, Zane would not forgive his darling daughter for this one.

Leo gritted his teeth, not entertaining a smidgen of doubt that Zane wouldn't be the victor. *It wasn't feasible.*

The 'bing' of the lift signifying they'd reached the top floor couldn't come soon enough. Barging his way through the opening doors, Leo dragged Skye along the regal-looking corridor to her deliverance.

• • • •

ZANE'S FIRST REACTION to Marco's words had been to laugh, but nevertheless, what was said caused a glimmer of doubt which clashed with his truth. Despite it being ludicrous, ridiculous and insane, the words burrowed deeper and against every power he possessed, grew in intensity.

It was all lies. Of *course* it was all lies.

In his mind, his finger inched towards the trigger of the Beretta now back in his hand, but in real life it remained unmoving.

'I'm telling you, she wanted it.' Marco circled Zane, the elation on his face clear. 'Shirley practically begged for my cock!'

Tiger glanced at Zane. He'd had enough of this shite. If Zane didn't blow this fucker's head clean off, then *he* would! *What the fuck was he waiting for?*

Regaining control of his faculties, Zane glared at Marco and raised his gun. This was how Marco played but he wasn't falling for it. 'You're a liar!'

'Remember how Shirley disappeared on the night of my fourteenth party?' Marco sneered. He raised his finger to his lips in thought. 'Hmm, and you never saw her again after that? Wasn't it then that she deserted you? Yeah, it was... Why do you think that was?'

'Shirley wouldn't have touched you with a bargepole!' Zane spat through clenched teeth. 'Skye is *my* daughter.'

'Who said anything about Shirley "wanting" to...?' Marco laughed. 'Yeah, I had a job to do. However, I reckon she changed her mind halfway through when she realised I was a better fuck then you!'

Blood pooled in Zane's palms as his nails dug deep. 'You want me to believe that you raped Shirley? I think not. You're trying to wind me up.'

The deep laugh from the back of Marco's throat rumbled around the room. 'We had to think of a way to stop the pathetic relationship you were in. You were lined up for Sofia Buscemi and that was business. Something had to be done and so I did it.'

'Who's "we"?' Zane snarled. 'You and your imaginary friends?'

'Not at all.' Marco shrugged. 'Our father.' *That would get Zane, the prick!*

'What?' Zane roared, the first glimmer of white rage pushing through. Their father had the upmost respect for women. The last thing he'd have done was instruct Marco to rape Shirley – or *anyone* – no matter how much he didn't approve of something. 'You really are fucked in the head! You expect me to believe that our father would have called *that*? He'd have been horrified! Don't you dare insult his memory by suggesting anything else.'

'Insult his memory?' Marco yelled. '*You* were the one who let him down by jeopardising the Buscemi association. Our father needed Shirley gone and what better way to do it? Maybe you should ask *Shirley* why she and her family disappeared so suddenly…' His face split with a sneer at the flash of doubt behind Zane's eyes. 'Why do you think the mad, fat bitch has been sitting in a posh house since? You really think that thick cow would have amounted to anything other than a bog cleaner? So, ask yourself where she and her family got that kind of brass from.'

As Zane lurched in his direction with a roar, Marco took the opportunity to deliver the final part which, if it didn't bring the man to his knees, nothing would. 'Our father - *my* father, paid off the Wilsons. He paid them to leave London and fuck the hell off. And by the way, he *did* know everything and was most impressed with my part in achieving the desired outcome.'

A wide smile then formed on Marco's face as Leo walked into the open plan room with Skye. Even the gun in the gorilla's hand wasn't enough to spoil his victory. 'Ah, here she is!'

Zane's head shot up in panic. 'What the fuck have you brought her here for?'

'I had to!' Leo looked from Zane to Tiger. *What the fuck was this? Marco was still alive? Why hadn't Zane dispatched the cunt yet?* He grabbed back hold of Skye's arm. 'You're not going to like this, Zane, but this bitch ordered Erin's accident. She's the mole. She's working for your piece of shit brother! I found messages from her on the dead guy's phone. She's a bloody traitor.'

A high-pitched whining noise kicked off in Zane's ears. No! That wasn't true. This was part of the long-standing mistrust between everyone and Skye. 'Stand up for yourself then, girl,' he barked, only then noticing how relaxed Skye looked. 'Tell him someone else must have had your old phone.'

'Well, I would…' Skye shook herself from Leo's grip and moved to stand next to Marco. 'Except that it's true. I hate you, Zane. I hate Erin too. I hate the lot of you! I'm only here to help my *real* father!' Her tinkling laugh clashed with the coldness in her eyes. 'I heard what was said about money as I came in too. My pointless slut of a mother had tons of cash. It's just a shame the selfish bitch didn't tell Marco of my existence. She must have been too embarrassed to admit being the local bike and shagging both brothers. I wish she'd told Marco though, because if she had, I'd have got the life I deserved long before now!'

Zane found it impossible to move his eyes from Skye's hand on Marco's arm. He wanted to gun Marco down. Skye was confused. Marco wasn't her father and she'd betrayed no one. None of this was true.

It wasn't possible.

The question was, why was he giving this piece of shit of a

brother airtime?

Zane was paralysed with shock, unable to pull the trigger of his gun. Instead, his eyes met Marco's, willing himself to react. *The cunt was lying. It was bullshit.*

It *had* to be.

Yet despite all the protests within his head, the shrill whining noise between his ears ricocheted around and gained in volume as the truth became inescapable.

Marco was Skye's father?

And *his* father had sanctioned what Marco had done?

Zane went to move forward but found he could do nothing but continue being deafened by his crashing heartbeat.

'I'm leaving now,' Marco said flippantly. 'You're not shooting me and neither are your trained thugs.' He jerked his chin at Tiger and Leo. 'Have the penthouse - see it as a parting gift, but I'm taking my daughter.'

'But I thought we'd live here now!' Skye gasped. 'I...'

'We don't need this place, sweetheart. Let this prick have it.' Marco squeezed Skye's arm. 'We've got bigger things in store.'

'You're *not* taking my daughter!' Zane roared, finding his voice. *But was she his daughter?* He stumbled, his legs starting to give way. 'Skye?'

Skye stared at Zane with the iciest eyes imaginable. 'I'm leaving with my *father* – which is not you! You're a fucking embarrassment and a liar. After what you did to Marco, you deserve everything you get! Anyway, it's not all bad. You have another kid on the way, remember? That's if it's yours or even makes it into life being as that liability of a bitch is carrying it!'

Leo and Tiger stepped forward in unison.

'NO!' Zane growled, his eyes speaking a thousand words. 'Let them go!' He couldn't risk anything else happening to Erin. Skye would see sense and in the interim, he had to protect everyone, no matter what.

Sensing his victory complete, Marco gave Leo and Tiger a long, measured stare, then hoisted the holdall packed with money onto his shoulder. With his other hand, he picked up a small bag containing a few clothes.

He jerked his head at Skye. 'Let's go. I'll buy you whatever you need.' He then turned to Zane. 'I'm not quite as incompetent as you believed, eh, dear brother. Looks like you don't have everything after all. Never mind.'

He stalked towards the door. 'By the way, you can take the girl I left in my bed, if you like. Perhaps you can get some use out of her? Accept her as my parting gift to you.'

Halfway out of the door, Marco turned. 'Almost forgot…' Shoving his hand in his trouser pocket, he extracted the keys to the penthouse and threw them at Zane's feet. 'You'll want these, no doubt? Enjoy.'

Marco and Skye left the penthouse and moved down the corridor, their laughter gradually fading, leaving Tiger and Leo battling to work out why the hell Zane had let his brother walk.

FORTY TWO

IT WAS QUIET on the journey back in Leo's van. Leo and Tiger agreed between them that Zane was in no fit state to make decisions. He'd been all but catatonic since Marco and Skye left the penthouse and nothing had changed. But they had to remove the unknown girl from the place. She was still out of her mind and couldn't be left, so a plan was quickly devised.

Leo glanced in his wing mirror, seeing Tiger's van two cars back. Tiger was bringing the girl to Dalston, whereas *he'd* got Zane. Briefly taking his eyes from the road, he glanced at Zane sitting next to him, a cigarette burnt down to the filter between his fingers.

'It won't be long before we get back,' Leo said, taking the road to Dalston. He didn't expect a reply and it was a good job because none was forthcoming.

Zane heard what Leo said but it was impossible to process. Everything that had happened tonight was impossible to digest. His face felt like it had solidified and turned into a static mask, set forever in the same expression.

None of this was real. *None* of it. It would eventually come to pass that Marco had lied about everything. It had to because... because what else could happen?

It was easy enough for Marco to make up a story by twisting the few facts he had. It wasn't a secret that Skye had issues, therefore it wasn't difficult for Marco to manipulate her into believing the bullshit he spouted was the truth.

'I'm hoping Erin will be awake and back to normal tomorrow,' Leo said casually, realising he'd spoken only to break the silence. But if thinking of Erin and remembering the huge part she played jolted Zane from the switched-off, vacant stance he was presently trapped in, he'd happily say *anything*.

Seeing no flicker of acknowledgement, not even a slight shift of the permanent frown Zane wore, Leo inwardly despaired. He knew Skye's betrayal would hit Zane hard, but he hadn't factored more poisonous arrows being thrown into the mix.

It was clear Zane was struggling to believe any of it, let alone the bit about Skye not being his daughter. *And as for Guiseppe's part in it...*

'Skye *is* my daughter,' Zane said, his gaze fixed out of the windscreen into the dark night. 'Marco has convinced her otherwise, but she'll see sense. It will just take time.'

Leo knew Zane wasn't talking to him but to himself in the hope that vocalising his thoughts would make them true. He chewed the inside of his cheek, the raw area formed from doing the exact same thing over the course of the day becoming more painful.

The question was, did *he* believe what Marco said?

In all truth, yes.

The concept of Skye not being Zane's daughter hadn't crossed Leo's mind before but now it made sense. Even though she had many of Zane's features: the piercing blue eyes, the dark hair and the stubbornness, so did Marco...

It also explained why everything had gone badly wrong ever since she'd arrived; why she hated Erin and also why Shirley hadn't told Zane of his 'daughter's' existence.

Shirley said nothing because Skye wasn't his.

But then why did Shirley hate him so?

Keeping his eyes on the road, Leo took a deep breath. 'You heard Skye admitting feeding Marco information and gave orders to those men to take Erin?' He'd said this already, but it hadn't sunk into Zane's head. He *had* to take on board what she'd done.

He glanced at Zane staring blankly through the windscreen. 'Zane? I said th...'

'Skye is *my* daughter.' Zane's jaw clenched, the vein in his temple throbbing. 'I've never believed anything that bastard of a brother of mine has ever said and I'm not starting now.'

At a loss, Leo continued driving. What, if anything would convince Zane that for once Marco wasn't lying?

• • • •

'THANK GOD YOU'RE BACK!' Martin jumped to his feet when Zane loomed in the doorway of the sitting room. The relief that he'd returned unscathed heightening on spotting his obviously broken nose. *Did this mean Marco was no longer in existence?* 'Your face... it's... Did you... Is he...? Can we talk? I've got to tell you abou...'

Clocking Leo's expression as he appeared behind Zane, Martin faltered, his dread returning. 'Wh-where's Skye?'

Seeing an almost imperceptible shake of Leo's head, translating as *'shut the fuck up'*, Martin stepped out of Zane's path and watched him head straight for a bottle of whisky.

'Is it Erin?' Martin gabbled, desperate for a hint. The sudden thought that this might be nothing to do with Marco and something a lot, *lot* worse gained traction in his frayed mind. 'Is she all right? Has something hap...'

'Erin is fine as far as we know.' Leo glared at Martin for the second time. *Couldn't the prat take the hint that things were not good.*

'I'm glad you're back, Mr Morelli,' Fiona piped up from the armchair. She wouldn't overthink the state of this man's face. She'd prefer to remain unaware of further unsavoury occurrences. 'Perhaps now we could discuss...'

'Skye has left with Marco.' Zane's voice was monotone, past caring that Fiona Bolt and Shirley were still in his house. He might as well tell everyone what had occurred. That way they could all fucking leave and let him be so he could work out how to cancel the spell his brother had put on Skye.

Once he'd worked that out, everything would be fine. Things would get back to normal: Erin would be discharged from hospital; Skye would see through Marco's lies and return where she belonged – with *him*; the new baby was on the way… They'd be a family again, like before.

Pausing, he took a long drink from the whisky bottle. His nose and face hurt like fuck, but that was the least of his problems. Whisky would take the edge off the pain. It could take the edge of *everything* whilst it was at it too! 'Marco's made Skye believe he's her father! He's been talking all kinds of shit. Erin was right - Skye's been working for Marco. He's done a right job on her, but she'll realise her mistake soon enough.'

Leo glanced at Tiger in the hallway carrying a still unconscious Alyson. Zane was still hell bent on refusing to accept the inevitable? *Christ, this was bad.*

'Alyson? Is that Alyson?' Seeing the woman in Tiger's arms, Martin rushed over. 'It *is* Alyson! What's happened to her?'

Tiger's rugged face was lined with stress. 'You know who this woman is?'

Martin nodded. 'Alyson Read, Skye's friend. She's the one Skye said came to London to visit her uncle, but she's supposed to have gone home. Where was she?'

'In Marco's flat, drugged to the eyeballs.'

Martin's heart banged within his chest. 'What about Skye? Has she really left with Marco?'

Leo blanked Martin. He wasn't answering anything else. If the bloke still gave a flying fuck about that little bitch, then he should do it on his own bloody time! And being as Zane was fixated only on drinking, it was up to *him* to take control of this shitshow.

Fiona cleared her throat. 'Mr Morelli, what you said about Skye being Marco's daughter is true.'

Shirley snapped out of her zoned-out state. 'Fiona! Don't say anyth...'

'Now's the time to tell him the truth!' Fiona barked. Seeing the state of Zane Morelli, it was clear he was never part of his brother's games. 'Can't you see he didn't know?'

Shirley's silence only infuriated Fiona further. Well, if Shirley wasn't going to speak, *she* would. 'Your brother raped Shirley, Mr Morelli. Skye is the result of that.'

'I found Hazel's wedding documentation in Skye's bedroom too,' Martin cried. 'I've been trying to tell you. Erin suspected Skye of having something to do with forging Hazel's signature for the documents that got Marco released and I… I think Skye did it.' He swallowed dryly. *This was the worst bit.* 'Skye put the documents in one of my drawers… I-I think she was trying to frame me for killing Hazel… But I… I think *she* did it.'

There were a few moments of silence before all hell broke loose.

Zane dived across the room, catching Martin off guard. 'How long have you known about this?'

Fiona shrieked when her son was grabbed around the throat for the second time that day. Her terror grew as Martin crashed to the floor with Zane on top of him. 'STOP!' she cried. 'It's not his fault!'

'You have the fucking balls to say my daughter killed Hazel?' Zane raged, inches from Martin's face, his eyes sparking with fury. 'You choose to accuse her of that now, yet you said nothing before?' He couldn't believe it. *Wouldn't* believe it. Not Skye - not his daughter.

'I...' Martin clawed at the hands around his throat, his eyes bulging. 'The signatures...' he croaked. 'There's a page of them. Practice signatures. It...'

'That could be anyone. It could be *you*! It probably *was*

you!' Zane roared.

'Leave him, mate.' Being as Tiger's hands were full, Leo was the only one available to use his brute strength to pull Zane off Martin.

Zane span around, his eyes wild. 'My daughter knew how much Hazel meant to us. She thought the world of her too, so she'd hardly kill her! This is crazy! Skye's a tiny slip of a thing. Is it not bad enough that it's been said she was part of Erin's abduction and not my daughter? For fuck's sake! I know some of you haven't much time for her because of what she's done in the past, but...'

'It's true that she's not your daughter.' The voice that came from behind was small and quiet, but everybody heard it.

Time stood still in the heavy silence following Shirely's words.

'What Fiona said is correct,' Shirley continued.

A bead of sweat trickled down Zane's forehead onto his face to settle in the dip of his scarred cheek. 'Y-You *slept* with him?' he gasped. 'You were with me! We...'

'It was the night of his birthday party. I… I had no choice.' Shirley was more in control of her voice, body and trembling than she'd been for many years. Nearly two decades had passed without speaking of that night until recently and even then, the details hadn't been mentioned. *Until now...* 'I was looking for a toilet. You were busy talking to someone. Marco appeared in the corridor and dragged me out of the fire escape into a car.'

'Whose car?' Zane's voice was flat - devoid of tone and feeling.

Shirley's chins trembled as she shook her head. 'I don't know. I... I was taken to a factory... He threw me to the floor... and then... then…'

In the following silence the clanging bells and whistling returned to gain momentum in Zane's brain. He dragged air into his lungs. 'Why didn't you say?' he croaked. 'You just disappeared. You could have told me!'

'He said you were promised to Sophia and that I had to go.'

Fat tears rolled down Shirley's face. 'Marco said that what he was doing was to make things easier and you wouldn't want me after... after...'

'I don't give a fuck what he said!' Zane roared. 'If you'd told me...'

Shirley took a deep breath. 'We left London shortly afterwards. Your... your father paid my parents to leave the city and never to speak of what happened. Then I discovered I was pregnant. My parents wanted me to give up my baby, but I couldn't. I just couldn't, regardless of how it had come to be.'

Tiger and Leo exchanged looks. *Guiseppe Morelli knew about it? Marco had spoken the truth? Holy fuck!*

Zane's mouth moved but nothing came out. His olive skin paled. 'Skye could still be mine.'

Shirley shook her head once more. 'No, I… I'd already had my monthlies since the last time we... erm… She can't be your daughter. She *isn't.*' She finally looked at Zane properly and saw the pain ravaging his face. 'I-I've hated you for years because I believed you were part of what Marco did, but you didn't know, did you?'

Zane put his head in his hands, his world imploding. 'No, I did not.' *Skye wasn't his daughter. Skye was Marco's daughter. No, no, NO!* 'Does Skye know about this?'

Shirley swiped the tears from her cheeks. 'Not from me. I refused to discuss anything to do with her father. I wanted her to have nothing to do with any of you! Skye didn't even know the Morelli name, until unbeknown to me a family member mentioned you several months ago and she went from there. I tried to stop her... I...'

'I'm truly sorry for what you have been put through, Shirley,' Zane muttered, the flashing lights behind his eyes becoming brighter as everything he thought he knew, believed and lived for was sucked into a vortex. *Skye wasn't his daughter. Shirley was raped. His father had known everything, yet protected Marco.*

Leo broke the cloying silence. 'Tiger, take the girl upstairs and put her to bed to sleep it off. We'll work out what to do with her later or in the morning.'

Zane swung around, his eyes filled with an emotion that could equally pass for despair or rage. 'There will never be a morning again!'

With an angry roar, he grabbed the whisky bottle and launched it at the wall, showering broken glass across the room. Following that, he staggered forward to lean on the sideboard where he vomited the contents of his stomach over the rug.

Forty Three

'FROM WHAT I GATHER, Alyson's had problems with her phone.' Martin glanced uncomfortably at his mother and Shirley who were both listening to the conversation. 'Yes... yes, I know, but her and Skye would have missed the plane if... Yes... It's only for a few days... I... Yes, I realise that it's... They'll be back soon. Yes... I'll make sure she gets in touch.'

Ending the call, Martin doublechecked the line was disconnected before speaking. 'They weren't happy,' he said miserably. 'I'm not convinced they believed me either.'

'You did the right thing,' Fiona said, pleased Martin had agreed to make the call. Not that she condoned the blatant lie, but not putting the girl's poor parents through additional worry - especially when no one knew how Alyson was this morning was the kindest thing to do.

'It doesn't help that they don't know me,' Martin grumbled. 'I've only met Alyson a few times and I don't remember ever meeting her parents.'

'But as Skye's boyfriend, they would have *heard* of you, so you phoning was better than me or Shirley doing it,' Fiona reasoned. 'They'd be more worried if one of us had phoned.'

Hearing the term 'Skye's boyfriend', Martin stiffened. He

had been Skye's boyfriend, but not anymore. From what had been said yesterday, he never was - not in the true sense of the word. His part in Skye's life was to serve as a distraction and supply the cover she required to make her appear normal.

And 'normal' was a gulf away from what Skye Wilson could be described as.

All this time she'd been living a lie. Not only that, but Martin was convinced she'd murdered Hazel and tried to frame him for the deed in the process. If she'd succeeded, he'd be in jail by now. Or dead, depending who had caught up with him first. And if Skye's plan where Erin was concerned had worked, she'd be a *double* murderer.

Martin shuddered. He'd pictured his whole future including Skye: marriage, kids, growing old together... Now all he had was memories of something that didn't exist in the first place.

'Where is this place that Alyson's been taken to?' Shirley asked. 'What even is it?'

'Mr Solenzo is a private surgeon who deals with injuries for Zane's people.' Martin shrugged. 'It's somewhere in London but I'm not sure exactly where.'

Shirley frowned. 'I hope it's decent. Alyson deserves good treatment. She's ever such a nice girl. This sort of thing doesn't happen to people like her.'

'I'm sure it's fine,' Fiona smiled. No, things like that didn't usually happen to people like Alyson, her or Martin. Even Shirley, yet now they were all embroiled in a world that had been alien only a short time ago. Except not so much to Shirley, who, unfortunately, had first-hand experience of what some of these people did.

Almost tasting Martin's devastation, Fiona sighed. He looked drawn, pale and exhausted. It would take him a long time to get over this, if ever. Skye was his world and future and now it had gone that prospect worried her.

Shirley fared differently. Since informing Zane about what had happened over eighteen years ago, she seemed purged. It was like a magic brush had cleansed away the ills and demons which had haunted her for so very long. And if it didn't sound trite nonsense, Fiona was convinced some worry lines and wrinkles had already vanished from Shirley's face; the lifting of the burden taking ten years off her appearance.

When she'd reached the conclusion that Zane, despite him being an enemy up until yesterday and undeniably possessing ways of life that she could never agree with or condone, he hadn't had any part in his brother's despicable actions. He was almost as much of a victim as Shirley.

Seeing that big, strong man throw his guts up from devastation; brought to his knees by people he'd given his heart to, was heartbreaking. The sight of such a feared man so utterly broken was not in any way enjoyable. 'Has anyone seen Zane today?' she asked tentatively. 'I've been up since dawn and haven't laid eyes on him. I don't even know whether we should remain in his house.'

'It's fine you being here,' Martin mumbled. 'Even if it wasn't, the state Zane was in he won't notice. But no, I haven't seen him. He went off with Leo last night, so he's probably at the hospital.'

'You mean we're on our own?' Fiona gasped. 'What if Marco comes looking for trouble?'

'Tiger's around. He returned for that very reason after taking Alyson to Solenzo's.' Martin found himself staring at the envelope still on the side containing the proof that his life was a sham. He no longer cared whether Marco turned up and killed him outright. He already felt dead, so being dead for *real* made little difference. Right now, there was little, if anything left of an existence worth staying around for.

• • • •

LAST NIGHT, Leo made sure he and Zane went to a room in the Thames Canning Works well away from everyone else. There was a steady stream of runners coming to pick up batches of cocaine to fan out dealers in territories which Zane controlled and he couldn't have them seeing anything.

Further men weighing, cutting and bagging the next batch of coke ready to distribute were still hard at work, and from what he'd gathered it was running like clockwork. The coke was going out, the money rolling in - everything was on target. But things would become skewed if it became known that the boss had lost the plot.

Containing his grunt, Leo stretched out his stiff back. All night he'd been sat on this chair. He estimated that he'd dozed off for half an hour here and there, but even that was doubtful. He couldn't take his eye off the ball. And that ball not only included the possibility of an appearance from Marco, but also involved watching Zane.

Leo had expected Zane to kick off and raze the canning works to the ground since working out by process of elimination that this was the place Marco had dragged Shirley to and where Skye was conceived. But Zane hadn't kicked off - he'd just drank and drank. And drank some more.

Two big bottles of whisky he'd put away before passing out and the minute he'd woken up this morning, he'd started again. It wasn't even mid-morning and Zane was already steaming drunk.

Thankfully, if there was a preferred outcome to this, Zane was *morose* drunk, rather than *angry* drunk. This was preferable because the combination of his raw strength, coupled with rage was a mixture even Leo would struggle to now contain. He already had a knackered back, a pounding headache and was starving hungry, so could do without getting his teeth knocked out on top.

He frowned, catching a whiff of his own body odour. He fucking stunk and needed a shower.

Opening a bottle of water that he'd had the sense to add to the order from the off licence for delivery last night, he greedily slurped at it. 'We'd best think about getting freshened up,' he said, injecting a believable amount of motivation into his voice.

Receiving no response, he stared at Zane still steadily drinking whisky with a glazed look in his eyes. 'Mate? Shall we get freshened up so you can go and visit Erin? She should be awake by now and will wonder where you are.'

As would the hospital...

Zane had hardly left Erin's side since she'd been admitted, yet since leaving yesterday he'd dropped off the radar with not even a phone call to check on her welfare.

Zane turned slowly, his movements jerky. Placing the bottle on the table took several attempts. He blinked, struggling to focus. 'Not going to the hospital.'

'What do you mean? Erin will be expecting you and...'

'How can I go like *this*?' Zane pushed himself to his feet and staggered to the table for support. 'Look at the state of me! Look at my fucking face! I can't let her see me like this.'

'Have a couple of cups of coffee and a shower. That will sort you ou…' Leo's voice tailed off spotting an additional bottle in the bin. His heart sank. *It was empty.* The half-bottle of whisky Zane had on the go was not the only one he'd consumed so far this morning.

Fuck. That put a different slant on things. 'Shit, mate, you've got to go. Erin will be worried sick if you don't.' Leo dragged his fingers through his knotted hair, the prospect of drinking himself an enticing prospect. But someone had to remain alert.

He watched Zane attempt to light another cigarette, the lighter wavering two inches away from the end of his fag. Never in all the years - even through all the shit that had happened, had Leo known Zane to get this wasted. It didn't bode well.

'I canna face telling her waz happened. I shoulda killed him. Killed them both. What do either of them mean to me anyway? Bollocks to it! I don't give a fuck!' Zane drawled. 'They mean nothing! I shouldda just done it. I'm a loser! That's me - a fucking loser!'

Leo pursed his lips. Marco had long since figured on Zane's list of people to give no time to, but Skye was different. Zane had believed her his daughter. He'd fought for her on every angle and to discover she was not his child after all and she'd merely used him for the purpose of destroying him, as well as everyone that he cared about, underlined one very important fact: No DNA test was required to prove that Marco's blood ran through Skye's veins. 'You must tell Erin. She needs to know what's happened.'

Zane stumbled heavily back into the chair and reached for the whisky. 'She's better off without me!'

Leo got to his feet. If Zane wouldn't update Erin, then *he* would.

• • • •

ERIN'S FIRST THOUGHT when waking at an ungodly hour was that she'd shortly see Zane. Since unexpectedly regaining consciousness last night, the hours of the evening had dragged by excruciatingly slowly. That the nurse's four attempts to call Zane to let him know she was awake had gone to voicemail, was worrying.

It was that which played on Erin's mind during the remainder of the night. That, and the unexpected news that she had a child growing inside her.

According to the nurse, Zane was here every hour available to man beforehand, so why was he not here now? Why had he disappeared when she needed to talk to him so desperately?

It was imperative he was made aware of what she'd been told. Yes, telling him that Skye was not his child and there could be paperwork in Skye's bedroom which might shed light on Hazel's murder would be dreadful for him. But she'd rather it came from her than anyone else.

Even though this news would be devastating, there was also light at the end of the tunnel.

Erin placed her hand on her flat stomach.

Pregnant? She could still hardly believe it.

A warm glow radiated through her thinking of the future with a little Zane or a little girl running around. She didn't mind which.

This baby may not have been planned but he or she had

survived the accident and was on the way, so it was brilliant news. A ray of sunshine in a world which was dark and foreboding: a little miracle created between them.

But where was Zane?

Erin's eyes flicked to the clock on the wall. It wouldn't be long before lunchtime. Surely he should be here by now?

Going against orders, Erin swung her legs out of bed, the floor tiles feeling cold and alien under her feet after two days of lying in bed.

Using the bed for support, she shuffled towards her coat on the chair in the corner. *What if Zane had moved on Marco and walked into a trap?*

What if Marco had killed him?

Panic bubbled.

Or being as Zane had already been informed about the baby, what if he'd freaked out? The relationship between them hadn't been plain sailing, so what if having a child with her was the *last* thing he wanted?

Erin reached her jacket and shoved her hand into the pocket.

She was being ridiculous. The nurse said Zane was over the moon about her pregnancy.

As her fingers closed around her phone and pulled it out, Erin's relief faded to find the battery dead.

Shit. She couldn't get in contact with anyone now.

When the door suddenly opened, Erin turned, aghast to be caught defying the orders to remain in bed, but her heart then surged to see Leo. 'Oh! I wondered when you two would get here!' she grinned, her worries disappearing.

'What are you doing up?' Leo gestured for Erin to get back into bed.

It was only as she moved back towards the bed did Erin realise that Leo was alone. 'Wh-Where's Zane?' she asked, her worry immediately reigniting.

Pulling up a chair, Leo waited until Erin was settled back into bed. He'd have to be blind to miss the panic on her face. The entire journey here it had gone round in his head where to start with telling her what had happened. He was still none the wiser. Neither had he liked locking the door behind him when he'd left Zane in a stupor at the canning works.

When Zane woke up, realising he'd been locked in like a prisoner, he'd go mad. But that was a risk Leo had to take. It was better than going on a drunken rampage looking for vengeance or whatever was going through Zane's mind.

'Leo?' Erin pushed. 'Why are you here and not Zane?'

Taking a deep breath, Leo began to speak.

Forty Four

PETER BOLT slammed the phone down for the second time, his face a portrait of rage and frustration.

First Fiona and now Martin? This wasn't good enough.

Martin was one thing – the lapse in behaviour since becoming involved with that girl with the mentally bereft mother was nothing new. Unfortunately, Martin's lying and odd behaviour was now a frequent occurrence.

But Fiona?

Stomping across the lounge to stare out of the window, Peter's face crumpled into a harder scowl. 'Craft workshop in Oxford, my foot!' he hissed, glaring at a patch on the driveway where the gravel had skittered off onto the surrounding grass.

Bloody embarrassing, it was. How dare Fiona do this to him!

He patted his jowly cheeks, sure they were still red from the humiliation of bumping into Fiona's friends, Marjorie and Janet, on his usual jaunt to fetch his newspaper.

Oh, he'd seen the confusion on their faces when he'd commented they were back early.

Sure, they'd tried to backtrack when he'd mentioned accompanying Fiona on a craft workshop, but it was obvious they knew nothing about it.

And they knew nothing because there was *no* craft workshop...

How stupid of him to be glad that Fiona was back this morning rather than this afternoon. He'd been looking forward to a freshly cooked meal, rather than the frozen ones she'd left in the freezer. Nothing beat a freshly cooked dinner - one which he couldn't burn due to his ineptitude in reheating things.

That was before he'd realised Fiona had lied.

And it didn't take a brain surgeon to realise why...

Snatching up his phone once again, he redialled his wife, his teeth grinding as it remained unanswered.

He could text instead, but what was the point? It wasn't like she'd respond - or if she did, it would just be more lies.

Peter's breathing became ragged as he continued pacing the lounge. How could she defy him like this? Fiona knew he'd forbidden her to have anything to do with that lunatic, Shirley Wilson!

Because that's who Fiona was with and she'd gone exactly where she'd badgered him to take her for so long.

London.

Not only had Fiona lied and gone ahead but he'd bet his last penny that she'd gone with that... that *woman*.

Peter dropped into an armchair, the material of his checked shirt straining across the paunch of his belly.

Fiona had gone off on the back of a ludicrous pack of rubbish regarding gangs and strange people.

For *what*?

That's what he wanted to know.

Martin was fine - they'd seen him with their own eyes only five days ago. Just because the stupid boy had disillusioned ideas of giving up university to live in London and marry that girl, didn't warrant following him there. When Fiona returned later, he'd wait to hear what further lies she'd spout before telling her that he knew *exactly* where she'd been.

But, Peter suddenly thought with a crawling sense of dread,

what if Fiona failed to come back? He didn't have the first clue where to find her and if no one was answering their bloody phones, where the hell did he start?

• • • •

ON ONE HAND, Erin was desperate for Leo to leave so she could process what he'd said. On the other, she wanted him to remain so that she didn't have to think about it.

Zane had allowed Marco to walk? He'd allowed the man to go, taking Skye with him?

Erin smiled weakly at the nurse writing the latest set of observations on the clip chart at the end of the bed. It was the same lady who had tried and failed to reach Zane yesterday.

'Your man not been in to see you yet?' the nurse asked with a twinge of concern.

'Something has kicked off at work,' Erin said. *It was only a white lie.* 'Now he knows I'm okay, he can get on with things.'

'Who was the man here earlier?' the nurse pressed. 'A friend?'

'My fiancé's colleague. He was passing and popped in.'

'He didn't look very happy...'

'He normally looks like that!' Erin laughed, finding that difficult to achieve. *Nothing was normal. Not one thing.* 'Look, erm… When do you think I can go home?'

'Home?' The nurse's eyebrows raised to just below the level of her hairline. 'Not for a while yet I wouldn't think.'

The nurse continued talking, but Erin stopped listening the moment she heard 'not for a good while yet...' She couldn't remain here any longer. It was enough of a shock hearing from Leo that Zane had lost the plot and was too drunk to come to the hospital.

Locking Zane in the canning works to ensure he didn't go on a rampage was bad. Zane didn't drink to that extent. *Ever.* He barely drank at all.

Yes, learning the truth about Skye would hit hard, but this was not good and Erin needed to be there for him. She *wanted* to be there for him.

The nurse was right. Leo wasn't happy and despite what he'd said, he looked more miserable than usual. It was hardly surprising.

But after Zane convincing himself that Marco had brainwashed Skye into this, it must have crucified him hearing further evidence. Including Shirley's.

Erin's eyes filled with tears. If only she could speak to Zane and show him that he – *they* - would get through this. But how could she do that whilst stuck here?

'Hey! What's the matter?' Frowning, the nurse moved to the bed and took Erin's hand. 'Don't fret. You'll be home soon.'

Erin nodded, the tightness in her throat squashing her words.

'Aw, I understand,' the nurse soothed. 'You want to be back in your own home with your man. Pregnancy hormones amplify feelings, but it will pass.'

Erin stared at her hands. *If only it was that simple.*

She cleared her throat. 'I don't suppose you have a phone charger I could borrow, do you?'

'I'll see what I can do,' the nurse smiled.

• • • •

MARCO PULLED OUT his carved stash box from his bag and cut a thick line of cocaine on the table in the suite he'd booked at the Ritz. 'First thing I'll do is source suitable premises.' His eyes danced with glee. 'After I've had some more of this, of course!'

Forgetting any coke stashed around the penthouse was not an option. There was no way he was leaving that for Zane. Now the truth was out, that fool would grasp anything he could lay his hands on to blat knowledge from his brain. But it was silly - Zane had the fucking penthouse, Alyson, plus a corpse! *What else did he want?*

Hoovering up the loaded line of coke, Marco gave one last throaty snort for luck and wiped his nose.

With the guttural pig-like noises coming from the man who was her father, Skye winced, the sound setting her teeth on edge. But it wasn't just the sound that was grating.

She fidgeted in the leather chair in front of the suite's balcony doors. Marco said he didn't do drugs anymore and had never been a big user, yet that was all she'd seen him do these last few days. He'd done nothing but snort that shit since they'd got here! Drugs interfered with thinking straight. And thinking straight was the name of the game. Marco was becoming a liability and that, she didn't like.

Nothing could screw up the plans she'd harboured for so long. Everything had pretty much gone well so far because *she'd* made damn sure of it.

Annoyance rumbled. *She'd* done all of the work. *She'd* gone through hell infiltrating that snake, Zane's, life. She'd even prostituted herself to Martin as part of the cause. Yet what had Marco done?

Her eyes narrowed. Not a fat lot, short of getting off his tits, drugging up and screwing her mate.

Along with how Marco was acting lately, her amusement over Alyson's debasing was also beginning to lose a little of its shine. Especially as now it could well come back on *her*. 'I'm concerned that you left Alyson in *their* hands,' she said. 'What if she goes to the police?'

Marco frowned. It was a bit of a shit leaving Alyson behind. He'd quite enjoyed fucking her. But then again, she'd started asking questions and that was a no-go. 'Alyson won't remember enough to do fuck all, therefore she's not worth considering.'

Although being as the girl remembered him giving Skye a slap, the thought was a little worrying. But he wouldn't mention that. 'Why do you care anyway? You said you hated the girl.'

Skye bit her lip. Yes, she did hate Alyson. Or at least, she'd wanted to piss the girl off. Alyson's life was so nice; so *normal*. Even *Alyson* was so bloody nice…

But had Skye really wanted the girl ruined the way Marco

had done it? She'd thought so once, but now… Now she wasn't so sure. But that looked to be the least of her problems.

Marco inhaled deeply as the cocaine picked up pace in his brain. He wasn't having Skye put dampeners on things. 'Anyway, regardless of leaving her with "them", as you so succinctly put it, they're not likely to encourage the silly bitch to go to the Old Bill. It will only incriminate them.' *Being as they'd yet got Callie's corpse to find…*

'You remembered the films you shot of Alyson, I take it?' Skye pushed. 'They would count as evidence.'

'No, I didn't, but don't stress. Zane won't notice.' Marco's eyes sparkled. 'Not while he's got other pressing matters on his mind.'

Skye's hands curled into fists at Marco's lackadaisical attitude. 'You can't be sure Zane and his cronies haven't factored that in. I haven't done all of this just to get nicked or for things to fail because of stupid mistakes!' she sniped.

She'd had enough of this. Marco was too manic and uncentred. The concept of having made an error in getting involved with him and this whole thing nudged once again.

But it wasn't too late. She could leave and start afresh. And that she had to do before Marco's craziness got them both slung in jail.

Skye moved to get up. 'Look, Marco. I don't think this is working out for me.'

Marco lurched from his seat, his hand grabbing Skye's throat. 'Shut you fucking whining! You sound like your crusty bitch of a mother! Don't think you can fuck off as and when you please! You're in this for the long haul, you stupid cow! And for that, you should be grateful, considering you weren't supposed to even *exist*!'

A nasty chuckle rumbled from the back of his throat. 'You whores are all the same. You need to learn to obey and do what's necessary, like I did. I fucked your mother because of business. I entertain *your* presence for the very same reason. If you continue to offer nothing but grief, then I'll farm you out to work on your back!' His eyes glistened with malevolence. 'It's not like you'd have the strength to prevent it. Your mother never did…'

The crushing pain around Skye's throat paled into insignificance. *Did he just admit to forcing himself on Shirley? No, he couldn't have. That would be one step beyond.*

'Shirley was a stupid fucking witch!' Marco's rant continued. 'Do you know what needled me most? She was happy to willingly open her legs for my brother, yet had a problem doing so for me! Well, fuck her and fuck her moaning. She got you out of her "ordeal", as she likes to put it. It's a shame that you're just as fucking bad! Listen, I ain't got time for sad little cunts like you bringing me down.' Cutting Skye the iciest of glares, he dropped his grip. 'Remember that I wasn't the one who screwed up with the cheque at the bank, nor did I sneak in non-warranted orders resulting in getting two men killed!'

He paced around the sofa, his eyes fixed on Skye. 'You'd do well to remember who you are, sweetheart, and that you're only in my life and here with me because *I* sanction it. That can change any time of my choosing.'

Marco snatched up his box of cocaine from the table. Looking back over his shoulder, he sneered. 'Now, being as you deemed this part so fucking important, yet couldn't manage it, I'll make a call and get that pregnant slut of Zane's dead once and for all!'

With that, he stalked from the room, leaving Skye staring after him in shock.

She rubbed the red finger marks around her throat, realising the thought that she may have made a horrendous mistake was now a fact. Because if she wasn't careful, she'd end up on the receiving end of Marco's madness too.

• • • •

'YEAH, IT'S FINE,' Leo said to the newly appointed foreman of the cocaine cutting team. 'He's been arranging stuff back there.'

Without waiting for a reply, Leo turned and hastily made his way down the corridor to the back room where he'd locked Zane. He could hear the banging and shouts of abuse from all the way up here.

Christ! He was trying to draw attention *away* from Zane's lapse of control, not underline it!

Perhaps locking the man in here to go to the hospital was a bad idea. But then, someone had to tell Erin why there had been no show.

But if this got out...

Gritting his teeth, Leo reached the storeroom, the banging and cursing at an ear-splitting level. With the key in hand, he paused and braced himself for the fallout.

Okay, let's get it over with, he thought as he inserted the key in the lock. Quickly pushing the door open, Leo entered the room and rapidly secured the door behind him. 'Have you any idea of the racket you're making? I'm trying not to draw attention to your presence here!'

Spinning around with the mangled remains of a chair in his hands, Zane staggered towards Leo, his bloodshot eyes wild. 'Like I give a shit about that! How dare you lock me in here, you fucking rat!' he hissed. 'Who the fuck do you think you are?'

Zane swayed precariously and steadied himself on a workbench. '*I'm* the boss of this firm, not you! You dare to take it upon yourself to fu...'

'Stop this!' Leo yanked the remains of the chair from Zane's hands and stared at it before tossing it to the floor with the rest of the stuff that had been destroyed during his relatively short absence. 'Rant all you like but it won't solve anything!'

'Oh, and you'd know all about that, wouldn't you?' Zane slurred. 'You're a fucking joke! Call yourself loyal? Fucking locking me in here like a cunt? I'm the boss. ME!'

'Then act like one!' Leo roared, his face flushed red. *Not loyal? Not fucking loyal?*

Zane's eyes narrowed, his mouth slack as he fought to focus. 'Okay, if that's what you want, fine! You're fired! Get out of my building and out of my life!'

In any other situation; with any other person speaking these words, would have earned an uppercut from Leo, no matter who they were coming from, but this was Zane. This was Zane - his mate, his buddy, his adopted family.

Lurching forward, he grabbed Zane by the shoulders of his jacket and pulled him close. 'Fine by me! I'll go, but not before I sort this shit out for you. Being as you're too pissed to go and see the woman you love yourself, that's where I've been. Erin's worried about you, you silly cunt. She wants to help. We all do!'

'Get fucked!' Zane roared, his fingers pulling at Leo's hands. 'You have no right to interfere. It isn't you that just...'

'It might as well be me!' Leo yelled. 'I'm doing your job and sorting your shit because you're feeling sorry for yourself! I'm watching your back and doing whatever I can to help you, so don't you speak about loyalty. Yeah, I'll go. I'll walk the fuck away and out of your life as you wish, but only when this is done and everyone is all right. Now sober the hell up because we're going back to Dalston! If not now, then first thing in the fucking morning!'

Zane opened his mouth to roar further drunken expletives in Leo's direction, then something somewhere inside him flicked the switch.

In slow motion, Leo watched Zane's face crumple, the visible sagging of his shoulders giving the impression of him shrinking as the anger fell through his body and poured out of countless holes in his legs to puddle around his feet on the floor.

Zane stared at Leo, his glazed eyes filled with pain. 'Skye's not mine. She's not my daughter,' he croaked. 'What the hell am I going to do?'

It was a good job Leo still had hold of Zane's shoulders when he crumpled forward against Leo's chest. No sooner had Zane's broken nose made impact against the front of Leo's T-shirt did he hear a sound that he'd never heard before.

It seemed the natural and only thing to do was to wrap his arms around Zane as the sobs wracked through his body.

FORTY FIVE

FIONA FELT STRANGE waking up on the sofa in a strange house, but waking up seeing Shirley rather than Peter didn't feel as odd as it had the first time she'd done it in that crummy hotel. It was still strange – even more so by being in Zane's house for the second day.

Martin had offered them his room, but Fiona had declined. Her son had already lost enough. Besides, she felt more comfortable downstairs knowing that monster of a man with the strange name – Tiger - was in the hallway keeping watch. That had been the only thing offering the ability to snatch a few moments of rest. That's when the swirling mess of her brain allowed it.

Another new day and she was still in London with no idea what should happen from here. She could hardly leave Martin in a state, yet he showed no sign of vacating this place and judging by the amount of calls she'd ignored from Peter it was clear he was going spare. But what could she do?

'Did you get any sleep?'

Shirley's question caught Fiona unaware. 'I didn't realise you were awake.'

'I couldn't sleep,' Shirley admitted, her voice and

mannerisms now exhibiting no trace of the nervous, skittish wreck of the woman from before.

'I expect Skye must be on your mind?' Fiona muttered. That girl had shown her true colours. She'd been fooled almost as completely as Martin, but it was Shirley she felt most sorry for.

Shirley heaved her bulk off the chair she'd been in all night. 'It's almost a relief.'

'A relief?' Fiona frowned. The things Skye said to Shirley, she was surprised it hadn't sent the woman over the edge.

'I've been waiting for this for years.' Shirley smiled sadly. 'Of course, I hoped it wouldn't happen and prayed I'd done a good enough job of outrunning genetics and that nurture over nature would prevail, but in my heart I knew. Seeing Skye again proved what I've expected all along.'

Her eyes hardened. 'She's a vindictive, nasty piece of work - her father's daughter through and through. I thought by telling myself how lovely, sweet and beautiful she was over and over would make it true, but the *real* Skye had to surface eventually. I just wish she hadn't hurt people in the process. Like your Martin. He's a good boy. He didn't deserve it.'

Fiona's throat tightened. No, he didn't, but then nor did Shirley. Nor did *any* of them - including Zane Morelli. 'She tricked all of us, me included.' After this, she'd never take anyone at face value ever again - forever doomed to eternally question her own judgement. 'And Zane? How do you feel about him now?'

Shirley exhaled slowly. 'Dreadful for blaming him all of this time.'

'It wasn't your fault!' Fiona exclaimed. 'Anyone would have reached the same conclusion, given the facts.'

Shirley shook her head. 'I-I loved Zane desperately and the thought that he'd sanctioned... I should have known better. He's the genuine one. Out of all of that family, he's the only one with morals and a heart.'

Fiona stopped her eyebrows raising at 'morals' being used

in conjunction with any of these people.

Zane, despite her better judgement, *did* possess morals and a heart. More perhaps than most and she was guilty of assuming otherwise - just like everyone else. 'What's done is done,' she said chirpily. 'Feeling guilty solves nothing. What matters now is what everyone does from here.'

And that, she didn't know where to start. 'We should find out how Alyson Read is. I feel responsible to make sure she will be all right and work out how to deal with her parents.'

'Yes,' Shirley agreed. 'I was thinking the same thing.'

'She had a coat. Ah, there it is!' Fiona picked up the leather jacket that Alyson was covered in when she arrived last night. 'We should take this to her. That way we can see how she is.'

'Is that hers?' Shirley eyed the jacket. 'It looks too big and...' Freezing, she paled. 'That's *his*. Marco's.' That leather jacket was all she'd seen and smelt when the bastard loomed over her in the hallway last week.

Fiona dropped the jacket to the floor like it was contaminated. The thought of touching something which had been against Marco Morelli's skin was sickening. She opened her mouth to speak but stopped when the sitting room door opened.

Tiger walked in, followed by a vacant-looking Martin. 'I've had word from Leo. He and Zane are on the way here now.'

• • • •

SKYE STARED OUT over Green Park, thinking she should feel accomplished to be in a suite at this world-famous hotel, but she wasn't. Not now.

She barely dared move; on edge for when Marco returned. He wasn't in this suite, but he was undoubtedly *somewhere* in the hotel and if she made a run for it, he could spot her.

Her brow furrowed.

But where would she run to, anyway?

Wasn't being with her real father what she wanted? To be away from her crazy mother and rid of Zane Morelli - the people who had prevented the life of wealth and luxury with Marco that had been intended for her?

Skye turned a solid silver salt cellar left from the earlier room service Marco refused to allow the staff to collect.

This kind of life was what she'd wanted and now she'd attained it. She'd even achieved a couple of extra nice-to-haves - like fucking over the oh-so-perfect Alyson Read.

Except that was before she realised *she'd* fucked up by believing the wrong Morelli. Her life-long resentment had been channelled against the wrong people and now the truth was out from all sides.

And the truth was that she was the result of rape…

Skye didn't notice the first tear falling at first. It was only a single tear.

But it was a *real* one.

A second tear followed the first. And then another.

Soon they were flowing thick and fast: genuine tears, along with raw pain gripping her insides like a vice with barbed claws.

Skye gulped air into her lungs as her all-encompassing sobs thundered through her like never before.

Adept at crying on demand was a different beast to this soul-destroying, crushing hurt which squashed her from the inside out. Crying for real only made things worse because she was crying for herself rather than anyone. And that meant she was just like him.

Marco.

She'd even killed for him, for God's sake!

Skye sat bolt upright. *But wait!* As she was crying - as in, *really* crying, not the usual fake tears, did that not mean she harboured true emotions under the layers?

If so, then maybe all was not lost and she could turn this around and fuck Marco's plans.

Dragging her hand under her nose, she willed her body to move whilst keeping alert for Marco's impending return. She hurried to the telephone on the mahogany writing desk and paused. If the calls were itemised, Marco could find out who she'd phoned.

But as he was so coked out, would he check?

She didn't know, but with no phone of her own any longer and with little to lose, she'd risk it.

But who would she call?

There was no point in phoning Zane. It was tempting to warn him of Marco's plans for Erin. Then again, it wasn't like she cared. It would be great for that horrible bitch to finally die and take the unborn brat with her and she had no wish to stop *that*, aside from pissing Marco off by ruining his plans.

But phoning Zane was stupid. It was unlikely he'd answer – not to her. Even if he did, what would she say?

That she'd realised Marco's lies? Realised that *he* was the problem all along and that it was *him* who'd set Zane up, not the other way around? That she now knew her mother had been raped and *she* was the twisted result?

Fresh tears threatened to spill.

Yes, all of that was true, but she wasn't admitting that to *Zane* of all people!

What about a taxi? She'd call a taxi and arrange to be picked up from somewhere around the corner, rather than outside the bloody Ritz! She must be careful.

Skye snatched up the receiver, then quickly replaced it. Using the phone wasn't worth the risk. It was easily detectable and her plans could be thwarted she had chance to get out.

But the money couldn't. Marco hadn't even *glanced* at the money he'd brought with him since they'd got here.

Skye gritted her teeth with determination and moved into Marco's bedroom. *It was now or never.*

Opening the walk-in wardrobe, she knelt down and pulled out the holdall. To get out of here whilst she still could, she needed money. And not just a few quid – a fucking *lot*.

Transferring bundles of neatly wrapped fifty-pound notes out of the holdall, Skye mentally totted up the amount as she went. *A million should suffice.*

She'd fucking earnt it.

Marco was now a danger to her, plus she'd stupidly somehow allowed him under her skin and with that, afforded him the ability of hurting her. And that could not go unpunished.

Forty Six

IT WAS DIFFICULT acting normal and making small talk. Almost impossible in fact. But it was imperative it appeared like this was a normal day. Since last night's wobble and voicing about going home, Erin must pretend that she'd accepted this would not happen for some time yet.

She smiled at the woman wheeling a tea trolley into the room. 'Milk with two sugars, please,' Erin said sweetly, glancing up from the magazine she was staring at, yet not reading.

'It's a nice day today.' The woman poured tea from the urn into a mug and handed it to Erin. 'I'll open the curtains a bit wider for you. Don't sit in the dark when it's lovely and sunny outside.'

Erin glared at the woman as she opened the curtains. *Like she could go outside!*

Except she would. And very soon if everyone left her in peace so she could get out of here. 'Thank you,' she muttered, sipping at the week, yet scalding tea.

'The doctors are doing their rounds in an hour, so I'll leave you to it.'

Erin forced her face into another smile as the woman

backed her trolley out of the room.

Right, so she'd got an hour to find a chance to get out of here without being stopped.

The minute the door closed behind the tea lady, Erin swung her legs out of the bed and moved to the sink.

Splashing water on her face, she glanced at her bag where her phone sat inside - fully charged, courtesy of the kind nurse from last night.

That nurse wasn't on duty so far today, Erin wanted to get out before she came on shift. That woman had been kind and the last thing she wanted was to cause grief for a patient absconding during her watch.

It wasn't like this was prison. She was allowed to discharge herself if she wanted to. They couldn't stop her. It would be sorely advised against but short of being a bit weak and dizzy, she felt all right.

Either way, she had to get back to Zane. Zane needed her and she must be there for him, like he'd done for her on countless occasions.

Unzipping the bag, Erin didn't think she'd be so pleased to see the odd selection of items in there. In any other situation, a man bringing random useless items would irritate beyond belief. But this odd collection couldn't be more perfect in *this* situation.

Refraining from analysing why Leo or Zane thought it helpful to bring a man's baseball cap, T-shirt and a pair of jogging bottoms for her, rather than her own clothes, Erin shrugged.

That didn't matter, but she *was* worried about Zane. He hadn't picked up when she'd called last night nor this morning, but from what Leo said, it wasn't surprising. She'd be back with him shortly, so she'd just phone Leo to pick her up when the time came.

But to do that that, she firstly had to get out of here.

She'd give it half an hour for the breakfast bustle to die down and then she'd whip these clothes on and be gone.

• • • •

LEO WAS NOT OVERJOYED that Zane had been drinking again this morning after last night's meltdown. He didn't think he'd ever seen Zane disintegrate and it wasn't pleasant.

But what the outpouring of grief and despair *had* done, was show that he'd finally accepted what Skye was and what she wasn't. Including not being his daughter.

What it *hadn't* done however, was remove Zane's knowledge that his own father had been party to what happened to Shirley or the additional hideous things Marco was responsible for. But accepting the truth about Skye was done and that meant something. The rest would take time.

Zane had to stay sober, but at least he wasn't fuelled by wild anger today so was in a fit state to go home. And that was a good job because they both smelt like utter shit!

Once Zane had freshened up, he could go to see Erin. She'd talk sense into him. Whether he realised it or not, Erin was who the man needed right now.

Leo glanced at his watch. If they made a move now it would be sparse on the canning work's shop floor, which was better than waiting until the place was awash with people. The less questions, the better. 'Right, time to move.'

Zane looked up slowly, the stubbly growth on his face coupled with his tired, red eyes ringed with purple bruising making him appear wild and unkempt. 'Move? Move where?' He didn't want to move. He was spent - physically and emotionally. His memory was patchy about what had occurred with Leo last night, but he knew he'd committed the cardinal sin and broken down, acting like an out-of-control, emotional fool.

It wasn't that which bothered him. He could be anything he liked with Leo without judgement and for that he would be eternally grateful. But this recent inability to contain his feelings bothered him. Leo was right. If he couldn't keep it together then he was fucked.

Marco was out and Erin and the baby remained targets. *The baby...*

Skye wasn't his daughter... She was nothing to do with him... She was Marco's daughter...

Pushing away the renewed prickle of combined rage and despair, Zane cleared his throat. He remembered something else. Something he should never have said. 'I don't want to fire you,' he muttered.

'Yeah, I know.' Leo shrugged. 'Don't worry it's forgotten. Life's too short for that shit. Other things are more important, so let's get you back to Dalston.'

Zane stiffened, unsure whether he could go anywhere. In this storeroom he didn't have to face anything or anyone. Occasionally, he could even pretend that none of this ever happened.

Leo hesitated before speaking, knowing the suggestion could go either way. 'Have you thought about moving back into the penthouse now the place is clear? It's four times the size of the house in Dalston.'

'I don't want to be anywhere Marco has tainted,' Zane snarled.

'Yeah, I get that, but what with Martin and the rest of them there you need more room. Especially with a baby on the way.'

'No! There's no reason for Martin to be there anymore. The same applies to his bloody mother. And Shirley. They're nothing to do with me.' *And as for the baby...*

Zane clenched his jaw so tightly it made his head hurt more than it already did. He snatched up the whisky and drained the meagre remains of the bottle.

'Just a suggestion.' Leo took the empty bottle from Zane's hand and chucked it in the bin. 'Forget I said anything. Let's go.'

He'd fucked up there. He shouldn't have mentioned the penthouse or anything to do with it. Zane needed to remain in a subdued state, not get riled up again. He certainly didn't need to drink any more than he already had.

Unlocking the storeroom, he steered Zane out, hoping he could whisk him out to the car park before anyone accosted them.

Hopefully, by the time they reached Dalston, Zane would have forgotten any mention of the bloody penthouse.

• • • •

'YOU STILL HERE?' Marco sauntered back into the suite and raised his eyebrows at Skye. 'I thought you'd be taking advantage of the beauty treatments. There's a spa and stuff downstairs.'

Moving to the well-stocked minibar, he pulled a bottle of house champagne from the cooler and rang the bell. The Butler who came as part of the price for a suite could open this. He could fetch an ice bucket whilst he was at it too.

Noticing Skye hadn't responded, Marco made a point of smiling. 'I'll call Harrods and book one of their personal shoppers to sort out some new clothes for you.'

'Erm, yes, that would be nice.' Skye scrabbled to hide her confusion. *Marco really was insane*. Did he not remember that only an hour ago he'd grabbed her around the throat, admitted to being a rapist, called her all the names under the sun and threatened to whore her out? Yet now he was being as nice as pie, like none of that had happened?

The Butler suddenly appeared in the suite and hurried to uncork the bottle of champagne. Producing two crystal flutes and an ice bucket on a silver trolley, he expertly poured the drinks, twisting the neck of the bottle with a flourish.

'Anything else, sir? the man asked, respectively averting his eyes.

'That will be all for now, thank you.' Marco pulled two fifty-pound notes from his back pocket and shoved them into the Butler's hand. The man nodded and with a small bow, backed out of the room.

Skye picked up a glass of champagne and sipped it. It was lovely, but nothing could get rid of the unpleasant taste lingering in her mouth from today's revelations. She'd like to down the whole bottle, but she must keep her wits while she waited for an opening to get out of here.

Hearing the front door of the suite shut behind the Butler, she decided to play the same game as Marco and act like everything was normal. 'I might check out that beauty centre later then, like you suggested. What are your plans?'

Marco hoovered up yet another line of cocaine. 'Waiting for the call to tell me that the job's been done.'

Skye bristled. *He remembered that, then?* 'Oh, okay... When... erm... when will that be?'

'I always say there's no time like the present!' Marco grinned. 'There's someone on route to the hospital now. That cunt of Zane's who upset you will be dead within the hour.'

Skye took another sip of champagne, her mind swirling. *So, he'd put the hit into motion? That at least was good news.*

Marco watched Skye carefully. She was good, he'd give her that, but she couldn't hide everything. Oh, he'd worked the stupid, ungrateful little bitch out, but he'd let her to walk into her own trap. 'It's amazing what money can buy, isn't it?' he said, his eyes reflecting none of the raw rage that he now held for the creature he'd accidentally produced.

He should have known better for anything female not to attempt to get one over on him. It proved the dilution of his genes within Skye made a gulf of difference. *Silly bitch.*

But whatever her plans were, they would fail. *Fear not, dear daughter, I've got your number*, he thought, his smile turning into a sneer.

Forty Seven

LOOKING MORE LIKE a slender man than the beautiful woman she was, Erin took one final peek out of the door of her private side room before making a dash for it.

Heart thumping, she made her way up the first of many identical white, sterile corridors in a direction - *any* direction to lead her out of here.

Hoping her hair didn't come loose from under the baseball cap, Erin moved quickly but not unnaturally towards the exit door of the department. The rim of the baseball cap rubbed against the bandage on her forehead and the rucksack casually slung over her shoulder was giving her backache, but she had to act like a visitor passing through.

These trainers were too big and the oversized clothes swamped her slight frame, but if she could get out of this particular part, she stood more chance of escaping from the entire hospital.

Reaching the door, Erin stopped, her heart sinking. There was a code pad and a swipe card unit to open the door.

Shit.

Hearing footsteps, it was difficult not looking over her shoulder to see who was behind and whether they recognised her. Instead, she appeared like her presence lingering at the exit door was normal.

'It's the green button,' a voice called from behind. 'To exit, it's the one on the left.'

Erin's eyes darted back to the code pad and swipe unit. *Of course! There it was marked, 'door release'. How had she missed it?*

She slapped the button with relief before the Good Samaritan got close enough to recognise her, then without looking behind, she stuck her thumb up as means of thanks.

Don't look back, she silently chanted as she yanked the door open and continued down the corridor.

Right. Almost there - just to find the main exit and then she'd call Leo.

• • • •

LEO THOUGHT Zane had been unnaturally quiet the entire journey, like he was locked inside himself. No doubt everything was running through his mind, but whilst he drank no further alcohol and didn't get angry, it was safe to take him back. He must visit Erin. She'd get through to him.

Leo's heart then lurched with the ringing of his mobile, praying it wasn't Tiger with news of something else having happened. Zane's state of mind was such that anything further would push him over the edge.

He snatched up his phone. 'Hello?' Listening, Leo could hardly believe what he was hearing. He couldn't react - it would only stress Zane out. 'Where? Okay, give me ten minutes. Yes, everything's fine.'

Putting the phone down, Leo chanced a look at Zane, grateful he hadn't asked who had called. He'd go mad if he knew Erin had discharged herself from hospital. Leo wasn't over the moon about it either. Erin should stay in hospital until she was 100% recovered, but what could he do, short of what she'd asked and go and pick her up? Good job they were now only minutes away from the house.

'I need to charge my phone,' Zane muttered, his voice strangely mechanical. 'It's been dead for ages. I must get on with work.'

Leo blinked. 'Work? Aren't you planning to spend time with Erin first? You know, whilst you process everything that's happened?'

'No time for that,' Zane said. 'She's better off where she is and without me for now.' He couldn't put his finger on it - didn't *want* to put his finger on it. All he knew was that he couldn't be around anyone at the moment. His brain was raw - like coarse grade sandpaper had scoured every millimetre. His skin too. His whole body felt the same - inside and out.

He pulled his hand down over his stubbly face. It hurt but didn't hurt at the same time. There was no part of him which was joined up or belonged any longer. The disassociation was strange, yet equally meant nothing. It was like drowning without water, just within himself.

Leo wondered whether he should be worried about Zane's comment. It was an off the cuff remark, but it was clear the man was deeply wounded. He'd feel better once Erin was by his side, and that she would be shortly.

Leo pulled up outside the house in Dalston, thankful they hadn't had to park down the road. 'We're here now. Let's go inside.'

Zane hesitated for a moment but then to Leo's relief, jumped from the car.

Glad to see Tiger at the front door as they made their way up the path, Leo jerked his head, giving the silent sign that he needed a word.

Leaving Zane to enter the house, Leo pulled Tiger aside. 'He's okay but a bit twitchy. Keep him calm and don't let him drink. Erin's discharged herself, so I'm off to get her now.'

With that, Leo hurried back to the van, leaving Tiger to deal with Zane.

• • • •

'GOOD TO SEE YOU, MATE!' Tiger said, his expressionless face useful at times like this. 'You having a shower?'

'Shortly,' Zane muttered, kicking his boots off in the hallway. He'd had them on for so long they were welded to his feet. It should be relief to be rid of them, but he felt little either way.

He stared at the familiar hallway. Being back in familiar surroundings did nothing but remind him of what he'd lost. And what he could still lose. What he had probably *already* lost.

Because the rest was no doubt lies too.

They were all in on it - *all* of them.

Sensing movement, he barged into the sitting room to be met with the sight of Martin, Fiona and Shirley, plus a photograph of someone he immediately recognised clutched in Shirley's hand. A photo of someone that up until two days ago had been part of his life.

The most important person in the entire world.

Lurching forward, he snatched Skye's photograph from Shirley's fingers, his face red with fury. 'Are you taking the piss?'

'What are you doing, mate?' Tiger stepped forward, instinctively protecting Shirley from Zane's wrath. It was like someone had flicked a switch within him.

'You brought that into my house to rub my face in it?' Zane screamed in Shirley's face. 'Do you think I need that kind of shit?'

Martin looked in panic between Zane, his mother and Shirley. *What was Zane doing? He was acting like Marco!* 'Zane, Shirley didn't bring th…'

'Shut up!' Zane swung around, his blue eyes ablaze. 'What the hell do you know? What the fuck do *any* of you know?'

'Mate.' Tiger tried to steer Zane out of the room. 'Let's go and...'

'Get the fuck off!' Zane threw off Tiger's grip like it was nothing. *They were taking the piss! Each and every one of them were taking the piss. Thought it amusing, did they?*

Zane lurched from one scenario to another in his head. Had they known the whole time about what Skye was doing and let him think that she was his? Had they allowed him to love her and believe she was his daughter - someone he'd walk over hot coals and die for, yet knew it was bullshit?

They were still here - in his life and in his *house*... Were they sharing anecdotes? Passing titbits back to Skye and Marco on an hourly basis for amusement value?

He stared at the photograph of the girl he had stupidly believed was his own flesh and blood.

Never again.

Never again would he fall for this crap. These *lies*. He'd had the right idea in the first place by letting no one under his skin.

He looked at Skye's perfect features on the photo: her glossy raven hair, those ice blue eyes so closely matching his own, the way her lips curled up just that little bit in one corner – to the jaw-dropping perfection of her beauty that he'd been so proud of. Now… now all he could see staring back at him from the shiny photographic paper was scorn, contempt and not a young female embodiment of himself, but Marco.

Always Marco.

With a roar, he ripped the photo in two and then ripped the halves into two and then again and again. Ignoring Shirley's horrified protests, Zane continued ripping and tearing until the picture was nothing but small pieces of confetti covering the rug.

FORTY EIGHT

AS HE WAITED for the call to come Marco buzzed with anticipation, cocaine and the effects of the third bottle of champagne of the afternoon.

His eyes flitted to Skye who had got up from the chair by the balcony to look out of the window. 'There's a view of Piccadilly from the other rooms,' he said. 'It's great for people watching.' Something he'd shortly be doing because whatever happened, it was only a matter of time.

Being as Skye hadn't responded, Marco placed his champagne down and moved across the sumptuous rug to the window. He placed his hands on her shoulders. 'Did you hear me?' he asked, noting how easy it would be to throttle her for being such a cunt.

Immediately regretting flinching, Skye knew she must pay attention. 'Sorry,' she laughed, her usual fluid tinkle sounding scratchy and forced. 'I was off with the fairies.' *Why was Marco still here?* He had to go somewhere eventually, even it was to the toilet for thirty seconds.

Thirty seconds gave enough time for her to leave. *Just.*

The ring of Marco's phone deflected him from the comment he itched to make about Skye's pathetic attempt to get one over on him. Moving away, he pulled his mobile from his pocket. 'Is it done?' His eyebrows pulled into a frown. *So, Erin Langley had slipped out of this one as well?*

Luckily, it wasn't the end of the world. There would be further opportunities to remove that bitch. Besides, it was Skye pushing for that task to take precedence, whereas *he'd* happily drag out Zane's torture.

If he looked in the beautiful gilt-framed mirror, he could just about make out Skye's face mirrored in the reflection of the window. She was listening to everything, there was no doubt about that, so his reaction and the next instructions to his gun-for-hire must be vague. Good job he'd previously briefed this man, wasn't it? Now he must rely on instinct as to the timing of Part Two.

'Okay,' he continued. 'Just move onto the next job we discussed. Yeah, that's correct. Not sure about timings but it will be soon. Head there straightaway and wait. I'll let you know when the window of opportunity arrives.'

Reading between the lines, Skye felt a glimmer of hope. She waited for Marco to end the call before speaking. 'Problems?'

Marco easily pulled on his scowl. 'Yeah, you could say that. The slippery cow has done one!'

'You mean Erin's left the hospital without anything happening? How?'

'Oh, the usual.' Marco shrugged. 'It looks like the jammy bitch discharged herself. My man arrived to spot someone who looked very much like Erin Langley being picked up down the road by someone whose description closely matched one of my dear brother's flunkies. Makes it seem like they had a tip off...'

'But who from?' Skye gasped. 'No one knew your plans!' And it certainly wasn't *her*, even though she'd considered it.

Marco could have laughed at Skye's stellar performance as she continued her angry diatribe.

'I don't understand why you're not annoyed!' Skye sniped. 'You're not letting them get away with it, are you?'

Marco set up another line of coke on the table and shrugged. ‘Didn’t you hear my instructions? I told my man to move on to Part Two.’

Skye raised her eyebrows. ‘Which is?’

‘To go to the address in Dalston that you very kindly supplied and gun Langley down there. He’ll remove all of them.’ *Except his man would be doing no such thing.* That was *his* to have should he desire it. And that he hadn’t decided yet.

‘I hope your man, whoever he is, gets it done this time without any issues!’ Skye stalked across the room. *This was it.* She’d never get a window to sneak out of here. Marco was lurking around here like herpes. She might as well use the blatant approach. He was too distracted to think of anything but this dickhead he’d paid to do his bidding, but one thing was for sure and it wouldn’t be *her* doing the work for nothing any longer.

She now had money and just needed to walk the fuck out of Marco’s suite, his threats and his psycho fucking schizoid life.

Taking a deep breath, she nonchalantly pulled her long hair into a ponytail. ‘I’m so disappointed, I think I’ll go and get a massage from downstairs, like you suggested.’ She had to go now. Like, *right* now.

‘Good idea,’ Marco smiled, pressing send on the waiting text. ‘I’ll defer your appointment with Harrods until the morning.’

• • • •

AS HE SPED TOWARDS DALSTON, Leo kept one eye trained on his rearview mirror. He knew what he’d seen - at least what he’d been as sure as he could be that he’d seen regarding the bike pulling up just after spotting a strange version of Erin in the bus stop down from the hospital. What he’d seen and sensed was that trouble was afoot.

The mannerisms of the biker immediately triggered alarm bells. After all, it took one to know one and he knew every tiny variant and microscopic sign underlining when someone spied their target. *Erin was that target.*

That fucker had sent a hit to the hospital, so if he'd arrived just ten seconds later...

Leo glanced over to the passenger seat. Erin looked more like herself since removing the baseball cap and freeing her long blonde hair. 'Why the bus stop?' he asked, containing his angst-ridden annoyance. 'Bit out in the open, weren't you?'

'I thought the disguise that you or Zane unwittingly provided me was quite good, but you know as well as I do that guy would have got me in my hospital bed or on the street, if you hadn't shown up.' Erin downplayed the gravity of the situation she'd thankfully evaded, but the implications gnawed deep.

Once again, that Leo prevented her from being added to Marco's body count was not something she would forget.

Her hand instinctively rested on her belly. She would never be safe. *None* of them were. If only Zane hadn't let Marco walk from the penthouse alive.

'You worked it out it was a hit?' Leo's eyes remained glued to the road ahead as they spread towards Dalston. *Yep, Erin was switched on. There were no flies on her.*

'The small signs of people out to kill me have become easier to spot now it's happened so often.' And that was the sad truth of it: that had happened far too many times. Soon, one of those times would succeed unless something changed. The thought of exposing her child to such an existence brought with it a fear that overshadowed all others.

'It must be dealt with,' Leo muttered. And that was a fact. The gun Marco had hired - because it had to be him or Skye behind it, would have the Dalston house, as well as their other locations as the next ports of call. The bike wasn't following them, so that was one thing, but if not today, then it would be soon. Zane needed to act. He needed to act *and* think. Most importantly, this woman and her unborn child must be taken out of the line of fire and away until the threat was removed.

'How is Zane?' Erin asked quietly. 'I tried to call this

morning, but he didn't answer. Is... is he okay? With me, I mean?'

Leo shot Erin a look. 'Of course he's okay with you. He loves you to distraction. His phone's been dead, but I won't lie… this shit with that little bitch has knocked him sideways. He'll come through - especially once you're back. Today he's calm and not drunk. He's at the house now but doesn't know you're coming as I thought it best being a surprise.'

Erin smiled, hoping it would be a *good* surprise. She couldn't wait to be back at Zane's side. Whatever he was going through they would deal with it together.

'We're nearly there.' Leo remained upbeat, deciding the first thing he'd do when they arrived back was arrange extra guards for the house.

• • • •

SKYE PURPOSELY didn't look behind as she walked across the marble floor of the Ritz's reception in the opposite direction of the beauty spa.

It was fine. Marco was so wrapped up in shovelling more coke up his nose he had better things to do than follow her. Besides, it was his idea. And being as he was so fucked in the head and lurched between Mr Nice Guy and Lunatic #9, she'd taken her chance whilst he was wearing the Mr Nice Guy suit.

She wasn't waiting around for Marco's alter ego to reappear. She was done.

Ignoring the top-hatted man opening the gold door for her, Skye clattered down the steps onto Arlington Street and paused.

Which way now?

Not caring if she drew attention, she ran the short distance up the side street to the junction with Piccadilly. Green Park Station was just down there, so she'd get on a tube. It didn't matter which one - all lines led out of this place eventually.

She had no passport with her. She didn't even have a change of clothes, but she *did* have money and her life, so she'd start again.

Breaking into a sweat, she barged into people, ignoring their tuts, glares and rude comments. Usually, she'd retort with a cutting remark, but there was no time for her that. She'd unleash her irritation on some unsuspecting fucker once she was nicely settled and clear of this godforsaken place, as well as out of reach of the man who turned out to be a bad bet.

It could have worked out so well, but it hadn't. Marco was a loon. He'd turn on her at some point and that, Skye wasn't waiting for.

Yes, it was a shit, but she'd got enough brass to get her settled. She'd go somewhere new and start afresh.

She pulled her bag close to her side as she continued up the street seeing the jutting underground sign coming into view. She had a million quid here – more than enough to set herself up somewhere and look the part. Plus, it wasn't difficult to get an emergency passport.

Perhaps she'd go to Cannes? There were plenty of rich, stupid fuckers there who wouldn't be averse to her charms. It wouldn't take long to fall on her feet again.

Some things worked out and others didn't, but she was fucked if she'd dwell on this episode longer than needs be. She'd already put far too much effort in.

Speeding past the other side of the Ritz hotel, all Skye could focus on was the Underground sign twenty yards ahead. That, and making sure no Albanian riff whipped her bag off her shoulder.

A bike overtaking the double-decker bus behind her didn't even enter her mind.

Forty Nine

TIGER HAD TRIED to prevent Zane from raiding the meagre remnants of spirits in the sideboard, but after the photograph incident it was impossible to stop. Shirley was having a meltdown over the destruction of that picture, Fiona was going crazy and Martin - well, Martin was seemingly unable to do shag all, the useless twat.

Leo wouldn't be happy. Erin was on route back and there was no way he'd knowingly bring her into this with Zane losing it again. But Tiger hadn't been able to call and warn the man. He only had one pair of hands and they were busy trying to shake some sense into Zane but failing miserably.

As Zane necked the remains of the second half-bottle of rum like it was water, Tiger snatched the empty bottle from his hands. 'For fuck's sake! Give it a rest! You heard what Shirley said!' he reasoned. 'She told you Marco snatched that photo when he was in her house last week.' He jerked his head towards the crumpled leather jacket on the floor. 'That's his. That's the jacket I took from the penthouse to cover the girl.'

'Marco put the photo in his pocket,' Shirley sobbed. 'It was my favourite photograph. My only one and you've ruined it!' She may have lost Skye and accepted the girl had turned out exactly as she dreaded, but Skye was still her daughter and always would be.

Zane leant on the sideboard, his arms supporting his weight as the room span in a never-ending circle, the speed of the jerky images on a constant replay he could not stop.

He didn't want excuses. He didn't want to hear any more. No one would lie to him again.

Coming up behind him, Shirley started pounding Zane's back. 'What's happened to you? Why are you behaving like this? How could you do this? Haven't I been through enough? Skye is still my daughter, regardless of what she's done!'

'Yeah?' Swinging around, Zane pushed Shirley away where she stumbled against the wall. 'But she's not *mine.*' He suddenly laughed - a deep belly laugh. 'And you know what? I'm fucking glad she's not! I hope that girl gets exactly what she deserves, the little fucking bi…'

'That's enough!' Fiona screeched, pointing her slender finger in Zane's face. 'Everyone can see you're devastated, but don't take it out on those who care about you.'

'Care? *CARE*?' Zane screamed. 'I don't want anyone to care! I need no one. I never have!'

'You're drunk!' Fiona spat. 'It's disgusting! You should be sorting things out, not wallowing in your own misery. I think you sh…'

Fiona's ill-timed lecture was promptly cut off as Zane grabbed her by the shoulders, the fury in his eyes silencing any further words she may speak. 'Don't tell me what I should or shouldn't be doing. This is nothing to do with you or any of you!'

'Get off my mother!' Springing to life, Martin threw Zane's hands off Fiona's shoulders.

Righting himself, Zane surged forward to headbutt Martin in the face and Fiona screamed as he collapsed to the ground covered with blood. 'You absolute beast!' she screeched. 'You don't deserve to be a father!'

The rage in Zane's eyes turned from red to white as he

dragged Martin off the floor. 'Why are you all here? You're nothing to me! None of you!'

Tiger moved forward. 'Mate, leave this now.'

'I want them out!' Panting with exertion, Zane threw Martin against the wall with a resounding crack. A framed photograph of a landscape dislodged and smashed on the floor. 'For the last time, get out! None of you have anything to do with me, so get the fuck out of my house and my life!'

Grabbing Fiona, he dragged her across the room and shoved her in Martin's direction. 'Get out! And take your pathetic son with you.' Spinning around, he then turned to Shirley. 'And you! Out! Get the hell out. Now!'

If these people didn't get leave this second, he'd kill them. He kill them all. Nothing mattered anymore. Nothing, nothing, *nothing*.

Suddenly, hands were on Zane's shoulders. 'Pack this the fuck in!' Tiger roared, it taking all of his power to hold Zane in position. He was like a man possessed. 'Erin will be here any second now. She's discharged herself from the hospital.'

Seeing a flash of something – realisation perhaps - behind Zane's eyes, he continued. If he could just get through to him. 'This isn't you. You're not like this. Just calm down. It will be all right, you hear?'

Zane's eyes met Tiger's, his cold and measured gaze signifying he'd passed the point of no return. Now he was calm, but this sort of calm was more dangerous than anything. 'I said,' his voice was clipped, 'I want these people, including you, out of my house and out of my life. If that doesn't happen immediately, I will kill every single one of you.'

The grip on Zane's shoulders tightened. 'I ain't going anywhere. Come on, mate,' Tiger reasoned. 'Don't let the woman you love walk in to see you like this. She's pregnant and doesn't need this stress. Think of your future with her and your new baby, not the past.'

'There is no future and there is no past,' Zane growled. 'I should never have got involved with Erin. I don't want her, nor the baby. It's not mine anyway. She's lied about that, no doubt, like everyone else. I don't want either of them. I don't want *anything*.'

Tiger's eyes narrowed, the urge to punch Zane in the face, fierce. 'How dare you say that sort of sh…'

'It's okay, Tiger,' Erin said as she walked into the room. 'I heard what he said.' And with that, she turned and calmly walked away.

• • • •

A SLOW SMILE spread over Marco's face the second he spotted it. Holding a fresh glass of champagne in one hand, he tapped the building ash on his cigarette in the direction of the crystal ashtray. He didn't check to see if it fell into the intended place. People got paid to clear shit up so let them get on with it.

Nothing would distract him from the view over Piccadilly.

People watching was cathartic and non more so than *now*.

Raising the glass back to his lips, Marco sipped, enjoying the expensive bubbles bursting against his tongue.

Skye should really learn that it wasn't good for the ankles to run with high heels on London pavements. Still, it wasn't like it made much difference.

He fleetingly wondered what was going through her mind as she headed towards the tube. He'd half-expected her to take another route, but clearly her delusion knew no bounds and she'd granted him a clear view of her escape attempt.

Did Skye really believe she'd get away with this? Did she really, *truly* think that he - Marco Morelli - would not work out that she was planning to jump ship? Did his darling daughter honestly believe he'd be that bereft not to be ten steps ahead and watch her every move? Did she not realise he knew what she'd planned even before *she* did?

He glanced up at the tiny red light concealed in the centre of the elaborate chandelier. It was barely visible unless its prior existence was known. He'd ensured there was one in every room of the suite – including the bathroom.

They may be tiny and unobtrusive, but the crystal-clear footage sent livestream from each and every camera directly to his mobile phone was the *opposite* of unobtrusive. It showed everything…

And although he'd had his suspicions of Skye recently, without these cameras he would have had the proof of what she'd planned.

And now he did…

'Oh, Skye,' Marco chuckled, the smile pulling further at the corner of his mouth. 'You really have been a silly girl.'

Marco took a long drag of his cigarette and held the smoke in his lungs before slowly exhaling it to pool above the massive window. He watched, almost in slow motion, as the motorbike drew level with his daughter.

Although he was many floors above street level, the slight turn of Skye's head towards the crash-helmeted figure drawing parallel with her, showed that she'd realised. And that she knew.

If she had time, she may even look across the other side of the road and up, belatedly realising that he had a ringside view of her destruction.

But Skye had no time. *Not now.*

Marco saw the flashes: one, two, three; he saw the bike accelerate away. Then the bus following temporarily obscured his vision.

Move, move, move!

The bus passed and came to an abrupt halt outside Green Park Station.

There were people running; *screaming.*

Marco remained unmoving and raised his cigarette back to his lips. The windows of the suite were soundproof, but if they weren't or if he opened one, then he was sure within seconds, he would hear approaching sirens. But he didn't need to hear them.

Because it was done.

He glanced at his watch. Now all he had to do was rush

down to the street and play the role of a horrified father who had just witnessed his daughter's killing from the window of his suite at the Ritz.

He'd play the part well. There was no fear about that. He'd also lift that bag he could just about see on the ground underneath Skye's body before someone else helped themselves to it or the police had it. Finding that sort of cash on her would raise questions as to her life. Without it, the killing would be resigned to one of those 'wrong place, wrong time' events.

After all, the money she'd swiped was needed back in *his* bag.

Marco slipped on his Italian leather loafers and shrugged on his jacket. Stubbing his cigarette out on the rug, he left the suite and made his way along the corridor.

Skye had been useful, there was no doubt about that, but all things eventually lost their value.

Humming a cheerful tune, Marco stepped into the lift.

FIFTY

LEO AND TIGER always had Zane's back but on this particular occasion, they were finding it hard to justify the words which spilled from his mouth last night.

No matter how hurt; drunk; how *anything* he was, what he'd said about Erin and the baby were inexcusable. That woman had given everything to him. She'd risked her life, gone above and beyond for him - for *all* of them and he treated her like that?

'Has she woken up yet?' Tiger glanced up the stairs towards the bedroom before glancing at Zane still spark out on the sofa. He bristled, the urge to punch sense into his friend of old not having diminished during the night.

'I don't expect she slept,' Leo muttered, equally as angry as Tiger. But it was more than anger. It was *disappointment.* 'I never thought I'd say this, but I fucking hate Zane right now.'

'You and me both,' Tiger agreed. 'I don't know where things can go from here. He didn't mean what he said, but, trust me, with things like that, apologies won't come close to righting it!'

'Zane's hurting.' Leo shook his head. 'We both know what happened with Skye has crucified him, but Christ, it doesn't excuse what he said. If I was Erin, I'd walk away. She can't stay here while he's like this.'

He folded his arms across his chest. 'We should move her into the penthouse, I'll stay there with her to make sure she's safe.' He paced up and down the hallway, his resentment growing. 'We've been holding this shit together whilst he's been losing it and I'm sick of it. I appreciate he's been royally fucked over, but if he's going to treat everyone like dirt, especially Erin, then he's on his own. She's one of us.'

Tiger nodded. It was true. Erin *was* one of them. But there were others who had been trashed during this nightmare too. 'What happened to Shirley and the Bolts? Chucking them out like that was callous. Shirley's been through hell and Martin – well, much as I didn't think I'd ever say it, he's not a bad lad.'

'They went to a hotel. Fiona said she'd call her husband to collect them.' Leo grimaced thinking of Peter Bolt. 'What I remember of that bloke from the one experience I had, he's a pedantic bastard and no doubt will cause problems.'

Tiger sighed. 'Something *else* we'll have to deal with whilst Zane downs in alcohol and self-pity. Fuck's sake! The only reason I'm still standing here is because of Erin. You're not the only one who wants to walk away.'

'Please don't do that.'

Tiger and Leo both swung around to see Erin coming down the stairs. Reaching the bottom, she placed her hands on their arms. 'Don't abandon Zane now. I won't.'

Zane's words last night were indeed devastating. To say he he regretted becoming involved with her and didn't believe the baby growing inside her was his, sliced through her like a knife. He was her world and imagining one without him in it was incomprehensible.

All night she'd laid there stuck between devastation and hopelessness, peppered with agonising hurt, until she reached the conclusion that if she wanted to be with him, she had to let this go. She knew Zane didn't mean those things. However, it would be easy to react and walk away out of principle. Why would any self-respecting woman stay with a man who accused her of being unfaithful and saying those hurtful things?

She was no pushover and certainly not the sort to shoulder abuse from a man or *anyone*, but Zane was different. Zane was *everything*. Zane was the soulmate she never believed she would find and for that reason, and that reason alone, she would not abandon the man she loved fiercely and who'd given his soul to her, risking his life for her on countless occasions just because he'd temporarily lost his way.

She would not be that woman.

Erin turned back to Leo and Tiger. 'I won't leave Zane and neither will you. For once in his life, regardless what he says, he needs us. *Each* of us. We will be here for him and help him get through this shit.'

'But how the fuck can you forgive him for what he said?' Leo growled. 'I wouldn't.'

'Yes, you would,' Erin smiled. 'Maybe not straight away, but you would. Tiger did.'

'That was different,' Tiger interjected. 'And I *haven't* forgiven him.'

'It wasn't different. What Zane did to you was personal, hurtful and shit, like this is for me,' Erin said. 'But you *have* forgiven him to a point, if not completely. That you're still here shows that. I will do the same. All I know is that I love Zane and this *is* his child I'm carrying.'

Her hand fell to rest on her belly. '*They* put that idea in his head and I'm not letting Skye and Marco ruin anything else. We must remember Zane's been lied to his whole life. He's broken right now and we need to put him back together.'

'Zane doesn't deserve you!' Leo snorted.

'I know I don't.' Zane appeared from the sitting room, bleary eyed and looking like death. 'I don't deserve Erin and I don't deserve either of you two either. All I can say is I'm sorry.' He dragged his fingers through his hair. 'It's not anywhere near enough but I am sorry. I'm *so* fucking sorry. I didn't mean any of it, but that's no excuse. Not even slightly.'

'No, it's not,' Erin said. 'But we're still here, aren't we?'

Zane nodded, thinking once again that regardless of anything else, he was possibly the luckiest man in the world. He'd gladly spend the rest of his life making up for his cruel words as long as Erin and these men remained by his side.

Pulling Erin into his arms, he held her close. 'The thought that you and our baby would die terrified me. But to make you walk away because of my stupid, shit behaviour…' His voice trailed off, his emotions overwhelming. 'I'll put it right – all of it. I'll make it up to you somehow. I'll sort this shit out in my own head and be there for you like I want to be.'

He turned to Leo and Tiger. 'That goes for you two as well.'

Marco and the girl he'd believed to be his daughter would somehow be relegated to the past. As would the part his father had in it. It would be difficult, but with Erin's help, his baby and his two trusted men, he'd get there.

It was time to move forward.

EPILOGUE

MARCO PUT HIS FEET up on the table, lounged back on the chair and smiled. He wedged his mobile in his neck so his hands were free to cut his next line of coke. 'Yeah, it's all done. The police think her death was a freak accident.'

Listening to the voice down the line, he chuckled. 'Yep, Skye did everything I asked so I'm all set and ready to take London by storm. When are you coming over?'

He then frowned. 'Giving you grief again, is he? Still playing the possessive husband? Nah, don't apologise for that. Losing the deal is old news. Him cutting me out was expected, so don't stress. I have other plans which involve *you*. So...'

Momentarily stopping to snort the line of coke, Marco then continued. 'I presume your promise to me still stands?'

A wide smile formed on Marco's face which reminded him he'd need to get his broken tooth fixed before publicly showing his face to the world. 'Glad to hear it! Now we can move forward and, sweetheart, I can assure you it will be worth the wait. All the irrelevant people we've fucked in the interim will be forgotten.'

He found his hand making its way into his trousers to ease the pressure of his rapidly engorging crotch. Soon there would be no sneaking about, no stealing moments as and when it allowed, no more sham marriages or relationships just to pass the time and tread water.

This one he'd waited a lifetime for and was the icing on the fucking cake. 'I'll see you soon, okay and then the world really will be our oyster!'

Ending the call, Marco closed his eyes, the concept of gaining the prize of all prizes now within his sights. Soon he would openly walk around London with the woman who should always have been his. No plastic porn-star fantasies with this one. This woman was the real deal – the jewel in the crown.

Soon, there would be no one to stop him.

If Zane somehow managed to right himself from the trashed mess of the life now left to him, it would only be to masquerade as an obscure person that people would rapidly forget.

Marco had no idea why his brother was offered the cream in the first place. He and Sofia were better suited and always had been. That was proved by the years their affair had continued.

Once Diego Delgado, who Sofia only married because she had no choice, lay dead back in his tinpot homeland, Marco would take the man's empire, his staff and with it, London – along with the rest of the fucking world.

Zane could try and impede that all he liked, but, Marco thought with a wry snigger, the prick didn't stand a fucking chance.

The best thing his brother could do was to slope off into the distance and live with that bitch getting fat with his kid, in a village somewhere way away from here and evaporate.

The time Marco had patiently waited for was here and he was taking every last piece of it.

NEXT IN THIS SERIES

SCARRED #5

THE LAST PROMISE

With Marco Morelli seemingly off the scene for the time being, Zane is determined to ensure his firm and life are stable and that he's financially secure in order to provide for Erin and what the future will bring.

There's a lot riding on that - firstly he needs to quash the rumours doing the rounds about his ability which threatens to derail the lucrative deal with Diego Delgado. Zane is relying on that deal to remain to ensure his foothold back in London.

But Diego's wife has plans of her own.
As does Colt Shoreham, who has returned to take up the offer that his brother promised him many years ago, should he ever need it. However, Tiger has issues of his own to deal with: one, his past and two, in the shape of a young woman who Marco treated so badly.

But out of all of them, who will be the one not honouring their promise?

MORE FROM THIS AUTHOR

ALLEGIANCE SERIES:

TAKEOVER | FALLOUT | VENDETTA | PAYBACK | JUDGEMENT

Daddy's girl Samantha Reynold hadn't bargained on unexpectedly needing to step into her father's shoes and take over the family casino business.

Pampered and spoiled, Sam knows nothing about the rules of this glamorous but deadly new world. She has a lot to learn and even more to prove. But she won't let her family down, especially when it looks like they could lose everything to their biggest rivals – the Stoker family.

Eldest son Sebastian hasn't got time to pander to pretty girl Samantha as she plays at being boss. Rumours are swirling around the streets of Birmingham that have the power to rip the Stoker family apart and destroy everything they've built.

MORE FROM THIS AUTHOR

RETRIBUTION SERIES:

AN OLD SCORE | FINDERS KEEPERS | THE FINAL TAKE

Three families... One prize...

Teagan Fraser had no idea what she was getting herself into when she took on an assignment as a live-in carer for Dulcie Adams – a retired dancer from a Soho club. Dulcie has waited forty years for her lover, Michael Pointer, to return, but she's been living in hope for a time that never came and left looking after something important, which Jonah Powell and his firm want back.

In addition to the notorious Powell firm, there are others wanting to claim what they believe is rightfully theirs and they'll do anything to get it back. If only Dulcie wasn't around it would be a lot easier, but she's difficult to shift...

A lot can happen in a short space of time and Teagan might wish she'd never become involved.

MORE FROM THIS AUTHOR

HUNTED SERIES:

THE STATUS DEBT | THE FAMILY LEGACY | THE TARGET OF LIES

Lillian Morgan would do anything to regain the status she lost by marrying beneath her and to cover the sordid details of her husband's death. This includes blackmail and the hand of marriage of her own daughter.

Tori thought her life couldn't get much worse, but someone is not being honest and secrets have the power to rip everyone to shreds.

Especially when life is built on lies.

*** This series contains written depictions of graphic violence, sex and strong language. It also contains some themes that may be uncomfortable for certain readers.***

MORE FROM THIS AUTHOR

DOWNFALL SERIES:

UNTIL THE END OF TIME | ESCAPING THE PAST | VENGEFUL PAYBACK

Dive into Seth and Jane's train wreck of a life, where drugs, alcohol and obsessional love means this downright dangerous pair will do *anything* to ensure nothing gets in their way.

They do bad things. *Very* bad things and their promise to love each until the end of time turns into a war against each other.

A war neither of them can win.

*** This series contains written depictions of graphic violence, sex and strong language. It also contains some themes that may be uncomfortable for certain readers. ***

About The Author

Over the years Edie has worked all over the UK as well as in several other countries and has met a lot of interesting people - several of whom have supplied ideas for some of the characters in her books! She has now settled back in central England with her partner and children, where she is pursuing her writing.

Edie writes gritty gangland and urban fiction and her series so far include her latest – the *Scarred* series; the *Allegiance* series, the *Retribution* series, *Hunted* series and *Downfall* series.

When she isn't writing, Edie enjoys reading and is a self-confessed book hoarder. She also enjoys crochet and music as well as loving anything quirky or unusual.

Visit www.ediebaylis.co.uk for the latest news, information about new releases, giveaways and to subscribe to her mailing list.

Edie Baylis

gangland | crime | urban

THRILLER AUTHOR

Connect with Edie

https://fb.me/downfallseries

https://www.goodreads.com/author/show/17153586.Edie_Baylis

https://twitter.com/ediebaylis

https://www.amazon.co.uk/Edie-Baylis/e/B075FQHWCZ/

https://www.bookbub.com/authors/edie-baylis

https://ediebaylis.co.uk/

info@ediebaylis.co.uk

https://www.fantasticfiction.com/b/edie-baylis/

https://www.instagram.com/ediebaylis/

https://www.tiktok.com/@ediebaylis

https://www.pinterest.co.uk/ediebaylis/

Join Edie's Mailing List

Subscribe to Edie's mailing list for the latest news on her books, special offers, new releases and competitions.

https://ediebaylis.co.uk/signup.html

CWA MEMBER

ACKNOWLEDGEMENTS

Firstly, special thanks goes to the ladies (you know who you are) - who were brave enough to allow their names to be adopted by some of the characters in this story after winning a competition on Facebook. (I must point out that these characters are in no way anything to do with, or connected to, their namesakes in real life!) Just want to get that out there!

Also, many thanks to the people that kindly read my drafts of *The Hard Truth.* I appreciate your time and feedback.

As always, thanks to all of the supportive friends and readers who give me the incentive to keep on writing. And, of course, love and thanks to my family.

Thank you for reading *The Hard Truth.* I hope you enjoyed reading it as much as I did writing it!

If so, would you please consider leaving a review on Amazon and/or Goodreads. Reviews from readers are SOOOO helpful and especially important to us authors and without you we would have nobody to write for!

Thank you once again and hope you enjoy the rest of my books.

Edie xx

Printed in Great Britain
by Amazon

45496808R00229